J. J. ARMAS MARCELO published SHIPS AFIRE (*Las naves quemadas*) in Barcelona, Spain, in 1982. The epic novel, which the author calls "an assault on history itself," was written with the help of a grant from the Ministerio de Cultura de España. Armas Marcelo is the author of three previous, highly acclaimed novels, *El camaleón sobre la alfombra, Estado de coma,* and *Calima.*

"This is a novel that is historical, but also one that is full of sharp, Bunuel-esque humor . . . Aside from the narrative, the most fundamental thing about the book is the language and, within that, the baroque sensibility that Armas Marcelo has achieved. One can't help but be reminded of writers like Lezama Lima, Carpentier, Cabrera Infante, or Sarduy."

Mario Vargas Llosa, introducing
Las naves quemadas in Barcelona
in March 1982

SHIPS AFIRE

J. J. ARMAS MARCELO

TRANSLATED BY SARAH ARVIO

AVON BOOKS  NEW YORK

Originally published in Spanish in 1982 as *Las naves quemadas* by Editorial Argos Vergara, S.A., Barcelona, Spain.

AVON BOOKS
A division of
The Hearst Corporation
105 Madison Avenue
New York, New York 10016

Copyright © 1982 by J.J. Armas Marcelo
English translation copyright © 1988 by Sarah Arvio
Front cover illustration by Robert Goldstrom
Published by arrangement with the author
Library of Congress Catalog Card Number: 87-91464
ISBN: 0-380-89741-5

First Avon Books Trade Printing: June 1988

AVON TRADEMARK REG. U.S. PAT. OFF. AND IN OTHER COUNTRIES, MARCA REGISTRADA, HECHO EN U.S.A.

Printed in the U.S.A.

OPM 10 9 8 7 6 5 4 3 2 1

to Rosa
to Juan
for everything

"There was a psychological reason also for the destruction of the ships; without means of retreat, the soldiers would have to fight desperately."
Maurice Collis

"Upon the ruins of the god, only the profaners remained, sacred."
José Angel Valente

PART I

Ab Urbe Condita

After the Rejonistas, shaky-footed, invaded the lonely sands of Salbago's shores, several anarchic, topsy-turvy, all but endless years, that seemed to have fallen asleep like slow clocks forgetting to keep time, had to elapse before life there, on that deserted island discovered by dint of the delirium of Captain Rejón, was to show signs of some everyday normalness, and a rational order, the basic administration of persons and things, floated, all over the territory.

From the first moment, the streets of the city they were to found were scratched out helter-skelter, without rhyme or reason, at loose ends, by the oceancrossers settling into Salbago like flowing lava. They truckled to the fickle urges of a lawless will that henceforth would hound them forever. They shut their ears to the wise instructions of Herminio Machado, trained in the best Italian schools, aged before his time due to disillusionment, to the down-right fiasco of his most civilized dreams: the thwarted raising of the ramparts of a city rampant and unreinable, the headlong layout of streets that nearly always led no place, and to crown it all, his feckless endeavors in the construction of the Cathedral, for which he had picked out a gorgeous grey stone which a few short months after being cut and squarely set in place was attacked and cankered by a surly yellow lichen, marring and crumbling it. From the days of the colony, the city was glaringly ugly.

Later it was impossible to repair so many botches or to chastise those responsible for the mess. The flaws lingered and rigidified and became rockbound tradition. A vast esplanade remained, the Grand Plaza, where supreme pun-

3

ishments, at the bidding, hour in and year out, of the
Holy Inquisition were executed, and all the while the city
grew mastodonic, scattering higgledy-piggledy, in the
image and likeness of its inhabitants, who streamed in
unstanchable spate toward the island shores. The streets,
snaky and tipping, dragged loosely upward from the sand
beaches and vanished into nameless mountains, at the
rim of the island's lost forests, a wild tangly vegetation
that halted at the awesome frontiers of the Badlands, a
deserted volcanic zone where life had been razed by the
age-old fire raging over it and strewing the infecund seed
of a ghastly drought. An impenetrable maze.

Meanwhile Salbago, in the years following the tremen-
dous revolution in the arts of navigation, became a port
of call. Its wharves were as much a longed-for respite as
an obligatory stopover (with tried-and-true dry dock) for
the ships crammed with adventurers of every stripe,
which, after laying in a great store of food and whiling
away a few days in mercantile transactions, in scraping
the hull, and the mandatory amatory jaunts of the sailors
through the slummy streets of the Bagnio, headed on out
for a land perennially unfound, still absent from the
charts, foreglimpsed as illusion solely in the fixated minds
of those who persisted in the daredevil conviction that
beyond the immense barrier of the sea, beyond the
unmovable line of the horizon, lay other unknown lands,
monstrous continents where virgin clusters of precious
exotic fruits awaited the lustful hand of the newcomer.

On the nervous days of the discovery of the island, the gleaming owl eyes of Simón Luz, the Jew, flew up from the depths of the waters and swept without a sound over the sea's dense evening mist. Then they hooked into the distance like an animal's claws. With seasoned ease, his eyes stroked breasts, rolling, gentle, white-crested, fleeting, faraway, formed by the waves on the scarps of water. Eyes that see in the dark, skilled clairvoyant pacing like a phantom caged on the interminable nights on the ship's deck, Simón Luz scented the different dampness of a land long sought, many hours before the telescope would unknot the agonized boredom of the crew. The premonition tore the netting of his analytical mind. In his skin waked hot pricklings of urgent lust. His soul sizzled with so much ambition inheld.

Some years before the birth of the irrepressible Discovery fever, the Hebrew did not possess the accuracy with the compass or the flawless knowledge of the then shadowy seas he trotted out in his banterings with the sailors, during one of which his peculiar lucidity of expression pricked the interest of Captain Juan Rejón. His god-given gifts stood out in bold relief, however—for engineering prowess—as a builder of round ships in the Portuguese port of Sagres, beside Cape San Vicente, where the horizons cross and crack the straight logical line of the centuries.

Thus he was here now, on the quarterdeck of Captain Rejón's Castilian caravel. Thus Simón Luz muttered between his teeth, "Land, Rejón, land." His fists clenched, fingernails digging almost with no pain into the palms of his excited hands, every syllable cracking inside him like

5

a whip, whip-snaps of joy bursting from his lips. Rejón
trembles. His dry tongue swabs like a sponge over the
tender roof of his mouth. Between trembles he pulps the
sweet pomegranate flavor of honor and glory.

"Yes, Captain, land," reply the black eyes of Bartolomé
Larios, Master Helmsman. "Terra firma, and it's ours, at
last."

Some years back, mixed up in the mumbo jumbo and
fracases of Berbers and Turks, swept up in the adventure
and illusion of war, Juan Rejón would not have fueled
such a vision. He would have simply given the order to
head on and on in the endless voyage. But today, in the
almost painful dissolution of disbelief and skepticism—
tough vine clinging like necrotic nerves to the slow
rhythm of his continual fiascos at sea—Juan Rejón gave
in to fascination: he opened the portholes again to the
dreamt-of landscape of glory and his craving gaze shattered against the dark flank rising in the distance out of
the calm mirror of the sea. This, surely, was his preferred
liturgy during the last days of the passage (doubt, meanwhile, pointy vulturine beak screaking desperation), when
the whittled cross, scornful or weary, like a horse bucking
its unrelenting rider, sailed counter to Larios' orders,
lagging and lurching in repeated concentric circles, ripples
instantly vanishing on the surface of yesterday and the
day before yesterday. Rejón huddled in the tremble of that
sham self-confidence (by now tattooed indelibly into the
nervous wrinkles of his face weathered by sea salt) he had
sculpted with single-minded effort in the warm sordidness
of the dimlit Sevillian brothels, the buccaneer nameless,
bad-tempered, bonethin, in the filth, in the hodgepodge
delusions of the ups and downs of every day, the drowse
of swilled firewater, and the disenchantment of the
constant waves of rumor and prophecy of unknown lands
floating within reach of his hands. Or in the crowded
dispatches of standoffish ship recruiters (to him especially), a frothy-headed market in the blood of adventurers, where so many prowl like hungry wolves swapping
tales of treasure and trumped-up dreams, golden lands
acting on their souls like a glittering magnet of speculations (it was here, on one of those lost days, that he came

across Luz, the Hebrew, a deranged prophet shouting over his faded portolanos the exact location of an immense land hidden in the middle of the Sea of Shadows; here that he sized up the loftiness in his eyes and the firm intuition of his expoundings). Or in the unbearable bouts of greed fever that sweated in his mind after his vesperal, solitary walks along the misted docks of the Andalusian ports: push off, no time to lose, for the bizarre chimera, not caring to what delusory dimensions this could rise during the long blistering watches on the caravel's planks, toward territories absent from the known planispheres and which only he (forgetting the most basic cartography, the stars and their uses, shrugging off the complaints of the expeditionaries, their picayune grumbles, their sense- less, superfluous prayers, frowns, and curses, stammered mutterings that coiled around him as he passed, his mind blanked on the open sea to the magic of compasses and alidades, astrolabes, sextants, and other navigational instruments he had never bothered to master, blinded and dazed by the wisps of ether redolent of land that day by day the winds blew with teasing calm from the most distant, untouchable horizon) could see taking shape on those same sea maps of dreaminess (so clear, so precise, nonetheless, to the Hebrew), phantasmagoria colored by the daily green of the sea—black gleam of its depth—the starry indigo of the silent sky and the unseen dun-grey of land, the pirate brandishing as universal cosmogony the ignis fatuus glowing fitfully on the brows of the adven- turers, in their fevery intuitions, that which rests, sleepy but smoldering at the bottom of so many days and nights vanishing into thin air, fading into disillusion, into the green waters, and the starry indigo sky that denies them glory.

Rejón looks again and again into the glass at the sudden vision. He still questions the reality and true nature of the apparition looming in their path like a capricious, outlandish monster. Perplexedly he peers into the limpid transparency, the flawless crystal, the crepus- cular light bringing to his ambition-fevered eyes the possible dimensions of the floating silhouette: an impla- cable sphinx in the middle of the sea, stippled with deep grey cast by the silvery gleamings of the spring sunset, a magic promontory afloat on a sea lightly rippling, gently rolling, twisting into whitening cinders of surf only as it breaks against the shore. Yellow sand beaches. Almost all its contours smooth, Rejón the corsair murmurs to himself, wrapped in frills of fascination, standing erect at the quarterdeck beside the beaming smile of Simón Luz, the Jew. Middling cliffs, Simón, over there on those distant slopes, climbable for the peasants. Pluck up heart, Rejón to his ambitious soul, to himself, lips parted murmuring orisons of happiness, learned by heart and mulled over and over as he waited for this selfsame moment, fever again streaming up and down his spine, discoverer of continents, doer of great deeds, conqueror of peoples, constructor of new cities as indestructible as his dreams.

"Salbago, Simón. Just where you pictured it."

"Right there, Captain," replies Simón Luz, the second-sighted. "Island or continent, makes no difference now."

Elbows on the rail, all the muscles in his body stunned, trembling and trembling, gaping at the hypnotic land, Rejón stands unflappable before the yearning that brims like boiling oil out of the burning eyes of the sailors, which rivet on the spirited face of the bearded corsair, hang on its least twitch—shining now, unshrinking, with that brilliant dizzying aura of conquistadors. The undampable lust he had gone to such lengths to contain during the long excruciations of the voyage, as despair ground against the efforts of the men, drinks up in one swill the crew's longing for land: open cracks the grey line of the sea before even he himself had foreseen it. Larios casts his eyes to the deck before the Captain's unswerving tenacity. As for Simón Luz, he never let on to the misgivings that may at moments have nagged at his insides. Superstition, black insolent bat wheeling over all their longings, holds the ships beneath its solo command, in a lost corner of that strange, mysterious ocean, at the edges of a dark, abysmal world.

By now Rejón's mouth is mostly salt. Fiddling, fondling together, his fingers coil, collide against one another nervously. Fingers clasp around that Greek seafarer's amulet, paw at that olive-green stone mossed with time and the legends of the sea that little by little have encrusted into its creases, becoming its true essence. A stone snatched in combat from the pirate Spiriakós, and his life in the bargain, near the shores of Oran. Fingers coiling like claws, scraping over the callused skin of his hands, winks and signals having something to do with the secret rite of pagan exorcism lying indecipherable in the buccaneer's soul. Now, with those fidgetings of his fingers, he is trying to shoo away from himself and his ships the mirage, if such it is. He abhors the fearsome legend of Saint Brandon, scattered like accursed seed, swimming over the seas, port to port, century to century, listened to in panic by seafarers the world over. A moving whale that looks like land. An Irish monk said mass thereon, blessing a nonexistent geography, the nightmare of all lost sailors. One day land would appear portside, and then, hours later, as if by the workings of some strange magic, without in any way altering the caravel's course, starboard. Or they would hold a close wind, luffing to the shores of the mirage. Then the vision would pop up suddenly at the stern, now far out of reach of the terrified adventurers, as if the boat had crossed—through invisible fog—a blurry semblance of land. A huge whale dragging its weighty extremities, snorting and spouting like an ancient curse into all the recesses of the Atlantic. Jasconius, Simón Luz had said more than once, is his name, and he never wearies of swimming these latitudes. He rolls like waves. He will rise over the horizon, then plunge, suddenly, on a sheer whim, beneath the dark water. Leaving not a wake. Moving island, flying tongue waking fever in the terrified loins of the sick sailors, phantasmagorical place draping itself in mists when least expected and vanishing from the sight of humans.

"Hundreds of sailors," Simón Luz went on, "have seen it, Captain Rejón. And hundreds claim to have set foot on that cursed land the sailors call Ilha Nova, linked to the legend of the Seven Cities. I have even heard, Captain, that they have drunk fresh water from its streams, tracked footprints more than twice the size of ours on its trails. An island whose surface is studded with crosses, as if it were a marine cemetery concealing many secrets. Everyone concurs on the story of the storms that unleash there at the end of the day, as the sky begins to darken, forcing them to cut loose and make for the sea, abandoning to their fates those mariners who could not reach the boat on time. I myself, Captain," the Jew pressed on, "have held in my hands some damaged copies of the Pizzigani Portolano, lettered with the island's name: Brandany. The ghostly face of the monk glides over its geography, blessing the monster, which steers north-south always. In the middle, Captain, is a curvature. And on either side, a mountain, like certain camels of the Orient. Clouds, whorls of smoke, banks of fog crisscross it constantly, keeping it cloaked like a phantom whose hazy shadow straggles over the sea and scatters on the horizons."

Any moment now Rejón could lose control over the snarl of nerves knotted in his throat. Liquid, what is left of his muscles, depleted in the adventures (that stiff coldness that spikes all his outward movements with tightness). His face is a puckered mask, a fiction, about to fly off through the pure air of the new glory now floating near his hands. The brittleness is fading from his features due to the strange cluster of sensations that clump and heave and spew in the deepest deep of his self, there, in the murky convolutions of his entrails where not even his feelings dare reach. He is deluged by confusion on this triumphal afternoon of his corsair life. Sweet savor of pomegranate, sourness of this same sweetness, triumph unrivalled, extravagant honor, endless glory. Was this the fitting moment to rake up all his previous fiascos, to be caught up and swept away by the legend of Saint Brandon? Was this the moment to dawdle over his alleged and outsized ambitions, dreams of discovery and conquest of the Promised Land, years of desperate waiting, trip after trip to Arzila enlisted in obscurity, a mercenary like any other, the repugnantly heady smell of the Berber pirates, all the useless battles waged on land and sea for the benefit and stupid honor of the Portuguese lords, in return for which he had gleaned a few crummy coins that had in no way made him forget the uglinesses and lost blood, the wounds and thirst, and that had, conversely, cloaked him in the infamy of a hard-core, incurable pirate? He had fought for them and they had doomed him to wander port to port branded with a curse. Was this not the day to forget the vile scars on his memory, now, when hope and grit were wholly borne out, vindicated?

Untold documents, various and sundry versions of the map of the world (lines clumsily drawn by hands that have never splashed even in fresh waters), planispheres of childish dimension (always abandoned halfway, ambitions drying up, lost amid dreams and fears, lukewarmness and indecision), chronicles of journeys, seamen's charts jotted with imaginary endless routes on which the boldest, finest keels vanished without a trace, wakes closing soundlessly around themselves and retreating into the void, waters again virgin as though they had never been furrowed, never slit by caravel, fusta, carack or galley, mute their lips of foam: to his mind these vapid scribblings concealed no arcane secret. Nor did he lend much credit to the highbrow speculations of those who thumped, from festooned pulpits, a geography they slicked in their arguments with a nearly impenetrable veneer of lies, hoax and fraud hoisted to a level of dogma that verged on religion. Not Macià de Viladestes, the Majorcan (mere good will of an idealist, grounded in faith in God); nor the strange lines marking capes, cliff heads, gulfs, bays, wilderness, estuaries, of Angelino Dulcert (description of one more sour experience, equal or even inferior to so many others); nor Ptolemy before him (whom the epochs had seen to putting in his place, his jumbled, informal assertions verging on the ludicrous, mere hunches, when all was said and done, of a cultivated philoterre); nor the incorrect, unfinished charts of Valentín Fernandes; nor Estrabón himself; nor the fragmented legends of the Nordic seamen, to his mind inconceivable (to which, even so, Simón Luz acceded a certain authority in the matter of seas); nor Giacomo Giraldi; nor Andrés

Bianco. A fraud, all their scintillating studies, all their maps of a secret sea, an unknown earthly geography that made no mention of the hidden presence of Salbago Island, busy as they all were with the creating of continents. Smoke-scribbled hypothesis that the true history of navigation was showing to be false, drapes of wind glazed with European book learning, which like a stage backcloth brandished an absence of knowledge. And for years, this whole maze of madnesses had been succored in the salons of Europe's imperial gluttons, eager to spread their luxuries and sterile extravagancies into new, still unfound worlds. And yet he, the so-called pirate Juan Rejón, a thousand times spurned in the anterooms of shippers' and shipbuilders' dispatches, he and his mania for new, golden lands had brought to light his truth: that solid land on which they gazed.

Rejón shifts his eyes to the sweaty, ecstatic face of Simón Luz, the Hebrew. Beyond, also on the quarterdeck by the wheel, he gauges with his eyes the shape of the loyalty in the face of Bartolomé Larios (with him before, in Arzila, so many times on the brink of capture and enslavement, crouching in fear in the light of the half-moon flooding the sea, with him now too, at the hour of glory, at the gates of fame).

But it is still too soon to advise the Bishop or the Deacon, says Rejón to himself. Better to relish, if only for a brief moment, the sphinx' whole surface. Possess the whole expanse of her, as though he were her true master, as though his eyes and his will could kiss the tangy flavor of a sacred and exotic fruit. Observe with the inner smile of liquid lust breathed with slowness and contentment by the court painter who, after repeated sessions with the palette knife, cashes in for the many-layered portrait of his lord. His senses are dizzied by infinite pricklings. Acidic juices that have never before today coursed in his body seep to the skin, sopping with his sweat and sliding toward desire, that constant pulsing wherein the power of pleasure far outstrips the instant of sane sensibleness. Juan Rejón's thoughts melt in pleasurous shivers. Likewise those of Hernando Rubio, known as Paleface (his nervous hands gripping the foresail sheet), whose fate as Inquisitor no one yet suspects. Likewise those of Martín

Martel, the Campmaster, who, never imagining his future disgrace—lonesome death by cockroaches and savage beasts of the night—is already turning over in his mind how to best deploy an army which will wage mock combat only, against the enslaved men of the vanquished Blue Empire. Likewise those of Sotomayor, the Lieutenant. Likewise the Architect, Herminio Machado, poring endlessly over his charts, spread open on the deck of the caravel, blueprints of a city, a cathedral, ramparts, a street-plan never to match his imaginings. Likewise Bartolomé Larios, the Helmsman, fanatical fantast, inseparable shadow of Juan Rejón, his double, believer in all the pirate captain's dreams, to the point where he turned the Leonese's moonstruck obsessions into personal conviction. Likewise Tomás Lobo, Sorcerer from Biscay, ensconced in silence and the loneliness of the evil eye, enlisted for the first time in the adventures, in the mad latitudes of the Discoveries. And Pedro Verde. And Julian de Cabitos, Rejón's right-hand man. Likewise the thoughts of all the callow hidalgos and hungry peasant boys sailing on the caravel of Juan Rejón and the five coming along behind. Ecstasy singing wildly through his chest. Swirling the senses, no catch, no kicker, ravening smiles on all their radiant faces.

Any moment now a little tremble will begin to ripple through him (it is indeed land, Rejón), quivers calling out a unanimous cry of the senses, hysterical chortles from the innate wildness of his being: a foamy drunkenness metamorphosing his body, weathered in so many pyrrhic adventures whose long futility is just now fading in his memory.

Nevermore, for even an instant, will he be Juan Rejón, mercenary captain. Forever will it vanish, this notoriety hanging upon him like a dead weight ever since it became known in Castile that he was in the pay and command of the Portuguese enemy. Ever since he aided the pirates of Oran in deflowering certain hidden coves on the coast of Andalusia, and mapped the water routes by which to burst by surprise on the innocent calm of the white villages of Majorca, his infamous name wherever it went dragging an accursed rumor behind it, rattling like the tail of a serpent. Nevermore Rejón the violent, fierce,

cruel, brutish, rash corsair, the dangerous voyager a
thousand times pardoned by the Crown, adventurer who
never lived up to his sworn vow, liar, thief, sailor-dreamer
and shammer, pirate to whom no one could trust property
or monies, merchandise or enterprises, save for you,
Bishop Juan de Frías, who backed my adventure, who
believed in my madness for land, deeming that on the
high sea fever would devour my will, and that you would
so easily avail yourself of my caravel, of its ruin, you who
know nothing of the sea! And you, Deacon Bermúdez, you
humbug, you scurvy castoff from Spain's gloom-filled
monasteries, its churches looted and penniless thanks to
your extraordinary greed. If from the beginning I had
heeded your counsel, of shysters and hick confessors, just
think where we'd all be right now. Shackled to the gates
of hell for sure, lost in the abysses of this blue and black
immensity, straying sleepless over this godforsaken ocean,
for your hennish squawks, our drowned bodies bloating in
the murky deep, our wried faces peering out of the watery
mirror, the face of the enemy.

Do you not see, in hindsight, how you have disgraced
yourself before my young hidalgos, my peasant boys, who
are here because I roused in them the lust for adventure
and not because of your feckless prayers? Will you not see,
for once, Bishop, that you have been wrong, that you lack
sufficient knowledge to exercise command in matters of
the sea, a world unsuited to you, hidebound, god-
communing friar who all during the voyage has seen a
storm in a squall and a curse in our quest for the land
we've now found. Do you see that your maps, your bibles,
your missals, your breviaries and manuscripts smack of
error and lost routes? Do you not see, Inquisitor, that the
earth has no end and that beyond that unknown vastness
some new land is always cropping up, that beneath the
seas no infernal abyss hides, no monstrous creatures lurk
but those that dwell in your sick imagination, that no—
lands in plenty float out there waiting for reckless adventure to move all our blood? But you, puffed-up Juan de
Frías, think you've got heaven in the sack, thought you
would pass your holy time for prayers yammering yarns
of the sea, what can you know of dreams and sailing,
quests and cravings, defeat, and the throbs right here in

the soul—but you've purchased yours with your niggardly money—that blaze the trail to glory in this world, the glory of men, Bishop! Yours is the prie-dieu, the barren drone of devotions, buying the mercy of what you do not believe so as to guzzle up our conquest with us, this History you were never man enough for, hero in petticoats! If it goes bad, blame the sailors. If we have success, you'll seize it for yourself. Now, Señor Bishop, as you begin to dream of baptisms, prayer books, inquisitions, cathedrals, Juan Rejón is law—not rashness, not hunches, but more truth, more life, than your virtue of a white-washed sepulchre! Juan Rejón is a safe port in whom to moor henceforth, forthwith, and I at long last shall claim as my own the purest, brightest air of this land just now discovered thanks to my boldness, my madness, and my perseverance. Were it for you, Bishop, we would now be back in the Port of Santa María telling fish stories so as not to be the laughingstock.

The corsair, in his silent soliloquy, spews a deepdown uproar of glory-spasms, seasoned as he is in the summits of the most thundering flops. The syrupy, cloudy juice of pleasure slides slowly up his spine to the base of the brain, then swirls through the body, making it tense and quivery all over, a rapture that overturns at a stroke all the riddles and blunders of the voyager wont to find, at the end of the sea-green trail, blank nothingness, wan disenchantment and death. All Captain Rejón's senses sheathe in fascination's golden tunic, in the echoed shudderings of pleasure that flitter like ceaseless butterflies with every pull of breath, overwrought, inebriate on fierce wonder inflaming and smothering all through his body, casting him a new image in the eyes of his men, that beau ideal that crowns the chosen discoverers of the Spains.

Paleface—Hernando Rubio—hovers around Rejón. He watches greedily, lustfully. Eyes bulging in their sockets. Drawn nerves visible in clenched muscles. Like an inland bird that has sopped his feathers in a puddle of water, scrawny, scraggly, always on the brink of a swoon, the discovery for him means redemption and survival. He pines for the smell of woman. It's an island, Captain Rejón, says Paleface unctuously. An island for you, señor, and for us who trailed you blindly to these new frontiers bowing now to conquest beneath your command, who shut our ears to the false sermons, flung out the tall tales and fears bulging in our gut, baffling us.

Hernando Rubio, the sailor, limps unmistakably. The sickly, hamstrung tendon in his left thigh mars the natural grace and distinction of this onetime student of medicine, dashed down now from his status of old-line nobleman. He is nothing but a dim shadow of the young, sleek, blond, smiling figure who climbed awkwardly on board Juan Rejón's caravel close to forty days ago, in the Port of Santa María, just as the buccaneer was giving the command to undo the ropes from the bitts, unfurl the sails, and make for the sea on what many muttered (Bishop Juan de Frías secretly among them) was a voyage with no return. To sail away forever was also the golden dream of Hernando Rubio. To leave behind a wretched, thankless, flat, dreary, grim, narrow, Manichean and Cainean land, and go seeking another dimension, in quenchless quest for another life in new as yet untried lands.

If Hernando Rubio had not been a weak man, if he had assuaged his slakeless thirst for the skin of a woman by

19

bathing himself daily in the holy water sprinkled by the
Bishop as he said his blessings, the temptation would not
have coiled with such dark power in his mind, his soul,
or the empty hollows of his belly. He would not have had
to brook Rejón's gibes, the Bishop's anathema, or humil-
iation by those who, by dint of blood and class, were far
and away his inferiors, he who hailed from hidalgos and
shieldbearers in the service of Castile and the union of
Spanish lands, who bears the emblem of his age-old heritage in the randy palms of his hands. And above all, he
would not be hobbling beside Juan Rejón, before Bishop
Juan de Frías, the patron of this venture (the original
monies by now squandered) whereas heretofore his advice
and counsel had been heeded with utter attention and
ballast, with silent respect, by the expedition's captain.
He would be sailing into port with all his honorable goods
clean and intact, not needing to cap his left knee with his
left hand, which he did not solely to ease his mind, but
to allay the continual pain in his totally unstrung muscle.
To the eye, he thus disguised that hideous old-burro
hobble that would accompany his steps now forever.

Tomás Lobo was at fault for his maritime mishap. He
had found him hiding, skulking in the stinking shadows
of the caravel's inner depths, in the deepest, remotest of
the holds, where the light barely reaches, where with
every dash of the sea against the hull's creaking timber
the noblemen's blinded horses neigh, fretful, and kick at
the planks, filling the bilge with their rotting feces.
Sprawled there on a sackcloth throw bought in the
markets of Cádiz, dead to the stinging smell of horse
dung, Hernando Rubio, lone priest, common dreamer,
celebrates a private mass. He attends his own ceremony
of pleasure, his daily rite of devotion. At the drowsy hour
when the sailors take their siesta, slowly he descends the
steps, entering his world of shadows and personal idols.
As the ship sways, the near noon light, sidling through
the open portholes, strikes his eyes for an instant, then
plunges him again into darkness. He chooses the mute
complicities of the hold, the sounds muffled, dry and
hollow, the multiple but now familiar stenches of horse
sweat, the blurred bulk of the supplies in his care ever
since the Andalusian stevedores, with might and main,

with ropes and pulleys, lashed them to the iron hooks and
rings of the orlop. There, in the turbulent silence of the
holds, Paleface has been transforming himself, shedding
his playfulness, shooing off his friendliness, his eternal
smile, his flair for people. The wickedness has poisoned
his young body, limiting his imagination to making up in
this way for the mandatory absence of woman, hopping up
the already overblown passions of a sailor seasoned until
now in wenching and debauchery. His face, once shining,
is scoured and transparent. His expressions wrinkle and
shrink, his frowns sour numbly, pale as wax, white as
marble. Dully his green eyes gaze off into oceanic pits of
disillusion. Livid, lonesome, like a Greek caryatid,
Hernando Rubio the seaman has bitten the bait of his
inexperience and fallen, at a stroke, into the swamps of
temptation, which now, in the peaceful hour of the siesta
and the stifling heat of a dead calm, exact all his life
forces, enthralling them to the urgent fulfillment of the
ritual. In the slithery caverns of his thoughts run wild the
ceremony's first shadows splash, giggling feminine forms
sloshing and rolling, gorgons with a thousand flowery
breasts, their vulvas waggling before his terrified, closed
eyes. For him alone the naked bodies dance. For him
alone, unseizable, soft, ethereal, smoky shadows fleeing
swiftly across the imaginary stage and ensconcing themselves behind the scenes, only to pop out again before
Paleface's eyes, rousing in his olfactory memory the jelly-
like smush, the quenchless gush of a woman's sex. With
a thousand silken fingers, the hands of the shadows caress
him, craze him with sharpened fingernails, contort him,
cradle him in the darkness of the hold, singing lullabies
that lace with the moans of passion and thrusts of pleasure, there, far from the others, like a leper lusting for
his own demise. Gliding toward him myriad breasts he
has seen a thousand times before in the light on the face
of the water, the erect buds of a thousand nipples puck-
ering like roses to his lips, virgin breasts sashaying across
the water between the mist and the illusory allure of the
mermaids, the lines of their bodies liquid and voluptuous,
hair streaming over their sometimes exotic, sometimes
familiar faces. The swashing of the sea against the outer
hull does not divert his attention, but comes to his ears

transformed into the mesmerizing murmurs of women in heat, goading and arousing him.

The old wizard Tomás Lobo has frankly suspected him for some time. He covets his sudden silence and indrawnness. More than once, Paleface has felt the brujo's eyes riveted on his back, impaling him. He ogles him as he works, as if he wished to ferret Hernando Rubio's secret from the pleats of his paleness.

"He's turned mum," says the spy to Larios. "He's hexed and now he won't talk. He brings us bad luck," rasps the Biscayan into the Helmsman's ears. "Maybe he boarded ship with a secret. A secret which will sink us all. We must cast him away, señor, away from us. A boat and a few supplies so he'll dry up on the open sea and this jinx will quit us. Drink up this holy herb, señor, so as to sight land."

"Not a word to anyone, Lobo," Larios orders as he sips the hot fennel tea. "Watch him, but don't let him see. And when you have it all, I want to be the first to know. You could be right, wizard, and we're cursed for his mysterious practices."

At the bottom of this selfsame secret throb Tomás Lobo's unconfessable feelings, lingering twinges, shared not even with Bartolomé Larios. If he wishes to unveil the mystery of Hernando Rubio, unearth if he can that unknown treasure caught sight of amid shadows (pore with slow pleasure over that penis longed for night after night), share those sobs linked to the memory and absence of woman, love, him too, lustful little hawk, that wild creature moving jerkily, fitfully in Paleface's hands, beg for a meeting, ask what will never be had, impossible coupling on the open sea, laments scattering their notes through the shadowy hold, a thousand sobbed phrases of an endless, tortured plea; if Tomás Lobo desires all this, slimy meddler, in hot pursuit, he must watch Hernando Rubio at last bite the wretched dust of desperation, once the spider lurking in the wizard's soul has spun its strategic web and bathed Paleface in his bilious venom. So he lies hid, waiting for the erstwhile student to enter the murky hold. From the shadows, he spies him like a hunch stirring in the distance, taken up in the preparations for his rite. In silence he watches the crescent climax, the arcing of the young milk-white body like a star open to the firmament. He's ready now to burst in on him in this pose, ridiculous once exposed, strange and strangled seconds after the brief light slips through the chinks, through the cracks in the planks, and strikes Hernando Rubio's lewd gleaming member, igniting firefly sparks— flashes, wee gleams of deflected light—on that smooth, spastic tender skin the wizard is loving now in silence. On the collusive sackcloth, on the dank floor of the hold he has converted into a chapel for his manipulations, Pale-face swags his young body, grinds his feverish form against the black planks on the ship's bottom. Lobo fondles the wrinkly geography of his own balls, his skin pulled tight by sudden passion, his cock a unicorn braying, horning in on its prey. In the shadows, a drool of pleasure dribbles downbeard out of the wizard's passion-parched lips.

"Paleface, you slimy son of a bitch! Heretic!" Lobo halloos from the shadows, aiming his voice at Rubio. "Have you perhaps forgotten the sermons of Deacon Bermúdez? Don't you know how Bishop Frías decries the sin of masturbation? You're a blasphemer, Paleface, an example of sin to all. Whack off your hands right now, I should. At last"—spite and satisfaction glitter in the depths of Lobo's eyes—"you will fall from favor with Captain Rejón, who you've been conning all this time, abusing his trust. I'm a wizard and from wizards I hail since the night of the ages, when your kin were not yet a worm-embryo. I loathe your airs, the fraudulent nobility of your sickly blood and the blood of your children. Hear me, lonesome sinner, I will spread your secret, I'll smear your unsheathed secret with voices of outrage. I will unmask the mystery of how you've spent your time penned up in this hold, the seal over your silence, the cause of your paleness. All will long for vengeance; you will be outcast. They'll see that you scrap your pride once and for all, and your worthless quackery, you jackoff."

Now the paleness of Hernando Rubio, where he lies petrified in his corner, is pure transparency. In his bones rattle unfathomable fears he has never felt before, flushing his face in searing shame. The shock stuns his reflexes, the first level of his basic movements, his capacity to react. He lies on the floor, scarcely breathing, his whole body shattered by the fiery stone of shame, unmanned, dazed by the lightning-sharp pain stabbing his left thigh's abductor muscle. Sure winner, numb to all, Tomás Lobo, on the brink of triumph, points again, right arm outstretched, at Hernando Rubio. His ejaculation stopped short, the drops of semen are icy tears trickling down his useless legs and chilling them. The corpus delicti of a crime he will never be able to deny, try as he does to swab away the evidence with the hem of his sackcloth throw.

"You're in my hands now, Paleface. Everyone will know what sort of phony hermit you are. You've kept it hidden from the others' eyes until today, but henceforth your honor, which you never deserved to blazon on your brow, will be unsalvageable. For the rest of Rejón's journey, you will see, during the conquest of the lands we shall discover once I have snapped the spell burdening us thanks to your evil arts, you will suffer shame and derision. Ash-coated you will drag yourself over the deck like a dog and lick clean every cranny of this ship with your tongue. This is no ruse, Hernando Rubio. Your luck is up. You're washed up, worthless for the labors of war, I say. I damn you for the rest of your days, quack-doctor . . ."

Paleface lies there, listening to the wizard's curses. He tries to cloak his nakedness with the sackcloth, his clothes whisked from him by the Biscayan's quick hands. Suddenly Tomás Lobo's gruff face flushes with lust. His voice sweetens. From Hernando Rubio's mind, the chimerical curves of the vulva have fled and a swoon chokes his senses. Lobo's breath quickens and his huge phallus huffs with lust under his thick clothing.

"Unless you would care to tend to me," the Basque goes on. "Unless you minister to my desires at once. For if not, I vow they will all be told. And first, your captain, Juan Rejón. This very day, the word will reach the severe ears of Bishop Don Juan de Frías, lord of the peasant contingent. For him, as you know, there is no sin more abominable on earth or on sea than that which you have committed here at all hours, no more costly mishap on this ship you've smirched with your shit than this masturbation to which you've shown yourself to be such a slavish, devoted servant. Never again, you hear, will he pray you to read him those precious biblical passages with your slimy tongue, blasphemer as he will now think you, your hands smutched from lusting in this loathsome, lonely pleasure. Do you follow? Nevermore will he ask you, you can be sure of it, to reminisce over your days in the Salamanca cloisters. Or to translate those goddamn Latin verses that seem to chase away his excruciating boredom. Are you still with me? Only if you pleasure me will the secret stay between the two of us, hugger-mugger, your crime unpunished if you share it with me."

Tomás Lobo is muttering into Hernando Rubio's ear. His cloying shaman-breath clings to Paleface's face: the black puke of a satanic animal oversloshing with lust. The demented passion choking Tomás Lobo's senses seizes his face with lickerish exasperation. His flushed features are so unlike Paleface's mute, defensive, inshrunk posture. Cringing, Hernando Rubio cannot even try to refute the evidence, dunked in a speechless tremble, letting the point of the wizard's sword pierce his injured honor. (You came here for this, Hernando Rubio?—the sailor brooding at the stormy eye of the struggle—for this horrid disgrace you crossed the parched lands of Castile to the olive groves of Andalusia, rustling beyond the cliffs of Despeñaperros, reached the port, the dirty, stinking water? For this you fled Salamanca, dull lecture halls, sad wine of chill nights, dissection of corpses? For this fate you nixed your puritanical habits, smirched the decent upbringing of a literate nobleman, sacked the discipline of the university, and changed your name, conqueror of delusion?)

"You have to do it to me too, Hernando," begs the wizard, grasping his shoulders softly, puffing stinkily into the fear on the face of Rubio the sailor.

Lobo moons with unleashed passion at the tired, limp member which rests, still pulsing, nearly hidden among sudden puckers, between Paleface's milky thighs.

"You have to do it to me." He jiggles, as he repeats the order, the sailor's frozen body, as it dawns on him that Hernando Rubio is in the grips of terror, deranging his features. Lobo too is totally transfigured.

So, Hernando Rubio, forget ie lovely swarm of womanly faces that an instant or so ago butt∿red your thoughts, beyond the sea, and your deepest feelings, with soft pleasures. Forget the forms of women you pine for, the female bodies a thousand times different and the same, their smells you crave. Focus on that pain bulging and bunching in your frayed tendons, so that you cannot move. Forget the alleged nobility of your forebears . . .

"I want you, I have always wanted you and I can't live any longer without you." Tomás Lobo joggles his body up against the boy's, pawing his face, which reddens with shame. "Do it to me now, Hernando, do it to me . . ."

Again revulsion and loathing rise, wadded vomit, in Hernando Rubio's gut, ascending through thousands of tiny bodily tubes, churning his insides. His chest puffs rank air, and his body, starting to react, sucks up, like a hunk of magnet, the flung fragments of his self. His eyes, cowed till now, blacken, and his right fist clenches, for one instant regaining all the power of his young body, and strikes square, like a cold rock whose scrape ignites kindling, like the crack and sting of a whip, against Tomás Lobo's wried face, scrunching his coarse beard and cramming his features. Tomás Lobo reels backward, scared, and tumbles against the stacked supplies—mute, motionless witnesses to this unmatched duel in the dark hollows of the hold. Hernando Rubio feels his wrecked muscle keeping watch over the inside of his left leg, where all motion seems to have dozed off forever. He knows too that his brusque refusal, his unforeseen response to the Biscayan's amorous advances have swollen the wrath of Lobo the wizard. Tomás Lobo could kick him in the face, scoring in his moment of paralysis. Or have the gall to crush in his chest, and the sailor could not spew one syllable for help. Silence matters to him most of all, that the dark forgotten hollow of the hold be the only witness to the fight. The worst is to cry out, or fight back. Silence is best. Lobo has turned into a brute beast again. Coming up from the blow, he buffs disgustedly at his face with the dirty palm of his hand—that callus-covered, blunt, peasant hand that for one moment grazed Paleface's firm soft desired epidermis.

"Señor," tattles the wizard, "Señor Larios. I know why the sailor is so vastly pale. He's a jackoff, a wanker"—all his vindictive fury lurking in the accusation—"the wickedness is sunken in his core. I caught him pleasuring himself deep down in the hold with the horses, where the stench of dung and crap is intolerable," Lobo whines, mealymouthed. "At first I thought he was shirking work, going down into the bilge to spit up his dreams in the darkness, out of our sight. Later a hunch led me to suspect him of buggery. Dare he fuck the hidalgos' mares to slake his sick passion? But no, of this I'm not sure, though it too could be. Today I hit upon what poisons his face and hangs a curse over the innocent heads of our sailors, who blame Captain Rejón for blunders never committed. It's an embarrassment to Señor Bishop. And to Captain Rejón himself, who placed his trust in him, who pegged too many hopes on Paleface, while he's done nothing during the crossing but dupe him . . ."

Nor will silence linger upon the lips of Bartolomé Larios, his unbending figure shadowed by the wheel, obscured now the black smirches on his past—the sly captain of other pirate adventures, invidious buccaneer who will not let a moment elapse before handing on the news to Rejón himself.

"Bestiality, señor. With the mares. This is the true cause of the skin malady we have noted in Hernando Rubio. He rubs himself with the beasts to slake his desire, in the filthy bottom of the ship, Captain. He took it no one would go down there to spy him out, because no one, Captain Rejón, but a sick man would stomach those hellish smells voluntarily. You always forbid the men to go down to the holds to rest from the sun when their chores were done. Meantime, he could go down there freely to tend the supplies. He was above suspicion!"

After many days at sea, Rejón's caravel plows waters woven with rippling interrogatives and murky, mysterious colors. Faces perhaps glimpsed by a sailor on the visage of the sea. Glinting smiles, menacing scowls, omens and unfathomable auguries. Images of altar saints like drowned men peering out of the mirror of the sea. Rowdy demons chuckling and shrieking and beckoning to the sailors to go with them to the ocean bottom and revel in their strange orgies. The boats falter, leaving not the least wake, unable to stand on a straight course, once the wind and the capricious coursing of the currents bring fears. Fogbanks rise suddenly out of the void before dawn like tatters of night, wrapping Juan Rejón's caracks in shadow until well into morning: as though tethered turning circles in some remote recess of the Cantabrian Sea, or lost along the hazardous trails of the Great Sun. Dusky, fragmented paths: the sea a forest in the dark groped through in terror and silence; the back-and-forth creak of footsteps on the worn planks of Rejón's ships. Out in front is the one he commands, relying on feverish hunches and making light of the evil glares and terse whisperings of the Deacon and the Bishop. Five smaller caravels scuttle tremblingly behind as though Rejón's ships were an omniscient guiding star. They wend the water, sails flapping wing and wing, with weary, desperate oars.

From time to time, like a reverberating error, the sea rolls and ripples around the ships. Hernando Rubio the sailor is no longer the private, cultivated entertainment of Captain Juan Rejón. And he has forfeited the Bishop's trust. His skin parches and cracks under the furious tropical sun. Amid syncopated visions, the wind and salt

buffet the sailor's face. He dreams of the torment of
Tomás Lobo. In waves of delirium, he hears the dying
gasps of the brujo from Biscay, as the mestizo smoke of
the holy bonfire rises into limpid skies over the new land.
The wizard's scorched flesh reeks heresy. The Basque
writhes helplessly: flames lick over his body. He shrieks
his last agony: he curses them all. Rejón, Bishop Frías,
the Deacon, even Bartolomé Larios. But above all and
above everyone you, Paleface you bastard, inquisitor,
murderer, never shall a one of you ever squirm out of this
piece of shit you've discovered. As you have condemned
me, so I condemn you: here I damn you to remain, mold-
ering, ever on the brink of death, stuck in this ground like
weeds. The crackling of the burning wood sends the
brujo's curse into the skies; it floats in the ears of all
attenders of the spectacle. Here too, among Paleface's
visions, are the Black Duke, in the seat of honor, and in
the crowd, Maruca Salomé, maybe his closest confidante,
stooped, her eyes runny with pussy spite. The Grand
Plaza, packed with the screaming rabble, sets the scene
for this vision. The sea has marked Hernando Rubio.
Cabitos lashed him here, to the caravel's mizzenmast. On
the sickly paleness of his skin fall the collective curses of
the crew, their spit, scowls, and ugly gestures. Paleface
dreams, he raves, he listens defenseless to the grandi-
sonant songs of the waves as they dash against the
warping deck, prophesying his future office. On nights
splattering the sky with deceitful stars, nightmares and
dreams come to him. As in a fairy tale, toward him float
the caressing melodies of naked mermaids dancing,
leaping out of the dark sea, reflecting in the bleary mirror
of the sleeping, cloudless night, always before dawn, at
the hour of mists; mermaids like smiley, never-tiring
monsters rubbing Hernando Rubio's bound body with
their hot breasts. Before dissolving into the dawn they
sing to him their hazy secrets, how to slip free of his
fetters and wrap himself in the dread density of the fog,
making no mention of the straits marked on the maps
over which Simón Luz, the Hebrew, pores, under his lamp
of pitch. Then again the vision of Tomás Lobo, the horror
of his seared face and the words of the curse pricking him
and stoking his fever.

Cabitos carried out Rejón's orders. Ten days and ten nights, damned vile jackoff. Mild punishment for your sinning soul, Paleface. Señor Bishop Frías will rest peacefully in his stateroom, his flesh protected from the inclemencies of the chill night under a heap of blankets blessed by holy hands, he will repose eyes shut, hands folded over his belly, when and only when you, unredeemable wanker, have paid the tithe for your brazenness. All expeditionaries will know, henceforth, that you have been damned like scum, you shall be fodder, fuel for the flames, warning, whipping boy, scapegoat. Masturbation, gentle or brusque, contorted or caressful, is the image of loneliness translated into deed and smothered in soft skins, recurrence of monologue and absence, Hernando Rubio, the straight way chosen by the damned of God, kneading the dough of delirium, molding out of their tormented minds oaths of urgency and desire, the she-mate of a thousand faces. The penalty for buggery, Hernando Rubio, is to burn at the stake . . . Utilize all your time lashed to the mizzenmast to contemplate your sin of indecency. Rue your disgrace, drive away those mirages that disembogue in the sea of the enemy. May your skin recover its natural hue, so that Rejón—who no longer even glances at your rags as he strides on the bridge or sips his tea of holy herbs to shoo away superstition, obsessed as he is by the land that for some days now he too has scented in the distance (as does Simón Luz, as does Bartolomé Larios), which, as yet unseen and crouching below the horizon, undoes his nerves, clenches his jaw metallically, mars the harmony and control of his feelings—grant you his pardon and favor again.

Whenever you, thirsty and ingenuous, plead for a pitiful drop of water, Larios the Helmsman sniggers. No pity in Rejón for the sinner nabbed in the act. No, snare him in his own sticky web. Lash him in the clammy ropes of disgrace and denunciation: be he hidalgo, mercenary, or common, lowly sailor, suddenly now every self-esteeming expeditionary is your enemy. They fleer silently at your lecherous sin, pious bastards, at your battered body, your left leg shrunken for good, the evil sunk there wrying the muscle.

Pray, anyway, for land to crop up on the horizon. Beg

the heavens, in which you will never have faith again, for the barrow that will save you from this punishment to rise out of the sea, though you'll be no good anymore for man-to-man combat, never make history for your alleged boldness in battle. Husband your skills as storyteller and minstrel for the secret writing. Task yourself now, and henceforth, first, to retain in your memory, then to chronicle, and last to archive the exploits of others. Scribe will you be, in your way, never triumphant warrior. Never will your robes cake with the dust of glory in the land of conquest, but in the libraries and archives your lords will oblige you to mount, that you alternate your historifying with the fearsome office of holy executioner. So garner, in books, the memory of others. For nothing else has Juan Rejón let you live. For no motive but this one has the captain curbed the urge to toss you overboard. This is your fate, your punishment, your future, and your revenge.

"Yes, it's an island, a huge island, you bird of evil augury," Rejón answers Paleface, his eyes glittering deliriously.

The corsair's face goes tight. His body smells of sulphur and the lustful flashes in his eyes strike like lightning rays on the motionless grey flank.

"I make this discovery, Paleface," Rejón preens, "in the name of the Crown. Larios, heave to. Stand by, drop the hook. We will wait here for the other captains. You, Martín Martel, work up a strategy. Make ready for the disembarkation, and for the battle against the heathen who inhabits these lands. I rely upon your arts and experience. Advise Bishop Frías presently. Fetch him to the prow for a look at this marvel."

The Bishop, his natural fatness pared away from days of obligatory fast, scurries up from the quarterdeck, still woozy from the heat of this place they now find themselves in. The water and scraggy strips of salted meat and fish shipped on in the Port of Santa María, short commons for such a long passage, have worked wonders on his peninsular adiposities far superior to the quadregisimal practice of fasting and abstinence. He looks out at the land, with relishing eyes, the palms of his hands joined over his chest. Hernando Rubio, now unfit for war, observes the joint madness of the crew, the Bishop, the Deacon, Captain Rejón, and Skipper Larios. Then the grey flank sinks (port and starboard) into the depths of the sea. Beyond, beyond the phantom of their obsessions, once again, is the vast blue sea, immutable, mysterious, flowing, virgin . . .

Before the flasks of wine swill down the parched throats of the Rejonistas; before the mirage cloaks itself again in the warm, nearing shadows of tropical night, before we celebrate this discovery with honorableness and delight, let us give thanks to God the Almighty, who guides us forever toward our destiny, pleads Bishop Frías.

"Let us pray to the Lord," commands Deacon Bermúdez . . .

Corruption skulking behind every shadow, at every crossing; bloody intrigue, constant cries for insurrection, heinous squabbles with their dark origin in the silliest nonsense; sedition, mutiny, murder, fracases endless and groundless, the flagrant fact of violence on a wild rampage. From the mud of Salbago rose a spiral of conspiracies and insurrections, watering the surface of the island, over a span of many years, with rivulets of blood, the normal order of things among its inhabitants, from the time the dreamstruck Captain Juan Rejón landed bloated with pride on the shores of this island which, in his sick delirium, he was on the mistaken brink of commuting into a continent, until the bold caravels of Admiral Christopher Columbus, on his first transatlantic voyage, cast anchor in these same smooth, welcoming waters. Slow years of bribery, of ambitions ensnarled behind Juan Rejón's single trunk of power. Insubordinations, silences, greased legends, insurgencies and superstitions slowly tinging a color much like iron oxide, like iron and fire, the motley, meaningless pawns in a game no one would ever deem finished.

The parmesanas, crossbows, bombards, culverins and cannon the Rejonistas had unloaded with fuss and hymns of glory, with such warrior gusto, onto the island beaches, turned out to be next-to-useless devices. Against no human were they necessary. And the wild neighs of those high-strung Andalusian beasts, drumming their ironshod hoofs into the soft damp sand, like an empty mockery of the violence inheld during the killing days of the sea-crossing, served no purpose. Lastly, against no real enemy who might come forward to meet them, against no heathen with face of war, was use made of the armies of peasants whose costly recruitment had been footed by Bishop Don Juan de Frías, his friends and kin.

After the thrill and joy of the landing, the mad whoop of war that ripped the skies, the gorgeous flutter of the standards and banners of Castile upon the blue backdrop of infinity, upon the yellow and black of the sand and soil on the island shores, long days elapsed, of jittery perplexity, edgy waiting, frustrated suspense, before Rejón and his trustiest counsellors were fully convinced that they were the only men on that chunk of terrain they had secretly begun to look upon as forbidding, dangerous, and damned.

Salbago was in fact deserted of human beings. The scouts dispatched, in the first moments after the hurried landing, up and down the island, came back bone-tired, bruised, white-faced with shock and surprise. Their reports, baffling indeed, rubbed salt in the patience of Rejón and his captains. They had seen only dogs. Better said, the shadows of huge racing dogs whose skin was entirely green. Dogs that yelp and tear away at the sight of a man. Savants of this terrain, in and out of the shadows and crannies of the scarped rocks they slip like phantoms, along the narrow ridges and rocky, unreachable trails. To track them for long is impossible. All sign of their fleet paws is lost forever at the dark mouths of caves and pits, and out rolls a thick, raspy growl, as if the silent stones were conspirators, guarding the dens of the green dogs, whose jaws are enormous. They bare their teeth in a weird grimace like a curse from hell, but never attack. With uncanny ease they vanish, and almost at once that howling begins, a soft purr from a thousand deep places, sudden and throbbing. Like a gigantic wheezing beast.

Simón Luz and Martín Martel, Larios, Lieutenant Sotomayor, Cabitos, and Rejón himself kept watch through several whole nights. And in the hours of greatest lassitude, when like invisible wizards fatigue, boredom, and sleepiness stroked at their brains frazzled by the futile edginess of the wait, by indecision, by the merriment sparked in them by the constant decanting of skins full of Andalusian and Riojan wines, when the questions crisscrossed, muddling any clear answer that might decode the mysteries of the day—no different from those of the day before, or those from the one before—suddenly, out of the shadows of night, like a thirsty warning stinging with impotence the sleepstruck recesses of their souls, surged the howls of the wild dogs, shattering calm, terrifying the men. The selfsame barks of the green dogs, sole masters of this hellish island set in their path by the devil, that same indecipherable language—wailings and prophecies that never quite come clear—they had listened to, a whit overcome, from the bridge of the ships moored in the harbor the afternoon of the discovery of the false continent of Salbago.

On the far side of the island, the earth was a long plain ravaged by silence and centuries of burning, as though a great planetary fire had swept through at some indeterminate point in the past, leaving it barren forever. Dominion of the devil, the shadows of the black lands stretched to the edges of the sea, where some sunken reefs, struck by the waves, sent up a dreadful crunch. There, Captain Rejón, said the scouts, not even the dogs dare go.

These same nights, the soundless shadows of the wild dogs prowl around the make-do stockade built at the behest of the Master Architect Herminio Machado (altogether remote from any labor save his obsession with the construction of Royal City, Salbago) as a forerunner-in-embryo of the city he had traced out square by square, on charts and mock-ups that were proof upon proof of the Portuguese's sagacity. During daylight hours, nearly all clear and cloudless, Juan Rejón's men, under the leadership of Martín Martel, fan out methodically through the island wilderness. They whisper of the inscrutable silences flung back to them at every step by the stones, rocks, abysses and black ashen earth from the far side of the territory, consumed, maybe, by that cursed, cryptic fire still reigning on the island and that just could be dogging their footsteps now.

The gullies and caves, the startling verticality of this terrain; waggling branches and deep roots of the ever-so-exotic trees they stumble upon in their terrified search, mysteries of a strange lonesome land sucking up in its silences centuries of codes inextricable to them, discoverers of Salbago. For days, Rejón's soldiers comb the woody surface of the island. Again and again they run up against the dreaded burnt frontier of the Badlands. Swords drawn, they press into the driest gullies, farthest from Royal. Now they track the green dogs without much vim. From time to time they catch a close look at that greenness flecked with tiny purplish spots of the fleeting hounds. They top peaks whose sheerness unlooses in them, seasoned as they are in the broad plains, a strange swoon that reels and reels through their minds, scrambling the four points of the compass, as though this new dimension had indeed seduced the discoverers. Martín Martel is the first victim of the nervous terror slithering and slicing like a steel scalpel into the brains of the landed expeditionaries. The dry solitude of the Campmaster's prior studies, his utter inability to combat so strange an enemy, drive him berserk. The warrior plummets into depressions he tries to salve, night-wandering, with the red liquid in the wineskins. In his midafternoon drunkennesses, leaves of shadow beginning to drift over Royal de Salbago, he chafes his body against the spiny fronds of palms of the camp stockade. Day after day his lunacy and lethargy threaten to desolate the army. He is still lucid. Some of his senses remain steady. Anyhow it's daft to watch the peasants chase up hill and down, hunting hither and thither for an invisible enemy that eludes them at the mouths of caves. It's absurd to see them shivering with fear before the echoing howls of silence, out of the island's darkest hollows.

Did the green dogs laugh at the frustrated conquerors? And they, the sailors, the soldiers, were they to go to shit on this damnable wedge of earth, this heap of rock swept by the careless sun and the lonesome wind, Captain Rejón? Maybe it wasn't better to abandon this land that stank of a curse inside and out, that shot the poison of despair into men of the stature of Martín Martel, his mettle scorched in a thousand battles, and him especially so far from imagining a death so terrible as that which would run him down several years hence?

"Maybe it's a punishment for our ambition. A curse from God for daring to fetch up on a land forsaken by his

hand." Bishop Don Juan de Frías nips in every moment
or so.

Simón Luz broods in the lamplight by Captain Rejón's
tent. An absurdity. A sad, senseless irony, that the long
trail should have dropped them off on this oceanic soil,
months away from the Andalusian docks, the memory of
which ebbs and flows in his mind. A disaster, that the
fickle winds should have brought them to this maze
without egress in which the only hard fact is the peren-
nial unnerving presence of silence, loneliness, and the
dismal howling of the green dogs, incorruptible creatures
of a land which closes around history like the waters of
the ocean, leaving the conquistadors without a leg to
stand on. In despair Simón Luz watches the wobbly walk
of the Campmaster Martín Martel, his crumpled face in
the clutches of grape liquor. He studies, squinting his eyes
in concentration, the hobbling, feeble steps of Hernando
Rubio, who later, and for years to come, would prove the
official scourge of Royal City. Studying the hasty maps of
this bizarre terrain, he notes the uneasiness betrayed by
the interminable dark rings under Captain Rejón's eyes,
proof positive of a worry eating him out from within,
never to quit him now for keeps, a qualm he unwittingly
passes like rabies to that whole lowly host, which instead
of working, mills, instead of living, lolls. An army beginning to come to pieces, to cater to their own opinions over
higher-up judgments and commands. Silently, night after
night, the Jew polices the fishy comings and goings of
Pedro de Algaba, who will be the first to mount the
dreaded steps of Salbago's scaffold. A son of a bitch
specializing in treason. A hardnose in that griping that
would prompt his death, who would not be happy till he
found it, who would not find it till he had roused the
troops against the Rejonistas, not stop hustling from place
to place, unslacking, obsessed, until he had incited the
sailors to insurge and return upon the lost trails of the
sea to the Andalusian ports whence, or so they said, they
should never have departed.

"The dogs, Captain Rejón," puffed the Jew, barely
budging a muscle, as if he were working up the solution
aloud; pontifical in the heat and quavering shadows cast

by the lamplight on the ground, "must be exterminated. Snuffed. Poisoned. Dead dogs, Captain, don't bite."

"The men are terrified," replies Larios, looking Rejón in the eye. "They're on the brink of mutiny. Algaba is rousing them against us and against this damned land."

"There is no damned land, Larios, only fool men," Simón Luz expounds, puffed up by the ordeal. "We're the sole damned ones. And this rank, our just desserts in this adventure, will be engraved right here forever." With a brusque, overblown gesture, hiking up his voice, Simón Luz grips his balls, conviction shining in his curvilinear face.

"And how are we going to do away with the green dogs, Simón?" Sotomayor asks presently.

"Fouling all the wells and streams on the island with poison," says Simón Luz without lifting his eyes from the ground, as though this pose lent greater authority to his words. "We must do it before the men are tempted to flee, and Algaba ends up with every reason for sending us all to the devil."

Rejón's limp silence is the Jew's answer. It's the very picture of the Captain's absence. Moreover, it is final. His will scuttled by these strange occurrences, so unforeseen, his brain benumbed by contradictions, Simón Luz speaks in his stead. Juan de Frías, the Bishop, is out. Caught up in sermons to the skies and biblical readings by way of amends, he beseeches God's pardon for a sin which, as yet unnamed among the commandments he knows inside out, is invisible, like the green dogs at the hour of truth, but which, in light of how things and events are unfolding, he is sure he has committed, he above everyone else.

"Maybe, Señor Bishop," Deacon Bermúdez throws in, "this whole mystery we seem to be wrapped in is only an illusion, a test sent to us by the Providence of the Almighty. Rather than a punishment it could be simply a step toward discoveries and higher glories. Praised be God, in that event. Now and forever," explains the Deacon, exulting in the thought of the savings entailed by a conquest not necessary after all.

For Tomás Lobo, wizard from Biscay, nonetheless, in this lonesomeness lurks a baneful sign. The hex, in his view, has not disappeared. Under that green purple-flecked skin of the wild dogs a thousand evil spirits lie in ambush, silent and surly, as yet unseen by the men. Spirits afloat, surely, at every twist and turn of these wild trails, these wilderness valleys lush with palm trees, all alike, their frond-shaded faces swaying with mocking smiles of knowledge and power, the litheness of their silent millennial shadows at odds with the stupefied steps of the Castilian horses.

"We'll fill all the wineskins with fresh water. This is the risk we must run: dump out the wine," explains Simón Luz. He looks at Rejón, trying to lure him into the virtually suicidal action he is advancing. The Captain seems to come to his senses, drawn by the Jew's zany idea. "We will poison everything else. Trails, water, stones, the caves they hide in, valleys and gullies. We will envenom the island. The effect will last but a few days. Long enough to finish off these damned dogs and their barks before they drive us batty and do us in for good."

"Laos Deo," the Bishop replies to the Deacon. I hope you're right. But I'm afraid God, in his infinite wisdom, is punishing us for a collective sin. Through his mind like a shadow sidles the memory of the journey and Hernando Rubio's transgression.

Not even Paleface, who had been charged with the specialized yet thankless mission of nosing endlessly around those scribblings inscribed in the remotest rocks, those signs that seemed to be markers down a forgotten trail leading noplace, had drawn any conclusion whatever after days on end devoted to his job of inspection. Likewise silent, sealed, and impenetrable were the hieroglyphs coded into the face of the flint-cut stones. No code exists, Captain, and it could turn out to be an irrevocable deviance to get mixed up in conjectures, in idle appraisals, señor. Besides, it's a perfectly clear fact that the whole territory is teeming with silent cemeteries, where only the whispering wind stirs, and the hundreds upon hundreds of mummies reposing in the dark bottoms of caves or ensconced in the chambers of those funerary mounds, so puzzling, so frequent on the island, señor, make me think that this silence ruling everything, even us, is on all counts voluntary. That is to say, it's only possible to interpret it as the wishes of an unknown people, an

ancient, sober-minded people who perhaps wanted to
vanish from the face of the earth, and withdrew into
oblivion, impelled, possibly, by a curse whose secret
signals are unknown to us, Señor Rejón. Maybe they did
not wish to be ruled by outsiders. Or simply the fire of
their lives flickered, then died out forever, lost all its force
and hope on this wedge of wasteland, because the place
ceased to have sway over them, forsaken as it was by the
gods or damned forever. Anything is possible, Captain
Rejón, even these speculations we have just been making.

"So we've wound up in a cemetery full of wise men" is
Rejón's only reply, his eyes on the ground, huddled in his
useless war cape, a sad simper of defeat on his parted lips.
"Damn it all!" he said.

At first it was fear of the unknown that kept the men
united around their captains, who were themselves pretty
leery, wary to a fault, keeping the army unified in
appearance only. But soon the aftereffects of this same
panicky fear set off a shiver of suspicion in the bodies of
the Rejonistas: a silence which at given hours before dawn
flittered the air over their bedazed heads, a pulsing whirr
of invisible wings grazing their ears for an instant. At
moments they quake with horror. They doubt their messianic standing as blessed conquistadors. Pedro Algaba
spearheads these plans for a sudden breakaway. He
schemes; from the cursed land he gazes with longing at
the ships peacefully swaying upon the harbor waters glittering in the lingering gleam of the full moon. His night
broodings draw in the humble peasants, their hearts unfit
to cope with such adventure, lured from the villages of
Castile, Extremadura, and Andalusia by the fierce will of
Bishop Don Juan de Frías, as if belonging to this expedition whose orneriness was now beginning to heave in
sight constituted a privilege unpeered to be blazoned on
their future shields, forged of naught. It's all a hoax, a
fumble, a monstrous blunder, Algaba whispers into the
ears of the drowsing peasants, this is a wretched land lost
in the Ocean of Shadows, a land that might swallow you
up the moment you least expect and never will you be
heard of again. A land brimming with spirits from other
ages that have nested here forever, burrowing themselves
in the mysteries we are raiding and profaning thanks to

Captain Rejón, with the colluding acquiescence of the corrupt Bishop Juan de Frías, who will wind up a heretic at the hand of the crazed will of Juan Rejón and that Jew lording it over us with his mumbo jumbo and endless machinations.

In fear-crimped flesh the return home began to feel like an irrepressible truth of the heart; an urgent physiological necessity to be met at once; an obligation of the spirit that sooner or later would induce the better part of the soldiery, now in all but open rebellion, to erupt. A pent-up rebellion the scope of whose true dimensions eluded all possible evaluation, but which Simón Luz knew all too well would mean the end of the adventure, the expedition's final demise. For the moment, the dispersal had the feel of a tumor, swelling and throbbing, an inner desire metamorphosing into a dark threat, much more powerful than the basic discipline that had to be preserved at all cost among the landed sailors, now soldiers of nothingness. A desire much fiercer than the fear bred on and on by the ceaseless barking of the green dogs in the numb dreams of the humble peasants and their masters. The ships, far shadows gazed upon from the shores of the island by hundred of eyes, became symbols of that brewing desire.

But all was not queasiness and crumbling in Rejón's camp, slumped and cracked as it was in a thousand unforeseen corners. Nor was all to be sagged morale or surrender to bleakness in the tortured soul of the Captain himself. Herminio Machado, for example, the Master Architect recommended to the Leonese Captain in Sagres by Simón Luz, turned out to be a genuine pearl in that army of cheap costume jewels clustered together in fear. A loner with big plans, head over heels in the obsession that had brought him to this island, the founding of the lost city of Royal de Salbago, he raised, slowly, patiently, stone upon stone, unflappable before the grumblings of the men, before the doggy echoes floating into camp, the first stockades of what, years hence, when the New World burst upon the Universe, was to be a port of call, an obligatory flap in the long transatlantic voyage on the far side of which lay the virgin lands of West India. Beside a nearly always placid sea, next to a vast natural bay where

the ocean had pooled and stilled its waters so that upon
them could sway, safe and serene, caravels, fustas, three
and four-sparred galleons, barquentines, polacres,
redondos, frigates, even brigantines, in short, the whole
spread of new vessels that the sudden marvel of the
coming years and centuries were to make its own,
Herminio Machado draws up his charts of the city of
Salbago. The first tents of palm and sailcloth sprang up
on the bare earth. Wines of La Mancha and La Rioja
tippled and titillated the men—who in their heart of
hearts feared the liquid would run dry—and sometimes
mollified the hidden terror inspired by this land of magic.
Little by little, the wineskins were drained of their rosy
liquid. As they sprinkled and spattered their optimism
into every hole and corner of the future city of Royal, the
men looked on a fresh world of friendly colors. The bronze
bell of the island's future Cathedral, the Rubicon (which
would suffer, over the centuries, attack upon attack,
assault upon assault at the hands of Frenchmen,
Englishmen, Africans and Dutch, and be ravaged, at the
first opportunity, by the famed pirate Vanderoles), was the
obsession of the Bishop from the selfsame day he left the
peninsular shores behind. In perfect repose, the bell
awaited its glorious moment of consecration cached at the
back of the tent of the ecclesiastical authority, who was
jealous of this blessed treasure he had turned with his
own hands on the glowing forge until it attained the form
he desired. Never, however, would Juan de Frías hear the
bells of the Rubicon toll from the high towers of the holy
edifice, because long, long before such an event he would
die beholding heavenly visions, hoodwinking even himself
in his last days.

Here, there, rose the heaps of grey stone extracted from
the nearby quarries, representing hope for the rubble-
work of the future, the docks and jetties over which at
last—all roads leading to Salbago—on a not-so-distant day
at the peak of the colonization, a many-hued screaming
herd would alight on these shores, the wives of the
explorers who had remained at home awaiting the good
tidings up and down the peninsular terrain.

In the wind, on the breezes of Royal, fluttered, peaceful
now—given their utter uselessness in other labors—the

banners and standards of the thwarted conquest of this
lone island, the possession of which was ever as free as
the notes strummed over and over, ear to the strings, by
the guitarist Otelo of Portugal, always the same song, the
same tune plumbed, in a thousand fresh variations, from
the depths of his Spanish guitar. In those days Otelo was
in big demand in the nighttime fêtes of Salbago, as he
was later to be in the cockfight yards and houses of joy.
Otelo had landed in Salbago, without name or past, in the
days of the colony, his firebrand character muffled in the
breezy sounds of a guitar. Night after night his voice,
tinged with sorrow and wistfulness, rolled from that
brawny throat, still youthful despite the long debauches
the aging guitarist always took pains to keep under
wraps. His greying hair, cropped close, bulging, jet-black
mocking eyes, pronounced jaw, the smile on his full lips,
revealed, in a word, nothing. Nothing did they add to his
nom de guerre. The tales of his rebel exploits, his sedi-
tionist feats, later perhaps to be sung by other guitarists,
had not yet begun to buzz through Salbago when the
Portuguese, as though untouched by time or history,
again cloaked himself in silence and took ship on one of
those hundreds of expeditions that berthed at the docks
on the way to the New World. So Otelo joined the folklore
of Salbago Island: the Portuguese rebel had passed like a
streak over the island territory, leaving his wake behind
him. One of those nights when it seemed that calm was
secured, and the inhabitants of Royal clustered and
chatted or drowsed or perhaps dreamed in peace, safe from
the rebellion plotted by Pedro de Algaba, Juan Rejón got
a close look at the greying head of Otelo as the singer
plucked ever the same tune with tapered fingers on the
strings of his guitar.

"What's the name of the song, Portuguese?" inquired
Governor Rejón, who was strolling through Royal as if he
hadn't a care, flanked by his closest men.

" 'Grândola Vila Morena,' señor," was the guitarist's
clipped reply. In the seat of his soul, something very deep
and dark alerted him that he was leaking one of his most
unutterable secrets, the first blush of a dream that would
never, till time ran out, have a happy ending (as he

fancied it) and whose existence, at that juncture in the days of the colony, was widely unknown.

"And what's your name?" Rejón quizzed him again.

"Otelo Carvalho, señor," answered the Portuguese, tone of voice unvarying as he gazed fixedly at the map etched in the face of Juan Rejón. In the secret dark gleam of the Governor's eyes, Otelo was trying to ferret out some clue, or whether the question hid an invisible double edge, some false underside primed by suspicion. Nothing, however, did he spot there. Nor, on the other hand, did the song or the guitarist's name have anything to tell Rejón.

Meanwhile, amid ups and downs and reversals, despondencies and renewed raptures, plans that never netted positive results, and daily disobediences, Rejón's men went on tuckering their bodies in a strategy they now replayed with their eyes closed: painstakingly they combed every inch of that surface pocked with holes wherein there was nothing to find but the deep silence of infinite mummies and tombs, paintings and symbols, petroglyphs roundly warning of the sleeping presence of a tradition abandoned in the rocky reaches of Salbago Island.

They were engaged in the launching of a unique operation framed by Simón Luz, which would dash Pedro de Algaba's plans for a getaway.

It was the Rejonista's first act of revenge against a land which, at first blush, they deemed an enemy and a curse. And it was a means of subduing it, of forcing it to its knees before them, the profaners. It was the peninsulars' first real and irrefutable victory over the rocky contours of Salbago Island.

The terrible keens of the wild dogs, racing terrified up and down the trails and slopes, shatter, a useless lament, against the massive walls of the valleys and gullies, heretofore such perfect lairs. Away over the sea's dark horizon drift their cries for help. Thirst claws at their throats; it is this very need which will lead them directly to death. All over the island, the dog's dying shrieks ravage and derange the silence. Into Royal, where the Rejonistas have taken shelter fearing the unbridled reaction of the green dogs, float the barks, muffled by distance, devoid of that magical force that had sparked such terror in the men in recent days. Unmistakable signal that the slow death masterminded by Simón Luz was taking effect, premeditated testament of a race of dogs, at once sacred and savage, to be made extinct by this extermination so cruelly contrived by the Jew.

Only a few pups were to survive the massacre, spared from the general destruction by their helplessness; petrified with horror, deep in the caves that until now had served as cellar and burrow, they listen, shuddering, to their progenitors' screams of death. The reason for this terrible shrieking they will never fathom, never grasp. These pups would later become the pets of Maruca Salomé and the Governor Juan Rejón himself, who could only fall asleep in his wizened old age if and when one of these magical animals, that had survived the massacre only to become the faithful guardian of the murderer of his race, oversaw his repose. Another of these loyal creatures fell into the hands of the Black Duke, who had purchased it from Salomé, at the price of gold, as a living luck charm. On untold occasions the Salbagans observed them out strolling together on balmy evenings through the streets and along the sand beaches rimming the city.

But now, at the hour of death, all over the island the shadows of the green dogs, in days recent and bygone immune to suffering, stagger slowly and drunkenly as they suffocate. This strange madness infusing them with deadly poison bleeds them forever of that enviable equilibrium of cosmic animals, that awesome sense of direction hidden solely in the marrow of ancient races, and that fantastic facility for climbing, down gullies, up hills, to the sheerest heights, into the deepest pits, places Rejón's peasants cannot possibly reach. Lost, at the hour of extermination, the proud airs of a free race, stiff the moist, steaming jaws, tongues sick with death, ruined gymnasts, muscles muffing and going slack. Blinded by fear, goaded by a strange urgency their skins had never known before, they weave through the ravines, twigs snapping as they wobble by; among nettle, balos, and verols, among dragon trees and willows, sorrel and linden trees, looking for gorse against which to scratch their bodies lashed by the venom draining down through them, silently, slowly. All over the poisoned territory, the green shadows slink like phantoms, gazing in the draining mirror of their deaths at the impossibility of resistance.

The Rejonistas, meanwhile, listen gleefully to the rattle of death coiling through the dogs' green skin, though the job of extermination had been executed from the start without the faith necessary to ensure the campaign's success: merely carrying out orders they were afraid would catch up with them. It was an exorcism of their own fears. Discord rampant over the island's parched soil, Algaba dared question Rejón as to the viability of such a drastic solution. Had it not occurred to him that they too could now be the victims of the poison, that they, the discoverers, could be left without hope of survival on this godforsaken land?

"Don't trouble yourself about that, Pedro de Algaba,"
Simón Luz puts in, his wicked eyes condemning Algaba to
death. "The blight will last a few days only. Long enough
to restore peace again. For all to return to normal. And
this cursed island, as you yourself call it, will be ours for
centuries upon centuries. The dogs will have vanished and
the men will never think of quitting our enterprise
again."

"And the rest of the animals? What will happen to
them, Simón? How the devil are they going to escape the
poison, annihilator?"

"We shall repopulate," the Jew replies smugly.

"Repopulate? With what in the devil will we repopulate?" asks Pedro de Algaba, voice faltering.

"With pigs and hens. Turkeys, pullets, rabbits. With
tamed alligators, if we have to. With whatever you can
think of, with whatever tickles your fancy." The Jew
breaks off, in a sudden rage, dead set on his plans, cock-
sure, surly, sneering. His face is a scalpel; from his fury-
squinted eyes dart filaments of light, straight into his
victim. "Those animals, Algaba, will be free of danger,
spells, and witchery. And so will we. We'll all agree about
staying on this island," he adds, his eyes two hot coals
slowly searing the lost fate of Pedro de Algaba.

This gathering of leaders, attended as well by Martín
Martel, the Commander (deadpan as a dummy, however),
Lieutenant Sotomayor, Juan Rejón, Captain and
Governor, Skipper Larios, and several Castilian nobles, is
a dialogue between deaf men, Algaba and Simón Luz, two
stances at loggerheads with no hope of meeting, the Jew
slowly inking his poison around Algaba's shoulders,
silhouetting his imminent death.

". . . And if there aren't enough animals here, if not
enough have survived when the operation concludes," the
Hebrew presses on, "we will ship them in from Castile or
Andalusia. Or from Africa, right here nearby." He points
to his homemade parchment paper maps. "There's land to
spare on this island, for all people and all classes. There's
no curse here, you'll see. All will be pacified once the dogs
are gone. Fear smolders in your imagination only. The
curse, you know as well as anyone, is a fabrication . . ."

Only when the smell of rotting meat floated in,

swathing the island with its deadly murk, the stench
swelling in the valleys, and glutting every hidden hollow,
following the streams of air downgulley, slinking up to
the stockade of Royal de Salbago and wedging its stinking
limbs into the tents, soaking the whole air with foul
unbreathable fumes; only when the Rejonistas saw the
vultures and buzzards and bitterns pirouetting aimlessly
downward and pitching into the sand, the black crows
swooping out of the cloudless skies to gnash apart the
poisoned carcasses of the magic dogs; only when a
dreadful silence, whose broken throb seemed to rise from
the very center of the earth, swept through the air
smirched by this stratagem of death, overrunning all the
realms of the island, from the peaceful, calm northern
beaches (where Royal had been built) to the far shores,
and into the Badlands, deserted, blackened and solemn,
charred by the sun and lashed by centuries of unceasing
wind; only when the air itself began to densify, to solidify
into an invisible crust that rested almost like a crown on
the heads of the swooning peasants, who gasped as they
sucked at the dank, impossible air; only then did the
Captain and Governor Juan Rejón again heed the counsel
of Simón Luz and open the gates to the small fort, giving
the pertinent orders for the removal of the carcasses of the
green dogs, which must not be buried on the island or
heaved into the surrounding sea.

Hundreds of green dogs, dead every which way, great
packs strewn over the island's rugged, teetering surface,
some still shuddering and twitching their poisoned limbs,
some already stiff and starting to decompose, others
wedged between rocks as if wishing to elude the enemy
by camouflaging themselves as land. This devastating
scene was the picture of success, the outcome of the necessary extirpation programmed by Simón Luz, the Jew.
Huge pyres pitched with shrubs and dried palm fronds of
every shape and size began to burn, sending wild billow-
ings of smoke into the skies, their usual pellucid blue
desolated by this outlandish stench. All over the land, the
peasant boys heaped up the dead dogs like trash, and lit
them on fire, following Rejón's orders. The last of a race
crackled and burned in the holy bonfire, precursor to what

was soon to be erected in the Grand Plaza, the exalted Inquisition's ultimate design.

But some unnamed expeditionaries disobeyed Captain Rejón's emphatic instructions. Many corpses were flung from the wooded highlands and cliffs into the sea, staining the water a bottle-green color which would terrify the men for many days. From the fires a dense black smoke rose over the distant peaks, for seconds and even minutes at a time darkening the light of the sun that beat down on Salbago. The oppressive odor of burnt meat, of singed heretical flesh, wild, nauseating, cloying, seizes the island's soft pure air, its scarped terrain a useless simulacrum of a newly liberated battlefield. The waters lap peaceful and calm against volcanic reefs, then churn and swash against the sand beaches, spewing mucky greenish froth—as if the dead bodies of the magic dogs were deliberately sloughing their natural color, and casting it down, staining them forever, on the shores of the land they had inhabited in peace until the hour of this unforeseen mass death. Those bodies, grotesque now, their limbs freakishly bloated with salt water, swing on the capricious tides ringing the island, float upon the green water like rotten tubers, whirl suddenly like a carnival chute. Among the fuzzy scribblings, the sudden foamings of whirlpools and waves, they ride away northward from the coast until out of sight of the peasant lookouts, then slowly circle back landward from the south, coasting on currents until they beach up, swaying gracelessly, eyes wide with rage, mouthing a last cry of horror, in the murky pools, among the rocks coated with sea lichen, along the shores tinged green from the fretting of their sea-softened skin.

"Algaba, you bastard," Simón Luz huffs, "this is one more insubordination we'll nail on you, son of a bitch," as if he meant to hereby hurry on the moment of his death.

For the gulls pecking at the bloodied bodies of the green dogs, for the vultures and buzzards plunging from the heights and wheeling hungrily over the poisoned carcasses, the beaches are a succulent, deceptive feast. They bloat with the same poison that killed the dogs; the red venom havocs their lives. Overhead they reel, never suspecting that the feast is a frivolous, treacherous ruse on the part of Pedro de Algaba. Minutes later the poison will have preyed on the gluttonous guts of the carrion-sated birds: splayed white wings plummeting, sinking instantly into the vast green sea, joining in death the holocaust of the green dogs, unwitting escorts of the vanishment of a race.

It took weeks for the Rejonistas' painstaking cleanup of the remains of the extermination, and to extract from their lairs the terrified pups, inspected by Juan Rejón from the first as specimens of a disaster perpetrated at his behest. An obligatory disaster that he himself had espoused. A sort of hazy, indefinable feeling—a mix of suspicion, guilty conscience, fear, maybe compassion, and a certain predilection for the recently discovered beauty of these strange animals he had doomed to death—invaded the depths of Captain Rejón's cold-blooded body, surging through his vitals in shivery waves.

One of those nights Rejón fell into a deep sleep. A nightmare crept into him. His long hair quivered and bristled like copper wires. After a still, airless afternoon, suddenly the night is hot. Rejón has shut the big palm tent and given orders to his lookouts that he not be disturbed under any circumstances. He is able to sleep calmiy for close on two full hours, huddled in his blankets, staving off the fever that struggles to lay hold of his body. Then with a jolt he wakes, as if a vast strange noise had exploded into tiny echoes in his brain. For the rest of the night sleep eludes him as he tosses in his bed or sits bolt upright drowning and almost suffocated in heat. He stumbles over the clothes and shoes he has left strewn around his chamber. In the dark he attempts, by all means in his grasp, to make out the contours of a geography growing stranger and stranger at every step. He feels his body rasped by the spininesses of the palm fronds that make up the walls of his tent, over whose surface he now sees horrifying packs of green dogs racing. That huge noise, raising a terrific swirl of dust as it passes, making him cough and hide petrified beneath the covers, seizes hold of his eardrums and bulges them till they nearly burst. Slowly, the noise transforms into a relentless barking, like a dirge, like the impertinent chug-chug of a train coming straight at him to spoil his sleep. The bitter barking of these ghosts raises too much racket for the guards not to waken, for those awake not to take note, but neither these nor the rest of the troops hear anything out of the ordinary emerge from the Governor's tent: the chaotic performance of this damnable orchestra is earmarked for his honor only. Now the barking is an hysterical weirdness, with an acoustically unbearable whirr. It pierces Rejón's head through some hidden chink he had never—asleep or awake—left uncovered before. Rejón keeps on moving, as if his life hinged on it. He tries to tear the veils of what he thinks is a nightmare, but it's a useless effort out of the depths of which the roar of barking surges again, recharged and unrelenting, overturning whatever it fancies, the pack of hounds transformed into the star performers of an extravaganza that fills the buccaneer with horror. "Thieves! Thieves!" Rejón chokes, between dreams. A panicky sweat oozes over his skin, but now the repetitive noise plays as though it were simply the sound of the wind ruffling the palm fronds of his tent. The sound thins, but still Rejón's voice will not reach outside the tent. So he's alone at the mercy of the merriment of the green dogs, who, mass-murdered in recent days, have returned from the blindfold of death to take vengeance upon their diabolical extirpator. Rejón wades, he splashes in the swamps of his own terror. Pursued by the pack, he veers flounderingly round and round like a ship in moments of shilly-shally navigation. Now the bark is no wail but a laugh, a guffaw of dread, a delirious chortle coming at him from out of the darkness, pricking him painfully with the jerky obsessive stab of a pin, mixed with the anguish of broken sword blades adrift inside his tired brain. His weapons are useless, for a sword cannot sever a sound. His frayed coat of mail and leather cannot shield him from the barks drumming on his chest. He burns in fever. Wide awake, he can't go on listening like this, helpless before the vision of these ghosts that have robbed him of rest and peace, as he slowly and inescapably crosses the bounds of madness, viewing at every instant of the endless night the yawning jaws of virulent dogs. Even so he cranks up his courage to dispatch them. At every step he trips over the slippery shadow of some wretched dog, possibly dumbstruck by Rejón's human presence. Incensed, close to blind, he gets up and runs, only to stumble again into the dark bottomless maze at the depths of the tent. Now the dogs are no longer green in Juan Rejón's eyes, but yellow and violet. Or the strange color of certain evanescences that appear in the sky, spanning the whole spectrum of the rainbow, but always with defiance in the eye. He is besieged again, from behind, by another pack issuing from the shadows of the void, out of the dry dust on the tent floor, and they harry him to exhaustion. It's a losing battle, practically pointless, but Rejón lunges in a feverish fury at the first animal to step in his path. This dog is an immense mastiff. A trick show starts up, to the amazement of Rejón, whose face by now is a mucky red blur: the animal metamorphoses, with frightful ease, leaving no trace of his prior form. For the briefest instant, he's a shrill whistle issuing from many mouths and whizzing round and round the big tent, racing faster than Rejón himself. The pirate lies hid in any corner of that fever-wrecked geometry, then pounces on the unseizable shadow of the green dog. At once, its coloring changes again, now cat, now huge chameleon whose century-cracked skin lacerates the palms of the buccaneer's hands. It's no longer so hard for him to comprehend the impossibility of victory over these snarling phantoms that have laid hold of him effortlessly. He clutches, as tight as he can, to the shrill neck of the whistle, but it rebounds like a ball off the tent walls. Now the dog, like a boxer in the ring, zigzags and lunges at Rejón. If the Leonese Captain expects to be hit on the right side, the teeth gnash him on the left; if Rejón scrabbles around beneath him, on the floor of the big palm tent, the green wolf will leap at him through the open roof, out of the starry sky, yank at his hair with such outlandish ferocity that the corsair hears the vertebrae in his neck beginning to squeak, the long dog striding back and forth across the passageway screeching with laughter, swaggering, now rolling, a giant-sized marble of solid crystal, baring its claws, invisible to Rejón until the moment he feels them smite his battered body. Little by little he is losing hope. Within him mounts an anguishing fear of death; he notes a great pain in the roots of his teeth and the salty savor of blood spattering the inside of his mouth. Now the bark is blue music, womanly, heavenly: the slow waves of a peaceful sea frolicking against the sand of an island effortlessly conquered. Now he hears the pack withdraw, without warning, and drift off into an imaginary distance. They clear the tent as if a miraculous "The End" had arisen on the horizon of the shadowy night.

Still quivering, he is waked by the first lights of a radiant dawn, but on his chest a legend is firebranded, words drummed steadily into his memory through so many hours of fever: "*Rejón, never shall you leave this land. Like the dogs, here you are doomed to live. Like the dogs, here you will die after all your futile, barren efforts. This will be your final testament, imprisoned and forgotten on Salbago Island, dream of Castile, your bones sunken in the dry steaming mud, your memories scattered in the dust . . .*" Its echo was the accusing voice of Algaba, hung by the neck on a rope made of hemp in the Grand Plaza. In the light of dawn, obsessively the Captain scrutinizes the bruises that have erupted on his body overnight, and the tooth marks of dogs. He lapses, slowly, as though having done penance, back into sleep, after long draughts of the exorcism he believes conceals itself in hot fennel tea.

It was an out-and-out triumph, the war declared by Rejón against the green dogs, whose survival the pirate now secretly resolved to shoulder, once the greeny animals had been tamed. Years later, Maruca Salomé would whisper pertly in his ear: "Governor, you couldn't live without those dogs." A battle the Rejonistas were to celebrate, overstepping Deacon Bermúdez' scrimpy, avaricious limits, with every variety of extravagancy. In fiery, rousing torrents ran the brandy they were able to wrest from the sly tricks of the Jew down the throats of the peasants and their lords. The salted provisions, already starting to reek of rot and mold, ceded to an inordinate consumption of fresh meat—peeving Deacon Bermúdez no end—captured before the dog massacre right there on Salbago Island. Now, on the nights following the victory, the wild mutton and pork roasted over the burning coals.

Bishop Frías, this same afternoon, forgetting about the crime, about the squabbles and superstitions of the men Rejón had dragged to the edge of a lost world far from the hand of God, offers holy sacrifices on an altar of fine wood designed by Herminio Machado and his cabinetmakers, after sketches he had seen in Venetian churches, an altar they had erected in the future Grand Plaza, a few short yards from the sandy beach. Unaccustomed to victory rites, the peasants bellow a Te Deum, riotous and out of tune apparently because their throats more anticipate a battle grunt than an ecclesiastical chant of the Gregorian ilk.

"Laos Deo," grumbles Deacon Bermúdez dejectedly.

"The worst thing about exile, Governor, is the lack of a decent confabulator," pronounces the Black Duke.

Even in these commentaries, seemingly without importance, his delicacy of spirit and intellectual refinement are in evidence. He sighs softly, wishing to be scarcely noticed, extends a slim hand—between courtly and feminine—takes up the bishop and pegs it in almost the exact center of the chessboard, a poison arrow for his adversary, a challenge to Governor Juan Rejón's white troops. This current Rejón is no more than a memory of the old Rejón, broken, gloomy, a vestige, a skeleton of what he had risen to be in the days of the Discovery and the Conquest, before the Admiral struck Terra Firma on the other side, and Salbago, by dint of the Discovery, became an immense bordello, an obligatory stopping place for voyagers bound for the New World. Now, in doddering old age, his rough, wizened skin is striated by a thousand little creeks, their beds dry, running longwise and losing themselves in the useless sea of his neck, hidden beneath his pleated shirt collar. A spurious map, on which are written all the frustrations of the historic figure he will never be, of the conquistador who got hung up halfway to a destiny grafted to the mirages that rose before his eyes as he went. After all, he himself, Juan Rejón, had been the first to tamper with his destiny of marked cards, having violated the contract with his own ambition and settled for shuffling sleepily across the open terraces of his golden cage filled with birds of many colors, the terraces of Salbago's finest little palace, built with care under the direction of Herminio Machado, Master Architect. The front of the Governor's palace looked directly over the rear of the forever unfinished Cathedral, and from its balconies one could view the near sea. Numerous terraces stand open to the invariable blue of Salbago's sky, and the plant life is tended as if this were a botanical gardens. The inner chambers, nonetheless, are devoid of light, and it is logical to assume that they were constructed for the Governor's solitude and contemplation, at a time when Rejón still believed in his triumph and fancied himself a leading light in the Conquest. In whatever case, the Palace's appearance betrays some interest on the part of the proprietor in distancing himself from the riffraff, in severing contact with a world he had no wish to inhabit. Corridors, passageways disemboguing in secret chambers, a feel for the surprise and solidity of the stone with which the Palace was constructed; cellars, silent pantries where the noise of the street never reaches, blind, dark staircases leading intruders to error; chambers just about always shut, like the cloisters in a convent, bespeak Governor Juan Rejón's thoroughgoing mania to isolate himself from the outer world, to reside like a myth, concealed from the eyes of mortals.

"Decent confabulator," Rejón replies, wagging his head back and forth, scratching his chin, reflective in the wake of the Black Duke's sudden offensive.

Through his old mind, like a spurt of acid churning his stomach juices, passes the blurry, now-dated image of his son, Alvaro, who had left for the New World, chasing ambitions he meant to fulfill at all hazards. In fact, it's a clear act of aggression, his opponent's strategical incursion, pitting his bishop in the center of the chessboard, a mad bull charging the terrified cuadrilla, incensed, exasperated, dashing wildly after the waving capes, careening, throwing the arena into an uproar. His eyes, Rejón's fevery eyes, tormented by this surprise attack, plumb the provisional placement of his immobile armies of wood. The fighting instinct is all the old warrior has left: amusement for self-defense. Time has no meaning, no longer figures in his plans, marooned forever on Salbago Island, lashed to the island's roots which enthrall and devour him, to his memories disarranged by the years, his rather unvenerable old age suspended at some indeterminate point in the infirmity of his organism in perpetual decomposition, thanks due to Pedro de Algaba's last curse. For him the years are blank medals, the record of a failure, empty pendants piling up on his weary breast, the stories of a lifetime, his, whose lot was the quest of grand feats, to teeter forever on the brink, in illusion, in a punctiliously planned process of make-believe conquest that never came to fruition. His first impulse, on seeing the bishop lunge like a reckless bull, was to kill him, to strike him from the game, this battle of honor he wages with his instructor, the Duke. Then, as the Black Duke himself had taught him at the start of this slow apprenticeship, he ruled against storming the trick-fraught ranks of that challenge and curbed his desire to kill, weighing the trick that lurked in each of his opponent's shrewd moves. The Duke had advantage enough being his teacher without his going and muffing it at the first opportunity. His yellowy eyes shift from man to man, silently studying his defense. For an instant, again a flash charging his breath with acid iridescences, his memory swells with the slow, tragic death of his Campmaster, Commander Martín Martel, and the unsavory events that turned Salbago, beneath the iron rule of his long, interminably long governance, into an expatriate bordello in the middle of the Ocean.

"Decent confabulator," he said again, as if the repetition of this little refrain could make his true intentions longer and deeper and more secret. The Black Duke looked in his eyes for a second or two. Then, with urbane grace, he lifted into the air his glass of Sicilian wine, conveyed it to his lips, and downed it with slow sips, accompanying the wine with nibbles of crabmeat. A tiny grimace, between pleasure and momentary repulsion, stole over the Black Duke's face, and for a few brief seconds a distasteful shiver rippled through his body, until the liquid finally nested in his stomach with its special concupiscent warmth of well-being. Then he looked at the empty glass and concluded that the game was simply a pretext for the conversation, an operation that each contestant employed to disperse his opponent's ideas, a sort of mutual distraction of attention.

His royal friendship with the Governor had begun suddenly. He had arrived on the island in the same boat as the wife of Juan Rejón, a flavorless woman, the useless

María Isabel, fat from age and neglect. With time, and with the loneliness, an incurable malady, pitted—although to differing degrees—in the souls of both Rejón and the Duke, souring them from the inside out, their mutual affection grew. A vivid image of the Black Duke on the bridge of the ship often floats into Governor Rejón's memories. He was not on the wharf to receive the exile in person. His obligation, albeit undesired, was to be on hand to welcome María Isabel, a lady pale as wax whose every expression bespoke unwholesome decency, a wife the island had nearly caused him to forget, a woman he received, in truth, without display or excessive formality. Hernando Rubio, whose new, absolute authority had gone to his head, personally took charge of welcoming the Duke, banished by the court and doomed to oblivion, to remoteness from the Peninsula. From the moment of the Duke's landing, bizarre secrets, rumors perhaps of ulterior design, reports relayed in a whisper, hearsay of various sorts, wound through the snaky, slanderous, muddy streets of Salbago, and out onto the open land stretching beyond the city limits, where, outside Royal's walls, all changed, strewn, perhaps blown away by the whistling trade winds gusting riotously over the island's fields and forests. By then the city had exceeded the bounds of absurdity and bore no resemblance in form or content to the ambitious plans of the ingenuous Master Architect, Herminio Machado, branded a madman and a megalo-maniac by all bureaucrats with sway over Juan Rejón. Now those streets, laid out, in principle, by an excep-tional mind excessively lucid for the madness of the age, played the peculiar yet ever-present game of awkward-ness and anti-aesthetics, willfully winding and slithering among wooden shacks infested with fungi, mold, and dampness, where the windblown debris and salt from the sea swept helter-skelter over the bumpy black ground trod by Salbago's lowborn, carnivalesque mob. The city of Herminio Machado's dreams, designed to the exclama-tions and acclaim of the elite of government men and worthies as if it were some new paradise, was a despic-able dump that had lost its personality before it ever really had one, a slum over the sea, ringed on the land side by a squatty, crumbling rampart built in part for defense, in part to justify founding Royal City itself, a fortress wall pitched in a big hurry, no thought to the future, climbing off into the hills and coiling around the rocks like a zany snake, slithering away from the sea and vanishing into the foothills, possibly pursuing the uncertain steps of an invisible Laocöon. A useless wall, even for Salbago's defense, as was demonstrated some years hence when Vanderoles' Dutch pirates invaded, pressing into the heart of Royal and setting fire to the Cathedral. Outside the city gate, the world of shacks sprang up spontaneously, the outlaw city, the dens of delinquency, sickness, vice, the most delirious diversions, where men—more and more of them all the time—cached their hushed pasts; hid their banned names from the authorities, or launched a new life of underhanded ambitions, in the miry mud, in the sour lonesomeness, waiting—almost always in vain— for the chance to slip away without a sound for the New World, the Promised Land they dreamed of in their endless delirium, and for which they were constantly drumming up plans and projects without a leg to stand on, initiatives that would never be seen through as imagined because they originated in absolute ignorance of the mad dimensions of the Terra Firma discovered by the mythical Admiral.

The Black Duke was banished to the island for political reasons. To remove him from the court of the Glutton Carlos V, to suppress his overweening memory, to snuff out his haughty pride, was the object of the punishment. Privileged and pampered since childhood, exquisitely groomed to govern and administrate one of the far-flung towns on the labyrinthian Peninsula which, to its own surprise, was becoming an Empire, he had bilked the plans of his parents, who in the end, by pure miracle, were able to save their son's neck from the justice of the royal scaffold. But at no time, in these terms, did the Black Duke ever allude to his trial in any conversation with Governor Rejón, not even in his most euphoric moments, when wine from Sicily and Alta Rioja drunken to excess lent its color to the cheeks of the bearded exile, the motive for whose punishment slumbered in silence and mystery or mulled in the fevery imaginations of the Governor's friends and officers. His defense, futile before the fact, collapsed before the cyclopean intransigency of the judges and royal councillors. Exile was the most fitting solution: a golden cage far from the Peninsula, but remote as well from the new Terra Firma discovered by Christopher Columbus beyond the seas, where the possibilities for resurgence of the defiant, still young Duke would be quashed for life, where in spite of his punishment—common knowledge—the purity of his blood and his high birth would be respected. His neck was spared, but his life ruined. Only Paleface, Hernando Rubio, was privy to the trial's secret. "They should have sent him to death, instead of to hell," was the vulgar retort that Governor Juan Rejón received, stunning him, when he expressed his curiosity to the Inquisitor as to the reason for the Duke's punishment.

So here was the Black Duke, on the quarterdeck, in the blue dawn of his arrival, garbed in black from tip to toe, a sour, greying somberness emanating from the depths of his enigmatical self, the stiffness of his manner cultivated to keep strangers at arm's length, the remote disdain of his frosty, penetrating eyes, interpreters of invisible, recondite realities.

"Who's that?" Rejón asked the Inquisitor, keenly interested by the newcomer's elegance.

"The Black Duke," replied Hernando Rubio, invoking an ambiguous reply to establish his authority. Not even Rejón could know the true name of the banished nobleman.

A Castilian cape, woven with courtly sumptuousness, protects the Black Duke from the inclemencies of the sea and draws, to his tall, graceful figure, the eyes of the raggedy crowd gathered on the Salbago wharf, as always when a caravel from the Peninsula or the New World lands on the island's coast.

"He looks like a nobleman," Rejón remarks.

"He is, Governor," Hernando Rubio tersely replies.

"Your wife is landing too, sir," adds the Inquisitor dryly. "Things will be changing. Your Excellency will have to behave with more discretion," Paleface finishes up, thinking of the slave girl Zulima.

Other flying rumors, colored with belief-staggering tidbits of myth, slowly drifted into Salbago, to the effect,

it seemed, that the Duke's punishment was for life, and
that the Court took the island for a hell full of smugglers
and losers. In the chitchat and slander lurked even juicier,
more licentious morsels: a wild scandal involving peder-
asty hid beneath the prim cloak of political causes for the
banishment, beneath that dark and indecipherable, but
manifestly hostile, standoffish solemnness, beneath that
chivalrous, elegant, proud demeanor—brows habitually
arched, evincing ill-contained contempt, head tipped
slightly up and back, hands outside his cape and spread
on his chest as if protecting, with fierce jealousy, his
inscrutable secret—of a gentleman wrenched from the
privileges of his caste and his superior realms. He took to
the lonesomeness of the place at once, and managed to
overcome, without much difficulty, an unwonted claustrophobia that stole into his soul on the serene silent nights
on the island to which he had been banished for whichever hidden reason. He was always calm, as though an
iron inner censor were overseeing, also in silence, the
resentment that must surely have been mounting without
cease in his breast. Nor did his words ever indicate that
he felt defeated by his long punishment. Encircled by new
honors that he himself, the Black Duke, had reinstituted
in his personal environment, his face turned purple with
displeasure when a lack of respect in one of his servants
or any other lowly Salbagan made itself too obvious.
Generally cryptic in conversation, virtually unbudgeable
in his convictions about all things on earth, whenever
Rejón recounted the exploits of the new discoveries and
the conquests that ensued, the Duke, characteristically
and skeptically, would arch his bushy black eyebrows and
pronounce, unmoved by the fundamental ambitions of the
age, "Taller towers have fallen, Governor. You have
already witnessed the Admiral's infamous end. Be content
with your lot, which is no trifling." Never the least inti-
mation of rebellion. Never encouragement for the
complaints Rejón would at times confess to him, too late
now to retract, egged on by an imaginary feeling of
complicity. His residence was a two-story palace, the
rooms ringing a wonderful courtyard blooming with the
lushest display of island botany. Like some weird obsession, from the moment of his arrival he undertook, aided

by his natural ability to dissemble, to get his hands on one of the descendants of the green dog massacre, the canine tribe pampered by Juan Rejón and his endless host of favored officials. A gorgeous specimen came into his hands thanks to the infinite arts of María Salomé, the sorceress. The dog now paraded, with high-toned stateliness, through the endless corridors of the Duke's mansion, like a keeper of his past. He called the dog Karl, and stroked him with especial delectation as they strode together along the corridors of the ducal manor he had personally been making into a museum, covering the walls with priceless canvases he had shipped in from the Peninsula, peopling the nooks and mahogany cabinets with framed documents extolling his heritage, his blood, and the glory of his family. Silver repoussé plates, Hellenic vases, sculptures without meaning in Juan Rejón's warrior civilization, filled this house of Andalusian design with echoes and mysteries scattering with old-fashioned refinement among the flawless furniture, metamorphizing the Duke's mansion into a place remote from the island time in which they had commanded him to live.

"He's like a man from another century, Hernando," the Governor remarks. Paleface is silent. "At least that's how he acts, as if he had nothing to do with all this."

Hernando Rubio, who had become the Grand Master of the Inquisition in the back rooms of Salbago Island, hushed the dossiers and records of the Duke's trial in the dusty archives in his personal keeping. The exile, meanwhile, encased cap-a-pie in his impeccable black cassock, which perfectly concealed the silken towelettes that swaddled his body sick with chronic hyperhydrosis, the cuffs and pleated collar of his white blouse peeking out from under the black stiffness of the cloth, his salt-and-pepper beard in trim at all times for the moment of his return to civilization, promenaded in silence on the saccharine sands of Salbago's beaches, in the perennially springtime afternoons.

Curiosity, which had nagged at Juan Rejón from the beginning, finally overcame him. The invitation he dispatched to the Duke to pay him a visit at home received a reply at once. It was now the distant past, the day the Black Duke, in full feather, not as if exiled to a new colony, not as though it were an undeniable insult to attire oneself in the courtly fashion among the rough adventurers that milled in Salbago's streets—like an army of the disinherited awaiting its final redemption—slowly mounted the stairs of the Governor's house, emanating elegance and dignity, every step revelling in ancient nobility, crossed the colorful terraces, escorted by Rejón's favorite—the slave girl Zulima (casting not the faintest lustful glance at her physical marvels)—and came into the presence of the Adelantado and his wife, the insinuating María Isabel, hollow-spirited, without a whit of grace, endowed by the Almighty God with very few corporeal attractions.

The friendship grew—and not Simón Luz nor any of Rejón's officers were beset by the jealousy so common among them—along threads tangled in an inextricable knot of mutual interest that neither the Governor nor the Duke ever stopped to unravel in their minds. The Duke honestly relished the cultivated coquetry he carried on with this hopeless rube who had ruled the country ever since the age of the discovery. He even found it amusing to teach society games to Juan Rejón, this churl who had attained the rank of Governor by despotizing a no-man's-land whose only inhabitants were some strange green dogs he had heard the sailors mention, amid mutters and myths, on the docks of Andalusia, in the moments before he set off for the land of exile. Juan Rejón, meanwhile, was captivated by the Duke's manners, by the next to always critical and philosophical language the nobleman employed in any inconsequential conversation, and the hieroglyphical games he inflicted, in the Governor's presence, on the officers of his elite, mentally squint-eyed middlebrows. This, precisely this, was why he liked to test out on his own lips some of those linguistic juggling tricks tossed off by the Black Duke like final decrees in a high-flown voice trained to give orders in the Spanish Court, not for banishment to hell in a port of call. Juan Rejón struggled to follow the Duke's superfluous lessons, as if behind them a secret alphabet lay hidden, a second meaning to things, as though objects, concepts, and their relationships had some other dimension, and to only a small clan of adepts was a profound exegesis permitted.

"Decent confabulator," repeats the Governor for the umpteenth time, his eyes riveted on the chessboard, his mind flitting among sequences of memory that shatter as they shuttle at him swiftly out of the past.

"Yes, Governor. Someone like you, for example, with whom a person of my inclinations can feel at home, and not get the feeling he's wasting his time. In whose presence confidences may indeed become simple soliloquy. Confession between equals. An exchange of civilities is what we call it, Governor."

"I see, Señor Duke, I see," Rejón assents, smoothing his own feathers, hoisted to a higher class to which he had always wanted to belong.

In fact, he was far from having understood. His response had been attended by a gesture imitative of the Black Duke: one hand, preferably the right, lifts partway into the air and drifts off into space, making invisible ripples that are erased at once, while his eyes turn in the opposite direction, focussing on objects having nothing to do with the conversation. This time, for instance, on the chessboard where the menacing bishop is holding at bay the lowly pawns encircling him, not daring to strike. A rabid wild boar ringed by fierce, barking hounds.

Now the Governor plays; advancing, with timid deviousness, one of his troops to block the overpowering invasion of the Duke's lone bishop. To stall the attack on this side, if nothing else. If only for the moment. Then he settles complacently back in his chair, satisfied with his move. "Taller towers have fallen," he whispers to himself, parroting the Duke's remark. Observing that the glasses are empty again, softly he snaps his fingers, another gesture borrowed from his "decent confabulator." Zulima steps from the parlor corner where she has been sitting in silence, veiled perhaps in shadows. Slowly (out of deference or difficulty) she crosses the vast carpeted chamber, freighted with the pride of having been and the pain of no longer being. Slowly she refills the players' glasses with the excellent Sicilian wine sent over to Rejón by the Maltese merchants who deal on the island, as long as—in exchange for which—the Governor refrains from meddling in their wheeling and dealing, and settling of accounts. "What a field day!" Rejón says to himself happily.

The two dogs that now accompany the Governor, like a reminder of his feat lost now in the age of Salbago's discovery and the island's subsequent settlement, a choice memory from his buccaneer life, move with freedom and gravity, stretch and lounge on the chamber's cushiony carpets. Zulima, the now old Zulima, shuffles back to her quiet corner, dragging her bare, callused feet. She's only a servant now. A slave, all said and done. A slave, on whom the dusty desolation of time, the legends and tales of her bygone epochs of youth and magnificence, bruited about in Salbago's streets and taverns, have left a hideous mark. Not a glimmer, not a hint remains. Nothing is left of that sleek, legendary figure, Arab with a touch of Negro, who roused in Salbago of the early days a degree of lechery not to be repeated for centuries. In Zulima's name were committed squabbles, street fights, scandals, duels, insanities of every stripe, wantonnesses and indiscretions, by the officers on whom Rejón, at that time fat on glory, had conferred the privileges of command and governance. She, Zulima, had for a long time been the prime attraction, the feature show, the prima ballerina of the Six of Hearts, an irrepressible house of fun that María Salomé, calling upon all the patience, industry, cunning and professionalism she could muster, had installed on the right side of the little plaza over whose open spaces looked the facade of the Hermitage of San Antonio Abad (where the Admiral prayed en route to Terra Firma, the New Continent, episode to give rise to controversy in later centuries) and on one of the side walls of Juan Rejón's little Palace.

The unrecorded date in the Christian calendar on which María Salomé made up her mind to disembark on Salbago Island, she already knew beyond a shade what she had come to do in these lands of disorder, rivalry, and danger. She was prepared with a vengeance to remain forever in this budding city, to tame it with the riotousness of her passions, to mesmerize it by shrewd use of insinuation and influence. Several petitions, by and large unbeknownst to her public, had priorly informed her of the urgent ardent necessities of the through-travellers and lodgers, and the wanton insatiability of the officers planted by the pseudo-Adelantado from Royal to the verges of the Badlands. This was why, upon landing, making as if she were en route to the New World, she declared that she would stay a short time only. "Long enough for a rest, and to pick up another ship for the New World," she said to the harbor official. And she said it with a convincing, feminine smile the like of which the nameless officer hadn't seen for an age, in spite of María Salomé's apparent years. She came accompanied, what's more, by six women much younger than she, who, as it later came out, were perfect practitioners of a trade which precisely because it was the oldest in the world—in age, wisdom, and authority—had also turned out to be the most difficult, given the doses of imagination, cultivation, specialization, and finesse ideally appended to its simple practice. They were, it was imprinted in their firm, plump, naughty flesh, the chief murderesses of hunger, boredom, and loneliness, which had spread like a resistant, runny scab over the skin of Salbago's roamers: men who had abandoned the hebetude of their provincial wives due to an erroneous interpretation of the realities of the century now drawing to a close; other men who, regardless of the presence on the island of their respective legal and legitimate wives, were fed up with the deadening boredom the island induced without cease. From the start, Salomé laid down the rules regarding her forbidden games, performed as marvelous midwife in the urgent making up for lost time, placing within reach of all men the chance of hotting up, then venting, all hollow, their hidden passions, firing up lust in the eyes of gamblers of cocks (perfect creatures she had providently purchased in the specialty markets of Andalusia), waking fever for the boldest games of the age. Bets raced around Salbago. From hand to hand passed ruins and riches, night after night. Evening after evening—and night after night—in the Six of Hearts, one shocking ever-changing show followed another. Salbago was a party and panderism was its prophet. Even she, a mature, accomplished strumpet, had suffered a metamorphosis from ongoing abuse of her body: rather than withering from the ravages of sex, she rejuvenated extraordinarily, as if some secret pact with the devil had restored all her vital fire.

"It must be the change of climate, Inquisitor" was the

Adelantado's reply to Hernando Rubio's insinuations. "By
now you know that weird, wonderful things go on in this
dump. Whereas some people are screwed for never
screwing, others get younger screwing."

"But the scandal's huge, sir, and the decent folk are
making more and more complaints."

"Balls," Juan Rejón bristles angrily. "First, these
people you're talking about, Paleface"—he called him by
this name to remind him of a very recent past—"were
griping about molestings and rapes every day. That if the
troops couldn't help themselves, grave measures would
have to be taken, because the fact is, they're abducting
and ravishing the proper ladies. Now, damn it"—the
Governor yawned and went on—"they're fretting about
the scandal. What's wrong with this country, Paleface, is
not only too little screwing but always the same ones
doing it. Go and tell them once and for all that Governor
Rejón has decided this island needs whores. And those
who were grumbling before, remind them they're troops
too."

All those who, on the island, or in prior days off it, had
been initiated into the art of whoring and body-to-body
eroticism—by practice, reading, or in thought alone—
preferred, for a long spell, the naked horizontal company
of María Salomé. Her tricks (always the most unpredict-
able), her numbers (always the most innovative), her
motions, and the surprise pleasures she employed with
her clientele had made her, necessarily, quite in spite of
herself, into a myth hard to outrival. It was even averred
that in the middle of a feint of love, she would mutate her
lovers into monkeys and pigs and, far from being annoyed
by the whore's magic game, by her gyrations and voluptuous moans, they seemed fantastically happy, screeching
like circus monkeys, or snorting scatologically like pigs in
heat. At bottom, in the hands of María Salomé they were
nothing but what the witch-whore wished them to be, by
means of an artistry only the devil could have granted
her, in exchange for her soul and for injecting perdition
into the souls of her habitués, according to the gibes of
Hernando Rubio, which were never heeded because María
Salomé had become a reason of state.

"Then she makes love with all of them at once,

Governor, writhing in beds done up in oriental silks and black cloth cushions, exquisite drapery, with tidbits and liqueurs that will damn them forever. If this isn't witchery, señor, may God come down and have a look," testified the Inquisitor.

The leading lights of these amorous feats harbored a vague memory of desire, as if all had been lived in a dream of pleasure, and yet could never quite make sense of the zoological mutation they underwent at the hand of the grand whoress Salomé. In fact, they were ashamed of having romped in a group like mere beasts, but the recollection of pleasure moved them to repeat the experience through many orgiastic evenings and nights. Evenings of infinite diversion, of unfathomable mystery—the kiss, possibly, or the curse, of fate—transpired fraught with obsession in the taverns and bedrooms (transformed into lush forests by the witch's whorish magic), the terraces, in every corner of María Salomé's extraordinary bordello, the Six of Hearts, the most reputable (and revisited) whore and cockhouse on the entire Ocean Sea in the days following the settlement of Salbago. On the brothel's facade were four windows (two downstairs, two up) and two doors (whence the name Six of Hearts, nohow suggesting its internal use), through which passed the slakeless throng of Salbagans, night after night. One entered directly into a courtyard arena, at the hub of which sat the cockpit. Beyond, the seats, planks resting on rectangular stones wedged into the dirt yard, functioning as bleachers for the bettors and carousers. Around the sides of the courtyard, under cover from the wind and rain, ran the vast bar known as the Six of Hearts: one could tour every corner of the courtyard and always find someone to serve him a drink, whether the finest Andalusian wine or some unheard-of alcohol or firewater the origins of which have been lost down the soundless galleries of unchronicled history.

It owed, in fact, to the Inquisitor's repeated complaints that Governor Rejón approached that encampment of overflowing cupidity, his amour propre piqued, his own desire spurred by an unwholesome curiosity the Inquisitor had instilled in his soul, not meaning to. So, one filmy afternoon when he was drowning in ennui, when the whistles of the macaws could not mitigate the mutinous ache of boredom, he slipped, thinking himself incognito, into the roofless courtyard of the Six of Hearts, where María Salomé greeted him without surprise and with all the honors due a man of his authority. She had recognized him at once and was congratulating herself that she could now count him among her most illustrious clients.

"I've been expecting you, Governor," she said with a smile.

As sole response, Rejón looked her up and down slowly and wickedly. Then, calm and collected, he announced to her in a rasping voice that he wished to see the upstairs rooms. The orgy was just then at a pitch. The bodies, liberated from the everyday law of gravity, coiled around one another, nibbling and sniffing, tongues touching tongues, tongues and organs touching organs. The women, as though he who observed them from the doors opening for him as he passed, in deference to his authority, were a usual customer who had come to join the session underway, milked with consummate lust the swollen phalluses of their chance lovers, from whose throats rose a ceaseless sound of flutes and harps, as if they were composing an erotic melody. Rejón easily recognized all these musicians, but his officers, who appeared to officiate here, in the recreational labyrinths of the Six of Hearts, with far more felicity and facility than in their usual posts of command, were completely unaware of his presence. There, whistling and singing, with their crotch-clusters absorbed in pleasurable friction, sprawling over one another bare naked and shameless, was the great majority of his highest officers, Salbago's social elite, all his flunkies, the enormous host of his friends, favorites, and party faithfuls, all those who had taken sides with him and against Pedro de Algaba the rebel, in that unfortunate disturbance that had robbed him for so many nights of the beauty sleep he deserved. Meanwhile, Maruca Salomé spied the Governor's changing expressions in silence, his hiddenmost instincts, Rejón motionless in the doorways of the procreative hells, hands at his back, fiddling his fingers nervously and toying with an olive-green stone which always accompanied him in battle, and served him, no doubt, as an amulet.

"Damn! What a ruckus!" Juan Rejón could not help exclaiming in view of the magnificent show.

María Salomé knew then that she had won him over for good to her lascivious cause; that the Governor was, indeed, one of her own: a whoremonger like all governors.

"The best is yet to come, Señor Governor," the grand whoress crooned in his ear.

Delighted, sometimes blushing, then bedazzled, and finally overcome, Juan Rejón made the rounds of María Salomé's den of pleasures, discovering in them a visceral encounter with lost time. Unrecognized by the screaming mob (possibly physically transformed into someone else by María Salomé's magic), feigning dignity and aloofness but nonetheless thrilled, Rejón moved down the aisles separating one row of bleachers from the next, digging his bootheels into the clay floor; listening to the cries of the frenzied crowd (little did he dream would be so numerous) rooting for the gamecocks. Surrendering, as he walks, to the insolence of the professional bettors, listening with half an ear to the words of the songs sung by the whores—all part of the same endless show—between cockfights, carefully observing the final drills, the tricks the trainers drum into their pupils minutes before the battle to the death, getting acquainted with the imported voice of the Master of Ceremonies, an Englishman by the name of Lord Gerald, who prior to the commencement of the fight trots out the features of each combatant, roused by the general mirth like any other customer, never relinquishing his phony dignity or his prudishness, led by the hand and the hypnotic smoothness of the grand whoress María Salomé, who guides him through the diverse and sumptuous realms of her enchanted castle, through the infernal circles of dice and cards, curses, oaths, and profanities, a wicked, wonderful hell whence he would never return if not called by the weighty responsibilities of his office.

Lord Gerald labors to maintain the deep silence that obligatorily precedes and at the same time forms part of the ritual of the cockfight, moments before the start. An entr'acte of spicy song has just concluded, and the ring flutters with passion. The fight is about to start up again and with it, the wild vice of gambling. The handlers ruffle the cocks' feathers, fondle them, coddle them, coo at them with the secret voices of haruspices, and then suddenly pinch them, yank out a few feathers, stretch the skin of their crops. In this ritual tournament for survival, the animals, gorgeous, accept the game of death as a profession, a destiny for which they have been carefully bred, fattened and trained with utter delight. Again the eyes of Lord Gerald, the English faggot who tyrannizes the sounds and silences of the fervent crowd, begin to glitter, as always when he is about to issue the fateful command to strike up the death-battle. Now he's giving the signals to the trainers to lift off the leather hoods masking the eyes of the contenders, who stand (as though in recognition) looking each other in the eye (as though they wished to communicate, to speak, *morituri te salutant*), and unloosed at the same starting line, unprotesting, with all the force of their ambition to triumph, charge, lunge boldly one against the other, dazed by the cheers of the crowd, and lock spurs, sand flying. Two pure-blooded gladiators who know their lives hang on a single thread, bravery, or—last resort—a stroke of luck. They thrust, they stab, they duck their heads to dodge their rival's possibly mortal blow; make the most of fractions of a second of mutual fluster, feint, hammer their claws uselessly at the air. Feathers ashimmer, the yellow cock sheers away from the brown cock's attack. But the brown cock skims across the sand, no reprieve for his enemy, proudly bristling his ruff. The sides are balanced until the yellow cock flags, and instantly the combatants hear a rabid cry for blood, as the public begins to side with one of them, this time for the brown cock's unslacking attack, like lightning striking again and again, as the yellow cock reels away, hiding his head, a respite from the brown bird's fierce appetite, *morituri te salutant* for centuries of minutes of fighting. The handlers are rooting too; a fight is never won until the enemy bows his head; a fluke strike of the sable, a sudden jab of the spur, can cut short the illusions of he who, oversoon, imagines he has triumphed in the ring. What at first was a cloud of dust raised by the fight, by the irrepressible thrust of its ferocity, becomes, over the battlefield, an amorphous mash of blood, feathers and scuffed-up dirt. At the most uncertain moment, when the public has already erroneously accepted the yellow cock's defeat, comes the mortal stab. Now. The animal wheels round and round the pit, banking his strategy on a single card. Spurned by the crowd, he knows he alone is the agent of his survival, and shrewdly, he seeks to win by wearing down his enemy, who has already exhibited his stock-in-trade. He bluffs him, he has him fooled, but no one knows it. Now: the blade wedges for an instant in the brown cock's head. Blood is the herald of death; incensed, again the yellow bird stabs, to the hilt this time, his triumphant spur. Death gushes red, the loser's body in the dirt, his strengthless claws kicking—instinctual self-defense—against an enemy that ruthlessly pitches into the dying cock until he sees him gasp his last, until he undoes him among the bestial roars of the spectators, the victorious animal still ruffled, strutting proudly now, his radiant body quivering, his eyes full of what winners know.

Rejón trembles with emotion. He tries to veil his enthusiasm, noting that María Salomé, still smiling, is watching him out of the corner of her eye.

"The best is yet to come, Governor," María Salomé hums in the ear of the already won-over Adelantado. Rejón clears his throat. He nods helplessly. Now the gladiator cocks withdraw, and songs soothe the wrought-up nerves of the public. Here he is again, Otelo and his Spanish guitar, subverting the silence. The Governor's memory does not fail him as he sees and hears the Portuguese thrumming. "As if time didn't touch him. He's bewitched too," murmurs Salbago's conqueror. And Otelo, from a dim corner of the bar, into the island evening air, like a challenge, flings that song of desperate love that in bygone days was the theme song of the insurgents in their dark hours:

> *When the black cock sings*
> *the day is done,*
> *when the black cock sings*
> *the day is done,*
> *but if the red cock sings,*
> *that's another song.*

If I tell you a lie
may the wind bear away
the song I sing.
Oh! What disillusion,
if the wind bore away
my very own song.

Juan Rejón is listening closely to the words of the
Portuguese's song, ignoring María Salomé's constant
courtesies and sweet nothings. Some memory of long ago,
clinging to him, even so, like a shadow, pierces his chest
like a cockspur, prods punishingly at his forgetful self like
a lance. In Otelo's guitar, the rending song lasts and lasts,
concealing a thousand clues to some long-ago events
which Juan Rejón, nervous suddenly, is trying to unravel.

In the ring two cocks
Stood face to face.
The black was big,
but the red was bold.
Eye to eye they stood
and the black struck first.
The red cock is bold
but the black is a traitor.
Oh, if I tell you a lie,
away may the wind
bear the song I sing.
Oh, what disillusion,
if the wind bore away
my very own song.

Algaba, possibly, in Rejón's sudden memory as he hears
the Portuguese sing, or a mere suspicion, or pangs of
conscience that have nothing to do with the words of the
song. Algaba present, almost, in every act, every occur-
rence to have taken place since Salbago was founded, the
image of the hanged rebel looming larger and larger as
Rejón walks away from the cockpit, as if to shake off the
phantoms that hound him. At the close, the chorus, like
a warning tolling outside of time, like an ugly premonition, the spectators singing along:

> *Black cock, black cock,*
> *black cock, stand warned,*
> *A red cock never cedes*
> *Till he's dead and gone . . .*

and all through Rejón's body passes a sour, unpleasant shiver, blurring his eyes, his memory, deadening his muscles, and the inheld rage strikes smack at his heart, gut, brain, smothering and stifling, haunting and hounding him.

In the near dark, dusk dropping slowly over Salbago, is the hour of the sublime last act. Silence, like a living being, commanding respect, again shows its face in the Six of Hearts. Calmer now, the spectators return to their seats, the alcohol beginning to mount to their heads. Even the officers who earlier on were making every effort to escape the world in the upper rooms of the brothel take the seats reserved for them in the front rows, some of them possibly interrupting the sexual ritual in which they'd been head over heels all afternoon. In pitch lamps the wicks are lit that are to make still more alluring the figure of the Moorish goddess on the hollow wooden platform that serves as main stage. Already the light falls on the incandescent, inscrutable, indescribable beauty of young Zulima, and before her, the gamecocks and bets have ceased to exist in the memories of the insatiable spectators. All else passes to second place, all that moves is relegated to silence before her, before Zulima, the Arab slave girl bought up by María Salomé following the Rejonista war, the African razzias of Martín Martel. She, María Salomé herself, has transformed her, patiently. She has primped her and primed her, with wisdom, in all the courtly arts of eroticism, and in the mysterious, voluptuous rite of the dance. She has ringed with rituals her image out of reach of the rabble. There, beneath the blueness of the sky and the flaming pitch torches, the half-naked body of Zulima reigns, shunning the obscene, total regard of men, save for those who have fallen in love through the ages with Zulima's brown skin to the point of madness and degeneracy, and have felt no compunction whatever about abandoning themselves to the sight of her, so that, day-blind, they live solely in darkness and

solely in ecstatic contemplation of the goddess' taintless
body, untroubled by the fatal fact that, once among the
chosen, they will be blind forever and in their dark solitude Zulima's sinuous image alone will shine for eternity.
This is the fabulous revenge of the Moorish goddess who
reigns in the greatest bordello of Salbago and of all the
Atlantic: strip to the skin and dazzle the eyes of those who
have enslaved and exterminated her noble people under
the patronage and at the whim of an arbitrary, unruly
history made always in the reckless image of its heroes.
The vision is always the same: the irrevocable story of an
annihilation, the vanishment of a race. Among gauzes and
celestial silks scattered hither, thither, on the platform,
in the deep, echoing crescendo of the drums, moans reverberating to the steps of the oriental dance, Zulima's
Muslim beauty captivates with strange hypnosis, stuns
till blind in the eyes the conquistadors and adventurers
who have filled the streets of Salbago with their miseries
and thwarted ambitions. The dance of veils is a perfect
rendering of the war of the razzias, and the violent movements of Zulima's hips, her savage guttural sounds, the
shrieks she hurls into the sky at the peak of rapture are
pursued with wild obsession by the eyes of men who,
enslaved like her, come evening after evening to the Six
of Hearts to inflame desire (never to be consummated) in
the cockles of their hearts. Last, right now, Zulima will
strike up an extravagant dance, a fierce ancestral boldness, an obscene supernatural provocation that drives all
the brothel's habitués equally mad. Lord Gerald, the
Englishman, with his precious manners and the painted
mouth of an aging queer, entitles it the "Banana Show"
in his own language. Now her round-and-round motions
are more frenzied. They radiate a magnetism exclusively
the knowing patrimony of priestesses whose religions
have lost their place in time. Zulima enters a trance and
her polished body turns the color of ebony, gravity-
defying. Sweat streams down her body, gilding it, the
torch-gleams rippling now over a boa snaking in the air,
levitating, she transforming herself into that boa whose
forked tongue is the desire of spectators who worship her
in abandoned submission. Simultaneously black goddess,
brown goddess, transparent goddess, legs spread-eagle in

the air, her veils, strewn on the platform like the ravages of her lost race, her body arcing and writhing to the uttermost, where carnality attains heights incalculable.

In the fervor of so indescribable a spectacle, in fact, the news reached Hernando Rubio, who since the days of the hanging of Pedro de Algaba had become a fearsome character with great clout in Salbago, intimate with the Governor's orders. Despite the Inquisitor's prompt complaints, it was plain that Juan Rejón had not banned the show or shut down the cathouse. And now, ravished by Zulima's rare beauty, Rejón is plotting for himself the exclusive privilege of her possession. Henceforth not even those who comprise his social elite, his personal court, the fawners and spongers, his party faithful, will enjoy the sight of her. A personal form of censorship the Governor will put into practice in his own behalf. Forbidden, from now on, for the eyes of the wretched ruck to graze Zulima's sacred skin. Because he, Rejón, the Adelantado of Salbago, he and only he will have the right to possess her, to be a devotee of the "Banana Show." Henceforth his wife, María Isabel, a crass, dried-up, barren undesirable frump, will be powerless. Same for Bishop Frías, and later his successor, Fernando de Arce, the Saguntine. Even the Holy Inquisition will be powerless to rescue him for God, to restore him to the reasonableness of his position and authority, to seat him again on the throne of Christian morality. Crazed by the movements of Zulima's vaginal muscles, held hostage in the heat of a sublime cave, all that was visible during the dance was the taut tip of a skinned banana slipping ever so smoothly in and out of the Moorish girl's vulva to the rhythm she gave it, until in her final transport, swooning, in the exact instant of orgasm, she would pull the fruit all the way out, along with shrieks of bliss, the delirium of Juan Rejón now and forever. Her firm, succulent youthfulness decapitated the will of the erstwhile corsair forever, enslaving him to her smell and to the absolute power of the feel of her alluring skin. An ardent cock would occupy forevermore the place of the fruit slipping playfully in and out of Zulima's vulva, bound in the spell of her pleasure. It got so the swing of her hips frenzied the Adelantado. In Salbago's cloudless dusk mottled by light and shadow, Zulima stole into Rejón's thoughts and opened afresh the old wound of forgotten passion, and as if by the workings of impossible magic, rescued Rejón's body for new exploits with that skin that would always remind the Governor of Salbago of the hot, distant sands of the Sahara. Not only was it the quivery zigzag of her torso or the secret writing drummed by the bare feet of the Moorish dancer into the dusty stage of the Six of Hearts as the dance worked its hypnotic power. It was her nipples erect like castle spires, dancing loose through the free universe as if with a life of their own, independent of her body, and her feet, hot cockspurs leaping into the light of the moon bathing all her body in its glow, showing glimpses of her innermost recesses, her pinkish tissues, her hidden sexinesses, the secrets of a whole body in tension as the music swells and the spectators pleasurably, wetly, shiver and swoon. At the climax of the dance, the sacred banana will make its debut, probing the goddess' moist interiors to the swing of the swirling of her hips and her rolling vagina. From then on, no one could retrieve Rejón from what for a long while they all thought was a giant mistake that would lead him to the very jaws of death. From the passion he was sunken in, there was only one escape: time, eroding emotions that now seemed invincible. Not the clergy, not Rejón's closest friends. Not his comrades-in-arms who had boosted the Adelantado to the pedestal where he now perched and who had not done what he had to Zulima due to lack of courage not lack of lust, as there was always an excess of this sort of lechery among conquistadors. Not even the criticisms of his closest men, those that came directly from his own officers, the parvenus who made up his ample praetorian guard being that they owed him everything, criticisms that filtered through the hinges of his own door and dusted with malicious slander every corner, room, terrace, bedchamber, parlor, passageway of his mansion. Not even the written reproofs that originated in Castile herself, faraway Castile, land of longing, admonishing him for his conduct, his public concubinage with that Arab slave girl who would be the mother of his only son. Not even the threats and oaths, which, had he been anyone else, would have blown a hole in his brazenness and put him back on the true path, the path he should have been following all along. Let alone the garbled gospel and teary invectives wreaked on him every morning by the useless María Isabel, or her repeated threats to abandon him. "Whenever you're ready," Rejón would reply, "let me know. I will place a caravel at your disposition to return you safe and sound to your peninsular abode. I'm staying forever. This is my land till I die." Then, crowing to himself: "It is good to make a bridge of gold to a flying enemy," a ditty he would teach to his son Alvaro when he was a little boy. So nothing could defeat the obsessive resistance of Juan Rejón, his heart tormented forever with love for Zulima the dancer. This was how the Moorish lass came to live in the Governor's house. And this was how the bizarre "Banana Show" became the exclusive plum of Governor Juan Rejón.

Hernando Rubio the Inquisitor would gnash his teeth. He would compose interminable reports on the case never would he dare send to anyone. They were only games to amuse himself by, lining up the possibilities for heresy such a situation might engender. He knew—he could vouch, moreover, on personal experience—that once Rejón got an idea in his skull, no one could get it out. This was a vulgar residuum from his erstwhile pirate life. Either the Governor's unwholesome passion spent itself, or all attempts to root out the obsession would backfire on the instigators and irksome critics. "Inquisitor!" he had shrieked at him, "They're green with jealousy, damn it! And that *is* an unforgiveable sin." So Hernando Rubio was reduced to the gnawing of a conscience, his own, to which Rejón had never paid the least attention. Rejón had used him (this he realized now, far too late) solely in those cases where it was absolutely necessary to recur to him, to the will and authority he himself had bestowed on him.

"When all's said and done," the Governor liked to remind him in dry tones, "you're no babe in the woods yourself; nor can you cast the first stone at me, Inquisitor. If you don't feel the need of the companionship of women, that's your affair. You're an old jackoff, or have you perhaps forgotten why you're lame? All you now are, your honors, authority, belongings, the fear and respect you command, even your life, you owe to me, you forgetful dummy, who rescued you from death and devourment by sharks when we were coming to Salbago."

Mortified, pocketing his transgression like a secret, buried in mounds of paper, files, inquisitorial dossiers, to Hernando Rubio, Juan Rejón's conduct was hands off, could above all be judged a trifling if one took into account that in the upper echelons of his administration such behavior was pretty much daily bread. "It's a matter of collective transference of responsibility," the Inquisitor persuaded himself, shrugging his shoulders.

Rejón notes again how the Black Duke persists in his attack, how a swift, precise move of one of his rooks suddenly jeopardizes the defense initiated by his infantry around his queen. The danger of a check is imminent. The truth is he has never been a great strategist. Not on the battlefield nor now, on the chessboard. His was adventure, the open seas, surprise as a means of survival. He had always let himself be borne along by a mood, unthinkingly undertaking the most impossible situations only to later, drawing strength from his own weakness, be reborn like the Phoenix, and turn circumstances around in his favor again. In fact, considering what good a knowledge of military science had done for Martín Martel, his Camp Commander, it wasn't worth racking his brain (whenever he remembered the death of his lieutenant, the Governor's throat constricted, a murky liquid seeped through his loins, shrivelling his facial expressions). Unhinged by this new attack, he moved a pawn as one does who stalls for time in a battle he knows he has already begun to lose.

"I'm an old man and I'm rotting, bit by bit, Duke. But it would please me if your grace would write my memoirs. That my triumphs and travails, my joys and my defeats be set down in history before I'm dead and buried on this land that has undone me," he said, interrupting the game.

The secret renegade smiles at him congenially, not without a certain coolness and superiority. Rejón exhales a long wheeze of fatigue, or maybe bad conscience. Again silence settles over the central parlor where the Duke and the Governor are playing. The Duke takes advantage of this pause to look sideways at the whining, almost squeaking shadow of Zulima the slave. He has heard so much about her that he cannot help but evince some curiosity as to her person. Zulima slinks slowly into her corner, at the back of the parlor. There she will sit, waiting for the two gentlemen to drain their goblets again. Her duty today is simply to be there, silent, submissive, distant from past memory, attentive only to the whimsies and appetites of her señor, Rejón. All that legend of a fabulous dancer and hetaira unrivalled that had once towered over Salbago like the crumbling ramparts of the city on the encircling hills is reduced to this lumpy, rotting, crabbed, slumped figure, trying to hide its unquestionable age in the shadowy skirts of dusk. It strikes the Duke, however, that the legend must be an exaggeration, that never could what he was now seeing in any way intimate what everyone claimed she had been: the wonder of Salbago for years on end, until the Governor himself clapped eyes on her and confiscated her for himself. Her eyes, henceforth, saw no other sun than that which shone on the terraces of the Adelantado's mansion, if we exclude Zulima's rare excursions outside the palace. Lost to the world, she romped in the beds, danced on the carpets, teased him, tantalized him with her smell and her skin. Now nothing remains of the ritual but the sad ashes of time and the long, long tradition sounded abroad—a secret shouted—by the natural exaggeration of whoremongers of all seas and all ages. Silence, meanwhile, hovers over the two contenders' thoughts. Now and then one of the green dogs, magnificent creature lying at Rejón's feet, protecting him from the cool air and the phantoms that pester him during these soirées, shakes his body to shoo off the pesky flies lighting cruelly into skin which has already begun to shrink and crack from so many years on Rejón's body. The Black Duke's eyes prowl the parlor. There, in that spacious room, that chamber aspiring to nobility, lies the legend of Juan Rejón, Captain, Governor, Adelantado, condensed into a coat of arms designed by Rejón himself: There, in those two upper quarters, are the Governor's feats and titles, the phantasmal history of the corsair; beneath, two quarters party per pale: sinister, three sable lances on argent; dexter, two dogs in vert, passant, upside down on sable, the crest on top with fluttering plumes of a color akin to old gold, the very color that time has slowly blazoned into Governor Rejón's ageless skin.

"Heavy is the head that bears the crown," remarks the Black Duke. Rejón looks at him with a touch of astonishment in his eyes. The Duke smiles again, condescendingly, and redescends to his opponent's terrain. "With health and time on our side, Governor, anything is possible," he replies to the Duke's petition.

His answer is, again, a riddle with a thousand meanings, a phrase caged forever in a thousand interpretations. The Governor emerges from one riddle straight into the next, without grasping the meaning of the prior one. Meanwhile, the Black Duke's mortal strategy, set out upon the chessboard, advances, slowly, imperceptibly, with complete aplomb, on the line of puppets that are his opponent's pawns. The Duke knows this is child's play, given the state of mental decomposition of his novice opponent. He knows he contends with the frail morale of a little boy, whose mood brightens at whatever illusion is propped before his eyes.

Martín Martel, the Commander, hero of the conquest and pride of the Discoveries, joined the immortal shades in an age when Juan Rejón had already attained the absolute rank of monarch beyond time. A fleeting moment, a glimpse, the sizzling and mingling of strange colors on an afternoon like so many in the history of Salbago, a dreamy languor scenting and soothing the atmospheres, the air bellying and bloating under its mantle of African heat. Dazzled, his eyes shattered into flying images, into tingling reveries coaxing him along, swaddling him in an electric discharge whose pleasure was very much like sex. He did not even need to draw aside the soft curtains behind which lay the void, limbo, and ultimate delirium. It seemed to him that this smoking darkness had been waiting for him forever, with ardent desire, never without hope of clasping him to its breast and sucking the rotten blood from his heart. So, he went in like an old beggar, the way an invisible being slips through any back door, without ceremony, trumpets, ritual, or farewell songs.

After all, he had never been a thinker and never wasted his time in contemplative dialectics of any kind. He was simply too obtuse. Grim, intent, if one did not concur with his megalomaniacal strategies, or if he was ever reproached for his inconclusive plans, he would harbor a dank grudge in the musty archives of his warrior soul, a schismatic sensation that dulled his lucidity in military matters, reducing him, in the end, to despicable downfall and squalid dishonor. At bottom, he had been a Camp-master all his life, nothing more, a military man of narrow scope, a simple troop commander too proud of his victories and who trembled with true hatred on contemplating defeat, a strategist soused on his triumphs, fattening them with episodes that had never occurred, a soldier specialized in justifying his moral failings and dreams of glory, dressing them with a slick of bad luck and cursed fate. So nothing could be expected of him but application and intelligence in combat, accountability for his own wildnesses, and the repeated staging of a horrific self-idolatry: glory chased like a virgin, to be raped as swiftly and deeply as possible. Never could anything but rudeness be elicited from him, indecipherable brays for responses, hunch when reflection was in order, instinct for self-preservation over dialectical process in the most elemental conversation. Ultimate personification of the Castilian fighters' law of iron, always eluded by the sublime logic of the history he sought, he never owned up to discouragement in combat, and even in his private life pigheadedly disavowed any shortcomings others tried to pin on him: "Envy's eating them up," he would mutter to himself, a hot wad of rage in his kidneys. Not even the reproofs of his superiors, couched always in terms of gentle, affectionate chiding, were acknowledged by Martín Martel's mulish character. "Your hair'll fall out, you sons of bitches," he replied inwardly whenever the protests of Juan Rejón or Bartolomé Larios fell on him, fall guy, on his hair thinning from pent-up rage, on his whole rough unkempt self. Inside him, like the wrath of Achilles the Greek, an incurable cancer multiplied madly, gagging his glands, beginning to make him aware of his total impotence in the face of that army of ragamuffins and conquistadors of straw, puny discoverers of utterly worthless islets that were to remain, for all of history, midway points in the great conquest, the great discovery that now they would never attain, dwellers of a thankless, mawkish land.

Besides, since the solemn day of the obligatory purge of the green dogs (although the brilliant idea had been Simón Luz', it was he, Martín Martel, who had brought it off), the cold, bitter barking of the dying hounds had echoed through the silent numbnesses of his spooked memory, breeding in his conscience, crazing him, the infinite crescendoing of a pain that dulled his senses, teth-

ered him to a hoarse tremble that deadened his entire
body. Each of those animals, each poisoned dog, came
back to life in Martín Martel's gut and churned his
liquids into convulsions, flushing his mind with horror. In
the presence of one of the surviving pups, for instance, the
Campmaster's face would blanch utterly, the sweat that
streamed down his face tinging the colors of melting snow,
and the vengeful snarls of those dogs strutting their
survival through the terraces, gardens, parlors and
bedrooms of Juan Rejón's mansion called back to his
memory the absolute futility of that stupidly aggressive
act which later, recast into full-scale conquest, would pass
into the historical reports that the Inquisitor and scribe
Hernando Rubio slowly wove with his bat-hand, spellbound by his sibylline search into the bowels of a history
concocted by their very selves, piecing together the
exegesis that would best serve the discoverers of Salbago.
Therefore he knew that he, Martín Martel, was a mere
cat's paw in the hands of Hernando Rubio. His will too
had been a cat's paw, utilized for determinations on military operations, from the moment the ferocious Simón Luz
began to counsel Juan Rejón. A nullity in the conquest,
that's just what he was: "It's all shit. We're all scum," he
consoled himself in moments of nervous depression, when
the barks of the green dogs pressed tightest round his
body. This was how that secretiveness began that led him
into madness, how that tumor of fury began to bloat in
his breast, against his superiors who had decreed the
lunacies it was then his duty to carry into action, to be
registered in the paper history Hernando Rubio was fabri-
cating in his honorific corner. All others were the enemy.
And all of them hells: first off, Simón Luz, then Bartolomé Larios, Bishop Juan de Frías, Deacon Bermúdez,
Inquisitor Hernando Rubio, Pedro de Algaba the traitor,
the mischief with the green dogs, the African razzias.
Even his old comrade-in-arms, the present Governor, Juan
Rejón. An endless list of hells and enemies growing longer
and beefier by the day, like a sinful, ravenous animal
smearing Martín Martel's thoughts and flesh with poison.
During his sleepless nights, anger swelled in his belly like
some other self, strange and unruly. Little by little the
night began to dim him, defeat him, dwarf him, to whittle

his face with sadnesses and darknesses. His surrender, wild and gay (only at first, of course), to wine and boozes transformed, from the crinkles of a shy sensation that would nag his senses now and again, into total submission, out-and-out slavery, distorting his features, which were naturally roughhewn, his demeanor, his very movements, until he resembled, in the full light of the full moon, a hybrid being, as much a dog as a man. Though disfigured, a third of his being remained faithful to the human species (here the anger coiled, like a poisonous snake); another third perfectly conformed to the characteristics of the vanished green dogs (a sudden gleam in the eye, heraldic vert on his warrior skin, a low growl garbling his words); and finally, a third that corresponded to a wolf from the Castilian steppe (inhabited by loneliness and hunger). Salbago's outskirts, the lawless districts, where wildness and anarchy thrived, the sandy stretches swept—night after night—by a hot, tireless wind, the stews strewn with shacks inhabited by men without names or hope, the whole underworld of misery and poverty that had piled up around Salbago and come to form part of the city proper, little by little came to recognize the nocturnal tracks of that strange figure, lonesome, dispossessed, tramping despairingly over the mud flats and damp sand like an old man with a mortal wound, a drunken wolf whose claws carried the pale scorpion of madness and panic into Salbago's slums. Hounded by miasmas of memory, dumbfounded by his own human defeat, he sought peace in solitude, howling and yelping as if hereby carrying out the long, gummy process of penitence deserved. The legend of the wolfman blazed like a trail of gunpowder. The rumor flew, embellishing and bolstering the myth, glossing it with feats Martín had never accomplished. "Let him rot," said the Governor upon receiving the news, "let him rot in peace. I know that wolfman and I know he could never harm a soul." So the dogman prowled loose, free, seeking impossible death at the hands of the soldiery and rabble, who would never pursue him, or take him seriously; or goading the Inquisitor to publish a warrant for his capture that would unloose the lust for bounty in the horde of starvelings and roamers. "He's a rebel without a cause seeking impossible martyrdom," Hernando Rubio branded him. In peace as in war, Martín Martel's destiny would always turn out the same: futile chase after glory, and ultimate ridicule. Unlike Achilles, the Greek hero, he was not begotten as mythic warrior of noble blood. Nor was his mother a goddess from the deep sea, who would come to his aid with a cry of vengeance whenever his son's soul wept. Martín Martel was the son of a lowborn like so many others, progeny of the Castilian steppe—like Juan Rejón— and his dreams were whetted by adventurelust and legends of other worlds. He took to the sea, heart set on faroff lands where he could settle, exalt his blood, and scatter his name across the pages of the most sublime conquest in history. Here he was now in that distant land, hungry and alone, toppled at the last from the grand pedestal of the elect. His ambitions and his glory had fallen by the wayside, amid defeat and oblivion.

When Juan Rejón, taking his cue, as usual, from Simón Luz the Jew and that whole host of lowbrow officials and arrivistes constantly fawning on the Governor of Salbago, commanded Martín Martel to burn the ships lest one of those ungrateful sons of bitches, the slew of them that came over here with us, lest it occur to one of those bastards, are you listening to me, Martín Martel, to escape and leave us in the lurch; when Juan Rejón gave the command without the blink of an eye, to chop off the heads, like fish for a banquet, of all of those whom he himself, Martín Martel, suspected guilty of Algabism, all they could accommodate in their minds being a stupid feeling of independence and rebellion, an exaggerated, unsuitable desire for power, which dissolved discipline and staggered belief, Martín Martel again felt on his face the pallor of marble, the stubborn chill of winter trapped in his bones. But he obeyed as though it were a divine decree to be honored over and above any other power. After all, when he received the order, the Hebrew was not at hand, and searching Bishop Frías' eyes he saw assent, complicity, and total agreement with Juan Rejón's orders. As usual it was a sham campaign that would serve to eliminate the agitators, root out all Algabistic tendencies. The Commander was, by the by, falling in the trap laid by Simón Luz' machinations, in his plan to rid himself of all Rejón's loyal servants, who might—anytime now—bilk his own indomitable rise to power . . .

Much worse (maybe this was the straw that broke the silent back of his patience) was the moral consequence of the triumphant expedition that Martín Martel, at Governor Rejón's behest, brought off on the coastlands of

95

the African continent. Sheathed in their darras, long, exotic sky-blue robes, the desert nomads, as the green dogs of the island had done before them, raced away terrified to take refuge from the atrocities of Martín Martel's men. They scattered among the sandy drifts, they hid in the endless Saharan dunes. They fled an invader their prophets had never reckoned with, unaccounted for in their sacred books or their oral tradition: historical shores, illusions fantastically conjured by their shamans (boundless seas, opulent cities adorned by women in pompous plume, collective treasures to satisfy the most extravagant aspirations) in an attempt to attach them to the land and convert them, by fable and fantasy, into a sedentary people, owners of a sea of sand blown by the moody tactics of the wind, forbidding, invincible.

"What's entailed, Martín," he explained, pointing to an approximate map, "is bringing as many Muslims as possible from the coast. Don't be choosy, Martín. Men, women, and children. It's all the same. Any and every human being you find on the beaches or in the dunes of the desert. Alive, naturally. Dead they're useless to us. They must serve as our slaves and justify our presence here."

These were the days of false glory, when Rejón's officers still felt like heroes of their own history. The awful burning sands of Sakia-el-Amra were a bloody feast for the Castilians thirsty for the victory they had in fact been deprived of ever since they shoved off from the ports of Cádiz. In battle formation, as if they expected retaliation from wild animals treacherously attacked, the hunters of Muslims fanned out through the desert as the Saharan women's terrified cries rose, manifestly futile, from their parched throats into the sky, a plea for help that for them was never to come. Brutally silenced by the quenchless roar of the sirocco, blowing thus in collusion with the invaders' campaign, abandoned to their destinies by their men, one after the other fell into the hands of the Castilians. Day after day, mounted on their Andalusian horses, the soldiers stalked their prey, destroying villages, setting fire to the pitiful jaimas, the round huts of the desert men, seizing prisoners, leaving behind them a wake of unknown terror and senseless desolation. Through an

open grave, the Saharans were herded over mountainous
zones, over interminable dunes, over dry beds of rivers
and gullies, to the shores where the desert sands pooled
with the white sands of the sea, beside which waited,
rocking in the peaceful coastal waters, the caravels
destined to become jails made of wood, symbol of the
enslavement of those desert beings who had nurtured in
their collective soul the indestructible myth of a vanished
empire, who had lived always in the hope of recovering it,
discovering it—albeit among ancient ruins—in some sandy
hollow where no one had set foot for generations, who
retained in their imaginations forever the vast memory of
sacred cities strewn over the desert like myriad whispering carpets, an oral tradition passed to the nomads by
their fathers and whose origin, perfumed with incense and
sandalwood, was lost amid the labyrinthine centuries of
Islam, the impossible legacy of an afflicted people who had
lived, hither and thither incessantly, clinging to the hope
of a resurgence of their historical structures, now
squashed forever, a people whose only true home was its
glorious past, vanished in illusions and dust, in the sweat
and drought of a never-ending Saturnian desert they
inhabited sometimes with fierce hatred but nearly always
with defiant love.

Without ceremony whatever, entire tribes were shipped
to Salbago amid the nasty cries of the ruffians recruited
by Martín Martel, their eyes cracking and exploding with
passion for the skin of Muslim women, whose dresses,
tattered by solitude and sadness, by the shivering cold of
the nights at sea, mid-voyage, bared to the light the dark
radiance that until now had been the exclusive reserve of
their men, the nomad warriors of the desert. Entire tribes,
whole families scattered by the desert over the years,
clans with all their pompous hierarchy of deposed dignitaries (sheiks, shamans, haruspices, chieftains and holy
men, one and the same in captivity) were dumped like
sacks into the dark holds of the ships. Not the adamant
pride of their imprisoned eyes, nor the glitter of hate, at
a white heat, that camped in the eyes of the recognized
superior castes, nor the silence in which they steeled their
hiddenmost longings for vengeance, could free them—far
from their natural habitat—from the humiliations and

degradation to which they had been condemned by the
white invaders, and neither peace nor truce was negoti-
able. Later, on the rotting planks of the rough, salt-caked
docks of Royal City, Salbago, these same tribes would be
logged in by the slakeless Simón Luz: nothing damped the
Hebrew's strategical obsession, whose intent was to justify
as such, and at all cost, in all its glory and necessary fol-
derol, a conquest that had never existed. His awesome
experience, acquired in the extermination of the green
dogs, had given him greater strength to proceed through
the tunnel toward murderous insanity, and had moored
him in the pleasures of destruction, to the greater glory
of Governor Juan Rejón and friends. In a sense it was a
means for his own survival, racing out ahead, scheming
and dreaming and plotting wild plans to deflect from
himself the suspicion or the definite certainty of his
Jewish blood, and the ultimate consequence that would no
doubt derive from it: his own death at the hands of the
Inquisition, growing in Salbago like a Gorgonian flower
thanks to the doggedness of Hernando Rubio, the onanist.

The Muslims, meanwhile, knew themselves again in
bondage. They accepted their punishment silently. The
inevitable disaster had fallen in on them like cursed rain,
and in the aftermath of the razzias, the Blue Empire
became, more than ever, a quest for perfection veiled in
dreams and webs of illusion. The expeditions to the
African coast were repeated, one after the other, until
Martín Martel began—his first blunder—to catch glimpses
of the true plan, the new extermination sired by the
Hebrew. He was, after all, the strong arm for Simón Luz'
machinations: he, Martín Martel, hero of the conquest,
was the agent of the new sacrifice this brainsick history
asked of its men. The Moors were not merely to be
enslaved. Like the green dogs, the slaves would be the
privileged few able to escape the pathological brutality of
Simón Luz and the sick indifference in which Juan Rejón
ensconced himself. This was when it began to come clear
to him that he was a war-toy in the hands of murderers.
But the protest reared up at the wrong time, in the wrong
place, precisely as the last expedition neared the Salbago
coast with its cargo of condemned men: he too was an
accomplice, and a perpetrator of this massacre. The sea

wind beat straight on, salting his face and beard. He remembered Pedro de Algaba, the traitor's execution, in fulfillment of the sentence drawn up by the skilled hand and limp conscience of Hernando Rubio. He glimpsed, in the same blur of memory, the face, like a whitewashed sepulchre, of Bishop Juan de Frías, Deacon Bermúdez' simper of false piety as he handed the cross to Pedro de Algaba to be kissed, as the noose tightened around the neck of the man who had been his friend and now was a mere convict. He scanned the lowered eyes of the Governor, who seemed adrift within that monstrous manifestation of hatred. He turned to the face of Simón Luz and found there frank evidence of the pleasure provoked by the imminent presence of the death of Algaba, whose eyes, at just about the peak moment of decease, insurrected as though trying to give voice to a curse: "They'll do the same to you, Martín, when they don't need you anymore," he said to him with a weird grimace lined with the first signs of the clammy pain of doom. He, Martín Martel, a name they had already begun to revile or ignore, was also party to this death which Hernando Rubio, that it serve as a lesson, had made into a circus act. This tied him closer to the Adelantado, bound as Rejón was to erect a monument to himself, to work up, at everyone else's expense, an eternal memory in the historical papers of the Spanish Conquest, so as to relegate to oblivion his mingy pirateering origins, a stele to a straw conquistador whose legend—underwritten by hideous detail—would never ever, despite his efforts, cross the unfathomable frontier of the sea eternally circling the insular lands of Salbago, though the name of Alvaro Rejón, his only son, would spread by word of mouth from the coasts of Africa, which he would tour tirelessly, to the islets, islands and Terra Firma of the Discovery. So it was upwards of impossible for Martín Martel to rebel, his hands and feet tied, mulling a foul taste of foam in his dry mouth, standing at the stern. He realizes that every knot in the net has been meticulously tied by Simón Luz' thousand cunning faces. If the Jew were even to suspect his thoughts, he hasn't a doubt of what the accusation would be, and the inevitable outcome: Algabism and the death sentence. What's more, the horrific ruse of the burning ships is branded in his memory, a fantastic sight that reels in his brain whenever doubt begins to bloom in his head like a flower freckled with evil splotches. The floating flames ripple in the deep dusk as slowly the ships sink, smoking, off-coast, and all hope of return, furtive or otherwise, frays in the adventurers' heavy hearts. The memory gives Martín Martel a constant headache. Hypnotised by the vision of fire sweeping over the sea, his skin sopped with the sweat of fear, the voice of Juan Rejón had yanked him from his stupor: "Remember, Martín, sometimes it's better for a man to die for his people than for a whole nation to perish for one man." He was alluding, most likely, to Pedro Algaba and the uproar stirred by his death. The Commander pitched his voice up a decibel, looked him full in the face, and dared to ask: "And the others? What about all those other poor devils we've killed?"

"They're lives without names, Martín. Scum. Chumps. They're not worthy of memory," answers Governor Juan Rejón. At that same moment, those who ventured out along the side streets of the fledgling town of Salbago might run across a hellish sight: a countless army of hanged men swinging obscenely from the posts of the fort. The Algabistas. Martín Martel had seized them and roughed them up. He had extorted confessions and sent them to hang . . .

After shipment to the Island of Salbago, men, women and children, heirs of the Blue Empire that had perished centuries before in the sands of the Sahara, were dispersed like sheep. They were already utterly certain that Allah had abandoned them when one day, just as they were growing used to breathing this other air, grounding and tempering their natural penchant for nomadism, they heard in the distance the hue and cry of those wild conquistadors of nothingness, their masters, who hurled themselves at them beneath the cruel command of Martín Martel, the Commander, sporting shields and coats of mail, their weapons cocked for the leap to glory. Open season. It was a mass murder, no doubt a slight variant on the Christian sport, hunt and kill the pagan, still practiced several centuries later by the British, happy as larks, in Tasmania. A mass assassination, an awesome slaughter that sank Martín Martel for good and all in the cane brew turned to profit right here on the island, with a corner on the market, by the Benjumeas, a family of Andalusians from Jerez de la Frontera, who had flocked to the city to settle in step with the conquest of Salbago.

Now he feels hemmed in by the headache forever, snuffed by the machinations of Simón Luz, the Jew, who would never dare to walk alone through Royal's winding streets or chance it beyond the walls marking the limits of the city and its law. Such is his cognizance of danger and his secret terror.

Drubbed by night, shunted aside, stripped of hope forever, Martín Martel conjures back in his toxic, liquorized memory, in great swoons and gut spasms that sour his throat and fill his stomach with venomous vapors harbingering his death, the legend of the blue men, a patched-together story (part fantasy, part legend, part myth, and part pure fabrication) that had been told to him, by way of smiles, signs, mime, and grimaces, out there on the high sea, the ships returning to Salbago, by a Saharan girl he had ravished on the sands of the African shore. Practically a child then, in the rocking caravel, she would later be known as that fabulous dancer of the Six of Hearts, and then as the very own darling of Juan Rejón, Governor of Salbago. She was the beauteous Zulima.

By now her people is slough. The chaff, the accursed shreds of a vast, exalted and unknown empire that perished with the coming of the new ages, evoked now only in defense of its tradition and memory. Its domains never had borders, but floated over the entire north-western coast of Africa, and its hypothetical frontiers blew away in the wind in many directions, as far as the distant lands of the East. At its broadest, it might take years for an expedition to cross the Blue Empire. She, Zulima, was the only daughter of one of the most illustrious and respected holy men, elder shaman of one of the principal tribes of blue men, a priest whose virtuous body was left sunken in the sacred sands of the city of Smara, in the middle of the desert, where none but the direct descendants of the highest caliphs may dwell in perpetuity.

So it was sacred, the blood that ran in the veins of the girl. Martín Martel was stunned when he saw her, moist and delicate, bathing in the shallows, refreshing her virgin skin, which peeped out beneath her robes, skin that had been possessed solely by the daily ardor of the Saharan sun. Horseback, he was seized by the black fury of desire, to have her then and there. So he scooped up the girl and plumped her on the saddle beside him. Mad horseman electrified by the sudden passion that had laid hold of his warrior soul, whinnying with tingly lust, he drove his chestnut horse romping and frolicking down the beach where the Saharans awaited their removal to Salbago. Then he trotted his steed away with Andalusian elegance to where the eyes of the men could not hinder his wildness. Zulima was, beyond question, his booty.

He revelled in the immeasurable madness of the princess' hot brown skin, swilled up all her salty flavors until the irrational thirst turned his delirium into swoons and trembles. Slowly the passion burned in his loins as he penetrated the Muslim girl's pulsing slither. An inner scream, long inheld, tore the silence, shattered against the dry desert's echo, all notion of time lost: all that endless space opening before Martín Martel, where the soft murmur of the hot wind stroked invisible corners, was reduced to this instant of life, to the boundless worship of that child body now streaming through the marrow of his bones swelling him with new breath, as though the act of love suddenly became, in the secret lexicon of gestures half comprehended, divine magic. Trembling, he explores every shameless fold of the pristine adolescence of the girl digging her fingers in the warrior's hairy chest. Frenzied, he sniffs her again and again, nips her, nibbles her, an animal in heat who initiates this rite of pleasure, cooling her with the quenchless wetness of his tongue and plunging into the hollows Zulima gradually bares for him, until he has sullied with pleasurous spit the whole body of this heathen princess who accepts, without a protest, the odor of blood and the conquistador's dusty sweat. Naked, he weds delirious rapture in the purenesses and softnesses of the Moorish girl. She, almost unknowingly, is performing the rites of womanhood. So, it was a violation without violence, the sun above sole witness shattering against the desert's bed of live stones, pounding its rays into the weary bodies. As the last act of that rare ceremony, they lingered in the shoals nearby, bathing and playing. It was there that he began to flirt with the crazy idea of keeping her for himself, race away into the dunes, perhaps, until his chestnut steed burst his nostrils and spewed the foam of death, stay here forever, skin browned for eternity by the rites of the sun, camouflage himself in a blue darra, a nomad like any other, be a turncoat in this bloody history that would never lend a thought to him again. The taboo thought stuck in his mind, snatch her, hide her from the grasping eyes of Simón Luz the Jew and the severity of Juan Rejón. Later, more level-headed, he leaned toward the idea of asking the Governor if he could have her, as spoils of conquest. The sailors began to eye him greenly; no longer found it diverting to flash sparks of desire at the girl who tailed him everywhere, as though happy in her role as abject slave. Lieutenant Sotomayor, meanwhile, took refuge in silence, an iron shield displayed as his greatest virtue; on the side, however, he grinned scoffingly.

It was all like an adventure dreamed in a night of passion, an illusion lasting exactly the time it took the devil to rub his only eye, an impossible wish crumbling like pillars of clay, blowing away like smoke, when they landed on the docks.

"They'll do the same to you, Martín, when you're not needed anymore. When they've bled you white," the waves echoed again and again, the faraway voice of Pedro de Algaba rising out of the near past and prancing over the waters.

Defeated by night, Martín Martel staggers, his bloated tongue ranting, his rotten soul burning in his bowels. Ringed by the swarm of roaches that will never quit him now unto death, slurping and slurping the buzzing flies, alone, wreathed in the haze of his memories, he rides the past, back over consciousness lapsed since the time the adventure drove him berserk and he placed himself in the hands of the Adelantado, Juan Rejón. From the pit of his inflamed throat he tries to scream that he will kill him, that the hour of rebellion is still at hand, that there's still him to frame the uprising of Salbago against Juan Rejón, stand in for Algaba, set fire to the Governor's house as he did to the ships, burn the foundations of the cursed Cathedral. My devoted soldiers will follow me to suicide, if need be, Rejón: your tyranny will fall, scoundrel. You, Rejón! You're the traitor, not Pedro de Algaba, you who made me seize him without a pang of conscience and sent him to the scaffold, you son of a bitch, you purged the dogs, you instructed me to burn the ships so the Algabistas couldn't get away, or so you said. But in fact, I see it all clearly now, so as to blame Pedro de Algaba before the unwitting eyes of all our men, so they couldn't cast the least aspersion on your blanket authority. His cries, despite the effort, were a nonsensical echo, a conundrum stinking of anise liquor and sugarcane rum, caught halfway to his desires, not even reaching the first dark corner around which he now totters, forgotten by all, in the silence of this Salbagan night, whose shadows spin dizzily by him, eyeing him like a dangerous stranger, like one of the hundreds of soused fortune hunters dallying around the cemetery and the Cathedral, like a leprous lunatic shuffling along slowly to his place of death, his body flayed, coated with the brown mass of roaches that will usher him out of life. She, Zulima, an old hag stooping almost to the ground as she walks, bears no resemblance to that Moorish lass he ravished in the sands of the Saharan shore, now nearing Martín Martel once again in his memory. She gesticulates obscenely, she guffaws at the absurd plans of the Campmaster, beside whom, like a curse returning to the scene of the tragedy, the green dogs bark and squeal, menacing, baring fangs that drip with fury, that will devour his flesh shrivelled and softened by liquor and years. "Crazy son of a bitch! Crazy son of a bitch!" echoes the voice of Zulima.

At moments Martín Martel regains his memories of lucidity, the lost memories of his childhood, his parents' move from the grimy port of Marseilles to the Castilian town where they blended in with the ruck and blanched their original French name to Martel: all his efforts at retrieval melt into sickly liquids that seep up his throat and souse him in hiccups. He tries with all he has in him, as though fleeing from the phantoms that will companion him in his exequies, to quell the queasinesses and dizzinesses coming over him, mouth pasty, lips crusty. The silhouette of the Cathedral, forever half built, the stone sick with the yellowy-green blight slowly and patiently crumbling it, tumbles toward him, squashing him. Reeling, he locates himself on Salbago's geography, sprawled over one of those unfinished staircases leading to those lovely terraces which Herminio Machado, always so prissy and vacant, will never see to completion. Now he remembers the Architect, profile of an Italian savant striving for all he's worth to be ahead of his time on this hellish island, a man who passed his life dreaming, skin and hair graying, proposing undoable projects amid the snickers of Juan Rejón's officials. Is this a vision, Zulima, old and horrid, badgering him, stripping naked, her greasy callused hands squeezing flabby dugs that hang to her waist, showing him her cracked skin, her woeful body, her bloody toothless gums, Zulima old and crabbed, leaning on a stick that serves as a cane so as not to fall on the floor or on him, Zulima beckoning him now, too late, to possess her, to have all of her at last, a galloping cackle transforming into the bark of a green dog?

Memory overlaps with reality again as painful tears brim in Martín Martel's eyes and he falls with a clatter between the steps ascending to the Cathedral's back garden, beside that other staircase that stops short along a half-built wall of Salbago's main church. Before him is Scaffold Square, and a little ways on, just to the left, appear the lights of the house of the glorious Governor Juan Rejón and a never-ending caravan of men dressed in darras, chortling with laughter, a throng singing threnodies with mournful keens whose notes kindle a cold dizzy tremble he doesn't yet know is the very herald of death, a slow ghastly death sneaking through the cracks of his liquor-sopped body: his liver churns and Martín Martel pukes on his body, splattering himself with tiny bloody clots, eyes bulging in their sockets, shadows distorting the figure of death, the lights of the Governor's house blinking on again, off again before his eyes, elongating trickily in Martín Martel's teary eyes, the lights wobbling like ships rocked by the sea, lights coming and going, and here is Zulima again, a hag shamelessly exposing herself and offering him some rotten corporeal morsels, some delectables stinking of sour milk and decay, the green dogs barking around her, slobbering poisonously and making him scream, uselessly, in terror. No one hears him. No one comes to his aid. Only the poker-faced, hanged ghost of Pedro de Algaba, rising before his eyes in a bubbly vapory murk, shrieking his curse: "They'll do the same to you, Martín, when they can't use you anymore." He himself, Martín Martel, already smells like a dead man, knows he's dead, in slow transit toward the void, hero of this brouhaha of shadows and memories, a ceremony of corruption and death that has come out to greet him, an unholy procession of devils. "No priest can save you from hell," squawks the hoarse voice of Zulima the Arab. "You're going to the devil, to the oblivion of all and the memory of nothing, a place yours forever."

The dry howl of the desert wind, the sea tossing him in its frothy waves, cresting higher, crashing louder, the hideous pain of his innards which are shimmying into his mouth, the memory of a people he helped to stamp out with his own hands, a people roaming peacefully over the African deserts, seeking a destiny in which only the adepts believed, a people that lived the memory of its communal past like a passion, a lie upgraded to gospel. The Africans' blue darras graze his face while thousands of repetitive visages of Saracens lunge at him, gnaw him, gut him, slit his chest from top to bottom, till the blood spurts from his veins, trample him gleefully like a cluster of ripe grapes in the winepress of death.

Ancient is the legend of the blue men of the desert. A legend passing now, scene by scene, across the lost mind of Martín Martel, patches of history vying for center stage at the hour of the endless death throes of Martín Martel, the profaner. Long ago, perhaps in the centuries before history, all the tribes flocked to the shores and inlets of the desert, alerted by a huge ship foundering in the aftermath of a storm that had illumined and darkened the sky for many days. For a long time they waited there, on the beaches, in silence. They had pitched their huts and their patience on the rim of a sea that was their enemy, because from the sea, said a vague tradition they set little store by, would come the hope of the desert men. They let an endless time drift slowly by, which for them had never been precious ("Squat beside your tent and your enemy's dead body will pass by you"), since what shone in their universe of truths was a hazy notion of atemporality: concentric circles widening through time, and eclipsing it. Time had been unmeasurable ever since they lost their center of gravity and through the centuries, from generation to generation, they roamed, searching for the lost corners of a forbidding desert, a home with no doors. Long years of waiting on the sands of those shores further tempered the proverbial patience of men who had given up the habits of war: all occurred in the certainty that one day a release from this lassitude would arrive at last, a perhaps impossible redeemer who would rise up from the bottom of the seas, indeed an angel of mercy who would lead them to the ends of time, and far, far from misery, who would escort them to a land none had promised them but which floated in their imaginations like a deity etched in their memories down centuries of sirocco winds, of mirages also unmeasurable, and dry desert. Then slowly they lost their fear and their hope. They retained a blurry memory of bygone glories, of treks to the verges of the desert to conquer a city its inhabitants would cede without a fight. Tradition of traditions faded away in their memory because nothing arose from the waters, the surf died down, and the depth of the seas drank up the remains of the ghost galleon, some of whose planks, washed ashore, were worshipped as relics. They came to understand that the sacred ship had always been empty, and determined to draw lots to choose up the expedition that would go in search of the foundered vessel, sunken before the astounded eyes of their forebears. In crude dinghys, the chosen neared the spot pointed out to them by the holy man, his fingers trembling over a map scratched in the sand, making it known that right there, on the floor of the sea, lay the riches and destiny so long awaited. The men drew closer, full of fear. Though not seasoned sailors, they reached the spot, and plunged again and again, searching for the remains of the shipwreck that floated even now in their memories. Afar, on the beach, the gathered tribes awaited the result of the ritual, observing the waves rocking the little reed boats and the men diving beneath the waters. Bundle after bundle were fetched out and set on the tottery surface of rafts tethered just above where the ship laden with mysteries reposed in the depths. Then they watched the boats returning to shore with their cargo of fate. As though performing an autopsy, the holy man's scimitar pierced the weathered skin sheathing these ancient bodies that shrouded their awaited legacy, and scraped away the sea algae adhered to them over centuries in the deep. Slowly surprise turned to bafflement. Up from the bottom of the sea after all these years they had drawn a single prize: yards and yards of luxurious silk, sea-color, sky-color, regaled to them by the ocean so that they would all dress alike, so that thenceforth they would be known as the blue men upon the desert sands. Like all men, but different too, fulfilling the ritual of identity as sole destiny. Then the long peregrination began again, the endless exodus over interminable parched beds of rivers, seeking oases where the tribes, almost always splintered tribes, could camp for short spells only to again take up their slow, tireless trek over the barren earth, enduring torrid heat by day, and a fierce onslaught of icy cold no sooner did the motionless shadows of night descend over the desert sands. That whole boundless realm was their hacienda, their home, their life. Until the curse of Martín Martel overtook them. Again a vision of huge ships whose approach spanned the horizon, but this time dread filled them, for the caravels did not replay the scene, did not sink, and Martín Martel arrived to enslave them, to pluck them from their land, to snatch away their tattered robes.

"Abandon all hope, Martín," the toothless voice of old Zulima drones again. "You shall enter the world of the dead, where you will shuffle on the path of the infinite washing your sins forever and ever, as just vengeance for your cruelty. Tomorrow, when the sun climbs over our heads once more, and the masons go back to their futile labors on the construction of the Cathedral of Salbago, though not in five centuries will it ever be finished; tomorrow, when this stinking town fills with hubbub again, with a thousand unlike tongues, the market tirelessly hollering its offers from over the sea, you will be star of the show, memory of the curse, when you turn up there sopped in sugarcane rum, your jugular bitten away by that swarm of vile vermin sucking your foul blood. From the corners of your mouth, in your last agony, will run a sour sticky drool, the bile in which your cruel will lives. You will die like a pagan, an infidel. Alone, soused, spitting up memories with bits of liver and clabbers of blood, horrified at what you are."

"They found him dead," moans old María Isabel. "He was unrecognizable to the eye and they took him for some beggar. His hands and feet were wolf-claws, and his skin was tinged greenish. I've sent for his body to be collected and given a Christian burial."

Rejón tries to hide his trembling. He feels a cold fluid slogging through the rigidified conduits of his old body, as if little clots slowed the blood. "It'd be worse if he died in a cathouse," the Governor muses, laying a cloth over the body. Then he walks over to the window. Far off, on a wine-dark sea meeting a sky which today strikes the Governor as less than blue, in his memory gasps a vision of the flaming fleet, burning in rhythm with the slow wind.

For a long time the ignis fatuus of a fetid, unbearable effluvium flitted like a phantasmal flying skunk through the dark labyrinthical passages of the unfinished Cathedral. Camouflaged among the infected stones—oozing a yellowy-green killer pus—it licked with pleasure along the blind cellar walls of the cursed church, in whose foundations nested rats and slimy bats and a whole strange sloughpile of human beggary huddled there in nocturnal witchery for the barren celebration of their own poverty. This was the consequence of the legacy bequeathed to the city of Salbago by Martín Martel, probably protected by the law, which always sides with founders of cities. Every morning, from when the sun greyed the day until it sank away, rumors were bruited about in the plazas, boulevards, markets, slaughterhouses, meat and fish stands, everywhere that people gathered. Conjectures that under close scrutiny would not stand up to the serious dimensions of fact, but which attested to the almost tangible existence, given that the stench was so thick it could be cut with a knife as though it were a solid body, of a fetid, deathless gas that intoxicated with revulsion and impregnated with rot—representing its greatest sacrilege—the noblest, most sacred geographical triangle of Salbago, the zone in which lay its still budding identity: that formed, as it chanced, by the grim silhouette of Herminio Machado's Cathedral, the fearsome ground of the Grand Plaza, and the Palace of Juan Rejón, the Governor, who had not succeeded in erasing the angry message that his Campmaster, in the delirious agonies of death, had stained with his own rotten blood into the temple stones, as a personal epitaph: "Shit island. You're all scum."

The gassy stench burbled and bred. The ground cracked in those very places chosen by the Holy Inquisition to judge and condemn, to burn and pillory heretics and insurgents of every stripe, sanctified places where Bishop Frías had sung Salbago's first mass, in the days of the colonization, and where His Eminence Don Fernando de Arce prayed on and on in convulsive monotony, who, like his predecessor, had sunk the greater part of his personal fortune—forged in the Reconquest of the Iberian Peninsula—in the battle against the satanic mold thwarting the completion of the Cathedral, while Hernando Rubio snuffed out rebellions by decree of death by fire, and Simón Luz dealt out sinecures and canonries; while Rejón imprinted his Leonese fingers into the skin—getting more leathery by the year—of beautiful Zulima, and Herminio Machado sweated and slaved over the useless, daft perfection of charts and blueprints of those royal, sacred sites, where in the hot wind of the incessant tropics fluttered the flags and banners of Aragon, Castile, León and Navarre. Certain beggars, their imaginations stretched by hunger and destitution—who forage by night for the food begrudged by the sky in light of day—claimed they had seen the shadow of the naked ghost of Martín Martel gliding along the Cathedral's inside walls and splotching them with the blood of his maimed, death-pocked body. Exorcisms and prayers were indicated. So Arce sprinkled with holy water and litanies each of the stones allegedly hexed by the ghost; sprinkled the walls, edifices, and streets of the city's aristocratic zone, impelled by a belief in the triumph of the messiah as schizophrenic as it was futile. By this time, Pedro Resaca was heading the administration of Rejón's Palace, and he was detailed to keep a watch out, in the lugubrious dark of night, for the hot air that had set off the legend. "I've seen nothing, señor," Resaca insisted. "People get wild ideas in their heads and won't readily give them up."

"Hellfire," snickered Rejón thoughtfully. "He's more famous dead than when he staged the massacres."

The rumors swelled, swept like a sly secret gale through Salbago, a port of call now for many years and for centuries upon centuries to come: Martín Martel's breath blew far stronger after his death and in the end his decease

seemed to hinge on his own will. The superstition
surrounding the existence of that dark phantom incar-
nate in the gravity-defying image of Martín Martel blew
up to such exacerbated proportions that Hernando Rubio
the Inquisitor had no choice but to outlaw all commentary deriving from the life, marvels, exploits and death of
Juan Rejón's second-in-command. Punishments ranging
from a simple fine to the more fearsome—torture, loss of
property and personal liberty—gradually succeeded in
squelching Martín Martel's illicit phantom. Over and
above legend, it had attained the rank of secret tradition,
going the rounds, a contraband blasphemy laden, over the
centuries, with fluorescences, glosses, and universal variations, whence Salbago had an almost palpable ghost
before it had a finished Cathedral, both immolated, years
later, simultaneously, when the Dutch fury besieged the
streets of the city and Vanderoles the pirate lit fire to the
ghosts of Royal for all time.

Supping on salt tuna, wrapped in rheumy, unmeasurable, unvenerable old age, forgetful of the epochs and years, as though this stony, insolent figure looming over the twists and tomes of his own history were feeding his immortality, Governor Rejón's insides rumble, in his guts where the sourest juices of his body constringe, where his flesh galls palely as he dredges up memories out of the hidden past. Slowly, halfheartedly, he turns over in his mind so many odds and ends of memory, until now lacking a fixed location, snatches of event, battered hunks of fact and circumstance which might throw some light on the curse—of incurable corsair—that has haunted him forever, as if part and parcel of his being, like an incurable blight, a cursed fungus, clinging to the belly of Salbago, a breeze rising into a roaring wind, splattering rotten dung all over the territory, flinging the hook into the eyes and souls of its inhabitants. Before his eyes, for instance, comes that fit of temper chiselling the face of Martín Martel, fury clenched in the chest of his second-in-command, the veins in his neck swelling like the wailing chords of a strange instrument that might spring off into the air at any moment, burped-up foam forcing through his mouth, beading whitely at the corners of his lips, splotching his beard, face all red with hate. Before his eyes comes the livid face of the warrior who had assisted him in all his insanities, the day he could abide no more and came to him to protest the iniquitous conduct of Simón Luz, the Jew, who was running everything to suit himself. He arrived on the threshold of his palatine quarters as he had come to the tents of his Captain in the days of the colony, as if nothing had changed between them,

117

though this time it was plain that rage hunched his body:
they had literally snatched out of his hands his little Arab
girl. This is what happened, Governor. On the docks, right
after landing. A girl destined from the start to become the
receptacle for the infinite randy obsessions of the Adelantado's officers, administrators, and insatiable bureaucrats:
this was the first Rejón had heard of Zulima. As Pedro
Resaca refilled his goblet with mixtela, slaking the thirst
in his belly and gently soothing his throat, Rejón caught
sidelong glimmers of the other part of the story, the inner
skin of a shadowy memory, the slow calling-back of
memories leading up to the scandal, at that moment
sorting themselves out in his mind. How he, Rejón, had
gone that same evening and fallen in love with her, how
a wild desire had glittered in his eyes the first time he
saw her dancing on the sand-strewn terrace of that fabulous whorehouse of universal renown, the Six of Hearts of
Maruca Salomé, mistress of tricks, gambleress of cocks,
essential madame: how that astonishing body had
unveiled for him a thousand secrets, down paths the wild
and woolly warrior had never dreamed of traipsing; how
little by little, imperceptibly, the vertiginous pain
clamped between his thighs at the level of his testicles
had begun to vanish; how the ardors of a feisty macho in
the violence of battle and prophetic adventures had given
way to other more personal, intimate satisfactions, thanks
to Zulima's perfection; how he had made her, in short,
into his special concubine, and she had assumed the functions of a Governor's wife, surrounding herself with that
guard of Moors, loyal men of her own race—or crossbred
with Castilian, no less—with whom she strolled (hereby
creating myth) now and again on Salbago's evenings of
eternal springtime; how on the day it became known in
the city that the Governor, Don Juan Rejón, Adelantado
of Castile, had taken as his natural wife an Arab dancer
whom all his officers bragged they had rolled in the hay
at one time or another—annulling, in passing, on the
exclusive authority of his own will, the sacred matri-
monial bond that united him to the barren María Isabel—
all observed a minute of silence (shock or metaphorical
bereavement, it was never known) and how then an
immense collective belly laugh rose from the masses,

reaching the Governor's ears, a cruel jeer at his conduct
(if the laugh was nervousness, or sheer impotence and
scorn, it was never known). Even so he did not desist.
Beneath it all, and such had always been Juan Rejón's
conclusion, lurked nothing but a low-down sentiment of
nasty jealousy on the part of his underlings, that gang of
bums there, with new names, first and last, thanks to him
only. "Screw them," he screamed from the darkness of his
bed, soothed and strengthened by the ever-renewing
caresses of that sexy silhouette tumbling over his callused
body and insufflating him with life hitherto unknown to
him. He recalls, for instance, that selfsame day he
brought her home, her rooms nearing completion, a vulgar
ornateness manifesting itself in the furniture and wooden
ceilings; how Martín Martel's sarcasm came to light in
that obscene, macabre joke which was to be the start of
the definitive rupture in their friendship; how two of the
Lieutenant's soldiers had come to the palace doors, totally
oblivious to the fate they bore and of that which would
befall them for a like outrage. In their hands was a
wonderful Saharan vase, a polychrome baked clay vessel
depicting scenes of love and revelry.

"Who sends you?" asked Rejón himself, his brow knit,
irrefutable proof of his severity and the suspicion needling
him.

"Martín Martel, señor. Your Lieutenant honors you
with this gift."

Within the vase, indeed, no poison could have been
more terrible for Governor Juan Rejón, not serpents nor
scorpions could have more injured his vanity than the
message, written in a slow solemn hand—worked up for
the occasion by some colluding clerk with notable skill as
a scribe—that lay at the bottom of the terra cotta jar, like
a piñata secret, the fatal words summing up all Zulima's
past in a single phrase, dedicated now to the Governor by
her first lover, with which to celebrate their apocryphal
nuptials, in which to toast the malmsey wines that Rejón
kept cached in the palatine cellars. "Something to break
on the day you wed the Moorish lass, Captain," read Juan
Rejón, ashamed, as the blood pounded in his veins, beat
in his temples, and surged to his heart, which bolted away
like a wild horse assailed by an unknown madness. In

instant retaliation, he had the two messengers detained and at once gored through at the hands, in fact, of that Moorish guard, his personal guard, that had flanked him from the very same moment Zulima took up residence in the palace. He commanded that once dead they be impaled in Scaffold Square and that he not be implicated in this act of vengeance. This was meet punishment for the bravura of Martín Martel.

"Screw him, screw him forever," Juan Rejón snarls, picturing his commander's hole-pocked body, half devoured, like a cheese, by the street rats of Salbago. "Such was the end you deserved, son of a bitch," he concluded to himself.

Now there was no way around it. They had left him alone. All but Pedro Resaca had left him, slowly, patiently, gradually, like a man with the plague slipping toward death, like the carefully planned scuttling of an old, battered ship, its prow sagging and about to sink into the waters ringing Salbago. He strayed through the palatial halls, trailing his loneliness behind him like a sleepwalker, the circle of his life constricting around him. He amused himself in the light on the terraces, listening to the off-key screeks of parrots and macaws, smiling wistfully at the birds that called to him as he passed, the sun on his forehead mustering scenes of his remembered life, altered faces hailing him as if in some truce between bygone battles, faces he liked whimsically to imagine were rendering him homage, belated and useless. Accompanied by those green hounds that were growing old beside him, he penetrated the dreamy chiaroscuro of his empty rooms, talking to himself, drunken on a strange anxiety through which he glimpsed his demise. Little by little, the web of his solitary destiny had been strapping itself around him like a belt, weaving itself to his shadow starched by the years, like a quenchless leech sucking his clotted blood, patiently squeezing out his body, shrinking it, scrunching it. Still visible were the prints of the chess players' fingers posed on the petrified, dead pawns in the parlor corner where, some time back, he and the Black Duke used to sit, before the mysterious nobleman vanished without a trace, and the game was left to rest upon the chessboard, inalterable and interminable forever, like ever so many things in Salbago, initiated with the most feverish intentions, left off halfway, between lassitude and lost interest, a very particular form of ruining things. And not until after his death would his own son, Alvaro Rejón, return to the island, who had been raised beside the sea, mesmerized by the waters, infatuated by legends of giant freakish fish, lured by the sea as if it were a magnet. Resaca had reared him up beside his own son, Pedro, and once they grasped the futility of this sluggish calm devoid of adventure and put their gear and thoughts in trim, cruised the west coast of Africa until they knew it like the backs of their hands, north to south. Then they launched into the continental crusade, the dream of gold and spices. The fever for riches havocked everything, shifted the shape and size of life and of things, which little by little yielded to the yarns, yearnings and fables that washed up on the shores of Royal de Salbago from the New World conquered by the Spanish. So it was no surprise that sons sold, for a few grubby coins, the haciendas just inherited from their fathers, after which there was nothing to do but cram onto the docks to purchase a ticket on the voyage to paradise—something severely punished by the Council of the Indies in Seville—or to bend with precious metal the scruples of sailors and captains. If none of this was possible, they signed up unpaid on one of those caravels bearing hopes and wild dreams that moored more and more often in Salbago Harbor to lay in goods and provisions.

Bartolomé Larios, for instance, made a hard and fast decision to leave after sorting out in his head that life in Salbago was a waste of time. In a spurt of madness (doing honor, in any case, to a long life now on its last legs) he dreamed he saw the Terra Firma of the Continent as if it lay at the height of his hands, swollen from the wheel. He wandered through the port, through the fishing districts, muttering to himself, coaxing himself into the truth of his most prized secret. Night after night he obsessed over the impossible journey. Night after night he concocted new schemes, jotting down conjectures and tales he heard in the shacks by the docks, later tailoring them to his own experience, remarks passed between whores and seafarers singing the sublimities of a boundless land. He would

wake rejuvenated, sweating and fevery, mesmerized by
his mission, by his wish for a transatlantic voyage, his
breath quickened by the conviction that that world lay
directly beyond the waves dashing daily upon the sandy
beaches of Salbago. He was mad. He had lost his mind in
the loneliest of senectitudes. One morning, shrugging off
his small household staff, and his nearest friends, who,
reading something new and peculiar in his gleaming
eyeballs, advised him not to go to sea today, he pushed
off, oaring, in a little boat not six meters fore to aft. "I'm
going fishing," he replied balkily to those who counselled
him to stay on land. A worthless compass, which had
given up pointing true north some time ago and devoted
itself to dancing fickly over the four cardinal points, was
the only navigational instrument he brought on board.
Apparelled in his old sailor suit, the fabric rigidified by
time and desuetude, he was convinced of the total success
of his undertaking. A single central pole, to which was
fitted a lateen sail Larios could no longer maneuver for
lack of strength, comprised his mast and spars. The old
helmsman vanished from the island as he had come,
leaving no trace. The sea, vast silent jungle, swallowed
him forever, and his memory, also forever, was left to float
peaceably on the green encircling waters. His boat, like a
loyal horse, returned alone to the harbor three days after
his departure and smashed against the outer reef.

"He was crazy," Governor Rejón said to himself,
recalling the incident.

And now, moreover, the Governor was troubled about
news coming from Europe, facts he did not care a fig for,
not a shit, he answered the accusations. The aristocracy,
and the King of Spain, Carlos the Glutton, charged him,
Juan Rejón, with maximum responsibility for a shocking
alliance with its roots in the mire of political intrigue: the
Black Duke, after his escape from Salbago, must have
gone to France, to the depraved court of King Francis.
"That little faggot, so that's where he wound up. With the
Frenchmen, that flock of sissies," said Rejón, wielding a
poor defense, looking down his nose at those accusations.
Then he would look intent, shield himself in a silence
assumably filled with concentric mysteries and fraying
memories. The wake of rumors reached the city, taking

Juan Rejón to task for the responsibilities of his position:
they slapped him, no bones about it, with the blame for
the flight of that archtraitor with the elegant manners,
who had disappeared from the island, scattering behind
him an obstreperous trail of scandals committed right
there, again and again, without being called to justice.
Rejón had always turned a deaf ear on the chitchat
brought to him by Hernando Rubio. "They're jealous of
him, Hernando," he replied to the lame-legged Inquisitor.
Was it or was it not true, for instance, that the Black
Duke denuded himself in broad daylight on the roof of his
house and was massaged by the concupiscent hands and
skinny, suspiciously feminine body of Lord Gerald, the
Britisher (no doubt of this, due to his demeanor and reputation) who had suddenly joined his household staff from
the cockpits and whoredens of the Six of Hearts,
summoned, according to María Salomé, by the Black Duke
himself, who had bought him up as one might an African
slave. "Love is blind, and all's fair," said Maruca Salomé
to Rejón. But blinded by his friendship for the Duke, he
did not wish to hear the truth brought to him day after
day by Hernando Rubio. "Those are courtly customs,
Hernando. A variety of cultivation we don't possess,"
Rejón said, scotching Paleface's intentions. But was not
this ample evidence of orgiastic, outrageous love,
forbidden even by natural law? "Each in his own house
and with his own ass," Governor Rejón would invariably
conclude, "can do what he damn well pleases." In this
way, fortune favored the Black Duke, no stranger, either,
to the Holy Inquisition, whereby only Hernando Rubio
could dare to lay a hand on him. "You," the Governor
would accuse Paleface, "are a jackoff and you only need
yourself. Anyone can do that, jackass." It was, by any
standard, an excessively complacent complicity.

For years, the Black Duke had patiently waited in his
island exile for the propitious moment to make his escape.
Games of chess, sublime readings, nocturnal promenades
on the deserted beaches, libertine interludes with Lord
Gerald—for this, and for nothing else, had he bought him
from Maruca Salomé—sentimental educations remote from
the hollow crassness of this land, frivolous expressions
which helped to shore up his reputation, of the respect-

commanding, enigmatic sort, unjustifiably held here. For years, all slander spewed into the ears of Rejón and Hernando Rubio by the voice of the street was taken as mere guff, tales dreamed up by the puny, unhealthy imaginations of inferior people who could not comprehend the Duke's nobility and balked at the mysterious grandeur of his banishment. Draped in his black gowns, almost always in long leggings, parading through Salbago a strange, superannuated dignity, easing, by way of Lord Gerald's massages, the fevery torridities of his hyperhydrosis—whose only symptom was his constant throat cold—the Duke never betrayed the tiniest glimmer of his revenge, a coat of mail he wore in his thoughts at all times, nor could one ever observe the least desire as the caravels came and went from Salbago. He gazed at them disdainfully as if he had never pined for them. All the while he was cultivating Rejón's trust, preparing himself for the one and only chance that would arise in his life of involuntary exile. Like so for many years. Like so until circumstances lined up, and the escape became more than illusion, more than a shadow in the imagination of this ever-unflappable man.

Nor was Lord Gerald to be forgotten on this land scorched by the simoon winds, when it was time to cross the forbidden limit of the Badlands, the impassable frontier of a forsaken zone of blackened, barren surfaces where none dared enter for fear of the void, of the sonorous solitude of that vast, vast no-man's-land—where the wind shuttled melodies that drove men berserk—or because at any moment, as the legend told, the hoarse voices of the doomed might surge out of any black hollow and drift away in that biblical drought, scatter like ashes or phantasmal memories. Groomed in the greatest of discretions, the aspiring fugitive had been drawing up, over many years and with utter painstakingness, a plan for irreversible flight. He had been waiting to meet up with the right person (the nameless captain of a French ship who tied up at the docks to fix some defects that had cropped up on the long trips on the southern stretch of the African coast). As a matter of fact, he was a slave trader who wanted to make over his life, go home to France, enter Marseilles like a national hero, recount his exploits

without being locked up and finally killed. From the roof
of his house, the Black Duke had surveyed the French
ship's repeated course, its comings and goings from
Salbago about every other month, the Black Duke's eyes
shimmering as though it were a mirage, the revery of his
desire, as if only a dream could bring before his eyes the
furled sails of the ship, the colors of the French flag
beneath which the pirate captain sailed, safe and sound.
All his visions of a getaway dormant, the renewed juices
of hope flooded again through that body that had never
let on, with the least flinch, to his irrepressible longing to
flee, his true intentions to go far from Salbago forever. He
knew, moreover, what the island authorities either did not
know or wished to overlook: Spain was virtually in open
war with France. The animosity and distrust between
King Francis and King Carlos that could only escape the
notice of rubes, of beings from another world who lived
their lives as if their country was the belly button of the
planet, from which all news and all reality stemmed. Very
well received would he be in the sophisticated Paris court,
that theoretician of warped prophecy, that frenetic champion of the dismantling and dismemberment of an
Empire—the Spanish—that had just begun to take shape,
this curious, inexplicable character—ever-so-cultivated,
precious to the point of priggishness, affected to the nth
degree—preaching at the top of his lungs the ludicrous
and—nonetheless—prophetical humbug that would now
drop like ripe fruit into the hands of the Gallic monarch;
an eccentric philosopher plugging the necessity of independence for an immense land, the New World, granted
by the Treaty of Tordesillas to Spain and Portugal, the
boundaries of the partition drawn with the blessed
consent of an impartial Pope—Rome, after all. Rome up
against which ran all the thinkers in history—though they
had never dreamed of conquering all of it, could not even
tally its exact dimensions; an irresponsible madman who
excoriated the gold fever, according to him the supreme
ambition of the Spanish. A unique, perverse thinker. In
short, a galling heterodox of the sort only Spain down the
centuries had begotten by the dozen: absolute, resolute,
incombustible despite the daily proximity of the bonfire.
This extreme rebelliousness was the unspeakable fore-

runner of an entire century of bloody massacres, historical gaffes, atrocities, insurrections, civil wars and wars of liberation, glories fading into defeat, botched beginnings and lost steps, conquests that conquered and trapped the conquistadors themselves. So, to the Black Duke one would have to confer the seat of honor, erect for him a polyglot pulpit, to broadcast his theory, *urbi et orbe,* in all the salons, all villages, towns, university lecture halls, every corner and cranny of the true capital of the civilized European world, the city of liberty and lust, of marble, of alabaster, of crazes and classics, perfumes and luxury, debauchery and hilarity, the smuttiest show, the canniest intrigue, the great city, where all the swindlers in the world passed for honest merchants, unpacking their fakeries for sale to the stupefaction of a spendthrift cosmopolitan public, a city always open where the tyrannical concept of sin had vanished forever, where the doubts and lucubrations that vexed the Black Duke would round out in glory, who would find in Paris the ideal complement to his character, at once subversive and contemplative, brilliant and captivating, in egalitarian discussion with professors and thinkers, savants, and people like himself who were conversant in other languages and other cultures, enjoyed a worldly liberal education in which tolerance was revered, with people made for the conquest of the spirit and not for the barbarous exploits and feats of gold and horsemanship that blew the tops off the minds of the Spanish. A whole century to come was to witness the slow ascent of the emancipation doctrine of the Black Duke, in whose soul bubbled the bitter bile of all the traitors of Spain, from Prisciliano to Don Julián, from the Count who switched to Islam to the Duke who double-crossed Spain for Europe.

The Black Duke and Lord are led by patience and utmost thoughtfulness. They traverse the suspicion-fraught latitudes of obligatory secrecy. They shun the easy error, eschew excessive hurry, which would muddy them in nervousness. They know they tread zones of delicate porcelain beneath whose brittle surface a chasm yawns. So, no matter the loss of a few more hours to carry out to a hair each complicated step of their forethought plan. Unlikely, crack cardsharks, they stake their lives on

one card, face up. Uncurbable hope spurts in their chests
as they walk, sporadic sparks spurring them onward, to
flee from this magnetized territory where the myth of
Circe, as they know firsthand, is sober fact. They step over
stubble, dried vines, seaweed adrift over the volcanic
ground in the sweep of the warm sandy wind; they flee
through the limpid light flung by the hand of the stars in
the tropical night. Here hugger-mugger and caution are a
sacred art, bone salt for the brave funambulists during
the hours when danger prowls near. The Black Duke had
studied the crude map drawn for him by the faceless
French mercenary over and over, so it turned out to be an
unnecessary risk to carry the evidence that could let the
cat out of the bag at any moment, pyroengraved as they
were into his superior mind each of the zigzagging trails
leading to the final evasion. On foot, leaving behind them
the rasping echoes of their hurried steps, cloaked in
silence and the sightless complicity of night, they first
cross the hated town where so many feckless years lie, so
much laziness scratched into the walls of hovels and
shacks, those hostile environs where both—the Black
Duke and Lord Gerald—had felt like actors in a play, fish
out of water, cards with blank faces, dinky specimens of
another, forgotten world, here where their customs and
habits were simply a travesty, leading nowhere but the
bonfire, and did not tally, in any way, with those of the
highest island aristocracy, born in the days of the Discoveries, an elite of bastards and wastrels, favorites and
darlings who had, as if overruling time, acceded without
interruption to power, rotten to the core, fraught with
insolvencies and contradictions from the time Juan Rejón
founded the city and populated, helter-skelter, the hopeless island of Salbago: a frontier city, always on the
periphery, a city that had stifled them, a city full of
squalidities and silly adventures, the two of them
hostages to the shadiest morality, forced to sail under
false colors, to enter the thick, take on the pose, of daily
hypocrisy, a city, all things considered, where the historical shake-up caused by the Discovery and Conquest of the
New World, beyond the Levant, gave rise maniacally and
mechanically to the dynamic unconscious impermanence
in which the masses lived, in devotion and subjection,

obsessed by legends of every feather, by the stories and sudden fevers of a universe to them beyond measure.

On narrow paths of volcanic rock, about to blurt round monosyllables of warning to the dogged step of the fleers, returning them again and again all through the night to their hypothetical point of departure—hours tangled in a nonsensical labyrinth sending them back over the frontiers they believed they had crossed—robes torn, balked again and again, but their spirits immune to fatigue or breathlessness, bit by bit they begin to gain faith in their desires, to enter that world of fantastic forms, full of gorgeous hermetical nothingness, not permitting themselves a moment's rest on the lunar peaks of that uninhabitable, alien landscape scorched by eruption upon eruption in the lost centuries. They pick out the trail, slowly, scrupulously, like twin souls led by the devil his very self across the parapets of hell until at last, at the first glimmer of day, they reach the far side of the island, Salbago's hidden silence, the rim of no return, where a monstrous cliff rises more than one hundred meters above the level of the sea, sheer, exhibiting the striae of an astounding sculpture like the giant organs of a vast church, in the open air, instruments sounding melodiously in the dashing of white-foaming waves, riffs of notes played by the air and the breeze upon the shore, on the beach along whose edge petrified lava twists and writhes into freakish forms, a museum of horrors, riddled with holes through which the warm water, foaming as it dashes, slips.

The Black Duke gazes ecstatically for a moment at those masks of twisting stone, like a prolonged mineral paroxysm, elaborate columns whose figures blend styles already classified by art historians and snatches of others, still mere sketches, to be fleshed out by future centuries. A gorgeous geological phenomenon, hidden from the lands of Salbago, visible only from this path that descends to the pebble-strewn beaches, a spectacle forever glinting with the sparks of the burning universe which in its hour burst the island and hurled it into the air, giving it a new shape, shattered into a thousand new pieces, flowing melted into the sea-foams stalling its course into the ocean. Now, the surf—like slough of the present-day island—sizzles, the ancient quiescent lava simmers as the sea crashes, leaps, licks with liquid salt the lower stria-tions of an immense wall, consummate architecture of an archaeological cathedral concealing the island's secrets within its crypt.

Just now, the two exhausted escapees catch sight of the messianic French ship, glittering and ruffling in the distance, a mere mile and a half from the coast, aflame on a sea shimmering in the lineal gleams of the sun in the breaking dawn. Beneath their eyes lies the beach of black stones, immense rim where a rowboat and three dozing men, now stretching their silhouettes among the shadows, have almost given up on them. All that remains is to overcome, path downward, that black specter looming beside them, skin that spectacular cliff of organs, risking their lives, as slowly they bear down on the boat's sleepy signal light. The fugitive adventure, the risk run across the volcanic highlands, through whistling winds and equivocal darknesses of night, had paid off. The Black Duke knew that a like event would never be repeated. He was dreaming of Paris.

He began to write his manifesto (dreaming of Paris), with much agitation, from the moment the boat took to the open sea and lost sight of the island—which slowly transformed in the Black Duke's eyes, into a nightmarish memory, behind him now forever—as if inside him some-thing dark and murky obliged him to remain behind the desk in his cabin, burning the midnight oil, redressing the transgressions, delving into the visceral depth of his here-sies. The nights and days, in endless succession, were for him one more incentive to finish his unfinishable oeuvre. Not exactly the memoirs of an embittered man, judg-ments skewed by long exile, prompting errors of perspec-tive as to reality. Not the splenetic essay of a broken man, a thinker misunderstood by the stony provinciality of his compatriots. Nor even the throbbing revenge of a traitor, a Spaniard of noble blood who had spurned his origins to quibble blackly with history and life. Simply the deaf-ening cry, the necessary explosion of a thesis of liberty, a dissonant voice whose outrageous theories bespoke a strange new vision of the world. He wrote night after night, day after day, month after month, as if nothing in

the universe was as important as leaving, signed and
sealed by his own hand, the thoughts he had for so long
kept filed in the archives of his mind.

On the island remained the troubled shadow of Juan
Rejón, Governor beyond all time, dreamer of specious
sagas, caught between his dogs and the trumped-up
memories of a conquest that never occurred, a history the
Adelantado slowly embellished with battles and feats
dreamed up by his mad, warped mind as it drifted off into
the corners of a time that was no longer his to live. His
fervors, horrors, phobias, fears, obsessions twined around
him like vines, fusing with his life story, a leafiness
slowly growing over the inside of his Palace, his lonely
strolls down stone corridors, the echoes of his footsteps
rebounding off the walls. Hunting for the tiniest clue,
Rejón nosed around in his house's grimiest corners. He
could not forget, since the Black Duke's departure, how
treachery had again and again steeped his life in hate.
Still arrogant, closeted inside those thick stone walls, he
dragged his shadow like a soul in torment, falling back,
now and then, on the futile episodes of existence. At
moments a fevery fear would light into him. Now it was
possible that what he believed was his great work—the
construction and possession of Salbago—could be snatched
away from him thanks to the madness of that bold individual who had spent years cultivating his intimacy and
trust. They might send for him from the Court, force him
to make the voyage home, oblige him to hide out in the
wild hills of León, or, far worse, wrest him from this exile
to which he had gladly banished himself for life, and ship
him to the Peninsula in a caravel, in chains. All this
could happen, or worse still: they could shove him for good
into a damp lonely dungeon where his bones would again
meet the obscurity from which he had risen. His name
would be excised from history following a short trial
where all witnesses would concur, and the military judges
would have no other task but to dispatch him to a dark
grave for life. Then Juan Rejón began to tremble, the voyage home swelling in his mind, menacingly real, the
journey to a land he had completely forgotten; he felt
the seasickness set off in his old body by the rocking of the
caravel, heard the wind blow in a rising storm soon to

worsen, to darken the sky, and make him retch like an epileptic. Prisoner of himself, Juan Rejón speculated, fore-glimpsing events never to happen, because otherwise the curse of Pedro de Algaba could never be fulfilled, the curse cast by the rebel so many years before, in the age in which he himself had unloosed the inquisitorial wrath of Hernando Rubio, known as Paleface. Later, recovering from his fit, still feverish but beginning to calm down, drenched in a sticky sweat that glued his clothes to his body, he drooped off into sleep, only to wake again shrieking in the palatial silence, and maybe stagger down the corridors, duck into the first doorway he came to, the startled puffing and blowing of the parrots and macaws making his runaway heart thump harder and harder.

All these visions were just that: whimsies induced by fear, death shudders of a loneliness that had been mounting around him and had climaxed with the treach-erous getaway of the Black Duke. "That queer has unbal-anced me," his voice spewed out as he burped up the air that had turned stale in his lungs during the seizure.

All his visions boiled down to this: hopped up tensions prompted by the Duke's departure in his mind outside of time. Not the King of Spain and all the New World, man in whose dominions the sun never set, would send for him nor take him to task for his ineptitude, nor would he ever be judged by the officers of the court, distinguished for the implacability of their determinations. Not even did his name exist, nor had it ever existed, as a solid entity to be reckoned with, in the mind of His Imperial Majesty King Carlos V, a European dead to dimensions not those delin-eated for him by the Old World, of which he had been chosen by fortune as favorite son. He never knew about islands, or Rejóns, or bishops named Frías, or Jews called Luz, or cathedrals inflicted by supernatural ills that stymied their completion, or voyages upon endless seas or hostile lands. His was a world of gourmandise, wealth, extravagancy, of constant abandon to the groaning board, to ceaseless victory, triumph served up on gold and silver platters by the mad Spanish conquistadors who hailed from the Castilian steppe, the barren plains of Extre-madura, the ports and villages of Andalusia. Carlos V had no cause for worry: God was always by his side, coun-

selling the Catholic with omnipotent cunning on every
step he should take. No mistake ever seeped into the ears
of His Sublime Majesty. So he had never heard of Rejón
or his false conquests. Only gold drew him to the New
World. Gold and the indiscriminate expansion of a religion that traumatized the minds and ancient traditions of
the natives of the New Continent. Therefore all of Rejón's
nightmares were—at bottom—illusions, a history that had
never existed in a book that had never been written. His
memories, beside the colonization of that world growing
gargantuan beyond the Levant, were a muddled para-
graph, of no importance, an insignificant impediment over
which in their chronicles the historians could blithely
skip. His conduct, whether or not it obeyed to the letter
the law of the monarch, did not count. If he killed or did
not kill, conquered or did not conquer, founded or did not
found cities, the outcome was always the same, the facts
read alike: nothing he did—by action or omission—had any
value at all. He simply did not exist.

So by nobody would the Black Duke's written heresies
ever be read. The Black Duke would never find himself
enveloped, encircled by that world he had dreamed of
always in Salbago. He would never recount, with the sort
of punctilios and the perfectionism that was one of his
most seductive qualities, the peripeties suffered in that
wild lost Atlantic place where he had remained for the
space of so many years that it wound up shuffling the
dates of his biography. His lampoon against Carlos V,
entitled *From Salbago to Paris,* an interminable tract
packed with invectives against Imperial Spain, its monks,
bishops, conquerors and rulers, would never reach its
destination. The ship the French buccaneer had put in off
the coast of the island, to salvage from that wasteland a
superior mind that was to divulge to the world the nasty
hypocritical lies of Catholicism, would be lost world
without end, sailing steady and sleepless into all corners
of the Ocean. His voyage, however, would never go down
in any important legend either; the history of those ages
would thin the flight of the bold, enigmatic Black Duke
to a shadow, more or less smudged, muzzy and immobi-
lized amid so many superior events, those which presaged
the light of a new age, thanks to the conquest of lands

whose indescribable dimensions their discoverers had never dreamed of.

So, *From Salbago to Paris* remained inside the mind of the Black Duke, an attempt to destabilize the Empire, a drop of oil dried up by the sun as soon as it beaded out, in this world full of new faces, newfangled customs, and bizarre conjectures. Nor did news of that legend ever reach Paris. That a Spanish heretic pass the rest of eternity digressing over the divine and the human, doubly enclosed in the prison of his cabin and the prison of the vast sea whereon his vessel would float for century upon century, always spied in the distance like a phantom, shunned by the crews of other caravels like a specter in the possession of the devil, was of no great consequence. That some serious investigators, years or even centuries later, with their revindications and intellectual troves, might boost the image of a heterodox lost on land or water en route to the city of Paris, also lacked true significance. So many, many other adventurers had lost their lives for the sake of whichever of the fallacies they had scrambled after that the story of the Black Duke, beefed up by his fanatical followers, exalted later by so many of the universities of the world, would never make the grade required to join the scientific tradition of Humanity.

Juan Rejón could doze and doze—as he had heretofore—amid his delusions of a frustrated conquistador. Who was the Black Duke, after all, to intrude on his little life and his imaginary feats? Pedro Resaca, the last of the faithful, shadowed him patiently in and out of all the palace crannies, his nursemaid, his cook. He was the only one who still understood Rejón, now metamorphosed into a bundle of eccentricities and superstitions. The only one, in short, with whom he shared that grief that blackened their bile: the departure of their sons to the ends of the earth. The only one who would be present on that fatal day, the day of the strange death of the Adelantado, Don Juan Rejón. Meanwhile, as time crept over the confines of the years, as if nothing ever happened off the island, as if this territory were the only inhabited land on the planet, Resaca came to hate the sea—in spite of being an old salt—as much as he hated his master. Both he saw every day, without recourse.

"The sea, Pedro," Juan Rejón would huff and puff, "hides a curse. The sea itself is a curse. All are lost in it, because this land they run from is their only refuge. They flee looking for death. You and I, Pedro, are the only ones left."

On the appointed day of his death, Juan Rejón rose from his bed with such a burden on him he could barely breathe. It was, to be sure, the weight of the premonition of his demise, and it gave him an excruciating headache. Ever since dawn, on opening his eyes, he imagined that a giant insect of unknown species (which he pictured as a puffy white beetle with human eyes and powerful elytra) had perched on his head while he slept, striking up a concert of exotic notes (like whirring or the tuning up of musical instruments), in fact, the prelude to his death. He was, as Pedro Resaca noted, not prepared. As always in the midst of these strange fits, he experienced sudden urges to finish tasks he would suddenly remember having left half done (forgotten maybe, many years before) whose original interest had mildewed in his soul.

"The Cathedral, damn it," he recalled, out of the blue. "What could have happened to it? I promised Hernando Rubio I would go look at the construction site." By some peculiar out-of-control mechanism, matters he had forgotten sprang into his mind, his memory's guilty conscience coming into play, his mind breeding, like so much disagreeable trivia, maps, charts, drawings, interminable sketches of the sacred edifice.

On those fateful days, he abandoned projects begun the day before with priority status and uncommon vim for a man of his age. Things of no consequence anymore, to tell the truth, to which he attached, in moments of senile daftness, excessive interest. He wanted, all on his own, without asking anyone and especially not Resaca, to clear up that doubt pestering him at all hours. "What was the name of that screwball in command of the troops?" Into his mind came this as-yet-open question. Like so, perhaps to chase away the evil shadows flittering about him from the early hours of dawn, he persisted in out-of-date pastimes that could even be considered normal quirks in someone unaware that by now he stood at death's very doors.

Like so, shivering, seated before the chess table, watching dopily as the armies gored each other in motionless battle, he passed the first hazy hours of the dawn of his foretold funeral. Like a quiet lunatic, utter bafflement and helplessness floating in his eyes, he stared at the placement of the chessmen he had nohow dared to touch since the moment of the premeditated escape of the Black Duke, when the game was left off indefinitely. Mentally he began to plot strategies for encircling the enemy, maneuvers on the silent field of battle, guessing at the Duke's hypothetical moves, setting traps for himself, but never touching the men, which were coated with a thick patina of dust and cobweb trapezes. He was determined never to move another chessman again. Not even a pawn—sacrificed without a pang of regret in times gone by—until he had won the game in his imagination or until, something he knew was highly improbable, the Duke returned and they could resume the battle as if nothing had intervened. Even there on the edge of that abyss, which was the authentic sensation of anticipated death, he maintained that useless pride, that Castilian hardheadedness which had acquired renown beyond the marine frontiers of Salbago.

Along these lines, he also kept on exercising—at least by rights—a power that in fact had disappeared many years before, as his men, one after the other, went away, died, abandoned the island, withdrew into silence, their hopes shattering, throwing off their leading roles on the stage of history, and old age took Juan Rejón by surprise, confining him almost forever to his Palace chambers, a wing fitted out to his predilections and eccentricities, keeping him, at the same time, apart from the world. Now reality itself exercised power by inertia, swaying it one way or the other by the sole virtue of the authority that still emanated from the invocation of his name.

At moments he believed he was already dead and

buried. The rabble, taken up in the congenial idea of his disappearance, distortioned their civic traditions and celebrated impromptu carnivals the etiology of which they found it hard to explain when order, late or soon, again reigned on the island. An exception never to be repeated, Juan Rejón was paraded through the streets of Royal de Salbago, in procession like a saint from Heaven through the city and its unruly meanders to demonstrate to any who might dare to revolt that his heart was still pumping, that he was alive and capable of punishing with the same cruelty and justice as ever, any defiance or gratuitous provocation. On this occasion he felt truly like Royalty, like a King or a Pope. Or a Saint. He waved showily with his arm on high (his eyes watery with emotion) to those who applauded and flung flowers as he passed, smiling proudly because the residents of that hellhole he had founded so many years back still remembered him, recognized him as their only possible leader, revered him like a god.

"You saw them, Pedro. They dance in the palm of my hand, as if no time had gone by," he commented at the end of that peculiar carnivalesque hoopla, as his major-domo, on his knees before him, struggled to pull his shiny boots off his chilled feet. "If I commanded them to jump from the top of the Cathedral walls, not for an instant would they hesitate to give their lives for me. They know this, Pedro. After I'm gone, nothingness, chaos. This they know all too well." By now, he was a human ruin into which the years had pitched with cruel pleasure. "Chaos, Pedro, chaos," he was still crowing over and over many hours later, calling back images he had seen during the procession.

It had all been a theatrical ruse on the part of Cabeza de Vaca, then commander of the troops of Royal de Salbago, and the episode had taken place nine or ten years before this day of his death, a song of victory over the Dutch pirates of Captain Vanderoles, who had held Salbago under a useless siege so as to force it to surrender by means of something which was quotidian custom on the island, a fact unknown to the European buccaneer on this occasion: hunger. So Juan Rejón, prinked like a peacock and riding beneath a baldachin, was obliged to

take part in the happy, hysterical hilarity that broke loose
in the citizens of Royal upon seeing that their necks, once
more, were spared, as away from the island sailed the
Dutch flotilla which, since the age almost directly after
the colonizations and discoveries, had ravaged all the
known seas with deft brutality, and, like so many other
buccaneers through so many years and centuries, had
fixed their covetous eyes on the conquest of Salbago, gathering, rightly, that the island was a rock of strategical
necessity from which they could launch their armed ships
toward three continents: Europe, Africa, and the New
World.

But Rejón, aswim in the soupy naïveté of senility, saw
nothing. During the long days of the Dutch siege of the
harbor, embarcaderos, shores and beaches of Salbago, the
Governor kept himself in prudent withdrawal in his
chambers, barely poking his head out of those rooms the
officers of his power-by-inertia had assigned to him for his
personal use. But yes, he could hear a roar like the sound
of combat, stentorian cries resounding all through the
city. Booms like artillery fire, like bombards hurtling over
buildings, like culverins shooting off, maybe from the
nearby sea, noises like explosions that sometimes seemed
to be passing very near the palace. He heard loud curses,
bustle of soldiers, and clang of armor, noting, with some
concern, certain of his palace guards scurrying from place
to place, coming and going on staircases and down corridors, from the cellars to the lookout towers, from the
ramparts to the lost recesses of his house. Oblivious to the
age he could be living in without knowing it, Rejón
rejected as evil and excessive the novel idea that on the
streets and wharves of Royal City, Salbago, a bona fide
battle was being waged, a war he had not noticed. "They
would have said something," he thought blearily as the
noises and rumbles crescendoed from one end of the city
to the other.

"Pedro, what the devil is making all that noise?" he
asked Resaca the majordomo.

"The sea, señor," Resaca lied barefacedly, knowing
what he did was but a small act of mercy for an old man.
"The sea's rough, señor."

"Rough? Hell, sounds like it's fighting the whole island."

Juan Rejón spoke leerily, peering out of the corner of his eye at Pedro Resaca's secret reactions. Then, with the excuse of personally feeding the parrots and macaws, he ventured out onto one of the Palace's more protected terraces. With every step, the roar of the battle swelled, to acoustical dimensions impossible to overlook, the racket rebounding off the terrace's inside walls, making the stone floors tremble. "Damn. These rough seas sound like an earthquake," Rejón remarked wryly. Each bombard blast tore the dense closeness of the still air, and rolled, bursting and popping, in and out of every one of the Palace's bedchambers, reaching the ground floor somewhat dwindled, and dying away (like thunder receding into the distance) in the crypt of Rejón's Palace, destined to house the mortal remains of this ersatz emperor who defied time, determined as he was never to abandon this world.

This was the first time the Dutch had dared to launch a proper attack on Salbago, as dictated by the war decorum of the epoch. For five or six days they held the island under silent siege, to induce them by means of this tactical dead calm into a surrender never to come about as anticipated. Then they unloosed on Royal a veritable storm of missiles and artillery fire, which shattered against the obstinacy of the tattered islanders. The pirates scrambled onto the beaches, sinking into the black sands. They even took possession of one of the docks. Here and there they seized a jetty, which served as momentary parapets, until the sea—in its violence dragged at their bodies, yanking them from their niches, dunking them like tiny, defenseless sea creatures. In a frenzied fit of euphoria they would later be the first to rue, they allowed themselves to be swept away by the heat of the battle, and dared to cry for blood through the streets of Salbago nearest the sea. What's more, a spectacle they would repeat many years hence with complete success, they attempted to light fire to the Cathedral Herminio Machado had designed in the early years of the colonization (as if in this squatty, never altogether finished fetish were lodged the islanders' will to resist), repenting no sooner did they see the slippery, unknown terrain beneath their feet, lost in the corners of the maze the Spaniards knew as Royal de Salbago. Beaten back at the hour of the siege by an angry, righteous mob, they threw in their heroism without a second thought, bowing too late to the evidence of a delusive mirage into which Vanderoles had lured them.

"I know you're tricking me, Pedro," Juan Rejón insinuated bluntly, as to the constant pandemonium. "That's the sound of battle, damn it. And it smells like a load of shit, which is the smell of death. The stink's gotten in here. The same smell that escorted Pedro de Algaba to the scaffold, the same smell that surrounded him in all his shenanigans and dumb insurrections. It's my fault. If I had killed him when I should have, none of this would be happening now. Instruct Martín Martel to cut off his balls on the spot, in my name, and bring them here so that I have full proof that my orders have been obeyed. Then have him string them from a high pole, damn it, at the entry to the port, right smack in the center of the Grand Plaza, that all may know the price of rebelling against the authority of Juan Rejón."

He raved incessantly amid the smell of battle and burnt flesh, which clung in his nose, rousing sensations of thought that, paradoxically, distanced him from the age. "Isn't he in charge of the troops, Pedro? Isn't that Martín Martel?" he asked, dazedly, discounting the more or less questionable fact that he himself was conscious of having lost the exact memory of times and things.

"No, señor," the majordomo patiently rejoined. He who now commands is the young Captain Cabeza de Vaca. Martín Martel is no longer living, señor. Or Herminio Machado. Or Simón Luz. He who spies and punishes is Inquisitor Montalvo. And the one who stirs up and settles down everything is a little maniac. A boy named Chaves, Cabeza de Vaca's aide-de-camp. "They keep the city," said Resaca dryly, "in total calm."

Rejón was silent for several instants. "Cabeza de Vaca, Cabeza de Vaca," he said to himself contemplatively while he distractedly sliced green plantain into tiny rondelles to feed to the macaws in the garden. "But, hell, wasn't that the name of the cleric we liberated from his cassock so

he'd devote himself to writing the history of the conquest
of Salbago, on express recommendation of Simón Luz?
That slimebag. That bat. That greenhorn who swore to
dedicate himself solely to writing the chronicles of our
feats and discoveries?"

"He switched to governing, señor," answered the majordomo. "Juan Chaves talked him into it. He told him that
men of letters had always been shit and scum, at the
mercy of men in command. He told him you spent the
whole day chewing the fat, that you said he ate out of
your hand like a macaw on your terrace, that he was your
slave and asshole commentaries like that which rile up
chumps and social climbers, and get their heads out of the
mud they're stuck in. Cabeza de Vaca is troop commander
now. He's not a queer or an egghead, and goes around
kicking up as much ruckus as he can. He even sleeps in
his armor."

"And Chaves? What does he do?" he asked, not looking
at the majordomo, giving all his attention to the macaws.

Pedro Resaca shrugged. "He's one of Cabeza de Vaca's
lackeys. A maniac with power and influence over the
captain."

"Damn. What a pack of faggots. Can't leave them alone
for a minute. I no sooner turn around and they screw me
up the ass. How times have changed!"

"For the worse, señor, for the worse." Pedro Resaca
replied, laconic, resigned.

"And me, Pedro? What's my part in this story? Am I a
stooge or am I still in command?"

"So it should be, señor. You are the Governor of
Salbago for life, señor."

"Governor of shit, governor of nothing," he mumbled,
chewing on a bit of green plantain. The macaws began to
peck at the fruit lovingly sliced for them by the Governor
of Salbago. Outside the palace walls the struggle
continued to unfold between the Dutch pirates and the
island's bold, brave, dogged defenders.

Do what he will, that rascal Algaba will always be a
born loser. Whatever he touches will smell like shit
forever, he thought. He wheeled slowly around to look at
the green ivy that covered the terrace's inside walls, from
the cobbled floors to the roof. "They're lovely, Pedro," he

exclaimed full of wonder, a childish streak in his voice, taking contented pleasure in his words. "The brush, Pedro, hand me the brush," he commanded Resaca. This was another of his favorite trances. When he slipped into it, he spent hours and hours in a pastime the palace soldiery judged, in whispers, an idiotic senile quirk. This chore demanded all the Governor's patience, as though the green leaves of ivy were precious furs, a gift for another of his favorite phantoms, Zulima the Moor, seldom remembered in Royal anymore, but about whom everyone had heard. The sheen of the leaves, as he rubbed them, gave way to the still glossier green of the original leaf. Nor was he ever concerned about the risk he ran as he worked, perched atop that crude wooden ladder. Entranced, hour on hour he shined, forgetting time, turning back to reshine a leaf when necessary. He swabbed off the dust clinging to the ivy leaves, scraped off the insects and mold, the spiderwebs, the scraps and turds—uglinesses left by the slow labor of pigeons, parrots and macaws. The chore might begin with the sun and end at twilight, a whole day passed in the most perfect of silences, in exclusive dedication to the cultivation of the rare cleanliness of the plants beautifying the walls of his terrace, space to which he had been confined almost without his taking note.

"They're pretty, Pedro. So pretty!" he cried, keyed up like a child, at the end of his useless day of beautification. "They belong in a museum. You might not believe it but they appreciate this gesture, my words, my caresses. They speak to me, and secretly tell me all that goes on in Royal de Salbago, all that everyone else hides from me, the usual treacheries, the fool ambitions of that horde of jackasses. They know Algaba's the one stirring up trouble and no one dares to knock his props out, not even that bum Cabeza de Vaca, who thinks he's making history where the rest of us couldn't. To hell with them all! I know only the ivy speaks the truth," he explained, looking at Resaca and wringing his hands, his wasted face wrying like a madman's. "But I'm not crazy, Pedro," he said, intercepting the majordomo's thoughts. "I listen to them and I'm happy they understand me. It doesn't matter that we can't speak. We understand one another

and that's enough." Then he remembered the words of the
Black Duke and cried out exultantly, "I'm a lyric poet too,
damn it."

The day the Fates had destined him to die, Rejón was
fearless. He saw a swarm of scrambled shadows coming
toward him, beckoning to him, but he discarded—as he
had so often—the ludicrous notion of disappearing voluntarily from the world. I don't know why the devil I was
going to listen to those damn whiffs of smoke, he thought.
He had the suspicion, as he so often had, that all that was
needed was a puff from his own will, and the spirits that
.had already eaten out his insides would crumble his
shadow into dust, without ever completely defeating his
stinky breath. "All I need is to be carried off to the devil
with you. I have you all down cold. There's no fool like
an old fool," he said to himself. He stood throughout as if
his survival depended upon his balancing there, as if he
knew that to let himself be swept along on the tide of
sleep flooding through him meant to stop breathing
forever.

In any case, this time the premonitions possessed
another dimension, attacking at any exposed angle,
striking at the weakest flanks, taking shape as pains that
sank into his body like needles of glass, forcing him to
double over frequently. He felt very strange chills piercing
his hollow spaces, paralyzing his smallest efforts and
reflexes. To shoo off the fear sifting into his soul like a
fine rain, he spent the day hollering and making foolish
demands, absurdities that could not be had, altogether
impossible. He was seeking, delusively, by means of this
peculiar ceremonial paraphernalia, to defend himself and
outwit death. First he wanted a full review of the troops.
"Let's see just who that fathead Cabeza de Vaca thinks
he is! Or should I say birdbrain! Doesn't even put in an
appearance to give the Governor the news! I'll have to cut
off his balls and chuck them to the dogs, so he'll spend
the rest of his days going through the world cursing the
hour he forfeited his pretty balls for slighting my orders,
to serve as an example to all those tempted to do the
same." After this tirade, he sank into a deep drowse,
forgetting his commands and promises of a minute or so
before. Little by little, arthritis had been wielding its

power over that living cadaver who yapped in fury to stave off the inexorable wound of death, because (he said) dying in bed is for old men and queers, for people who won't ever make history no matter how hard they try, Pedro, for men who did not seize the chance to clear out when the time was ripe. By now his whole body was a rusty contraption creaking at every step as if his muscles had hardened into some sideritic substance, as if his limbs had lost their natural flexibility for good. A hazy, infinite pain further soured the half-spoiled juices creeping sluggishly through him. Slowly the blood clotted in his veins as he shuffled around his bedroom like a sleepwalker, giving orders no one obeyed, directed to no one really. Dragging his feet down the dusty corridors he would suddenly rush back in a fever to sit beside the fire Resaca laid for him every morning, in hot weather or cold, in the bedroom of the Governor of nowhere.

The pair of green dogs had grown old with their master. Cain and Abel trailed the steps of their lord Juan Rejón with his same shamble, so that no one who witnessed this scene had a doubt that Rejón had transmitted, perhaps by osmosis, his own progressive illness to the animals who served him as lifelong guardians. When the Governor paced to and fro in his rooms, the dogs followed their lord. A clatter like crockery, like an out-of-tune orchestra in bad taste, was heard throughout the house, leaving behind it a gamey reek of urine and flakes of rust dust. Because, over time, the dogs identified more and more with Rejón, with his senile eccentricities, although deep in their recondite tribal memory, inherited from their exterminated race, they kept cached the sulphur of revenge, possibly waiting for the Governor to become solely his own self's spit, unable to cry out or defend himself. At no time, for instance, had they unleashed the ferocity that during all those years at the Governor's feet they had fed against him in their black hearts. They never revealed the pangs of resentment concealed in the depths of their eyes. For this reason too, they enjoyed the absolute trust of him who still believed himself the master and keeper of Salbago Island; they were his protectors by calling, and whatever he commanded, if only by a next-to-imperceptible shift in his eye, they saw to at once. The

ramping, savage, mythical past of their race remained as
though cast in stone at the time of the colonization (the
selfsame age of Larios' lunacies, Otelo's provocateur
songs, María Salomé's gorgeous harlots, Tomás Lobo's
worthless witcheries, the traitorous uprising of Pedro de
Algaba, the ghost of Martín Martel, Bishop Juan de Frías'
messianism and his bell, and the not lesser derangement
of his successor, Fernando de Arce, who heeded, step by
step, the deluded dream of Herminio Machado, the razzias
plotted by Simón Luz, the Jew. All that surrounded Juan
Rejón in his rooms were names of dead people, catalogues
and lists of the demented and disappeared, apparitions
swinging capriciously from the ceiling beams and
demanding their share in the unwreaked vengeance, all
chronicles Cabeza de Vaca had promised to transpose into
written, nearly sacred history before time itself left them
strewn and forgotten among the dead leaves, the forgotten
verbiage of the past. Juan Rejón steered through a sticky
liquid with bumbling movements bringing him, at every
step, warped memories of battles and clashes, colonizations and piracies, an endless list of things he had never
done, not wanting to, or things he had carried out blindly,
without scruples or reflection. He spoke with them, with
his memories, as one speaks with a person who stands
before him in flesh and blood, in a hushed, respectful
voice, calm even under criticism. He bore his predeath
ordeal as the necessary revision of a history that would
never be written. He snatched, in flight, the memory of
the Black Duke, who had declined to serve as his confidant and chronicler. "What a queer," he announced
loudly. "He blamed it all on politics, but I know why he
was banished here, to this beastly African islet. Because
he was a notorious faggot. They married him to the
Duchess of I don't know what, a widow they say was still
a real good-looker, and what he did was show her his
impotence. Hellfire! And the rest of the time he dribbled
away thinking about absolutism and tyranny, and all that
guff he tried to get over against King Carlos."
    He applied himself to his soliloquies as though testi-
fying before the final tribunal, enacting a rite that would
probably (or so he might have been thinking) bring him
peace. But when a shadow enveloped in fragrance of roses

approached his warped mind, he would know at once that his darling Zulima's round had come. He would be left lying dumbly, sleeping in a timeless, soothing ecstasy far from everyone and everything, like a catatonic schizophrenic it would later require centuries of patience to coax out of his stubborn silence. The morning of his death the vision of the Moorish girl came again, her naked dances, her tantalizing contortions, her songs only he could hear (he explained) because they had been composed for him alone in the garden of Heaven. "It's Zulima, Pedro," he said before he sank again, almost forever. "Zulima's coming." A little later he fell into a stupor Pedro Resaca knew to perfection, during which he fed him in almost total darkness on hot soup made of whelk, mint, and fresh milk, a breakfast prepared for the Governor by the majordomo with ingredients for the dissolving of dreams.

For him, in this trance of his one desire, all the other apparitions that pestered his nights and days disappeared. All the excretions of his body, greater or lesser, came out on his bed, on himself. The long paralysis would always wind up the same. His breath dimming as if he was on the brink of death. He would be beginning to wake from the soporific vision when a spell of fierce panting overcame him, marking, in mounting climax, the beginning of the end. Next came a long, frenzied, spasmic tremble, rousing strange pleasure in all his rotted limbs. Last, he would ejaculate a thick, whitish-yellow starchy fluid whose stink spread through the room, soaking everything. This olfactory announcement the majordomo knew was the end of the dream. The fit (thought Resaca) had passed and Zulima's spirit had vanished as it had come, leaving no trace but that sad sample of pleasure on Juan Rejón's skinny legs. "The dead woman fucked him again," Pedro Resaca muttered between his teeth. Like this he could abide the revulsion and nausea seeping into his throat, giving him a fierce urge to retch, as he cleaned up the den of delirium and Rejón's body, so shrivelled that it looked like a vegetable, squirming amid dreams and nightmares. After the cleanup, in obedience to the absurd orders of Inquisitor Montalvo, a rigid and arbitrary officer, came the Christian exorcisms (something in which Rejón had never believed), the holy aspergillum, the balm of salvation brazening what remained of the demons in the chambers of the man possessed, the invisible signs of their wicked, supernatural, and bodiless presence.

Invariably on waking Rejón was met with the same question: "How was it this time, señor?" A question of courtesy. And Rejón invariably replied with words Resaca knew by heart. "Same as ever. Same as ever. Zulima is a goddess." With slight variations upon earlier occasions, he spelled out in detail the whole ceremony of love performed on him by the dead woman, leaving his body with a ravishing hunger. "All that glitters," the majordomo murmured to himself, "is not gold."

On this special day in the life of the Governor of Salbago, Resaca had been preparing for him, during his oriental morning dreams, some of his favorite treats. He had a hunch, from early morning, that the Governor was performing the rite of his final fevers, and he wished to take leave of him with all the honors, treat him to a sumptuous feast Juan Rejón had always relished. It was the season for vieja, a tender white fish that resided solely in the seas off Salbago and Sardinia, an island in the Mediterranean Sea Resaca had heard his lord the Governor mention from time to time. He poached two pieces, medium-sized with reddish scales, and placed them to soak in a vinegar marinade, with a side of potatoes the majordomo customarily boiled in their skins in seawater. While Rejón nibbled on bits of crabmeat, pulped and simmered in its own juices (another of his favorite dishes), Resaca boned and scaled the fish and sprinkled it with a sauce made of parsley, anise, and the finest of olive oils. Last, the exquisite viands were splashed with Riojan wine.

Cain and Abel strode fretfully around the room where Rejón appeased his gluttony. They had smelled, perhaps, the hour of their revenge and were edgily preparing for it with the same delectation they sensed in the Governor. Again and again, they peered around at Resaca. The majordomo noted a steely, cutting gleam in the eyes of the hounds he had never seen before, but possibly a characteristic of these creatures he would have sworn were tamed forever.

After his meal, Rejón slipped again into a pleasurous

doze. Full and content with everything, either he never
detected what was closing in around him, or (as was
nearly always so in the many final years of his old age)
he was playing dumb, employing a strategy that had often
given him the desired result and which acted, in fact, like
a charm: by not thinking about the things he did not want
to have happen, they never happened. Strange wisdom he
had culled by experience during his countless crossings
and scams, and which had, up until the present, reaped
benefits that had made him into a monarch for perpetuity, without a scepter or a crown, but who had outlived
all the evil ages, wars, sieges, scourges, all the disasters
a dignitary of his caliber had to brave in the course of his
life. "Now I wish to sleep," he said. That noise of tossing,
swishing leaves in the imaginary storm of his brain had
ceased and peace, unconsciously sought, has settled into
his spirit.

"Shall I remove the dogs, señor?" Pedro Resaca
ventured, forebodingly.

"No, no. Leave them, as always. At the foot of the bed."

Pedro Resaca did not insist, despite his intuitions.
Furthermore, his particular wisdom had taught him not
to meddle in the destiny of others, for the things that
were to occur would occur anyway in their given moment,
fulfilling each step that the life of a man brands upon his
brow at the hour of his birth. Resaca sensed that his hour
of truth, the moment of his ultimate and final struggle
was about to commence, and that the Adelantado who had
founded Salbago wished to face his single destiny alone.

Not until next morning did Pedro Resaca again enter
the Governor's quarters. The sheets of Juan Rejón's bed
were drenched in blood. His body was torn apart, limbs
strewn over the wide chamber, mangled remains of a
grisly battle the dead man, with the last fight he had in
him, seemed to have levied against creatures of supernatural power. Whoever they were, the murderers had
savaged the body of the old Governor, ripping it to pieces
and leaving them swimming in a sea of blood. He saw
deep gashes of incisor teeth in the severed hands of the
Governor, possibly put there at the moment in which he
attempted to fend off his enemies. The torso, disembow-
elled and bloodied, covered with scratch marks, testicles

and phallus nowhere to be seen, lay in the exact center of
the bedroom, essential relics out of which spilled a mess
of reddened guts already beginning to reek. Of the dogs,
as though the past of their progenitors had swallowed
them up, nothing was left but the bloody tracks of their
paws, helter-skelter all over the room. The Governor's face
was the crowning touch, the final consequence of this
sudden rampage. The eyes floated outside their sockets on
flesh so puffy the Governor's face was unrecognizable. A
probing smell of burnt sulphur wafted through the room
like invisible smoke, and a sinister alternative crept into
Resaca's mind. Either the spiteful dogs had unloosed their
pent-up fury against the Governor, obeying orders lurking
in the mazy darkness of their blood, and destroyed the
diminutive body of the Adelantado, or he had been barba-
rously murdered by men consumed by impatience for
power, unable to wait for a death for which there was not
much longer to wait. Due to his own survival instinct,
enlarged by the absence of his master, he did not wish to
accuse the guards. They, señor, had heard nothing, seen
nothing all evening. Surely not at night, when the Governor's chambers were kept shut by his orders. They, the
guards, had been there all along, fulfilling their duty,
keeping watch over the rooms outside the chamber where
the Governor slept. So they were not answerable for what
happened inside, and they had seen no one go in or come
out.

Pedro Resaca pictured both scenes at once, the two
possibilities he had thought of. His hair bristled like
copper wires. First, the green dogs in a mad fury pouncing
on that living cadaver as it lay sleeping. He saw his
horrified eyes the instant he felt the vengeful teeth and
savage claws of Cain and Abel. Then he saw the animals
poisoning his puckered body with their rabid drool,
tearing his muscles, ripping out his limbs. He heard, like
a spasm, the silence with which the unsuspecting Juan
Rejón faced the fiends who had been for years his faithful
guardians, as their teeth gored his body. Finally, he saw
the dogs padding stealthily away down secret corridors,
their revenge had.

Almost simultaneously he heard the steps of the traitor
crossing the galleries in the darkness of night, arriving at

the doors of his room. He pictured his silence, his
rapacity, the command by which he would induce the dogs
to disappear before the crime was committed . . . He
expunged—an exception that proved the rule kept by him
all through his life—the name of the traitor, which blurted
into his mind again and again. And, as if there was
nothing to keep him in the Palace any longer, he collected
all his things, his fishing gear and all the other objects he
had brought to Rejón's Palace in his day, and abandoned
the noble edifice where he had lived for so many years.
He went back, an old man now too, to his fisherman's
fate, to the district of the Haven, there outside the
ramparts of Royal City, to the port crowded daily with the
nameless horde, strivers after adventure. The smell of the
sea and the warm breeze dried his glassy tears as they
fell into the sand. He knew very well that only like this
could he salvage his life, by the sea, flinging memories
like ashes to the wind, not even waiting to see how
Cabeza de Vaca would celebrate the exequies of the
founder of Salbago, or what final honors he would bestow
upon the remains of Juan Rejón, Governor and Captain
General of Royal de Salbago.

All day a pungent smell of sulphur spread through the
city. They said Rejón was possessed. That, as was to be
expected, the phantasms he had been possessed by always
had killed him in the end. That a giant insect had
appeared in his bed, of unknown species but most like
a puffy white beetle with eyes of a man and powerful
wings . . .

Alvaro Rejón came home from the New World a shadow, stricken by many solitudes, silent and dark as the grave where the cadaver of his father, Juan Rejón, had at last been laid. No sooner did he set foot on Salbago's black sand shores than he felt, plummeting through his tired spirit, a deep perturbation prompting corporeal discomforts akin to seasickness or some sort of obsessive cooped-up feeling and bloatedness. He could barely choke down that sudden fierce desire to bolt, now impossible. Over twenty-five years of unbroken absence were all the bags he lugged on his back that day of his homecoming, the island geography—long brooded over in the New World—hazed, swept just then by a coarse, massy mist, a smothering rain of ash slung to the skies by the never-ending nearness of the African desert, whose shores, years back—in the unrepeatable fullness of an age enduring in his memory only—Alvaro Rejón had combed, secret by secret, poking into all its sacred crannies, guided by the deft hand of Pedro Resaca, lowborn fisherman who had risen even so to fill the post of majordomo to his father, Governor Juan Rejón, almighty lord of the island, Adelantado of Castile, Conqueror of Salbago.

He had not had time to bask in the so-often-recollected landscape of his childhood and youth. Let alone know all. But he could tell that with this return, which now seemed a senseless, superfluous act—stupid product of sentimentality—life had wound up clutching him in its cruel, rusty claws forever, having forced him to roam from illusion to illusion, mirage to mirage, to pluck himself up again after every fall as slowly he sagged and withered into a shadow of himself. The day of his homecoming, dawn peaking,

151

Atlantic salt still pinching his face, Alvaro Rejón had to grant that Royal City, Salbago, however diminutive its dimensions beside the new colonies and mills of Terra Firma and the cities that had cropped up there since the days of the Discovery, had experienced an extraordinary change in external physiognomy during those long years of absence. Under the faceless surface, the original flaws had multiplied a hundredfold, sprouting blotches and smirches which though at first blush seemed fleeting blooms, had found a home in that dungheap, Salbago.

So he had to get used to watching (with signal broad-mindedness) people of every stripe and feather swanking elegantly through the markets and streets like posh gentlemen, popped up out of nowhere, trailing their pricey frippery in the dirt and yakety-yakking in local slangs he was no longer abreast of. Or barking—with crass, bossy authority they had delegated to themselves in the inner kingdoms of the dirty port taverns—for wines and cane liquor, marc, anisette, rum, guarapo, orders of salted fish sprinkled with piquant red spices likewise from the New World, or platters heaped with chunks of octopi, boiled and smothered in onions and green pimiento juice. All those pubs of olden times had thrived under the aegis of the new age, blooming therein palaces of illusion, adventure, opulence and power. As if the years had not passed, as if the water clock had stalled its slow but ceaseless shuttle, there stood the legend of the New World, loftier than ever, a religion more today than ever before. In those dim collusive interiors, the walls sweating with commingling stenches, men bound and determined to rise from obscurity at whatever hazard gambled hard their individual destinies, devoting themselves, around the clock, to cards, creators of fortunes and failures turning into hard fact, swapped overseas interests—solely glimpsed through the rose-colored lenses of the imagination—and tillable island terrain, schemed sugar mills never to resemble the plans dreamed up by those tinhorn merchants, or set out, verbally, the first preparations for expeditions to carry them cunningly to the coasts of Tiris-el-Garba or Sakia-el-Amra, where a quick razzia of thirty negro slaves would surely come to crown the success of the enterprise to which they were now clinking their glasses with lively cheer. Above anyone, Alvaro Rejón knew these dreams, life's swindles, gullies, valleys, gorges, and vapory meanders.

Royal, Rejón was thinking just then, had ended up a market without scruples, a racket in filthy lucre, a versicolor bazaar of airs and graces which anyone, their first and last names recently affixed to dubious marks of identity, could buy or sell, in any seamy stall, for the price of the day.

He had wanted to spring a futile surprise on people (his abandoned family and friends, the Governor's servants) who no longer existed. Dimly, as if coming to after a long stupor, he was beginning to see—before ransacking the ultimate reality of things—that his father had vanished from this world skewed by the new age of navigations and constant discoveries. Even he, Alvaro Rejón, direct descendant of the founder and Governor, had become a nobody, one of so many streaming through Royal City, strangers to the citizens of Salbago, some overnight lodgers, others fettered forever to this sad, sodden do-nothingness, chance inhabitants of a land afloat on the sea as if by the agencies of magic, an island reviled, and in a breath, revered. This, since its more or less bumbling beginnings, had been the most paradoxical, self-refuting feature of its being. There, like a statue of icy marble, stood this Salbagan irreconcilability, after so many spins through time, enacting the eternal rite of its presence in the quotidian life of Salbago.

He drifted through the grimy streets as if buoyed along in the air by the bustle of the crowd. Lonesome, glum, starting to feel a little like a leery stranger on his own soil, or a journeyer just landed in a new country, he walked along puzzled, distracted and dreamy at once, stray-footing spunklessly in and out of the pitiful cafés. Inns, saloons, bars, brothels he still kept stashed in some corner of his memory (thanks to the famous escapades of his boyhood), or these other new bagnios rising before his eyes as though popped up out of nowhere, here, there, on every corner, shacks, markets, stands loaded with rubbish and gewgaws, proscribed meeting places, whorehouses of every feather, were food for his dazed eyes in his futile search for familiar faces, which, to tell the truth, existed

only in his cobwebbed memory, prompting inside him a
psychological phenomenon of difficult explication, yet
which deluged all his thoughts and perceptions. As a
matter of fact, in Alvaro Rejón two memories now coex-
isted, intermingling their influences and passions, two
modes of thought, two distinct cosmovisions, two contradictory speculative methods for receiving external sensations. One was the old memory, all he had breathed freely
in the years of his youth, the memory of that Salbago that
dozed beneath the unsparing whip of his father, Juan
Rejón, when his—Alvaro Rejón's—mere presence was
ready cash, letters of marque expiring at the exact
moment of his leave-taking for Fernandina, also called
Cuba. The other was marked by his decided mania for
adventure, spawned with the reckless voyage to Terra
Firma, the New World, its lands and peoples, its mesmerizing glows, its rarefied reality, a whole endless sequence
of events that had transpired or were simply imagined in
deliriums of grandeur—ingested, all the same, by his
analytic mind and converted into snatches of memory—a
catalogue of names and data, flukes and hunches which
in the remoteness of his current claustrophobia not only
seized hold of his hebetude but pumped up half-truths into
vivid reality he had never, needless to say, wholly lived.
So, finding himself in the vast lands of the New World,
furrowed by beds of rivers that were seas and harlequin
geographies lush with the greenness of the ever-growing
jungles, it dawned on Alvaro Rejón that he was a transplanted islander, and maybe this was why—it was coming
back to him now—he had never thrown in with the plans
of that mestizo prophet, Camilo Cienfuegos, though at a
given moment his secessionist theories had worked him
into a lather. Now, after his sad return to Salbago, he was
struck in the soul by the conviction that having ceased to
be what he thought he was (a transplanted islander), he
had become a continental by compulsion, a person divided
between two distinct and distant worlds, a transplant—in
a word—wherever he was. Then too, his marks of identity
so clearly tagged for power and glory at the time of his
departure in pursuit of adventure had watered down over
the course of time, dissolving at last into the well of
disappearance and oblivion.

World-weary roamer and plunderer, Alvaro Rejón had forgotten that in these temporal latitudes his upwards of a quarter century of unbroken absence stood for a lifetime, a century, a millennium even, completely blotting away the memory of things, demoting them to myth, altering people's names, distorting faces, transforming old places—abandoned by history as it trundled on—into new ones, altogether unknown to him, leaving not a trace or sign of the past. Into his mind at that moment, a sort of echo tearing suddenly through the shreds of his time-battered memory, flashed the counsel of old man Resaca to his father, Juan Rejón, when the Governor, in a tizzy of feverish inclemencies set off by his own frustrations, courted adventure as a means of escape, of flight from Salbago, the Black Duke's baneful influence seeming to have stuck fast in his obsessions. "Governor," said Resaca the majordomo, "a dead man lies in a hole. An absent man in oblivion." Perhaps it was this crushing warning, Alvaro Rejón mused, that had kept his father consigned to Salbago, where his name would make history as a second-rate conquistador. Salbago had been his father's security, acting as an anchor against all those urges that had blurted into his soul throughout his long life, exhorting him over and over to flee, as Helmsman Bartolomé Larios had done in his day, away from that damned land blighted with enemy shadows, green dogs, and blurry but always present memories.

Alvaro Rejón took a look at his own physique, clear illustration of the decay wreaked upon his person by the relentless forces of time. His hair, now all grey and raggy from neglect, galloped dirtily in the wind over vast balding patches, the peculiarly blue hue that had crept into it having spirited away the memory of that long blond mane that shone so splendidly beside the fickle glitter of the New Continent. That hair, emblem of his present personality, suggested an old man who had just stepped out of a cave, superannuated in the age under way. His eyes—sunken in their sockets and scored by an infinity of tiny yellowish veins bespeaking the slow advance of his cataracts—taking in the scenes passing before them, now accepted the contemplation of a world unlike the one he had left so many years gone by. His face showed the basic attributes of preternatural elderliness, in step with his garments. He was the sad slumped acme of misfitness and spinelessness.

He was beginning to feel tired, dragged down by the piling-in of memories, by the voyage, by all those sensations that sparked insecurity and did away for good with his dreams of implanting himself again in his ancestral island home, where he had been born, where he had worked up the grandest, most fantastic dreams of his life, far now from the wildnesses and delirious adventures he had lived in the New World's unplumbable dimension. True, this was the same land as always: Salbago. True, his name was the same: Rejón. But this dump, Royal City, which he had left behind to boost himself up into another, ampler life, had become, after so many, many adventures, the worn flip side of the same coin: here too were the hollow daily hustles, the sudden oversloshings of lust, the most improvident madnesses sprung from plans laid always in the air, a whole string of bungles typifying a pugnacious race spreading through the world like rampant, indestructible ivy. The fortune hunters, and their perpetually implausible notions, the prophets pining for new lands (nonexistent as they pictured them), the hucksters and all their hanky-panky transformed into fabulous visions, seamen, by and large, who in the wistful afternoons sank themselves to the gills in liquor and firewater so as to rouse their dreams, amid soliloquies of treasure and riches ungaugeable by any numbers known to date. An opulence of smoke in reach of their hands but always nixed by a last-minute stroke of bad luck. In Salbago, midway between the New World and the Old Peninsula whence everyone, early or late, had come, in the staggering shuttle of those coming home with their heads tucked, or those who in spite of everything were always ready to start out, rumors, spats, quips and cranks, tall tales that had become eternal verities, popped up here, there—even in a single day—creating new versions, new variants that Alvaro Rejón, almost better than anyone, knew inside out. It all boiled down to that chimerical fever, veiled in mantillas of fierce, cruel mirage, drawing them Westward. Then he remembered, in the lead-grey glisten of evening, in that ceaseless murmuring of markets, lost in the throng that would never look his way again, how he and Pedro Resaca had dreamed up that fabulous voyage, overleaping the warnings of the old majordomo, how they had fanned the flame of all those tales of more than twenty-five years past which, seemingly untouched by time, were still being told and retold in Salbago, bemingled with every ilk of bogus detail. A lifetime of lust whisks up in his thoughts as they bound away now along the convoluted coasts of the Caribbean, dipping into the warm, heavy waters that ring Margarita Island, skimming over seas always just discovered by madmen who wound up losing their sense of direction and nose-diving into the mazy purgatory of delirium. In his memory, he splashes in the murky churning waters at the mouths of great rivers, banks thick with tribes of Indians idling in stilt houses the likes of which the amazed discoverers had never clapped eyes on before. Coming in clear too, in this abominable anonymity, is the image of Puerto Vigía, the embarcadero built by him and Resaca on the eastern coast of Venezuela Colony, facing the rising sun, their first settlement, a fortress where all day the winds tussled, crossing their sharp tusks, slakelessly riffling the mangroves and young sugar crops. Were they sure to build, out of Puerto Vigía, an empire of wealth the reaches of which would vanish upon the farthest horizon of the plains of Venezuela? Puerto Vigía was their first hideout, the place where they awaited the rapid assimilation of what to their minds would comprise the force of the continent. They had landed with their single treasure, a precious cargo of squalid negroes snatched from the coast of the Sahara. According to laws decreed by the Court, it was a matter of protecting the Indians, time and again, moreover, friends and accomplices of their own conquest. It was a question of rescuing them from the perils of slavery and winning their souls for Christianity, license and pretext for anything and everything. The conduct of those early slave traders was above reproach—of law or conscience— safeguarded by the selfsame stamp and seal of the Crown, beneath which glowed the influence of Bartolomé de las Casas, a priest mad on all counts, a harping, nagging friar who from the outset would defend the Indians, premising his argument on their natural condition of physical weakness, and on the other hand asserting that the physical strength of the black African with respect to the natives of the New Continent was five to one. Hence to be a slave trader was to usher in an era of commerce in flesh without souls, was to build an Empire per las Casas, to lay the foundations of a formidable palace the likes of which had never been glimpsed before.

Into his mind as he wandered absentmindedly among the little stands of tropical fruits shipped to Salbago from the Continent with a certain regularity (always en route to the Peninsula) flashed his later landing on Fernandina, his brief stay among the drifting population of Our Lady of the Assumption of Baracoa, obligatory port for all those who aspired, admittedly or no, to make the leap for Terra Firma, plant their feet on the coveted Yucatán, and get drenched in the dives of Vera Cruz. He remembered, as though time had exempted him again and halted before the cloudy eyes of his memory, the bilked deals, the double crosses, the buying and selling of privilege, the traffic in clout, the rows between conquistadors, the schemes woven at night and scotched at dawn by the very agents who had instigated them in the darkness, the squabbles and legends, the incredible stories of Hernando Cortés, the rebel, life with Mademoiselle Pernod, the devastating tale of Camilo Cienfuegos. His thoughts trotted away over the lands of the Yucatán and washed up caressingly on the Vera Cruz docks, where his cravings were so easily sucked up by the fervid convictions of those who, back from splendorous Tenochtitlán, were embarking on an even more otiose odyssey than the irresistible impulse that had led them there: to tell it all in words, to endeavor, like apostles of a new religion, to persuade all the others that everything said of the region with the purest air in the world was gospel truth. That there, in Mexico-Tenochtitlán and its environs, fantasy had magically painted itself in fast color, though the hooves of Hernando Cortés' horses had been trampling it all into their image and likeness. For the conquest was both a liberation and a necessary profanation. Rejón remembered, in nearly the same instant, the story of the burning ships, the tale few dared to utter aloud but which he had heard many times from the mouths of old Christians since his days in Baracoa, his and Pedro Resaca's eyes glittering with the longing their chests could no longer contain, their bodily fluids in a fever, stoking their ambitions. Was not the story of the burned ships like a cross, stirring their blood, a sort of symbol, an event like no other that fired up the two explorers and insufflated them with the force they needed to press into unknown jungles and climb, slowly, patiently, haltingly to the flanks of Popocatépetl and Ixtaccíhuatl, cross the arid plains, pass by the village of Quauhnáhuac—chosen by Cortés as his private residence, to be known in centuries to come as Cuernavaca—and at last abide the swoon set loose in their spirits by the sudden vision of Tenochtitlán, paradise of dreams afloat on the waters, city built by demigods in the center of a splendorous sacred lake, raised in honor of divinities who, judging by the blessings, until the coming of the conquistadors had heaped their gratitude upon its powerful, happy, proud dwellers? Burning the ships, thought Alvaro Rejón, was a strange destiny, brainchild of heroes blinded by faith in their indestructible messianism, a zany proposition that could be brought off by the hand of a true leader. To burn the ships was to prompt permanent exile, to proclaim oneself god, to surpass all possible profanation, to sever the road home, to land, perforce, in glory, to stir in the most secret spleens the quivering bittersweet taste for flight forward, to seek as sole means of survival the impossible mutation of men into gods, into deathless fearsome *teules* now and forever, to pitch, in short, into the overspilling of undampable irrationality that any Spaniard eye to eye with Hernando Cortés carries hidden in his simmering loins.

In Salbago again, back through the door for those doomed to silence, out of pocket, with only words for recounting the fantasy which, though real, nobody was going to quite believe, save maybe boys like the one he had been, he sensed—on the doorstep of preternatural senectitude—the senselessness of all adventure. In his memory the names of those who had risen to stardom clumped together with those who in spite of touching on the same traits, same places, same risks as the ones who had made a splash, playing their luck in similarly like situations, had never crossed the unfair frontier of anonymity. At that moment, leafing back through his memory over a whole heap-up of anecdotes, feats and exploits—tiredness beginning to drag him down in pretty near the same places where his vim for adventure had been waked, years before, as he gazed at the western horizon—he could not but adjoin his name to the list of flops, vanquished by time and the Conquest.

Through the air and ambience of Salbago floated a fidgety breeze, sending flurrying over Royal City the jumbled aromas of salted meats and fried fishes, of oils and spices muskily mingled, a live effluence breathing, today as it had yesterday, a thousand make-believe formulas for flitting over the sea to the Promised Land. But Alvaro Rejón was shorter and shorter of breath. His limbs, rasped by rare sensations touched off by his landing on the island, barely responded to his directions. No question but that he, Alvaro Rejón, was out of place in Salbago. He was no one. And this state of just about out-and-out beggary would stay with him for the rest of his days, as he listened dejectedly to the news that kept on coming, willy-nilly, from one or the other world, the Peninsula or Overseas. Overseas now had the ring of a territory undiscoverable, a spate of nightmares, an unrealized dream in the shambles of which he had thrown over everything, given it up for lost, a place fluttering to life lush with color and fresh images, where the road had no end, where the laws were written on the spur of the moment, on the stones, as the profaner thrust to the heart of the Continent, discovering by sheer instinct a primitive world that would in fact conquer them, the profaners, who would lift their voices in warped triumph over the demise of gods who had already fled their places of power.

There, Overseas, likewise thrown over to his own bad luck, but (unlike Rejón) totally convinced of the blunder implicit in returning to the island, Pedro Resaca had remained, the majordomo's son, his partner and pal, ruined now, half dead, but preferring downright poverty on that continent thronging with surprises and unforeseen events sooner than brook the disgrace of an empty return, trumpeting the failure of his life. "I'm staying here forever, Alvaro, in the kingdom of nobodies," Resaca said to Rejón when the latter broached the notion of a journey home. So this was Pedro Resaca's last word, a man who had always wreaked his will on the elements. As a boy he had made a fierce resolution: he would be more than just a fisherman's son. He was born in Salbago, but had always wanted to scrap his islanderness, shunted, inturned. Even now, in his dreaminess, his blurriness shuffling and scrambling up time, Rejón managed to summon back the remark that Resaca had pronounced on board the lateen-rigged carack bearing them to the New World, as the island withdrew into the distance. As if in some ceremony long planned, he pulled off his oxhide boots. Unshod, making his eyes at once utter a verdict and cast a curse, he shook out the island dirt and flung it into the sea, like ashes of a plaguey body. "Out, dust of Salbago!" he said, gazing hard at Alvaro Rejón. And that other slogan he was remembering now, nutshelling all his passions when he found himself at a dead end: "These boots are made for marching," as good as a command, taking on faith the legend of Cortés, burn the ships, if need be, morning, noon and night.

He recalled—again only for an instant—the changing colors on the face of the water, foam-silver to wine-dark, passing, in kaleidoscopic vision, through emerald-green, through all shades of blue that exist in the universe. He swam over seas they tagged with new names as they sailed them, believing as they always had that they were the first to deflower them with their keels. Then he imagined that all the experience he had netted through years of voyages and peripluses just might help him to kick off some new enterprise, come at life from a fresh angle, as if nothing had happened, set out on a new road now, sure to sidestep hardships and fiascos, defeats always unnecessary, blunders always unwarranted. A new journey, he thought, to the ends of the earth, to the end of time, till he washed up in the last unfound redoubt of the seas. He saw, always within the murkiness of memory, that all he had sought through the world were snatches of nothingness, just what he had now found on Salbago Island, erstwhile territory of his father, Juan Rejón.

He spent that whole day of his landing in an endless

litter of contradictory memories, winds of a tropical
typhoon whipped loose in his mind inducing fevers and
sweating. Little by little he sank into a drowse he was
beginning to know all too well, a sort of wooziness that
never fell off into a deep sleep, a little semidoze, a recess
of the subconscious where the binds of time snapped loose,
rope knots flicking through the air, fusing past with
present, mixing his now-forgotten youth and this feeble
old age, confusing hopes for a future never to come with
the failures he had garnered, one after the other, during
his long years in the New World. He poked, like a ghost
on unknown terrain, into the last stinking café still open
in the port of Salbago, day dawning, where the nameless
rabble, the homeless, hopeless horde, peopled the long
journey of night, cackling and poking fun at their own
downfall among sad shadows and shafts of light, amid
firewater and roast hunks of camel meat.

In those moments of utter ennui, when a dizzying fit of
wheezing hugged his soul, and he glimpsed death at close
quarters, Alvaro Rejón fell back on coca, an exotic weed
indigenous to the New World and virtually unknown in
Salbago in those days, on the Iberian Peninsula or the
rest of civilized, sophisticated Europe. The natives of the
lands of Nicaragua generally knew it as *yaat*, an obscure
Mayan term, while in some extensive regions of the Venezuela Colony, where, in fact, Alvaro Rejón had first
witnessed the Indians munching the leaves—not daring to
sample them himself—they called it *hado*. It was during
the long trek to Peru, on one of those lost odysseys undertaken with his partner, Resaca, that he began to cotton
to that gift of the earth Indians all over the continent
partook of, under one name or another, to stoke their
courage, to feel like gods for the great stretches on foot
(like that journey to Cuzco and Lima) over rugged, inhos-
pitable, alien, hostile terrain requiring extraordinary
exertion. Rejón remarked with amazement how men on
the brink of expiration defied the laws governing the
natural selection of the species no sooner did they begin
to suck the divine juice of those greeny leaves. The
natives had the custom of wearing around their necks
pouches that looked like little gourds, inside which they
jealously cached the leaves of the holy weed whereby the

so-called White Goddess wreaked her vengeance on all
beings, natural or supernatural, making them her slaves.
The coca, once its leaves were pulped by the expert teeth
of the Indians, had the look of boiled spinach, slowly
inducing a sensation of mounting well-being, giving rise,
spontaneously, to a strong, vital, lasting euphoria. At
first, with masked interest, Alvaro Rejón noted how the
Indians never went without those mysterious little
pouches he guessed were an amulet against the hex of the
jungle, being that the natives of the Continent were naturally and monomaniacally superstitious. Exhilarated by
the weed juice, almost without a mutter of protest, they
trudged like beasts of burden, climbing up and down
cordilleras, fording rivers, immune to the insects and the
imaginary evil spirits to which they always alluded at the
critical moment. In this way too—as though they were not
being humiliated and insulted—they endured in silence
the madness of that army of bedraggled Castilians who
with banners and weapons, crucifixes and virgins, trekked
diagonally and almost unknowingly across an enormous
continent which, then and for a long time to come, they
knew nothing or almost nothing about. Rejón studied,
ever so patiently, the reactions of those lethargic beings
who transformed into radiant, muscular little gods once
the coca commingled with their corporeal juices. And no
sooner did he try it, yielding to temptations he instantly
knew it was futile to resist, than he felt that all he saw
was real, that all he imagined was about to become so,
that the world was his (not comprehending now why it
had never been so before) and that dire thirst induced by
the jungle in creatures unpracticed in wandering there
vanished, fatigue dropped away, as if this bodily sensation had never existed. Then, again gradually, he penetrated the concentric circles revealed to him by coca and
its science, its various preparations and uses, the ancient
rite of races ignorant of their own origins, but who gazed
skyward speculating on their advent from worlds other
than this one. He felt a pleasure he had never known
before, nor would ever feel again, the first time that
untalkative native of the Andean altiplano, curiously
blue-eyed and dark-skinned, aloof and proud, as if in
continual contact with the divinity who had imbued his

eyes with the color of the sea, the wrinkles in his face numbering in the hundreds, unveiled for him all the secrets and mysteries of the weed, placing in his hands, also for the first time, the power to build his own natural paradise, for himself, without need of company, beneath his own free and exclusive will.

Yaquís, who before the coming of the Spanish Rejón presumed was an elder worthy of one of those tribes now lost forever, used a certain scallop-shell lime and the pulpy meat of sea snails and river snails, indispensable treasures the Quechua went nowhere without.

"This is my only law, señor," Yaquís spluttered in reply to Juan Rejón's inquisitive silence, as rival thoughts flittered about in the conquistador's mind. Never would the native grasp the real reasons that these allegedly forgiving gods whom the Indians had awaited during so many tireless centuries had now turned so cruel, like viracochas, wicked Incan devils bringing unhappiness to his peoples.

Caught up in the ritual, burning with devotion for coca, fired up by this strange daily ceremony he knew in infinitesimal detail, Yaquís officiated in silence. From another pouch, also worn strung from his neck, he dug a smelly, gummy wad of snail meat, and using a plant stem, blended it with the chewed-up green mash, the weed of the White Goddess, and stuck it all back in his mouth, rolling and squashing it between his teeth like a little rubber ball, until his body was sated with its juice of salvation. The entire Venezuela Colony and all the lands of the crushed Incan empire, enslaved by Francisco Pizarro, were planted with this weed of initiates, which became a necessity of life for Alvaro Rejón too, who cared not in the least that his teeth were visibly rotting, turning black and repulsively slimy. Yaquís, in a rare display of confidence, passed him all the secrets, free, the dark ancient effects induced by the drug, its possible admixtures, its usages, the correct measures to bring on the desired sensations. The weed became food for Alvaro Rejón, indispensable in his hour of harrowing nostalgia, psychological upset, boredom, fatigue, and sagging morale.

So nothing was strange, despite appearances, about Alvaro Rejón's manipulations at the back of that seamy Salbago café, the fulfillment of rites which to the other denizens of dawn were utterly unheard of. One more madman, of the hordes of them, they were probably thinking just then, seafarers of night, skin weathered by failures, by the mirages sweeping ceaselessly over the face of the sea, myths coming to life in transit between continents.

"It's my only law," Alvaro Rejón managed to squeak out, in reply to the barman's expressive silence. "My only law, señor," he said again, thinking of Yaquís' disappearance.

Barely a moment or so later, an almost forgotten blissfulness began to stream through his limbs, a delicious, caressful shiver filling him slowly with a vitality out of keeping with his weary years and the grey morning. His memories began to slip back into their usual slots, refiling themselves by common consent in their respective archives. Time, as though by magic arts, stopped its peculiar shuffling and went back to being mere consecutive (and hence belittled) phases, scenes of a roamer's life perhaps not to meet its end here, beside this immense sea which, by virtue of the staggering ambition of Admiral Columbus, had ceased to be unknown forever, deflowered, furrowed as it now was by hundreds upon hundreds of keels descrying in their compasses new routes by which to launch out over the waters in quest of fame, glory, wealth, and the promised land, a pack of fools, as always, mixing up value and money. This was all. A vicious circle, a constant round of comings and goings, a cycle of construction, conservation, and destruction.

"Nothing's new under the sun," said Rejón with a grin as he slowly pulped the coca, letting that juice of new life sit on the soft flap of his palate for a second or so. His eyes, meanwhile, had turned tiger-green, and their iridescent rays fell on the silent faces of the frequenters of the bar.

At once that original radiance he had lost during the last days of the voyage home to Salbago floated back up in him and he flushed again with his natural colors. A loquacity seized on his tongue that the chance parishioners of the dawn would have been hard put to imagine a few hours before, as this outlander with the unmistakable look of a beggar began to tell stories laced with twisted hyperbole, feats that boggled belief, exploits the echo of which left a blur of incredulity on the faces of the listeners, journeys that plainly displayed a knowledge of the entire navigable orb, presumably exact details of maps and marine charts as if right then, on the warped wood table where Rejón leaned, a fantastical world they had never heard described with such precision were being unveiled.

"And El Dorado, Captain?" blurted one of the nameless young sailors, baffled, mesmerized.

Alvaro Rejón took his time—maybe overly long—to reply. Theatrically he arched his eyebrows in the suspenseful silence. Then he let his shoulders slump over his chest, his face submerging in shadow. His eyes, in this new gaze toward nothingness, lost a tad of that fierce gleam they had when he spoke. Calmly he drew a breath.

"El Dorado does not exist, señores," he said, hiking his voice up a decibel above its natural pitch. "Does not exist," he said again, this time in lower tones, wagging his head back and forth before his startled audience.

"So, Captain, what the devil is over there? What about the gold and all those tales we hear?" a chorus of incredulous night lifers protested Rejón's assertion. A fleer floated over the faces of those present.

"A dead end," answered Alvaro Rejón. "That's what's over there. A huge hole where the sea ends and the land begins, beyond the reefs and cliffs, beyond the legends and

tales. And once the mirages they've been dreaming on
fray away, they fall in. Where we, scum Spaniards, spend
all our time looking for a swindle metal, a depleted mine.
Where we pitch towns in the hopes of creating colonies,
never guessing that the jungle is like lava shrouding the
earth. Where we become desperate men, without roots or
past, where we avail ourselves of the pleasures of the
Indians we have conquered, and wind up, only months
down the line, like them, victims of the vastness of that
territory, as if we had spent our whole lives hoofing
around that land which is ours, yes, ours but never quite.
A land unmeasurable. A land that we, sad conquistadors,
dream of hoisting on our shoulders and hauling toward
the Peninsula, when in fact what always happens in the
end is that we go over to their religion, their creeds and
customs, their haughty savagery and primitive vitality,
which like some ancient wisdom that will always elude us
worms itself into the core of us and makes us forget the
Old World, doubt the existence of Spain, of Castile, of the
King, of God, of everything. Such is El Dorado, señores.
And I'm from here, though you probably won't believe it.
Yes, from Salbago, whence I left more than a quarter
century ago searching for El Dorado, and for all those
years I roamed over the continent, journeying constantly,
launching missions and sugar mills, witnessing how other
madmen like myself pulled new cities from their sleeves,
new territories, new empires, new colonies, or conquered
lands that would never be theirs. All for a King who can't
so much as picture the vast reach of the world he thinks
he rules. I also lived for a time right up against the
history written by the chroniclers and monks. I've been
conqueror, pirate, slave trader, tobacco grower, and a
thousand other damn things. All for the King. All for the
glory and fame of Spain. I saw Cortés several times, in
Mexico. I was close to Pizarro too, both Pizarros. In Lima,
Gonzalo was ruling people of every feather, governing
jungles and cities cropping up in the middle of deserts. I
knew at close hand all those maniacs who dream on and
on of Spain in spite of having ceased to be Spaniards such
a long time ago, though they scarcely know it, because
they reckon that blood and a nostalgic, nebulous memory
of the past can have some meaning in the present, the

ultimate recognition they've always sought. They're
trapped in a huge delusion. Split between two worlds,
they'll never find peace for their tortured souls anywhere
off what they think they've conquered, a land with a life
of its own, with no need of them, a land that has
conquered, transfigured, hexed them for keeps. That is El
Dorado's only reality, señores."

A deep hush spread over the bar in the wake of Alvaro
Rejón's words, a speech uttered almost at a breath, with
hardly a pause, a harangue that unsettled the customers.
Maybe his words had gone too far. He had raised his voice
gradually as he proceeded, like a leader who suddenly
remembers he knows inside out the handling of rhetorical
weaponry, in which are cached the secrets of persuasion
of masses and peoples. Slowly too, with that deft determination owing to which he had towered over other men
for so long, he had contrived to keep his name under
wraps, by saving the surprise for the end of the session,
when the anticipation conspicuous on the faces of his
listeners might have given way to disappointment, and
then blowing sky-high the rising wonder of those pitiful
misfits by trotting out the name of the founder of Salbago
at the very moment when the interest sparked by his
words might begin to sag among all those devotees of the
moment, verily because the belief in one's own as-yet-
unlived ambition was more powerful than the experience
any another man might have.

"Yes," he said with a touch of wistfulness. "After so
long, I've come back to the land of my birth. I am Alvaro
Rejón, son of the founder of Royal de Salbago."

By then, by the moment of the unrolling of his true
identity, he had grasped that his father was dead. That
therefore his name no longer wielded absolute power over
Salbago. That other men, other caballeros, men unknown
to him, had palmed the island lands and he would never
be able to claim them back. By then too, half the incredulous audience had grown tired of the endless cock-and-
bull of this grubby stranger who now, in flat-out provocation, was asserting that he was the son of Don Juan de
Rejón, unaware that the utterance of that name fetched
up in the oldest men present a pale nostalgia for time
gone by and an ever-so-dim but nonetheless perceptible

cooped-up feeling. Rejón studied the tuckered, suspense-
filled faces of those wretched, wretched losers, dreamers
of land and treasure that time had turned into musty
utopia, deep drowse of drunkards, babble of booze drifting
off into smoke while tiredness, day after day, and with a
vengeance, hunched the limbs of these armchair adventurers and sank into their bodies that time-mellowed laziness that had become a quintessential islander
characteristic. Some, the oldest in that heap of human
carrion, its eyes roving from side to side in time like a
pack of hungry dogs, remembered Governor Rejón as
though in a dream, as if at a stroke all the overblown
tales, yarns, deeds, feats handed down to them by their
fathers came suddenly and spectacularly to life smack in
the middle of what for them long, long ago had become a
round-and-round of illusions, a perpetual trumping-up of
voyages and peripluses that would never come to pass,
marooned as they were on Salbago Island forever.

Thus it had been since the founding of the city, since
the days of the discovery of the island. For them, for the
nameless horde piling onto the docks in fear and fixation
on the impossible journey, to rake up the past—to go back
to the days of Governor Rejón, if only for a moment or so—
was a mistake, was the contention that any time past was
better than the one in the offing. The return of a Rejón,
the homecoming of the only scion of Juan Rejón, whom
the chronicles of legend had given up for dead on the New
Continent, represented nothing, save naturally for a nasty
tang of unwreaked revenge corporifying in their vitals.
Here, suddenly, was the precise personification of a loser
whose name was Rejón. A young man who had departed
the island brimming with talents and passions, and who
now, in that vicious circle all sensed but none could
pinpoint with total precision, came back as simple as that
to Salbago, wound up in the same rathole he had deserted
with a smile, the envy of people (possibly his own parents
among them) from whom they had inherited this relish for
doing nothing, for grumbling about everything, for pining
after other worlds they would never have the pluck to
explore, for woolgathering, for conjuring up lands and
riches they had never nor would ever lay hands on. Was
this the hex that Pedro de Algaba had bequeathed to

them at the hour of his death? This sudden, solo appearance of Alvaro Rejón, must it be read as the end of the myth of a breed of men who were born to spin circles around the chimera that they themselves, the lion-men, had trumped up in the age of the grandiose visions of the colonies? So was it worth it to risk one's neck in the perils of the discovery, or better for some damn fool pretty much like them, after long years of futile travels, to come spin them a few tales he had a mind to pass off as gospel, that he may not even have lived, but instead (marooned in Salbago just like them, moseying up and down the same Royal alleys and backstreets) had drummed up to boggle the minds of people who had never felt the giddiness of deliverance in their balls, never had the chance for a voyage to the New Continent, a land—the more they aged—ever more mystic and distant?

A corrosive dullness, as though they had ceased to believe this phantom tale-teller from faraway lands, corporified in the faces of these tipplers of dawn, and acted as a traitorous detonator of the dispersal that commenced minutes later, leaving him all alone, this sharpshooter of lies who insisted his name was Alvaro Rejón, who didn't so much as blench as he denied the existence of El Dorado (the only truth granted sight unseen in those days) who got lost in meanders and no one ever knew for certain if he roamed in reality or in the vast fields of the imagination. He was, despite the skepticism of those shadows without known mark of signature, Alvaro Rejón.

"Pack of halfwits," he thought, in a rare moment of lucidity. "Degenerates," he said to himself, an echo maligning his own breed, his past, his life, an echo beginning to garble his words, now that the long effects of the coca—which like some native or other of those lands now lost forever, he went nowhere without—had worn off. True, he knew by rote all about the cultivation and harvest of the plant and the leaf's subsequent usages. This was the only secret he would always hold sacred. Fully conscious now of his pariahdom, Alvaro Rejón flipped one by one, in a state of solitude that actually even titillated him pleasantly, through each and every one of the phases the future would allot him in Salbago, first and last land his eyes would ever see. Surrender himself to

coca body and soul, waste away and die on that territory
still everyone's and no one's, that island hatched from his
father's delirium as a rock of salvation for untold drifters
who would never be anything but that. Surrender to coca.
Raise on secret unreachable terrains the empire of the
green leaf, like a bottomless well into which they all,
islanders and continentals alike, fell, an irresistible urge
to which all of them always ended up loyal slaves. Such
would be his final destiny. His father's—he was remembering—had been the poisoning of the those damnable
green dogs, now a vanished race only a few pure specimens of which remained, which had been removed to the
castles and palaces of the Court, back there, in what was
beginning to be the capital of the Empire, a pesthole
thriving on the banks of the Manzanares, at the very hub
of a Peninsula that had ceased to be the *finisterrae* to
become the ideal homeland of the *plusultra*, a market-city
slowly gaining supremacy in the lands of Castile, predes-
tined by the ages to be the Court, the mad metropolis of
the royal dream of Felipe II. In that city (then known, and
to be known world without end, as Madrid) the green dogs
had lost their savage glare, mien of defiance, elegance of
freedom. Quartered away from Salbago, they lost all their
primitive presence, and acclimated to the cushy life of the
Court of Carlos, that wily European glutton who had
banished the ever-mysterious Black Duke for life.

"Resaca the majordomo is still alive, señor," the
bearded waiter hallooed from the bar, fifty or so years of
age, eyes bright even at this unlikely hour, bulging belly,
generous red jowls. "Still alive," he said again, smiling,
as if this information were a gift to Alvaro Rejón, as
though in his words and the way he lipped them lurked
a wish to hoist him out of the ennui into which he seemed
to be sinking again. "Still alive."

"Where?"

"In the same cave as always. Since the Governor died.
Near the Haven. The señor knows, does he not?"

Alvaro Rejón heard the barman's arch words chiming
at the hub of a commotion which, were it not for the
lingering effects of the weed, he could never have stom-
ached in an altogether conscious state. His eyes
recovered—in a survival spurt—as though an inner fire

were rousing his scrambled memories, that vivid (tiger-green) gleam, and guided by glints half forgotten but even so breathing memory clearer at every step, he tottered out of the café, without bidding the barman goodbye, much less thanking him for the service, which was, needless to say, unpayable. Dizzily he stumbled down some back streets of the Haven, that district still belonging, after all these years, to the fishermen's breed. He scrabbled about wildly for the way to turn in that maze of shacks and fishing boats, of squalid back alleys and harbor slums that had hatched a new and thronging Bagnio.

For Rejón, Pedro Resaca's memory became a fanciful fixation, allying the past and the present, and on which the future rested. It seemed frankly a miracle that Pedro Resaca, his father's majordomo, could still be alive.

He wrote at every hour of the day and night, spurred on by the thought of wrapping up his treatise before reaching the shores of Marseilles. The Black Duke, on the long and interminable voyage that represented his passage to liberty, knew for a fact that his posterity hinged upon what he wrote on the French vessel that had rescued him from the island. At his side, unnoticed, intruding not at all on his intellectual labor, Lord Gerald fiddled, his eyes ashimmer with the dreams he pondered in the long hours of silence when all the Duke's gusto was taken up with his work. He stole sidelong looks at him as the sweat beaded on the Black Duke's temples. He revelled in the thought that soon they would be together, cohabiting in the City of Liberty, far from the primitive promiscuity of the world they were putting behind them for good. The Duke scarcely sensed him there next to him. He scarcely looked his way anymore. But Lord Gerald understood. He himself would shoulder the Black Duke's obsession, his passion to finish his exposé at sea, during the last days of exile. The little book, the Black Duke's mission, had wrested from Lord Gerald those Salbagan nights of passion and surrender, sensations now embedded in his womanish soul and lived and relived in his dreams. He loved the Black Duke, even at the price of these sacrifices contorting his flesh. He understood him, but in view of this new fixation, Lord Gerald felt orphaned, shunted to second place. To the best of his ability, dissembling as much as he could, he bore this dampening of their relations with the idea that soon, at the close of this voyage, all would resume its usual course. He never had an inkling that the French vessel's trajectory would always

173

be the same, a round-and-round route into every corner of every sea, borne by the wind, and never to reach the port of their desire.

In a lather, the Duke heeded nothing that had no direct bearing on the text he was writing against Spain, against its institutions, ancient vices, falsified history, rigid orthodoxies, historical smoke screens. A revenge over and over which he had mulled in Salbago, land of exile, jail, sword swinging like a pendulum over his memory, his head. Caged now in another prison he fancied was his agent of liberty, he worked in a frenzy, pulse racing, cooking up tidbits, gleefully flinging curses, soaked up in the black chronicle that must expose to the world the truth of Catholic Spain. He had lost all notion of time. For all he cared the days and nights could pass with a blink of his tired eyes. His sole interest was to have time enough to finish his masterpiece, the final stroke the Europeans awaited to blot Spain from the historical memory of the world.

Little by little, the Black Duke sank in his madness. A madness he had unknowingly sought in every hole and corner of his existence and had now found, at sea, on board a French ship never to bear him to liberty or fame . . .

PART II

The Promised Lands

"I shouldn't have taught them all that," Pedro Resaca, the majordomo, rebuked himself thoughtfully, but belatedly, when it began to sink in that his son, also called Pedro Resaca, and Alvaro Rejón, sole scion of the Governor of Salbago, would wind up like so many, hightailing it, bolting from a roundabout life whose stillness tired hot-blooded animals.

He had reared them in all, or nearly all ways, thinking that by smattering their childhoods with sea sports and pastimes of fishermen the boys would grow up sure to confirm and conserve a land their fathers had discovered, conquered, and laid out for them. "We make worlds," Resaca brooded, "in the image and likeness of our ambitions. We can't read the future. Those worlds, their fetters, frontiers, customs, are useless to our sons, who scorn all we do for them. It's best to let them do what they like as they like. After all, they're the real masters of their lives," he reasoned downheartedly, shrugging his shoulders and turning his attention to untangling fish hooks.

Not wishing to, with not the remotest intention, he had swayed the boys toward adventure, stirring in their blood an indomitable urge to handwrite their own histories. At this late date, he shouldn't act surprised. If he heard an echo, someone—he himself—had made a noise. So he was to blame by and large for what was occurring, he said to himself. He had a hunch, his old sea-dog eyes blinking back the tears, that they had gone off for good and would never come back to Salbago together. The rage of the age had prevailed, to sail the seas in search of destinies they would possibly never meet. They, today's youngsters, were

made of a different stuff from the old men: wood that
rotted and warped more readily, but supple and nimble as
the gait of the Saharan gazelle, floatable and resilient as
corks, bobbing up again whcnever the adventure dunked
them. They had a sense of direction altogether unlike the
unruly, primitive one of their forebears, and if they had
resolved to depart Royal de Salbago, it was because here,
in this port of call more like a bordello than could possibly
be imagined, nothing and no one could keep them any
longer. None but the phantoms of the history and its zealotic spectators could live on this land savaged by laziness
and sloth.

He leafed back in his memory over all the lessons,
pointers, tips, sailing maneuvers, stories and sagas he had
drummed into the two boys, and which had weathered
their minds as they grew up, in a hurry, to be men. From
time to time, mulling the same memory over and over, he
drifted into dangerous byways with no way back, shocked
by the proportions to which certain past events had
swollen, rattled by the hard truth revealed, in the light
of present events, by the gleam he had seen so many
times, thinking little of it, in the eyes of Alvaro Rejón and
his son. He had to own, albeit begrudgingly, that Royal
bred two kinds of Salbagans: those who (unknowingly)
were born to stay put; to watch the others sally forth into
the future and settle for the idea (as they aged in all
senses) that they would be the next to go; who had been
born to moon among the rocks, high on the cliffs that
jutted over the sea, dooming them to live in the gullies of
these volcanic lands where (strangely shirking their more
or less shadowy task) the vine had begun to take root;
who, having listened to the age-old legend of Saint
Brandon hundreds of times were tuckered by one quick
glimpse of the rock on the sea's horizon, settling for
learning all the ins and outs of the myth by heart and
happy with as little as that; who, palms perched over
their brows, threw their own shadows, and passed their
lives pining for a voyage overseas they would never have
the pluck to make, as though held to the island by an
unseen power that over the years had come to look like
fact. These were the calm, tame, complaisant islanders,
happy to summon up history, hushed about their own

lives. And the others. The wild, frisky ones, the fidgeters
and fleers, who settled for nothing, who sent their
thoughts flying over the waters around them, day after
day, while secretly they plotted escape, who watched
themselves grow up slowly, curbing their lust for faraway
lands as they gazed horizonward and waited to cut free
from the island and never look back; who cooked up,
maybe more to sell themselves than anyone else, any
excuse, duck behind piddling incidents to work up some
bad blood and procure the will to go; who had the strength
to hold their tongues until the right moment came, stirring up no suspicion around them, until the decision was
set and they were absolutely sure that nobody could make
them turn back; who glimpsed, beyond the sea, on the
sea's far side, those vastnesses bandied about daily in
Royal, Salbago: the Empire being built by leaps and
bounds in the West, on the New Continent discovered by
the Admiral, the promised land for those who could prove
they were born to win it. El Dorado, jungles, deserts,
never-ending cordilleras, rivers greater than the ocean,
rain cascading from the sky like stones, illusions made
into hard fact by dint of the daring of a handful of rash
dreamers. Terra Nostra, bounteous mother, giving all and
asking nothing in return but the unforgoable will to
adventure.

Pedro Resaca and Alvaro Rejón had been hoarding the
necessary strength for their bodies and souls as they grew
up, the majordomo was sure of it, rendering up his fate to
a lonesomeness that like a vulture would swoop down
upon him and peck into his lungs.

Ever since they were boys, almost without noticing he
had primed them in the arts of the sea. He had furnished
their imaginations with the necessary wings. First, in the
blue-green waters lapping warmly against the shores,
seasoning them little by little to look at the island from
off it, coaching them in all its sea caves, currents, winds,
and whims, showing them how to hold the boat steady, as
that penned-in feeling rose inside them. Then he took
them out to where they could almost touch, with their
already toughened hands, the horizon's forbidden stripe,
pointing out by name each of the winds that rose by night
and by day. He taught them to dowse the lateen sail at

the crucial instant, before they themselves could be dowsed by those same winds and tides bristling with treachery. And when they knew firsthand that the sea was a creature more whorish than any of the wenches they had begun to romp with on evenings in Salbago's saloons, when they knew how to sway with the waves, and thus stanch their queasiness, he struck out with them for the shores of Africa, putting behind them the horizon they never dreamed it would be so easy to cross, before their eyes the endless fringe of a wild, virtually unknown land belonging to other strange races, other civilizations possessing other religions and legends: the red and yellow Sahara, firelit at dawn and in the dusks falling suddenly over the desert, a shifting orography swept every day and night of the year by the tireless whoosh of the simoon winds.

He, Pedro Resaca, first a fisherman, then a majordomo by the grace and gastronomical whimsy of his señor, Juan Rejón, took them to sea so they would shake their fear of the waves, learn to swim on the high sea, unmindful of currents, so they would master all the knacks and arts of sailing and fishing—what meaning the colors glimmering on the face of the water concealed in the deep, where the banks of palometas, whelks, and bleaks reposed, on what secret trails the hunted sardines, roncals, and mackerel slithered away from their enemies, in which caves lurked the red and black viejas, where the oysters, clacas, urchins and crabs, edible raw, bred. He took them to sea so they would tingle with the effort of fishing a tuna, nabbed from the pack leaping over the dark water like racing greyhounds. So they would grasp that the loneliness one feels out there, while the boat rocks at the mercy of what the forces of the deep sea dictate from moment to moment, was a false human suffering which once overcome could be transformed, paradoxically, into a faithful friend forever and ever. So that, in fact (now he saw it with clarity, with a light that crushed him with its force), they would dream of other worlds, conjure up their own myths inside themselves, and picture their ambitions turning real.

All this he had done, acting as their instructor in all the caprices the sea dredged from its depths, training them to be tough to meet what obstacles might crop up in a future crossing. Storms, galernas, squalls, swells, heavy seas, whirlpools, sudden downpours or surprising dead calms on the vast waters, rounded out the language and experience of the two boys, thanks to his teachings. And with time they, Pedro Resaca and Alvaro Rejón, lost the fluster and skittishness begotten by the sea and its whimsies, and learned to decipher, with commendable intuitiveness, codes and visions, specters and chimeras that—like delusions—rose before them in the long thirsty lonely hours as they spun through zones their keels had possibly never plied, the water quivering as never had they seen or imagined. Old salts from the first, they pushed farther and farther south, skirting the rickety docks that dotted the Ivory Coast, sketching in as they went, inch by inch, with boundless patience, the sea charts given them by nobody, so that the hour came when none knew the Saharan coasts better than they did, the vast bays opening their arms to whoever had the boldness to come so far, beaches, shoals, sandbanks, reefs, in their exact dimension and location. They knew, better than anyone, how to nose into the warm, still waters washing like caresses against the blond sands of Río de Oro, combing the coast till they knew it like the backs of their hands, as if on their own dominions. This whole realm, which many years before had struck Martín Martel, the Commander, as strangely sinister, was more than some pleasure park without secrets where they could roam wild, where nothing and nobody would dare balk their mission. There, on that vast sea sash marking the watery frontier between Salbago and Africa, Alvaro Rejón and Pedro Resaca began to pitch their own world of myth, to plot and prepare, slowly nearing an impasse that left them but one escape. The island held them like a tight old corset, where if they so much as budged they sparked suspicion and indignation, where, heady, scrappy, they felt trapped in a fidget, a spiritual itch all but unbearable.

Their few spells in town, away from the sea which molded them into another sort of men—masters of instinct and intuition—their presence became more and more pesky and exceptionable. The two went off on binges, on all-out benders, in the slummy locale that had belonged, in better days, to the witch-harlot Maruca Salomé, the Six of Hearts, where Zulima had danced, where Alvaro's father was smitten with love for her, though he never guessed that the Moorish girl was in point of fact his mother. Inside this dive, this bordello gone to wrack and ruin and all but forgotten by the high officials of Royal who had easily shifted the honor of their caprices elsewhere, the boys—as in some warmed-over vaudeville— mimicked the orgies their fathers had been heroes of in the golden days of the colony, dancers in a notorious choreography of pleasure-loving and pimping passed down to them vivid as ever. In Maruca Salomé's tarthouse lingered the flavor of memories and a classiness that harked back to a time that while in fact was probably pure hokum, the old men recalled as an inimitable, fabulous age. Hollering, ramping, raving, swept up in the raciest scandals, they scoured Royal's fishing districts— their turf—chasing the fallen women who lived outside the city walls in vile hovels where they took in their countless customers. They barged rudely into public places, squares, shops, markets, saloons, and nobody ever had the spine to speak up to them, let alone dress them down for their barbarities and frenzies. They nabbed and ravished, with letters of marque, all wenches they came across, whether chosen by the two together before the fact, or by chance. The laws they broke, however, had never been overly revered in Royal, Salbago, this domain now hemming in around them, altogether too small for their ambitions.

"Like father, like son," wheezed Hernando Rubio, now on his last legs. "Yes, señor," he fumed, "those lowlifes hatched these little farts strutting around this town as if it was their private estate."

"It would be to the good," Juan Rejón advised when he received word of the irate complaints and could no longer play deaf, "for the boys to be always out to sea, Pedro. There, damn it," he barked, slamming his fist into the nearest thing at hand, "at least they can't hurt anyone. If they stay here, they're going to drive Royal to the dogs."

It was a barer and barer fact that they were born to leave, fated to travel the seas and wind up settling down

in other lands more akin to their restlessnesses. By the
day, the strife and outlawry they instigated heaped up
around them, sheltered by that unfair impunity that even
so no one would dare rebut. Functionaries, constables,
wardens, magistrates, governors, lieutenants, officers of
the Holy Inquisition, church authorities, and whosoever
attempted to pull rank on Alvaro Rejón and Pedro Resaca
were nipped, trounced by that pair of hoods, twitted like
piddling little drudges by that pair of bees whose hedge-
hopping was more feared in Royal than the plagues of
African locusts (devouring all in their path), than the
droughts (cyclically cracking and spoiling the crop fields),
than the baleful winds (that often wafted over Salbago
Island sprinkling a blue fungus that withered the budding
tomato plants), and than the swollen tides (that every
year, early in September, ruthlessly destroyed the docks
and dragged the black sands out to sea, leaving the beach
full of stones that rumbled in the storm). They were worse
than any of these scourges and the townsfolk breathed a
sigh of relief when they saw them cross the line of the
horizon and vanish on the high sea. They felt, the citizens
of Royal, freed of tribulations. But not for long. Only until
a whimsy brought that devastating blight home from its
fishing trip, and back they went to their old escapades and
excesses through streets and squares and over docks and
into all the holes and corners of Royal de Salbago.

So the day they decided, of their own sweet will, to go
off forever, the inhabitants of the city gave thanks to the
Almighty for the bestowal of this unexpected gift, to be
spared of their presence. For some days they hustled and
bustled, overhauling the boat, fixing the flaws in the
planking produced by their constant sailing along the
African coast. Patiently, they tarred in each of the chinks
in the hull's remotest crannies. They mended the sail.
And then they purchased from the majordomo himself one
of his fleetest fustas, telling him nothing of their
upcoming plans.

"The sailors are off," crowed the now-doddering Inquisitor Hernando Rubio. "They're going away for good," he
hummed as soon as he heard the news. "Blessed be God,"
he prayed, hobbling and muttering. "This will be gall and
wormwood to the Governor, but it's the best thing for

Royal. Let them be off, let them sail to the New World
and sink, way the hell over there where I hope to God no
one will rescue them."

Next, for some long days, came the strange picking of
the crew. Silent, solemn, like real ship recruiters, sedu-
lous, like merchants versed in every step they must take
to bring their plans to fruition, man by man they signed
on their seamen. The townspeople pretended they had no
idea what Alvaro Rejón and Pedro Resaca were plotting.
And the two of them, taken up in their venture, began to
believe in it. Hush-hush, as though their lives hung on
the secret, they hired the last of their seamen from that
motley, shifty breed that roamed through Royal's worst
districts, sowing lawlessness and danger. Hernando Rubio
had guessed their plans, but it was more in his interest
to keep them under wraps. "It is good to make a bridge
of gold to a flying enemy," he reminded himself, rubbing
his hands together. But even the Inquisitor was far from
imagining that at least as plans now stood all these
doings (raved about in nooks and haunts, saloons,
brothels, churches, bedrooms and official chambers) were
not charted to take them pell-mell down the routes of
mirage leading over the sea to the New Continent.
Though Rejón and Resaca enlisted a vow of silence to no
avail, they didn't clue in the sailors either.

First they would go to Africa. First move, to gain those
shores they knew better than anybody. First measure, to
secure a goodly cargo of Saharan slaves they would then—
to their minds the true adventure sooner or later they
would have to brave—convey to the ports of the New
World, where small slave markets, cautiously, covertly,
were beginning to breed, as needed by the sugar mills and
the construction of the Empire's new towns and cathedrals. Alvaro Rejón was abreast of all this. It had been
described to him by some of the Spanish Empire's first
slave traders, smugglers from Catalan and Majorca who
several times yearly, under the rose, and as easy as that,
traversed the vast ocean which in former times had been
thought murky, and from the facts it was plain that they
knew every pleat, every puff of fickle breath, every surge
and dash, every storm and calm. Like fleers from justice,

steering clear of the obligatory stop on the docks of Royal de Salbago, and hence passing unseen, they landed directly on the shores of the Sahara, alongside the desert that commences in the zone of Sakia-el-Amra.

Alvaro Rejón was stumped that summer morning, on return from one of their excursions south. The sun beat straight down on his head. There, along the coast, lay two impeccably rigged caravels, gently rocking. They were, in fact, slavers. Later would come explanations, and vows of silence that must never be violated. On clear warm nights around the campfire, they swapped facts and fables—the pirates' feats, the secret underside of the ruses they would begin to unroll as soon as the natives of the African coast began to show their faces hereabout. By now they had noted the close, covert watch the Saharans kept over them, besieging them with eyes seasoned in great distances. It might take days this time to break down the barriers of their distrust. But sooner or later the Africans would succumb to the white man's presence, led possibly by instinct toward their fate as slaves. Still lying low, they would send out what the slavers termed the advance guard, the scouts, three or four spokesmen who within hours would be dazzled by the glitter of the goods regaled to them by these men from the sea, who asked nothing in return. The game heated up; the slavers catching each other's eyes cannily. Then at last, from beyond the dunes rimming the beach surged a shrieking mob, wanting a share, forthwith, in the white man's treasures. Chips of colored glass, fake gemstones, cheap rhinestones, rusty worn-out knives, bits of broken mirrors, snatches of fictitious, fraudulent happiness making them beam with bliss, oblivious to the deadly stratagem weaving around them. Over the desert sands the news tore like the wind, rousing the small bands of nomads who, guileless, mesmerized, streamed down to the wet sand at the water's edge,

converted now into a fête beyond compare, hoopla of
market or fiesta. Men, women and children paraded,
crying for gifts, while they themselves were the hidden
fortune sashaying gaily and trustingly on the very verge
of slavery.

The order to attack would not prove necessary.
Forgetful of all prior raids, woozy on cane liquor, they
barely knew what befell them as they were handed, with
hideous hilarity, into the smelly holds of the caravels.

That, said the slavers (eyes aglitter with greed, goggled
with ambition, their grandiloquent gestures at odds with
their appearance, as if they already held in their hands
these solely imagined riches), is how huge fortunes are
made in the New World. So Alvaro Rejón convinced Pedro
Resaca that they should bring off one of these razzias
themselves, to mark the start of their new life far from
Royal, Salbago. Reckless and rash, Alvaro Rejón did not
dare bid his father farewell, knowing for a fact that the
Governor would not grant his permission for the journey,
and that if the Adelantado had his way, he would pass the
rest of his days going to pot like him, old and proud,
without a water clock or sundial to count out the time of
his life, in a swoon of memories drifting backward into the
days of the founding of Royal.

So, one bright dawn in early October, when the tides
had lulled and the sands washed up again onto Salbago's
shores with their sclerotic smile, they shoved off, and
rowed slowly away from the coast. Once out of danger,
they hoisted the sails that would bear them zigzagging for
the nearby shores of the Sahara. Not until gaining land
would the hired seamen know what was to be their first
destination. Rendered as they were to the will of their two
captains, to them a sea was a sea and the water's sudden
changes of color meant nothing. Within a few hours they
had ridden out their seasickness, and were at home with
the bellowing commands and countermands of Rejón and
Resaca. They swung the sail windward or leeward,
heeding the cries of these two wizards who read the sea's
indecipherable signals without a miss. Straddling hope
and fear on an ocean apt at moments to fleck silver-grey,
they peered constantly into the eyes of the two captains,
trying to detect in their inscrutable looks a twinge of

gloom or misgiving. They saw none. Alvaro Rejón and Pedro Resaca steered their ships through realms they had sailed hundreds of times before. Visionary, as if the fates were always in their favor, as if all the demons of the land and sea were always on their side, they never muffed a maneuver and never turned back. Old salts as they were before this adventure, they knew flawlessly, by name, the reefs and islets marked on their maps, what distance divided one shallows from the next, where the perilous invisible sandbanks lay heaped. Between them they spoke a lingo unknown to the other seamen, and Alvaro Rejón let flap in the winds the long blond mane for which he would be so famous in coming years in the Caribbean brothels.

After some days of sailing, meeting no obstacle worthy of note, they spied the African coast. "We're in Africa!" whooped Pedro Resaca. A shiver surged through the crew, giving way to shock. Africa, the coast of the Sahara!

It then fell to Pedro Resaca to round up the men and win over the disgruntled. With a smile flaunting his pearly white teeth, he spelled out the motive for this journey, a surprise even to those who had suspected deep down, ever since departing Salbago, that they were being gulled. "You are here," hollered Pedro Resaca, "to become slave traders. Whoever's not up for this fight, speak now, and get out," he warned, knowing as he spoke this was an unlucky hour to stay on shore at the mercy of the Saharans. None who a moment before had begun to meekly protest, now that Rejón and Resaca had unfolded their plans, could bring himself to speak.

When, after many days out, they fetched up at Margarita, an island off the Venezuelan shore of Terra Firma, nobody came out to greet them. There were no cheers for their feat, no reproach whatever for their underhanded adventure. For part of the passage (which barely registered incident of note) Alvaro Rejón paced about rather bothered by the reactions starting to crop out in the twisted expressions of some of the seamen. All in all, none of this was strange. It always happened on long crossings. The other half of his mind was wrapped in a haze he could not wipe away until they came to their destination: the suspense wrought by his landing in a world unknown to him. He had his doubts too, those occasions when the most dauntless captains step out of the clouds, place their feet on the shaky deck and take stock of their plans, their souls blighted by bafflements. Slowly his skin, pale as it had been for days on end, flushed again with color. The waters now bore unmistakable signs of the nearness of land, broken bits of warped boards, trunks of trees and plant debris, marking the end of that limpid line, the distant, disheartening horizon that had almost unmanned him. Then he knew, in his heart of hearts, that they had come to the Continent, though they approached at an angle off the routes marked on his crude sea charts heeding the counsel of slavers he had met in the Sahara. Maybe, he thought, what was happening now was that the winds had nudged them, toyed with their two vessels, without him, who shouldered the blame for this slimy expedition, even taking note. These things were wont to happen, he said to himself with a tired sigh. In these ten or twelve days, sailing by sheer hunch, Alvaro

Rejón had felt the stinging of despair, a hair shirt stuck to his flesh, clinging to his soul like a barnacle, a leech sucking his blood and bleaching his face, the fever mounting from the soles of his feet and coiling in his head like a poisonous snake. Several slaves died to whom he could give nothing to drink, and he had to ration the few foodstuffs left for the remainder of the crossing. The jareas, dried dogfish, salted rockfish, cassava bread and rotting meat jerky induced a dire thirst Rejón could not slake with words alone.

Resaca meanwhile saw the shadow of Salbago on all sides. Feverish, he was quite sure they had never budged from the African latitudes they had supposedly left behind. Every day he woke at dawn, observing in wonder the slow trajectory of stars that did not figure on their nautical charts. Wracked by sweat and fever-bred nightmares, he believed he saw, in the mirror of the still wavering dawn, the distant silhouette of Salbago Island, sucking them toward it with voracious force. He felt that forgotten clutch of fear he had suffered the first time his father took him to sea and he viewed, from afar, the coast of the island he had never stepped off before. "I feel seasick," he confessed to himself in a whisper, casting an eye over the platform where their cargo of repellent negroids lay stretching and moaning, their sole treasure. "What shit!" was all that popped into his head at that moment. During that hazy time lost at sea, on the verge of forgetting which direction they faced, when songs like those of sirens began to waft over the deck, riding the warm winds that blew over the horizons, Resaca could think of nothing but the curse of Saint Brandon, to the point where he couldn't say for sure whether or not what he truly coveted was to catch sight of that legendary rock that shadows lost sailors and swallows them. Naturally he would rather stumble into that skittish monster, lord of the seas, than go astray and perish, thirsty forever on the shadowy immensity of the ocean. "That's not Salbago, damn it. It's Saint Brandon," he would think when at dawn the fever shook him, the fear stabbed him, waking him all in a tremble, with aches and pains in the head, while in the dim distance, if he paid close attention, he

could make out the fickle, fleeting glow of a mirage that
was beginning to haunt him.

After a night all during which they heard birds cawing
as though it were day, after the signs that floated by the
vessels informing them that land now lay very near, one
of those mornings when a punishing sun beat on the blistering backs of the seamen (when the yearning to mutiny
was ever so obvious, manifest in the transpiercing glances
the men shot at Alvaro Rejón and Pedro Resaca), they
spotted a tiny island in the distance, which at first blush
stood for salvation, ever so desperate. This time it was no
mirage. It was the island baptized with the floral name of
Margarita, thus to be known for centuries to come. They
were, in fact, in the Caribbean Sea, if a tad off their original route, their aim to strike upon Española Island,
otherwise known—in those days—as Fernandina. Still
unbeknownst to them, they were brushing the rim of a
misty realm teeming with islets, a ripening region where
the countless islands of West India clustered, this side of
Terra Firma.

Margarita, like Salbago (which lay for them now at a
smudgy, horrible spot in the east, on the far side of the
world), was a link, a perch in the sea before coming to the
New Continent. A drifter's island, serving as a roost as
much for the servants of the Crown of Spain as for the
corsairs without a known country committed to roving
and ransacking up and down the Caribbean, it was a
territory tendered by the sea to whoever had the grit to
cross it, or to any who wished a last moment for reflection
before undertaking the voyage home, to muster the
strength they needed for the challenge, or to think better
of their plans and turn back. The successive governors
dispatched to Margarita by the Crown turned a blind eye
on fugitives and outlaws, in exchange for respect for the
island's laws. They extended their hospitality to all travellers who turned up on the island, accidentally or on
purpose, whether they came from Spain—from Salbago—
or from nearby Cubagua, whence had begun, around
about the time Alvaro Rejón and Pedro Resaca put into
these shores, an unstemmable exodus of pearl fishermen
beaching up on Margarita Island—hopes dashed, fevery
ambitions scuttled—with the last gasp of their feckless

efforts. Inhabited half by Indians who shrank from the Christians, half by Spaniards who dubbed themselves Christians to safeguard their lives and live for a spell as subjects of the monarchy, above suspicion, the island deferred to Puerto Rico on weighty ecclesiastical questions, whereas in matters of law Santo Domingo held jurisdiction. Small, enticing, in the eyes of Alvaro Rejón and Pedro Resaca's mariners, the island looked like a sanctuary in the surrounding sea.

They debarked, nothing to it, looking about aweless, as if they had been there some time before. They didn't feel like intruders, thinking they had found a safe haven at last. The first scouts sent out by Alvaro Rejón discovered that Margarita, like Salbago, had two distinct regions. They came back to the beach tagged by a toothless old man yammering all the chitchat and tales that popped into his head. "Here," the lonely old man announced, pointing to the ground with his left hand outstretched, "here, maestro, the Villalobos rule. They're the lords and masters of all," he went on, chewing greedily on the meat jerky furnished by Resaca to appease his hollow hunger. "As for those," he said, pointing sneeringly to the string of slaves resting, lashed together, in the shade of the palms, a short way from the water's edge where the conversation was unfolding, "they won't let you sell them here in Margarita, maestro. The business you're looking to do is farther up or farther down. In Margarita that trade is practically speaking prohibited, maestro. The Villalobos are in charge here and they've got all the slaves they need. They don't favor anyone coming here to get rich." He went on chewing and chewing the strip of jerky with his toothless gums, slipping it from jowl to jowl, slowly pulping the meat and salt with the press of his jaws. "Yes, señor. The Villalobos have the say-so, just so you know, maestro," he said again, cackling convulsively and daffily, thinking he could thereby more easily dissuade the slavers newly arrived on the island. "Nothing to do about it." He wagged his head no as he talked. Then he ran his eye again over the slaves reposing in the sand like sacks of useless cargo.

"We've botched the trip," Alvaro Rejón said to Resaca in a whisper. He felt like he was about to burst. He was baffled again, riddled by doubts, sweat streaming down his face like tears and shimmering in the sun.

"Damn," Resaca muttered between his teeth. "We're up to our necks in this gamble, Alvaro. I won't take a step back. I'm carrying on."

"If I were you, maestro, I wouldn't talk that way," the old man nipped in cheekily. He had overheard the whole conversation. Resaca peered around at him, curbing himself for the moment, vowing he would die. "If you've come far, as it seems," he continued preachily, speaking to Rejón and Resaca without much interest, "take a tip from us who went this godforsaken route before you which, like they all do, you think you're going to carry off in some new way."

They sat in the sun, the ships moored a few meters off shore, the basin deep enough so as not to bar the keels from putting in. Over a smoldering fire roasted the skinned carcasses of some animals that looked like wild rabbits or hares. Beyond, in small clusters, the sailors awaited the outcome of the huddle their captains were holding with the old man.

"Get them out of here, maestro. Chuck them in the sea," the old man prompted, looking over at the Saharans. "The currents will sweep them away and not a sign of you will be left on the beach."

He never stopped eating while he spoke, sucking with pleasure on a sliver of jerky that hung from his gums. Then, unsated, he turned to picking at the hunks of meat roasting on the embers. He played mysterious, peppering his cryptic talk with prophecies as if he held his own hypothetical powers of persuasion in high regard.

"The businesses?" he replied quizzically, to Alvaro Rejón. "I just told you, maestro, the businesses all belong to the Villalobos. They rule us, they run us, and they're allowing us to walk and talk on this island right now, free of danger."

And, like a cunning historian or a weathered chronicler who had known firsthand all occurrences lived on the island since the coming of the conquistadors, he jawed on and on, in endless monologue, listing, prolixly, the name of every Villalobo on Margarita to have been landowner or gentleman, governor or viceroy. He began with the vanished Aldonza Manrique, daughter of Villalobos the barrister, first señor of the island. He skimmed over episodes, omitting the string of intrigues woven within the Villalobos family so that the dominion of the island might never slip from their hands. He spoke then of Pedro Ortiz de Sandoval, Marcela Manrique, Juan Villandrando, Villalobos, Villalobos, and Villalobos, one succeeding the other, year after year, lustrum after lustrum, to the governance of Margarita Island. He wrapped up his oration with a long sigh like the tracks of a caiman along the sandy bank of a river. Or perhaps it was his heart's last throb in honor, devotion, and surrender to all those names he had uttered with such historical bluster. "Those are the Villalobos," he said vacantly a moment or so later. "They've got a hundred slaves, and all the land belongs to them and their minions. This is all that's ours," he owned with a tinge of sadness: he was gazing out to sea. "You can sail it and fish it. You can swim till you sink. You can come, and if you like, you can go," he said wryly. "Keep in mind the law of the Villalobos. Here they're King. They command. They are Castile. Spain, maestro. For eternity." Then suddenly he sank into a stupor, a deep, long silence from which he did not emerge even to horn in on the muddled parley conducted by Alvaro Rejón and Pedro Resaca. He confined himself to nodding or shaking his head, hereby demonstrating that his words were no longer needed, since what it behooved the slaver captains to know about Margarita he had already spelled out, and then some, in return for those hunks of hot meat.

In a lull in the conversation he broke in again, only to declare that they had better scram if they did not wish to part with their negroes and morangos, their precious, forbidden cargo. The Indians, he said, had fled the island as soon as the Spanish arrived. The few they managed to enslave were in the service of the Christians and lords of Margarita, the Villalobos and descendants. The rest were men without a country, maestro, no country, no family, and no ambitions. Their lives behind them, maestro. "Like me." He smiled ruefully, with traces of lost pride. "Not too many can stand this do-nothing life on Margarita. I'm a poor old man and what I fish is plenty to eat. I hardly have a good tooth left. My memory is eking away because a lot about life will never catch my eye again. Here, the outlaws and pirates who come to hole up don't stay long. That's their deal with the Villalobos. Time enough for them to give up hunting for them, or to heal their wounds and troubles." So it was better they go, this was his tip to them, he said in almost pleading tones. Those who had thrived here during the fifty years of Spanish sovereignty (the Herreras, Riberos, Gómezes, Alvaro Milán, Andrés Andino), had pulled it off in the early days on the pearls of Cubagua, and now their offspring had time to spare to polish up their holdings, the estates passed to them by their fathers, maestro. "But that's all over now. There's not a fucking pearl left in the place." He grinned, squinting his eyes mirthfully, as if the wrack and ruin hanging over each of his words tickled him no end. "It's over," he said, bursting into delirious chortles followed by a puff of smelly breath and a wheeze. "Now they live on the salt they pan from the sea," the old-timer spluttered, on his knees in the sand.

Pedro Resaca drew Alvaro Rejón away from the fire to speak with him alone. "He's a demon, Alvaro. A apparition of this godforsaken land. He's mixing us up and bullying us because he knows that since we just got here we know nothing about this land beneath us. Let's head for the Continent at once. We'll build our own hacienda over there."

Rejón paced around thinking for a while. He went round and round in a circle, tracking a bigger and bigger ring of footprints in the sand. Then he meandered off down the beach, slowly, so as not to tax his nerves by hurrying. He had seen the strain coloring the face of his blood brother, Pedro Resaca. The turn things were taking vexed him, and he angled about for an honorable way out of this white hell into which they had tumbled. He wavered between shrugging off the old man's advice, and throwing in with Pedro Resaca's view that they should head on for the lands of the Continent he was sure, from the facts he had gathered from the slaving corsairs (if that information didn't turn out totally wrong, he thought) teemed with secluded bays, coves, and inlets where anyone, they told him pointing to their maps, could stake out their own hacienda without anyone turning up later to bother him, asking leave of no man at all. For the only law upheld among them—fugitives from the law, corsairs, buccaneers, and pirates of every stripe who ran wild through the convoluted seas of West India—was that of mutual respect, silence, and brotherhood, a complicity which if violated was punishable by death, and no one would check around to see if the vengeance had been just.

He came back walking with the same sham insouciance as when he walked away from this place where the embers still glowed in the campfire and the seamen he had signed on in Salbago were stripping the last of the meat from the bones of the wild rabbits. He noted a certain corporeal contentment in their faces. They were not hungry or thirsty. They did not suffer from cold or excessive heat. Maybe some humidity their bodies weren't used to, but this anyhow was bearable. He noticed that they had begun to be gripped by one idea: to clear out. They peered sideways at their two captains, trying to follow the conversation, a quarrel in whispers held at the water's edge.

Suddenly Rejón turned to them with a firm look. "We're off," he said. The order surprised no one. Not a murmur of protest was there against the men who had brought them safe and sound from the far side of the sea to a new life. "We're heading for Terra Firma, the Continent." Rejón spoke now without looking at them, surveying his maps and charts as if with his eyes riveted thereon he could pinpoint the route that would lead them to those coveted coasts, the eastern shore of Venezuela. They made for the sea, gaining their ships, their hearts hopping with revivified lust for adventure. With shouts and whacks of the sword, they herded the negroes back into the holds. Hoisting the sail, they headed out in search of a hazy realm, spurred by an obsession akin to that which in an earlier age had gripped Juan Rejón and his henchmen, almost one hundred years before, when unknowingly they sought Salbago Island. For good and all Alvaro Rejón shattered the possibility of ever reliving the fate bequeathed to him by his father: land in the same adventure, brand the same bizarre chimera across his brow. Up till now, though perhaps not altogether comprehending this, he had worn a memory of family demons pegged like amulets and ex-votos to his soul. Again the giddiness of adventure had triumphed, the crazed will of a captain who always chose the unknown evil over the known good. In Pedro Resaca's eyes, as though by miracle, that prophetic fire that had become the essence of his personality began to glitter again. The sailors' faces too flushed with the fresh color of hope, before the obstacles they would meet between here and there, in that narrow arm of the sea dividing them from the Continent, from Terra Firma itself. Slowly, as they pulled away from the island, an obscene scrawl receded from sight, formed, in macabre composition, by the dismembered cadaver of that toothless fisherman, cocky old windbag, whose bones would lie drying and yellowing in the sun forever, where no one would ever again spare a thought for his warnings, yarns, anecdotage or death.

They spotted it a day later than expected, at a point somewhat more westerly than Alvaro Rejón had proposed to Resaca on this second (and this time short) crossing. From the sea, very slowly their eyes scanned the spot that was to be their first haven on the Terra Firma discovered by the Admiral. On first glance they named it Puerto Vigía. It was a virgin cove where the sea's green waters scarcely stirred. As gently the boats parted the hushed waters, over their surface a small breeze whispered in this place whose loneliness, it struck Rejón, rendered it ideal. This was indeed a territory abandoned by God's hand, unseen two or three miles out to sea, flanked by two great pillars of rock which, like stone guardsmen, kept watch over the sea and the horizon. A scant space for maneuvering, no more than fifty meters broad, was the passage through which one entered the cove and reached the sand shore, where the waters lapped stilly, calmed the fitful churning of the waves outside the harbor, outside those natural walls shielding the beach from the winds that scrapped above, in the cliffs. Only a murmur reached the beach, the back stream of those same winds sparring in the sky. Here none but the wind waged battle. And a few days after settling in this lost spot on the coastline— perfect haven for corsairs weary of the drudge of sailing— a mood of safeness came over them, which their highstrung spirits were feeling at home with already. The air they breathed was pure and theirs. They threw together docks, roughhewn, urgently needed. Methodically they set out the rules that would reign in Puerto Vigía. For each chore, they parcelled out, by category, the slaves brought from the faraway Sahara. With utmost heedfulness, they

began to explore the near hills, up which climbed thick
green foliage, and the coves thereabout.

Puerto Vigía was not the El Dorado they had come
seeking. Nowhere around in this stillness appeared the
bustle of markets, the buying and selling of slaves
described to Alvaro Rejón by the corsairs on the shores of
Africa. Nor was there, for many miles around, any native
or Spanish population that might feel provoked by the
presence of unsavory slave-trading pirates shipping in
their clandestine human cargo spurred by an insatiable
craving to strike it rich. Nor were there pearls thereabout. Nor silver. Nor golden apples. Nor prophets pointing
northward or southward. All the easy myths they had
pictured in their dreams were figments of fever. The tales
and legends that had come to them from the New World
shattered against the reality of the stone pillars of Puerto
Vigía, a hideout in a far-flung world, a nest, a roost, a
point of departure for their upcoming journeys and jaunts
around the Caribbean Sea, and the endless curve of
islands that was West India. Slowly their ambitions, born
and bred under the wing of these fraudulent tales, faded,
and they turned to the pressing task of fortifying the
entrance to the cove. Like so, at least for the time being
(while they versed themselves in this new turf beneath
their feet) the wanderers settled in, left off roving like
nameless phantoms, and obeyed, to the letter of the law,
the orders dealt daily by Alvaro Rejón and Pedro Resaca.

The pirate camp, a sprawl of dark shacks and stockade
pilings stuck up helter-skelter, would be standing after a
month of sweat and toil. The necessary orders were doled
out, the men molding to the discipline Alvaro Rejón asked
of them. Now at last they were free men and could have
belongings of their own. They could choose, at will,
between pirateering—braving the sea—or roosting on the
land around Puerto Vigía. They were burning the past,
just as years past a man named Hernando Cortés had set
fire to his ships on the shores of Vera Cruz. They were
putting behind them the teases and chimeras of youth.
Miraculously amnestied from life in this secret, silent spot
in the New World, each could turn to his private
thoughts, spill his seed however he liked, hone his ideas
and home in on his will. Here reached not the authority

of the King, nor the orders of cocky captains, nor the
whimsies of governors, nor the Inquisition. Solely the sane
voice of Alvaro Rejón and the alert, clever eyes of Pedro
Resaca reigned. Puerto Vigía was the only place they
could call their own, the one hidden haven to which they
could turn in a moment of need, where none would probe
the source of sudden riches or spoil their dreams of repose.

Rejón, meanwhile, regained his lost peace of mind. He
had a funny feeling that death had been stalking him for
a long while, but that now he had escaped from the eye
of the storm. Fortune smiled upon him; he was sure he
had landed on his feet, alongside life's winners. He and
Resaca would commit themselves, in the coming years, to
culling and sorting everything useful gained from the
ocean crossing. With slow exactness, they blotted out
every leftover bit of memory from Royal de Salbago, now
and forever. They stood, unbeknownst to them, on a territory that centuries hence would set the jungle scene for
endless bloody battles, where the massive mighty shadow
of the Royalist honcho, José Tomás Boves, alias Boss or
the Grouse, a mad Asturian, would scour the seacoast and
lowlands of Venezuela with savage cruelty, a general
who—leading a strange army of mulattos and negro slaves
(whom he had liberated, and who hailed from Puerto
Vigía)—had held Simón Bolívar at bay for upwards of two
years, the son, and grandson, of the Mantuan lords of the
Valley of Santiago de León of Caracas, known to all as
the Liberator, whose secessionist doctrines would in the
end prevail over the political maladroitness of the Spanish
in the domains of the New World.

Mademoiselle Pernod, after many years of selfless devotion to the oldest, wisest, sexiest, and most artistic profession in the world, sustained a top-notch reputation. Her personality and her presence were required, were desired every place that wished to be thought sophisticated in a world that fought valiantly for fame, honors and a hacienda. Mademoiselle, at least in appearance, was cultured and cultivated without lapsing into the arrogance of exhibiting a level of erudition that would not serve her well in a new land where pillaging figured among the fine arts. Mademoiselle Pernod ringed herself with an invisible circle to prevent intruders and undesirables from approaching her or any of her cocottes whom, thanks to her fresh way of seeing things and understanding life, she had turned into grand ladies wedded to Spanish hacendados who had struck it lucky in the New World. Over time an aura of splendidness and untouchability formed around her, and her name and her fame as a deft, intelligent operator, a hetaira for whom love of whatever kind held no secrets, a dangerous woman nonetheless desired by the highest magistracies and fortunes of not only Santo Domingo but the whole Caribbean Sea, became legendary. Her gestures, her smiles, the light caresses she distractedly bestowed on the gentlemen she singled out for her conversation and friendship, exuded a certain perfume made of esoteric blends of rare herbs known only to her, rousing in these upstart churls a hitherto unknown affectation of decorum and civility. Coarse and conniving, sometimes stingy but almost always thieves, they became gentle, generous personages—imitators of the distant Courts of Europe—in the presence of

205

Mademoiselle Pernod, whose fame for rigorous refinement had overshot the borders of Hispaniola Island and—her name and her outlandish practices buzzing from mouth to mouth—bcen underwritten by tidbits of legend, by hyperbole and exaggeration, making the rounds of the Caribbean Sea and rousing mutterings and murmurings and fixations of admiration in all the sphere of the continental coast contiguous with the islands. Myriad marvels were reported about her which the primitive erotic imaginations of the conquistadors, buccaneers, hacendados and Antillean governors had embellished with bizarre details that could only be corroborated by those very persons whose stories they were, and who had witnessed, in Santo Domingo, one of her provocative vespertine strolls, Mademoiselle sporting a charming parasol in cloth of gold, sparing her, in part, from the punishing tropical heat. "She's a travelled dove," said the gossips, leaving their meaning ambiguous. Mademoiselle Pernod always dressed in precious, exclusive gowns made of exquisite gold thread, and she exhibited herself on the city's Royal Road on rare and counted occasions. On her neck, elongated and delicate like a polished alabaster carving, shone choice necklaces of the finest pearls to be found on the transparent bottom of the Caribbean Seas. She always wore shoes embossed with gold thread, and on their high heels her fragile legs swayed gracefully like a tame gazelle's. Her slim waist, ideal from the gentlemen's point of view, suggested the way to the subdued indecency of her small breasts, from which it was rumored that in moments of exacerbated amorous delirium flowed a white, sweet, abundant and warmly delicious liquid she would oblige her lover pro tem to suck, restoring his forces to return indefatigable to the sweaty struggle of the strongest of desires. It was, explained those who dreamed of experiencing it, the fountain of eternal youth, a sort of celestial gift only she possessed under the sun of the New World. It instilled, in those gentlemen who claimed to have enjoyed her favors, a general respect for her person and her reputation. And what's more, even after their complicity had ended, her lovers continued to so adore her that they would devote themselves to fanatically spreading her fame through all the ports and haciendas of West India. Like so her powerful prestige had risen, while those who had never seen her pictured her green almondy eyes, her turned-up little nose (indicating pride and strength of character), her mouth brimming with exotic juices—crowned by lips that whipped them into aphrodisiacal excesses—and her chestnut hair, slinking silkily over her shoulders and covering most of her delicate, desirable back, at whose end point the secret of a tiny curve began, in whose intimate hollow lay hid one of the most refined, bliss-inducing vices Mademoiselle was wont to conduct with her lovers. She was precisely this, precisely as pictured by the heated, and for once lucid, collective imagination of the Caribbean. She accepted only gifts of gold, solely objects in which gold was present, gold lockets, strings of natural pearls mounted on gold, gold bracelets, gold brooches, earrings, any sort of pendant as long as it was gold, gold rings and hoops, gold belts, sumptuous dresses shimmering with gold, shoes always of gold, rings, cameos, and gold statuettes, which she spread about in the parlors of her golden mansion, whose entryway was guarded by two life-size gold dogs. In payment for her favors, which she lavished solely on those who, after gently tearing away each of the untouchable veils girding her like a fortress wall, managed to elicit her interest and enter her turret, she charged gold as well, following a rational price scale based on the exigencies of her lovers, who were beyond a doubt entranced by the range of possibilities and new pleasures tendered by Mademoiselle in her private mansion.

Don Alvaro Rejón had installed himself years before in the city of Santo Domingo. He arrived in his own boat, which, though of reduced proportions, accommodated within a curious collection of rare objects, stuffed animals and furniture, which he unloaded showily, for all to see, once he had procured the home he had been looking for, to stay (or so he said) for some time. From the first moment, his presence commanded that respect elicited only by those personalities who comprehend that mystery is curiosity's best friend. Allied to silences and conversations drifting into the realms of fable and fiction, Don Alvaro Rejón revealed himself to be a consummate traveller, now very weary of adventure (he said), who was

passing himself off, this time, for what he really was: a
man who had turned up trumps in the New World via a
fortune he had made at the hacienda in Puerto Vigía, in
the Colony of Venezuela, and which later, with the
demand created by the construction of sugar mills, the
cultivation of tuber and grain plantations, and the
founding of new cities, had spread as far as Tenochtitlán,
Mexico. He demonstrated, quite effortlessly, that he had
travelled over the whole of Great Colombia, through the
jungles and cordilleras along the narrow rim of the continent, across the Isthmus of Darién, into each and every
one of the ports and secret refuges on the Caribbean Sea.
He would smile with a sneer of disdain, as though the
story being told was prompted by exaggeration and fear,
when his Santo Domingo barfellows told him of the
dreadful deeds of the pirates ravaging the Islands of West
India, all those ships that like fantastic shadows roved the
Caribbean Sea bent on plunder and murder. "That, dear
friends, is nothing next to what's coming," he would
rejoin smugly, as though he foreknew the future to come
swooping down upon that zone of the world. Don Alvaro
was a native of Salbago, on the far side of the Atlantic,
an island anyone who travelled from Spain to the New
World knew, if only in passing. So they had naturally
heard of Don Juan Rejón, his father, Governor of Salbago
and Adelantado of Castile, but they were innocent of the
internal dealings that had prompted his departure. When
the conversation lapsed into domestic episodes of the past,
Don Alvaro Rejón would retreat the first chance he got,
taking refuge, with some gravity, in his present position
and his upcoming plans. Like so, he cultivated around
himself a special aura of mystery and charm, rousing a
peculiar interest in people already by nature possessing
an exaggerated penchant for unwholesome curiosity,
prone, as the colonists were, to nosing around in their own
shit for the clue that would burst the scandal that would
crack open the secret sheltering gentlemen of substance
like Don Alvaro Rejón. Ringed by attentive and obedient
negro and mestizo servants, Don Alvaro Rejón spent his
days perusing his affairs, balancing the books of what was
deemed—with some exaggeration—an empire of slaves,
more or less hugger-mugger, strung like a rosary over the

little ports and marine hideaways of the Caribbean. He arranged and tended his most important affectations himself, the wee details of his public and private tenue, giving rise to laudatory remarks from his barfellows, with whom Rejón had little or nothing in common. After a few short months on Española, he knew the island inside out, riding unhindered on all the roads and over all the lands of all the landowners, to the ports and refuges farthest from Santo Domingo, in the constant company of two trusty mestizos, through whom he imparted orders and suggestions to his inferiors, his equals, or those whom, due to rank and class, were presumably superiors. He betrayed no sting of conscience in joshing about his principal profession, jesting and waggishly speculating about the potential for the slave market in these terrains in the near future. He (or so he claimed) knew of vast territories unsustainable without manpower that could guarantee discipline and labor, two of the principal factors wanting (he said) for the construction of a stable world the dimensions of which eluded any one of them. He spoke of Cuba, especially about Our Lady of the Assumption of Baracoa, the village where Hernando Cortés, Conqueror of Mexico, had been a scribe—before he was a fugitive, and long before he was the hero of Christendom and the Spanish Empire. He referred, with superb command, to the seas of the Gulf of Mexico, the curiousness of their currents, where alleged monsters dwelled in the deep which, though many made the claim, none had in fact seen. He enumerated, drawing on his impeccable knowledge, each of the cities Hernando Cortés had conquered—by force or by one of his famous ruses—to reach the very hub of the continental world, the city (as he described with every variety of detail) flowing with the purest air on earth, so much so that on opening their mouths the Spaniards felt an ever-so-sweet caress sifting down ticklishly into their lungs, and drowsing their spirits into a nirvana of breathlessness. He bounced, with infinite ease, from one part of the Imperial geography to another. He would talk of the sugar mills built by the Marquises del Valle in the outskirts of Cuernavaca, a town not far from the City of the Lake (where Conquistador Cortés himself reposed for long spells), or drift off into the tale of one of the expe-

ditions he had undertaken with his men to the farthest
verges of lost jungle territories or to the mouth of huge,
unknown and hence nameless rivers. He would wax prolix
on the subject of certain Veracruz specialties (at this
gastronomical juncture, he loved to describe the feasts of
crab with hot sauce he had sampled in those ports),
switching to talk, not without a measure of nostalgia, of
his Venezuelan properties, a spot he nonetheless returned
to during certain seasons of the year, depriving of his
conversation and his inimitable mythomania the Spanish
clientele who by now were no stranger to his songs,
stories, sagas, and tall tales of every color. To top it all,
his time spent in the tropical geography of the New World
had made him bit by bit into such an ace in botany that
the garden he cultivated in his private mansion in Santo
Domingo was unequalled throughout the realms of West
India. Surely, Don Alvaro Rejón was a gentleman who
had come into the world a century before his time. He was
a lay prophet, a perfect man of the future, a being who
had disencumbered himself, or so it seemed to all, of that
relish for heroism and daredevil fame in keeping with the
times, to take up instead a lively interest in serious
commerce, property, and an in-depth knowledge of lands
and peoples, never neglecting his principal perversion, the
distant origin of what would ultimately be his downfall:
women, and the berserk feeling waked inside him by
news, from one quarter or another, of the existence of a
distant, undiscoverable land, hidden somewhere in the
southern realm of the continent, studded with sacred
cities built, from the ramparts to the most primitive
dwellings, passing, naturally, by way of the temples,
entirely of gold. His secret obsession for the golden metal
was one of the qualities he shared with Mademoiselle
Pernod, the most cultivated whore on all the lands
conquered by the Spanish madness.

Mademoiselle Pernod presided over several houses of
assignation that had acquired fame, deserved and distinguished, for diabolical sublimity in all the gossip-shops
frequented by the hacendados and gentlemen who still
dreamed of becoming heroes of the Spanish Imperial
Crown. Known was her fanatic zeal for procuring and
providing services in those days unimaginable, sur-

rounding them all with rites of initiation that induced
delirium and slavish addiction in the Spaniards. In a land
where white women were a prize coveted second only to
gold (and in some cases of manifest eccentricity, second to
none), Mademoiselle Pernod had had the foresight to
administer with intelligence the commerce of sex, what
the vulgarness of the orthodox and anathema-crying officers of the Holy Inquisition and the flocks of mealymouthed friars swarming through the New World
unblushingly termed "the Empire of gutter passions." In
this as in all other aspects of her life, Mademoiselle
Pernod observed the world from on high, treating it as a
superior (she, the goddess) to an inferior (the world and
its supposed masters, men). Her word was law up to the
line which marked the blurry border of her own interests,
and within this vast, vast territory, staked out by her
natural method of granting the finest of her pleasures to
whoever happened to tempt her, she deftly managed the
immense possibilities of that profession the demise of
which the centuries would never see, from simple coitus
requested on the run by some captain or other stopping
over in Santo Domingo to the most intricate operations
culminating in holy matrimony, a dream breathed by over
half of her white cocottes in their moments of disenchantment and boredom, as they lay cooped up in the steamy
rooms—walls lavishly draped for that time and place—that
set the none-too-common scene in her bordellos. In this
way, Mademoiselle Pernod knew she was aiding the
Conquest and the conquistadors who had risen, thanks to
the Discovery, to a new station in life, forgetting the past,
forgetting the wretched remote peninsular villages and
snivelling families they had left behind on the other side
of the Atlantic. In this sense La Pernod was no exception
in that world of sudden glitter where fame and money
could be won overnight and conversely, lost again in a
moment's inadvertence that sent many of them back to
the obscurity from which they had risen a short time
before. Hence, with luscious adroitness she avoided letting
on to the real contempt she felt for these false marquises,
counts, captains, and gentlemen, squandering the provocative grace of a gesture of the hand, a stroke of the
fingernails on the dull heads of these velvety sirs, at the

same time her most faithful clients and confidants, who
understood almost better than she the slogan making the
rounds about her: "Within La Pernod, everything.
Without La Pernod, nothing." In her own way, La Pernod
was a sort of sacred Caribbean queen, possessing a beauty
as radiant as the gold she so adored. Even the stones
sweated when this chic madame passed by, of unknown
and hence always dubious origins, who doled out favors to
her privileged clients and sold white women to men who
charged her with the serious mission of securing them a
wife and a mother for their legitimate sons. For this
reason Mademoiselle Pernod did not admit into her
service just any girl who wished to join her stable of
whores. She drew a profound distinction between those
who would allow themselves to be led into amnesia and
total surrender, and the balky ones who would never
master this exacting vocation; between those who let
themselves be led by the hand, by her authority and
sagacity, trusting in the destiny Mademoiselle personally
guaranteed, sooner or later, and the pert girls who
mistakenly had it that they too were goddesses who with
time, instead of withering, would transform into made-
moiselles and thereby ultimately unseat their patroness.
The first, those deserving of her tutelage, she coached
with infinite patience in the most covert means of
mesmerizing the passions of the suitor who had gone
sweet on them, to the point of no return, a wedding before
the altar. The second sort, as though an inferior race, half-
breeds or negresses, she condemned to anonymous slavery,
penning them up for most of the day and night in the
scurvy dives she herself, La Pernod, had spawned
throughout the port of Santo Domingo. Unsparing with
the upstarts, generous to sometimes dangerous extremes
with those who acquiesced without reservations to her
total authority over them, Mademoiselle Pernod slowly
erected an indestructible commercial network, the tales
told about her and her cocottes buzzing over the Caribbean Sea. Known, though it could never be proven with
absolute certainty, was her habit of making love without
removing her gold high heels, the sight of which alone
tantalized men of every walk as she strolled down the
Royal Road. This was a bit of information that the lucky

man needed to turn to his advantage to extract maximum benefit from her amorous frenzy, which Mademoiselle Pernod lavished solely upon her handpicked. Another way (it was alleged) might be a clandestine dip in the secret waters of the pool sunk in the center of her mansion crammed with gold objects. Between sessions, Mademoiselle was indulgent with her whimsies, and would exhibit herself, dripping and smiling, like a mythological goddess in sacred waters, before the eyes of her lover of the hour, inviting him to bathe with her, and there, under the starlight and in the complicity of darkness, to perform a new variety of bliss (a ceremony reserved, frankly, for the very few, though many might claim to have experienced it firsthand), a proscribed ecstasy culminating in penetration from behind, through her smooth rectum, discovering—in pleasure and pain—the mystery of burning interwoven tissues where her lover's forces would constrict and converge at last. Day after day news and rumors of her own erotic feats reached Mademoiselle. Unrufflable, and always smiling with seeming and supposed semi-innocent naughtiness, she neither affirmed nor denied the words of those who had the spunk to bring her those tales. Her casual partners in pleasure she chose exclusively at her own sweet will, making them pay the highest prices. Only would she enslave them and torture them once they had tasted her breasts' sacred white potion and inhaled the effluvium emanating from her goddess body—primed in exotic perfumes and eaux de toilette—and at the very moment of penetrating the spread cheeks of her ass, they burned as never before.

Nor did anyone ever know for a certainty how Mademoiselle Pernod had wound up in the city of Santo Domingo, nor what true age was concealed in that taut body ever ready for love, nor what real name hid behind her glorious battle appellation. The oldest men in the place remembered her as always having been there, going so far as to avouch that she was already in Santo Domingo when they landed on Hispaniola. So the years elapsed for everyone save for her, who had never had children and whose escapades and caprices were always little known, at least if it was a matter of fixing a first and last name to the gentleman in question. But other

versions, far more twisted and slanderous, put into vogue
by some detractors motivated perhaps by spite, who had
dished themselves over for keeps to guarapo and cane
liquor, presented various scenarios tending to expand on
the idea that Mademoiselle Pernod had come to Hispaniola accompanied by a mestizo, young and strong as a
fighter bull, later to be known by all as Camilo Cienfuegos, whose black eyes full of rancor glittered like coals
as he sputtered mumbo jumbo and delusions of doctrines
rather advanced for the age and which, having been
judged dangerously heterodox had cost him his life shortly
after Don Alvaro Rejón came to live on the island. Cienfuegos (prattled the drunkards) may have been her first
illicit lover. Others, going still further, claimed he had
been her husband. But after their hypothetical split-up,
an uncrackable mystery closed around their alleged relations, and all the rumbles dwindled into chitchat which
crumbled as soon as any effort was made to lend them the
least semblance of authenticity. Mademoiselle Pernod and
Camilo Cienfuegos never exchanged a word, not so much
as a suspicious glance that might spur on the fabricators
of romance. Mademoiselle Pernod, dedicated body and soul
to the most refined of prostibules, betrayed no interest
whatever in this subversive character who brashly spoke
his mind in the harbor saloons and met under the rose on
haciendas of Spanish caballeros who, at least for the
moment, had fallen in with his secessionist doctrines.
Cienfuegos, whenever queried, would reply that he came
from Cuba, where he had been raised on one of the
island's first sugar refineries. He was a firebreathing
runaway slave, of dim origins, who no sooner did he land
on Santo Domingo than he was caught up in an incendiary language of harangues and squabbles, political spats
and perilous intrigue, firing up the hotheaded rabble on
the docks, tattered, faceless, inciting the slaves to rebel
against their masters and the dispossessed to rise up
against the Crown. Obnubilated by his own theories, like
a prophet priest who had lit upon the invisible threads of
a new religious faith, he yammered on and on, trying to
persuade them all, from Spaniards to illiterate half-
breeds, negroes and Indians, of a zany doctrine whose
maddest contentions always wound up in crude insults to

His Imperial Majesty and trumpeted the ultimate secession of the New World from the Metropolis and the Crown of Spain. A ludicrous madness that even so everyone wished to hear straight from the mouth of the apostle. So Cienfuegos would pitch his voice louder and impale with his eyes whoever contradicted his arguments. He flouted, with his fast, loose, brash talk, the genteel norms to which these parvenu gentlemen had already grown accustomed.

"You," screeched the incensed mestizo, "cannot see the future like I can, right out in front, clear as can be. You, señor, are a coward and a shit."

All their meetings ended with the supposed insurgents rattling against each other like the rosary of dawn, having gone there simply to debate vital issues of interest to all. In the wee hours, heads muzzy on swigged rum, scrambled the ideas they fancied they had elucidated, groggy with sleepiness and confusion, they would scrap and shout and even come to blows, vowing a fight to the death that would already have slipped their minds by the following day no sooner did the first effects of the hangover pass. When Don Alvaro Rejón was asked to one of these hush-hush meetings, he carefully observed Camilo Cienfuegos, who waxed that night even more brilliant and grandiloquent than usual. With his chums, Don Alvaro was blunt. "Cienfuegos," he said, during the card game which in the early hours of evening brought together several of his mainstays in his home, "is a man of the future. But paradoxically he has no future. He knows little of the workings of high politics and a lot about household tiffs. Even were he born in an age later than ours, when his ideas might enjoy more popularity and be better understood, his life would end the same. At the bottom of the sea." In the sleepy tropical heat of the Dominican afternoon, his words, pronounced with round, absolute conviction, rang of prophecy . . .

Fearing the passion that such a subject wakes incomprehensibly in the hearts of men (including those who soar above the others in intelligence), Mademoiselle Pernod flatly forbid all discussion of politics in her houses of fun. One could, on the other hand, strike up commercial alliances, concoct deals of every ilk, swap slaves or properties, buy and sell haciendas, launch plans for journeys and odd expeditions and live with all the superfluous loquacity that liquor and firewater bestow upon the souls of men who in such moments of inner ebullience believe themselves much freer than they in point of fact are. Within the natural discreetness that was the hard and fast rule in her parlors of pleasure, all was permitted. All but politics. "Politics," Mademoiselle Pernod would lovingly scold when one of her clients sloshed over in this regard, "is the mother of all vices," a slogan that served as a reminder, and was hung on placards, by strict regulation, in a conspicuous spot in the foyers of her houses. It may have been this special taboo of La Pernod's against politics that someone had twistedly put to use to clinch the link between Mademoiselle and Camilo Cienfuegos. "Maybe," they said, "she lost him to politics, and this is her way of wreaking revenge."

Don Alvaro Rejón, as one could only assume, was a habitué of Mademoiselle Pernod's, and though bedazzled by the libertine beauty of this woman of revery, he curbed his ecstasies, eyeing the madame on the sly with long, penetrating glances. Slowly his desires were turning to fixations, waking him in the dead of night drenched in sweat, his sex tantalized by those dreams that upset his sleep. That urge was now a reflex, a wanton instinct escaping his body with an urgent tremble and an ever colder and clammier sweat that ripped up his patience and fevered his most intimate glands. On these sleepless nights, listening to a thousand creakings set off by the edgy malaise that had burrowed itself in his soul, Don Alvaro Rejón repeated over and over the tip that Don Luciano Esparza, the unplugger-doctor whose profession had won him a fortune in the Caribbean ports, proffered him one afternoon while they were playing cards. "To reach her," said Doctor Esparza, referring to Mademoiselle, "one must have a great store of patience and be prepared to forfeit all to her beauty. Then it's a matter of luck. You must take it step by step, leaving in her houses of joy a fortune in gold, which not everyone possesses. All of us, my friend, fall in her snare, from the Governor down to the plainest gentlemen, who ask only to be near her. But Mademoiselle cunningly places little stones, tiny impediments in our path. Yes, my friend, so it is. We tucker out and wind up lugging off whichever little floozy we run across, when we see we can't touch the skirts of the goddess." Luciano Esparza was speaking from personal experience, Don Alvaro gathered, being that it was broadly rumored, to say the least, that the doctor's young wife had been, some time ago, a favorite cocotte of Mademoiselle Pernod.

"I'll be damned!" Don Alvaro exclaimed wryly, as if for him Mademoiselle's person held no interest. "It's harder to hump her than to climb Mount Carmelo! How my partner would love this story!"

In his conversations, full of frothy bonhomie, and in his more sober, responsible dealings, Don Alvaro Rejón would roll out the existence of an associate, whose first or last names he never happened to mention, as a prefatory excuse for not purchasing a batch of slaves that had arrived already limp and stinking in Santo Domingo's black market ("I am sure," he would mumble circumspectly, "my partner would not back this acquisition . . ." or to decline joint ventures put to him by some hacendado ("I'd need a little time to confer with my partner," he would demur thoughtfully), what to the astute listener, wise to these sorts of proceedings and hanky-panky, meant that Don Alvaro Rejón was not overly impressed by the operation in question.

It was, in form and substance, a formidable mode of thought. Far behind him lay the imprudences of his youth in Salbago, the crass cockinesses of that rude, unruly islander who had fled like a soul possessed by the devil from the far side of the sea and run aground at some hazy spot on the coast of the Colony of Venezuela, where he had dug in, and from where he had toured the greater part of the known geography of the islands and Terra Firma, allying his name to ventures and transactions always, or nearly always, crowned with success. That night, drenched in the sweat of unrealized desire, the semen wrestling to burst the glistening glans he jerked in his hand like a desperate boy, Don Alvaro Rejón lit on the idea of proposing to Mademoiselle Pernod a commercial alliance that would open the doors to her affections, an unlikely affair that would spark the interest of that unattainable goddess with whom he was head over heels in love, and which ultimately would spare him the long roundabout route with all its perils described to him by the pudgy unplugger, his bosom buddy, Don Luciano Esparza.

Between sips of hot brewed coffee, Don Alvaro Rejón wove, in the smirking dawn, the scheme that would smash the parapets girding Mademoiselle Pernod. He would propose, while not discounting the shock it would at first cause the madame, that together they launch a new establishment, not with women this time, but with sea cows. He would bankroll, and foot the expenses, of this palace of bestiality he had masterminded. To her, naturally, would fall the work and responsibility of management, and the inductive methods for persuading her gentlemanly clientele of the pleasurous magnitude of this perversion. Later, much calmer now, his cravings and night shivers abated, day dawning, he drifted off and dozed until the early hours of afternoon, when a leftover clap of that same shudder woke him suddenly sopped in sweat and again overpowered by the pestering tremble of desire.

Never till then had he exchanged so much as a word or a glance with Mademoiselle Pernod, apart from the amicable greetings that were a must between client and madame. Rather difficult this made it, therefore, to speak with her alone about the scheme he had drummed up, though it was a fact that Mademoiselle was alert to his seriousness in such matters, of his gentlemanly status, and all the social minutiae known in the public gossip-shops of Santo Domingo City. He hid, as best he could, the quivery reflex that drew a nervous tic in his face and fixed his expressions (on other occasions slack or tinged with conceit) with a shadow of insecurity, touched off, in his vitals, by the bedazzlement of finding himself alone and so close to the Invincible Darling.

"Yes, Mademoiselle. Sea cows." He modulated his syllables slowly. "Or bulls. The male too." And he opened his arms at the moment of his proposition as though surrendering to the obvious, that on these shores sexual perversion knew no bounds.

Mademoiselle Pernod looked at him hard, as though the

idea astonished her. Never before had she really taken note of this colonist, whose long blond hair betrayed his European descent. Never had she guessed that behind the evident—almost courtly—chivalry of Don Alvaro Rejón lurked such an eccentric and imaginative mind. Despite her long experience as a madame, she could not stifle—at the moment their eyes met—a pale blush, which she endeavored to mask behind a smile of professional politeness. Tastefully apparelled, scented with a perfume he had shipped to him by covert channels from faraway France, Señor de Rejón retrieved his composure during his conversation with Mademoiselle Pernod. With cultivated (even affected) delectation, he lifted to his lips the beverage of rum and coconut fixed for him by Mademoiselle herself. He displayed before her his most gallant manners, having no idea just then where he had learned them. Slowly, like an old hand, a man of the world, he sparked the enthusiasm of Mademoiselle Pernod, enraptured as she was, whitest of goddesses, by the eloquence of this slave-trader captain who recounted his feats without reverting to that self-puffery that was common practice among her other more churlish customers. As dusk fell, they sealed their deal with a far more sophisticated toast: herb liquor laced with the nut-brown pulp of the tamarind. Don Alvaro Rejón observed, meanwhile, how night was descending upon them and how the drink imbibed by Mademoiselle Pernod had loosened her tongue for confidences she shared with only her dear friends, her very most intimate friends, she commented with giggles of complicity. He noted La Pernod's stifled breath, the desire welling in her eyes, saw with bewilderment and flattered manliness the craving his person engendered in Mademoiselle, who in gales of more or less hysterical laughter announcing the preludes of her final surrender, peeled from her body the precious raiment that draped her, a show she held in safekeeping for her dear friends, her very dearest friends. And that night, the habitual drones of darkness rising about them, bodies naked and interwined, they bathed together in the pool of white marble hidden in Mademoiselle's hiddenmost mansion. She wore—as vaunted by legend—those golden high-heel shoes as he pumped her, splashing in the warm water,

moans of passion and pleasurous laughter pealing into the
night. Then she rolled over and washed him with rose
salts that brought a luscious white froth to the face of the
water. Over and over she played with his penis until she
had inflamed it again so that Don Alvaro Rejón would
penetrate her from behind—as the legend went—ramming
and ramming her in search of new juices in innernesses
few could boast of having explored. In the transports of
pleasure, from Mademoiselle Pernod's nipples flowed—as
recounted by legend—that mythological liquid the people
of Santo Domingo knew of by hearsay alone and to which
they attributed restorative properties, as if Mademoiselle
herself held within her the sought-after fountain of
eternal golden youth. Seven times running, in all the
positions Mademoiselle knew to perfection, Don Alvaro
Rejón shot his sexual humors into the secret concavities
of his beloved. All through the night, in the splashy
waters or between the gold silk sheets of Mademoiselle's
bed, around him he heard the cheeping of celestial birds.

Like so a passionate, stormy union was born, reviled
and envied by friends and strangers alike, a frenzy
undying in their hearts for a long time, enwrapping them
through the days and nights, as though for them time did
not pass, as though the things of this world were devoid
of any interest save for that which they themselves lent
it, as if both had forgotten their private affairs and abandoned themselves passionately and playfully to exclusive
delirious gusto for the variations of love. News of their
amours escaped Santo Domingo, twisting like a cyclone
across the borders of Hispaniola, brooking the jeers of
those who could not countenance the most whorish,
gorgeous hetaira on the Caribbean Sea dished up to a
gentleman of such rocky recent past, a slaver, in short,
who had captured the heart of Mademoiselle Pernod,
known by the hacendados and Antillean wooers as the
Invincible Darling, the only woman worth her salt in all
of West India, over the Caribbean Sea, from the Gulf of
Mexico to the shores of Venezuela.

The languid strolls of Mademoiselle Pernod and Don Alvaro Rejón gradually ceased to astonish the citizens of Santo Domingo, who in the cool evenings scurried into the narrow streets to eye one another, to greet pleasantly, face to face, as though the passions that divide people, turning them into little less than enemies each of each, did not—at that hour—obtain. It was a tradition they had been cultivating since the founding of Santo Domingo City, since the laying of the Royal Road and the peaceful plazuelas owing their existence to this: to nod to one another, to chitchat about the events of the day, the news that came in from Spain reporting on the religious wars raging in Europe, or from the south of Terra Firma, touching off frenzies of ambition in men who had put aside adventuring and its vicissitudes for a settled life and the amassing of a fortune via overseas trade in spices and other less divulgeable products. And here among them were Mademoiselle Pernod and Alvaro Rejón: she, smiling about brassily at all who, having stopped through one or another of her houses of profligacy, had become the Madame's potential victims of blackmail, her golden parasol afloat in the evening air, visible from any vantage on the Royal Road, rousing, in passing, the most ambiguous commentaries, and contortions of contained desire, her figure like a beguiling gazelle's, as if levitated, tenuously linked to the impossible cobbles of the Royal Road by way of those legendary little gold high heels, a tantalizing perfume accompanying the slow wiggle of this fabulous treasure on exclusive reserve for those exquisite lovers who comprehend that perversion is one of the aims of human love, hips asway and with a silent smirk of

complicity, at a given moment in the promenade, as
Alvaro Rejón swaps a word or two with local worthies; he,
eyes everyplace but not stopping to perch on anything or
anyone, as if steering oft-travelled waters, brows raised a
touch to evince pride or superiority, his longer, slower
steps keeping pace with hers, hands nearly always at his
back, a look on his face between ennui and mockery, as
though it was utterly necessary that they all know she
was bonded to him, that she belonged to him, and once
this point was made crystal clear, they could let fly with
their rebukes and slander for all he cared, for nothing
would it do to change his conduct.

It was around this time that, on a somewhat desultory
voyage (like nearly all things of the day) one of those
dolled-up pages that the Court of His Imperial Majesty
liked to boost to higher magistracies, charging them with
the ever-so-special mission of parading their European
pedantry through the lands discovered by the Admiral
and conquered by those mad captains who had abandoned
their native peninsular soil with the idea of hitting it rich
on the New Continent, stopped in Santo Domingo on his
way to Spain. This time the Ambassador was a native of
Valladolid, tall, slim, finicky to the point of unctuousness,
a trifle affected, presumptuous, and almost always
disdainful, with a lecherous pout on his vaguely uneven
jaw. His perfectly white skin he protected from the harsh
rays of the sun beneath a black silk parasol carried at all
times by an Indian slave placed in his service, at his
express behest and petition, in all the ports where he
halted to make his inspections, and where the orgies
arranged for him at his request were already becoming
famous. The women, the prepubescent lasses and callow
little mulatto lads with whom he was bedded down most
of the day and night did not suffice for the Ambassador.
What he asked, and unthinkably so, was that the pleasures put to him bear him simply one step farther in his
mad race into the abyss of degeneracy. In Santo Domingo,
Ambassador Diego de Medina pounced like a voracious
bird on each and every one of the disconsolate Mademoiselle Pernod's strumpets. Like an Imperial inspector of
Caribbean whoredom, he visited each of the dives that
gave quarter to pleasure in the city of Santo Domingo.

Slakeless, Don Diego de Medina sought any and every
experience that might rouse lust in his loins. In parlor
after parlor, ball after ball, reception after reception, the
Ambassador of His Imperial Catholic Majesty was bored,
once he had sampled, virtuoso connoisseur, the flavors of
every pleasure, singling out for repetition, as a prize,
those delicacies that seemed more capacious than the rest,
which he classified, with a fleer, as common fare. This
unrepentant stud, this oily character uncurbable in
private contests of lust, was able, nonetheless, to uphold
the rank conferred on him by the Emperor of the Spains.
There was no memory in Santo Domingo of any other of
Emperor Carlos' many envoys who had possessed such
enviable ardor, cause for general commentary, and which,
due to how drawn-out his trip was becoming, had begun
to alarm the townspeople, who were in this regard rather
disinclined to deride one of their racier entertainments.
Even so, this longness of body, spirit, and libido did not
dare to woo Mademoiselle Pernod, even knowing as he did
that Don Alvaro Rejón, her lover of notoriety, was absent
from the city on one of his mysterious junkets around the
Caribbean Sea, visiting those ports, hideaways, and
markets the Salbagan knew like none other. They told
him, tongues always forked, of Mademoiselle's generous
capriciousness with persons of high and noble standing,
the variety of her pleasures and pastimes, the revels and
orgies the Madame dispensed within the walls of her
forbidden haciendas where none but the lucky few could
enter. Like so, Don Diego de Medina began his long,
ceaseless peregrination from bedroom to bedroom,
chamber to chamber, balcony to balcony, surrendered to
sophisticated hedonism and those concupiscent niceties
that Mademoiselle Pernod dished to him daily in her
effort to escape, by any manner of means, being among
those impaled on the concatenate spear of this dignitary
of the Royal Court, whom, according to what Don Luciano
Esparza had told her, nothing could be refused. Guided,
all the same, by that foxy wisdom with which time and
experience had graced her, Mademoiselle, while heaping
smiles and exclusive entertainments on Don Diego de
Medina, had saved, for the imminent return of Don
Alvaro Rejón, the final fête, the ultimate ecstasy, the

sybaritic lust sure to be roused in the Ambassador by a wild romp with the sea cows.

Don Alvaro de Rejón swiftly established friendly relations with His Imperial Majesty's lickerish ambassador, dedicating long hours of conversation to cracking the reserve that those Pelasgian eyes—pigmented with Priapism—cast back at him whenever the Salbagan strutted out the stories of his life, endless tales, marvels he described to the Ambassador as though there in the flesh. That afternoon, completely relaxed, they drank hot brewed coffee, which served as a stimulant and a stimulus, launching them into as-yet-unexplored conversational waters. It was then that Don Alvaro Rejón decided to take the plunge and speak to Don Diego de Medina about the sea cows, the mermaids and mermen that he and Mademoiselle Pernod had trained for love with human beings in a paradise not more than fifteen miles from Santo Domingo City. "Not just anyone may enter there, Ambassador," Rejón sighed, winking at the depraved Vallidolidian. "Only connoisseurs and bosom friends," he added. Don Diego de Medina checked his surprise. Until that moment he had received only vague reports of the Caribbean sirens and all he knew went up in whorls of smoke as soon as he applied his rationalist mind and European erudition to an in-depth analysis, turning up the same conclusion as always: mermaids did not even exist, they were mythological creatures, and that was that. A mere figment of the overheated imaginations of Spaniards who had gone berserk in their efforts to subdue a land whose dimensions more often than not turned out to be illusions of the idlest sort. He remembered that the song sung by those beings was purely mythological. And so the only way to right the carnal wrong pumping in his heart was to take the bull by the horns, forget his courtly scruples, and play it to the hilt, as if he knew what was what. Mademoiselle Pernod, present as always, observed with drooped eyes the process of persuasion her lover cast over the Ambassador who, trammelled in the nets of this smooth talker who had toured all the worlds of the Empire, began to slip into a ticklish tenderness from which he would not be free until he had seen with his own eyes and tasted with his own

unquenchable senses the sweet madness of those beasts
trained for love. And Alvaro Rejón already knew that the
Emperor's envoy paid no attention to the stupid distinc-
tions between the sexes in human beings, which meant (if,
that is, deductions translate into deeds) that among the
mermaids and mermen Don Diego de Medina would attain
the swinish climax of depravity.

Don Diego de Medina, even skinnier now from his
incessant abandon to every sort of pleasure and profligacy, his skin pallid, his eyes ever eager to behold what
Europe termed delusions of madmen, spent six days and
six nights fucking and pleasuring those sea creatures,
whose glossy skin, smooth as a feather, kept his penis
always erect. Forgetting his station, he flip-flopped in the
pools with the sea cows, stroking the stiffened nipples of
those sea-ladies (as he preferred to call them) who sported
(in place of thighs, calves and feet) a playful, rubbery,
pronged tail they used, in the hot throes of love, for
fanning, or for inserting tenderly into the Ambassador's
softest hole. The ecstasy kept him aroused for weeks of
total orgy, during which his lecherous madness cut
through all commonplaces, flouted all taboos; from
frisking with the mermaids, he turned to nuzzling with
the mermen, who from the waist down exhibited the same
features as the mermaids, with the distinction of a tiny
penis, a mammalian softness the Emperor's Ambassador
took it upon himself to masturbate in delirious rapture.
One by one, each of those creatures fell before him, and
still Don Diego manifested no desire to quit that
mansionful of mythy pleasures made to his measure.
Exhilarated, intoxicated by the eccentric excellence of the
service, that dissolute being breakfasted, lunched, and
dined in the shadow of sea cows *en fleur;* there he drank,
slept, and dreamed.

"His Majesty Prince Felipe," the Ambassador remarked
to Don Alvaro Rejón one day, "would be tickled to own
one of these creatures for his pleasure and diversion.
Imagine, my friend, what it would be like to have in
Court, to shock all those noblemen wearying him with
intrigues of State and bunk like that, one of these sea
cows! What a riot! The Prince is a genuine enthusiast of
all things exotic on earth. He knows a lot about such

things, my friend. My dear friend! To have one of these
as a gift would fill the Prince with happiness," he said,
still feverish from his own experience, as he swabbed the
sweat from his brow with a white silk handkerchief
fringed in lace of baroque design.

Meanwhile, life in Santo Domingo trundled on, buzzing
with talk of the depravity that Don Diego de Medina,
Ambassador of His Imperial Sacred Majesty, had picked
up there, among those degenerates. Don Alvaro Rejón,
wise to the nervousness taking hold of the Governor of
Hispaniola, sent him daily and respectful missives urging
calm but which only provoked, in this island notable, a
flurry in his mind, envy in his heart for having been
excluded from those lascivious get-togethers, and irate
thoughts trapping him in dark, depressive zones.

In the end it was necessary to use all means of persuasion, all ploys, all the white lies and good offices of Don
Alvaro Rejón and Mademoiselle Pernod to separate the
Ambassador from this unlikely house of secrets where the
whores happened to be stark naked sea cows more
wondrous and dextrous in games of love than any of the
women Don Diego had ever favored. Restored to his
senses, now Don Diego de Medina was addled by
conflicting thoughts, unsettling his soul and the serenity
he needed to put to sea, to embark on a long voyage,
always dull and uncomfortable, to the lands of Spain, a
boring, dying country, as he was now inclined to think.
How the hell, to cite an example, were they ever to
believe him over there in doddering Europe, full of false
glitter and phony languages, torn by religious wars and
senseless battles, determined to prove and prove again,
with the help of science and libraries, that they were
rather far from comprehending the New World, how the
devil were they going to believe that he, Don Diego de
Medina, Ambassador by the Grace of His Catholic and
Imperial Majesty Carlos, King of all the known world, had
fucked, at a breakneck pace, dozens of mermaids with
slippery, sexy, smooth sea-creature skin, with roundish
nipples and smiling songful faces, who rather than legs
had long extremities that ended in a forked tail they used
for fanning his ass while he humped them? Who would
ever believe such colossal madness? How the goddamn, to

name but another example, would he prove to his friends
at Court that he had fornicated for upwards of six days
with little sirenian boys, hairless but for their lank blond
pubes, a sweetness without equal summoning waves of
strange, tumultuous pleasure at a temperature much
hotter than could be attained in the ritziest bordellos of
the cities of Europe and the Imperial Court? What did he
stand to gain if he had to keep mum about these events,
which he classed as sublime experiences, lest he be taken
for a daft, hopeless liar? Counts, dukes, marquises,
viscounts, gentlemen, pages, captains and even princes
who until now had been his friends and confidants would
shun his stories and desert him like a dog, which was
certain to incur, as an immediate consequence, his fall
from favor at Court. They would think he was deluded, or
feverish, or worse, possessed by the devil and tempting
the flames of the bonfire where heretics and dissenters
burn. And yet, when all was ready for the voyage home,
he was excruciatingly certain that it was not a dream he
had lived, but that he had committed all those forbidden
acts in flesh and blood; he felt them to be part of his life
even if the story had to be cached, a memory indelible, in
some secret attic of his mind. He was half crazed, a
changed man from the longing that had, in anticipation,
nestled into his heart. Only the genius of a man of the
world like Don Alvaro Rejón could have foreseen what
would happen to the Ambassador, the psychological
maladjustments that would warp his nerves.

"You may take one with you, Señor Ambassador,"
blurted Don Alvaro Rejón suddenly, as Don Diego was
musing aloud in his presence about the fooleries and infa-
tuations to which he had been led by the Caribbean
sirens. "Like that," Don Alvaro said with a smile, "no one
can doubt your adventures and feats."

This was the magic formula that Don Alvaro Rejón, his
accomplice, after all, had prepared for the Ambassador.
But still the Salbagan did not succumb to the invitation
extended to him by Don Diego de Medina, to accompany
him on his long journey home to Spain. He resisted, as
best he could, the temptation to travel to the Peninsula,
to see the Court, its airs and graces, its pomp, its smooth
and cultivated manners. He knew he was forfeiting the

finest opportunity of his life. He dreamed for an instant of the friendship of powerful princes, statesmen, counts, dukes, and all the high honors of the Empire. Don Diego de Medina could open doors for him, this was a fact. Drowsy and downcast, he turned to look at the city of Santo Domingo, then glanced back at the sea lying black and hostile in the darkness, and slowly he blotted from his mind all thought of the voyage that would have taken him back to Spain, to the Peninsula, a land upon which he had never nor would ever set foot in his life. "You can't run with the hares and hunt with the hounds," said Rejón to himself with a trace of sadness in his thoughts.

A wind seldom seen, icy and unremitting, that had whipped up on the open sea, making the galleys pitch and roll, chased the Spanish Imperial Armada to very near the shores of the Italian city of Genoa—the chosen city—which has been in a twitter for days over preparations for the welcome to be proffered to His Catholic Majesty, Prince Felipe, the hope of Christendom, soon to be lord of the supreme Empire of the known world. Despite the darkness of night and the autumn wind, the twenty-seven galleys and myriad ships that make up the main body of the Armada sight from afar the lights of the port and the city awaiting it with open arms, intoning its finest songs of welcome. Around about ten o'clock in the evening, precisely on the historic date of the twenty-fifth of November, 1548, under favorable skies, taken by the savants to be a very good sign, the Imperial Armada sails into Genoa. Naval exercises commence at once, and last on and on, the prowess of the seamen responding to the orders of their boatswains as a single man. With grand majesty and lentor, as befits him who stands captain, the fleet furrows the waters, making way into the harbor with perfect harmony and discipline, flag-bedecked from stem to stern, nobility glittering in the wind, its splendidmost standards flying. More than a thousand pennants flutter their insignia among the masts and spars.

Arriving is the Prince of Princes, glory of the Spains and hope of the Empire. Deafening salvos of artillery fire greet him, booming and booming through the plaza, while the ships now berthing at the Genoese docks reply to the joy of the welcome with earsplitting salutes of cannon and harquebuses, spattering the sky with such thick heavy smoke that now indeed from the ships one can barely make out the city, feverishly waiting, or the hills where the last lights of Genoa climb away. Now the solemn operation of disembarkation begins, executed with the same harmony and discipline as the entry maneuver into the harbor of the Italian port. One by one those who constitute the magnificence and pomp of the Imperial Court alight. Princes, cardinals, dukes, the Admiral of Castile, marquises, counts, bishops, knight-commanders, gentlemen, pages, wise and learned men who oversee letters, arts and sciences, captains, men of the cloth, officers of every stripe, doctors, scientists, inventors, craftsmen, painters, writers already of universal renown, musicians, choristers of the royal chapel, the full guard with firm resolute air, stablemen, cooks, an entourage of inimitable pomp never before beheld by the eyes of the world, an army of dignitaries who accompany, and constitute the personal service of, His Highness Prince Felipe, an entire illustrious cultured cultivated people travelling alongside their Lord, providing him, moreover, with fecund and lively companionship. Drums, trumpets and tubas keep time with the nobles of the Court, a spectacle the magnificence of which human eyes, in Genoa, have never before witnessed, a sublime cortège brandishing, on this august occasion, its finest regalia, its weapons cleaned, oiled, and shining. His Catholic Majesty, later to be known the universe over by the name of Felipe II, has doffed, for this occasion, a long purple velvet cloak with silks and trim that further exalt his serene face glowing with the satisfaction of the historic moment and, if only for today, camouflaging that deep brooding sadness that has pervaded the Prince (imperishable poison) ever since he was widowed three years ago, on his eighteenth birthday.

Every man in the valiant Genoese army, stationed in the post for which he has long been trained, now stands in wait for the lords of the Court, lining the shore, bearing witness to the lofty magnanimity of the welcome. Honor to whom honor is due. Hence nothing has been left to chance, nothing to fate, not a thread of protocol has slipped from the knot tied, during the time taken to bring the preparations to completion, by the Court specialists,

who of necessity preceded the Armada by many days, to
oversee disbursals, and the formalities of the ceremony
that would come to pass on the Prince's arrival. From the
harbor sands, three long, long bridges of wood reach
toward the waters of the sea, and out over them. The
middle one is naturally assigned to convey His Imperial
Highness to the Genoese mainland. It is garlanded with
flowers and wreaths breathing freshness, with flags and
banners hailing the presence in this ceremony of all the
lands of the Empire. Sided by broad windows, it resem-
bles an Italian pergola. At the foot, a baldachin draped
with precious cloths awaits, with yearning and respect,
the coming of the son of King Carlos, Felipe the Magnan-
imous, the Immense, the almighty scion of the Emperor.

All the city of Genoa feels that it cannot bear its impatience to view with its own eyes the glorious retinue and
join the procession. So they throng in the streets,
hallooing and hurrahing, where in the crowd no distinc-
tions are drawn for class or rank, the sage and illustrious
members of the Senate mixing in the mob with the ruck
who grime the city's slums with their daily vagabondage,
and the riffraff who since time immemorial have been the
absolute proprietors of ports. All sweatily squeeze and
jostle, wanting to partake, albeit anonymously, in a spectacle they know is unrepeatable, glad for once to be a
fundamental part of the occasion, in high feather, each
after his own fashion outdoing his own good taste, the
gentlemen tricked out as nobles, the rubes as gentlemen,
the bevies of hussies from the Genoese bordellos as ladies
whose honor has never visited the sordid bed of purchased
pleasure, as princesses the high-toned dames smiling from
their balconies bedecked with flags in a crisscross of every
color.

The Genoese authorities are mindful of who is their
guest, gather the importance of the name Felipe in this
age of religious unrest, and with this in mind have
readied the route he will follow, where the thrilled public
now flurries to greet him. Along this same route curious
pyrotechnical contrivances are neatly posted and set to go,
into which the most magisterial makers of fireworks have
poured all their knowledge and devotion. Here is a castle
hanging in the air, forsooth, aflame with colored fire,

while Felipe waves, pleasant and gracious, though always with that grim indrawnness at the depth of his darker looks, replying to the cheers of the crowd.

From the ships of the Armada, as Prince Felipe treads the Genoese streets, wending his way toward the Palazzo Doria, the music swings on, so many instruments playing together that never had the ages heard sounds more harmonious, sweet and complex, songs to which the rejoicing populace responds with ceaseless mirth. Arcades, carpets, tapestries, canopies, wreaths, flowers, an opulent, spectacular display meets the newcomers as they hike on, ringed by hundreds of flaming torches, that flood with light, that fracture the silence of the autumnal Mediterranean night.

His Catholic Majesty will lodge, as is only to be expected, in the parlors and bedrooms of the Palazzo Doria, likewise frilled and festooned for this unforgettable occasion. The cortège is now reaching the steps of the Palazzo and Felipe slowly mounts, pausing majestically a moment or so to evince a silent interest in certain paintings and artifacts, emblems of the long saga of Spain in the world. Gilded signboards lettered in showy characters in the Latin tongue extend praise, glory, and congratulations to the Prince as he advances, now entering the bedchamber where the walls, he finds, are draped with new tapestries woven of wools and silks, and where, like a mythological paradise, hang paintings in cloth of gold depicting in detail the journey of Aeneas the Trojan from the Hellenic coasts to the lands of Lazio.

He is not yet King. He has not yet been crowned Imperial Majesty, and he already senses, in the distance, the formidable grandeur of lands of which he has heard his father's ambassadors speak. Try as he might, from the moment he is crowned King until—after long years of rule—he attains the grave, he cannot make peace with his sorrow. Seated on his throne in San Lorenzo of El Escorial, he detachedly observes the Court of his Empire, Madrid, which has divested other capitals of this honor. Madrid, the Court from which the old King will try to dissuade the young Emperor, the Court silently eclipsing Valladolid, sapping Toledo's strength in History, growing further and further from Lisbon. He does not yet know that when he is Emperor, enshrouded in that cloud of sorrow that will accompany him forever, he will go to the bedside of the Imperial glutton to beg counsel of the experience of his predecessor in the seat of the Empire, and after conversing with the old man for several hours, will broach the question of the location of the Court. "If you wish the Empire to stand as is, put the Court in Toledo. If you want to expand it, put it in Lisbon. But if you wish to lose it, place it in Madrid," the ancient Imperial lion will submit, chewing the victuals brought to his chambers by his son, Felipe II, as a special treat. Now in the Palazzo Doria, elated, at the fore of that procession ashimmer with all the splendor of the Empire he is to inherit and whereby Spain, olympian and stately, displays her powers, amid doctors, savants, nobles, bishops and cardinals, Felipe, an aficionado of history and things worthy of exalted minds, brings with him three satyrs newly arrived from the Indies on board one of those many caravels that ply the Sea of Dusk with the same ease with which he, His Catholic Majesty, gazes from side to side, responding to the hoorays of the crowd. The satyrs, as they are known by all the Court, are two males (aged ten and forty years) and one female. And among these wonders spawned nowhere anymore but the New World, the Prince brings—rare curiosity for the amazement of the Italians—a dead mermaid in a crystal and rosewood urn, as well as many other exotic forms of animals and beings whose genesis God and Nature slated for the coming of the New Ages. The mermaid, also called a sea cow, boasts the body of a woman from the waist up, and her closed eyes make her look like she's sleeping. Below, the body splits into two huge rubbery tails, resembling those of saltwater fishes, and at the spot where these part is a mound of yellow fluff occluding from view the creature's sex.

Entering Genoa under Felipe's baldachin is the Cardinal of Trent, Cristóforo Madruzzo, bastion of Catholicism and horror of heretics the world over, whose weary, sleep-swollen face betrays the profound worry in his spirit prompted by the discussions of the Council and the severe problems it must confront if it is to quash the heterodoxy threatening to engulf Europe, a new outbreak surging over all the territories like a scourge of the devil. Respectfully, and as if to play down his pressing problems, the Cardinal joshes with the young Prince. His journey replies, in fact, to an invitation from Felipe, who in Valladolid, in the absence of Emperor Carlos, oversaw the royal nuptials of his sister María and the Archduke Maximiliano, his cousin, so that, by this form and fashion of union, the branches of the illustrious golden Imperial tree of the Hapsburgs might go on intwining. Dignified, charming, the Prince of Hope treasures within him a memory of that wedding, where in every instance duties of State outweighed the lapsed health of the groom. Maximiliano, sick with recurring malarial fevers, shivering and sweating at once, could not but attend his wedding on the stipulated date. It was an act of grace on his part, a royal sacrifice in every sense, to set aside his ravaged health and step up to the altar, as an obligation of the highest order. Naturally, the date was of the essence. Otherwise Prince Felipe, upon whom the eyes of all Christendom now turn to look, branding him Successor to the Imperial Throne, could not have attended the event, for his duties would have hindered him. His Imperial Majesty is already ailing, wracked by ills, sapped by the spiral of violence that has shaken Europe, and by the religious war triggered by the Reformation. No rest. No sleep. Yet he eats and eats, gorging himself with the same immoderacy and gulosity as ever. Moment by moment, like a lynx sheltering her lair from the claws of beasts, he surveys the movements of his enemies over the map of Europe, while reposing in Germany in the wake of one of his countless military or political victories, which he cannot even enjoy. He is the first to note the decline in his long life of Invincible Emperor (and unrepentant guttler), and he sees approaching the sorrow that will escort him to death, that eminence now beginning to throttle his blood. He hears word of the feats of his young son and is content: the Imperial Crown will rest upon a sound head, beyond a doubt. The Prince, at the hour of his sister's wedding, feels weary. He is tormented by loneliness, wherefore he would soon journey to the lands of Flanders. Hence he presided over the wedding with some haste, though the occasion evinced all the pomp and splendor befitting its heroes. Felipe (now reminiscing in the halls of the Palazzo Doria) conducted himself with a fincsse as sublime as it was swift, scarcely pausing to take part in the celebration or the festivities that followed the religious ceremony. Maximiliano and María, wedded now before God and the Empire, would remain in Spain in command of the regency.

Prince Felipe's voyage from Barcelona to Genoa is luxuriant and dazzling. He tours all the European domains of the Empire, over which he is to reign for ever so long, and on this periplus blazoning power and nobility he will be ringed by the loftiest luminaries ever to contemplate the ages together. It is a matter of illustrating the solidity of the Empire and the might of Christendom in whose name wars, conquests and massacres are waged, cities burned and other new ones founded, men are damned and beheaded or uplifted and hailed. Escorting His Catholic Majesty are statesmen (intrigants and exegetes of the history of nations, alliances, pacts, treaties and declarations of war, of blackmail and military dissuasion, peace and war), dignitaries of the Church and soldiers acclaimed for their stalwartness in a thousand battles. This, in fact, is the triad whereby Carlos, the Great Caesar, maintains the power of the world in his right fist, the selfsame power he will bequeath to his son. Here as well are the Duke of Alba, the Admiral Andrea Doria (rivalled by Cristóforo Colombo alone, as the Italians call him, whose name has passed into legend), Cristóforo Madruzzo, the Cardinal of Trent and scourge of heretics, the Admiral of Castile, the Marquis of Pescara, Don Bernardo de Mendoza, Don Berenguer de Requesens, and many Spaniards more, their names lending brilliance to History and to the Empire in the eyes of the world. These were the days of the preponderance of the one destined to be the Prince of Eboli, also occupying a top spot in the entourage, as do Don Gonzalo Pérez and Don Gonzalo Suárez de Figueroa, today Captain of the Guard and in time, for his stout services, his gallantry and loyalty, the Duke of Feria and royal favorite. In Felipe's cortège, in the highest rank for the magnificence of his eloquence, marches Doctor Constantino, upon whom the suspicions of the Holy Inquisition, ultimately to accuse him of Erasmianism, have not yet

fallen. His Catholic Majesty, cognizant of the bedazzlement induced by his stardom, of the awe inspired by his
presence in people of every ilk, has sought the company
of no small number of learned men, inviting them to
travel beside him. Here, for example, is the Valencian
humanist Honorato de Juan. And artists who have
already achieved wide and notable celebrity, the chief
example of whom might be the blind musician Antonio de
Cabezón, inventor of diferencias. He is accompanied
besides by the intellectual hauteur of Don Diego Hurtado
de Mendoza, by now famous all over Italy; posing as a
page, as yet incognito, is Don Alfonso de Zúñiga y Ercilla.
The names Sesa, Astorga, Luna, Olivares, Falces, Gelves,
among others, nearly all luminaries, reckon among this
unending entourage of nobility. The cream of the Empire
is flocking together to accompany the Prince of Hope on
this journey. Thusly in Savoy and Genoa, among other
cardinals and ambassadors of universal renown, Don
Fernando de Gonzaga, the Prince of Ascoli and the Prince
of Salerno join forces with the retinue. All but hidden in
the middle ranks, at the head of one of the two companies
of harquebusiers, is Captain Alfonso de Vargas, uncle by
blood and later the patron of a half-caste from Cuzco,
Garcilaso the Inca, who in time would be the first great
writer born on the far side of the Ocean, in the New
World discovered by the Admiral. Endless Galaxy of
celebrities immaculate, heads high, higher than their
station called for, Imperial Olympus of pomps and vani-
ties, Court adazzle with luminaries whose intrepidity and
intelligence have carved them a place in History, all
offshoots of Christendom and the Empire that staggers the
known world. All are now in Genoa, content and joyful,
moved by the welcome and hankering to strike up a
conversation with his Most Serene Majesty Prince Felipe,
who is gawking at his mermaid, the sea cow brought to
him from the New Continent, in his own caravel, by Don
Diego de Medina, the page, a gift from a certain Don
Alvaro de Rejón, a wealthy islander—native of Salbago—
on whose behalf Don Diego de Medina, still giddy from
the recent voyage and from the memory of those lands
that have gone so to his heart, has presumed to ask the

Prince for one of those nobiliary titles that His Imperial
Majesty shells out for favors rendered . . .

Amid all these mannerist caprices, amid all the pomp
and foofaraw of the Court that runs the world, in the
throng of dukes, captains, warriors, cardinals, bishops,
and priestlings (that sludgy character skulking like an
invisible shadow, turning from side to side his cranky
eyes that collude in every parlor corner, who spots heresy
in a simple look; dangerous character already beginning
to tower, to be feared by the cannier councillors; smoky
character, Official of the Holy Inquisition, untiring harpy
who goes by the name of Blas Pinar, and who hails from
one of the fiercer lands of Castile), Don Alvaro Rejón's
mermaid lies dead, encased in a crystal and rosewood urn
full of water that putrefies and must be changed over and
over. Wonderstruck, Felipe is trying to picture the dimensions of a world he will never fathom, in spite of the fact
that all the power of his Empire will hinge on the size of
those lands, as they are, and will be, its chief sustenance,
without which the Empire would be merely tinkering with
the cold countries of Europe that by now were secretly
vowing a battle to the death with the Spanish invader.
Even lifeless and motionless, Don Alvaro Rejón's sea cow
represents to the Court an expression of refinement
verging on myth itself. She, the mermaid, is the hard
proof that the legends blowing in from the New World are
not tall tales trumped up by the delirium of conquistadors
and captains attempting, with the help of chronicles and
catalogues, to empty the Imperial coffers on their own
behalf, to foot their new enterprises, new adventures, new
mirages feverishly ogled on a horizon that doesn't exist.
She, the mermaid from the New World, upon whom no
one dares bestow a Christian name because they still
can't settle on whether she's a monster or a person—or
both—has come to Italy—incorruptible cradle of Christian
culture—at the hand of the Prince of Hope, as a remote
blend of classical nostalgias and new mythologies, a gift
from God for the grit of the Spaniards who dared to trek
over unknown lands, a creature hitherto never beheld—
nor ever touched—that outsoars the simple truth and the
mythical ages retold by the Greeks. All Italy awaits her,
arisen in the so-called Indies of the West, beyond the sun,

the winds, the storms and the centuries themselves, only
to see her dead, like some exotic princess from other lands
whose mythy reality not only calls up wondering cries,
but is sworn to sight unseen. She's a splendid, outlandish,
thoroughly frivolous and eccentric game of the Counter-
Reformation, the wild card played by the Spaniards, stopping at nothing, in this magnificent tourney of frivolities,
in the welcome rendered to His Catholic Majesty, Prince
Felipe. The whole blessed affair has more than reason to
not feel bilked, if one takes heed of the staggering pomp
inspired by the age in the Court of Aragon and Castile,
the alliance from which it arose as though all were
prophesied in a book of the Bible, the eyes of the world
now turned, by express wish and command of King
Carlos, toward the sumptuous, imperious protocol in the
Burgundian fashion, its formalities supervised always by
the Duke of Alba, Grand Master of Ceremonies of the
Empire.

A cultivated man, his spirit astir with curiosity for new
things, who has felt longings, ever since he was a boy, to
clap his eyes on one of those animals he knows (thanks to
his readings in Greek classics) existed in another age and
therefore just might still exist in this one—though in some
other historical realm—Felipe fills with bliss as he looks
once again at this sole specimen of the mermaids who
navigate the seas of West India with thorough famil-
iarity, a sea creature he had gotten tidings of from
seafarers and roamers who turned up in Court, but the
sight of which outstrips any of the legends or lies mouthed
by those dreamers to date. Christopher Columbus, the
Admiral Isabel pinned her faith to, and all her queenly
indulgences, also happened to have seen from the deck of
his caravel how those mermaids and mermen leapt over
the water, recollections later glossed by the jealous Bartolomé de las Casas, the mad priest, on reading the *Diary
of the Discovery* and studying the Admiral's allusion to
three sirens—his fevery delirium having turned him into
a hopeless liar—since three was the number of singing
sirens who, on his voyage into nothingness, had tempted
the seagoer with whom Christopher Columbus wished to
be compared, Odysseus the Greek, who had lashed
himself, cavalier and smug, to his ship's mast to listen to

the love-melodies of those beings he had never seen. Christopher Columbus, however, wrote of the actual existence of those creatures, one of which Felipe was now showing off in Italy, as the most precious trophy ever bagged by the Empire.

The sea cow deserving of such Imperial grace was, nonetheless, beside the point and very far from appreciating the solicitude and subtle interest she elicited. Nor did she manage to see the frenzy of medical activity unloosed by her slow expiration on the Mare Nostrum, regardless of which the sapient doctors travelling with the Prince could do nothing to avert her death. At first it was deemed that a dead mermaid was not the same as a live one, but later it became imperative that the Court councillors reconsider. Her importance was attributed to the possibility of proving her dubious existence, and of astounding the Italians with the Spanish adventure, which by midcentury had so far outdistanced Land and Time as to discover and ship back to Europe the reality of this mythological being which has lain, until today, solely in the memories of those (scholars or dabblers) who have read the Greek classics and, like all of us at some time or another, lost their bearings on the boundary demarcating reality and fiction.

Don Diego de Medina was not incognizant of the woeful state in which the sea cow, after traversing the Ocean of Murk, put into the Port of Seville. During the voyage, the crazed Ambassador continued to make exaggerated, indiscriminate use of the sea cow for his relaxation and recreation. Every night, with the excuse of inspecting the creature, His Imperial Majesty's randy envoy played at love with the silent siren with whom, one of the oddities of life, he had fallen brutally and bestially in love. At dusk, every day of the long crossing, Don Diego de Medina would fall to sampling the various rums and firewaters he was delivering in special flasks to Spain, as a gift to His Majesty King Carlos from the New Continent's many new hacendados. Muddled by the liquor, titillated by the recollection of his hours spent in Mademoiselle Pernod's house of revery, he raved. Back to his mind, aquiver with heat and nostalgia, came the almost touchable memories of all the women he had undone in his days of wine and roses.

In ecstasies over the recent past, strung like a madman from those memories unravelling as the prow of his caravel drew toward the docks of Seville, he had the mermaid, whom he had christened the Sacred Monster, playing on her capacities for love and lust, brought to his stateroom. Benumbed by vapors of firewater, in love-struck soliloquies he addressed her as if she were a person, and watched with rapture the arduous exercises the sea cow attempted to perform in that narrow crystal and rosewood cell it had been necessary to construct for her removal to Europe. Spellbound by the incomparable sight of her glistening sex, that juicy, smiling, vertical mouth beckoning him (this, finally, was his surmise) to the lubricious game of pleasure, the Ambassador peeled off all his clothes and climbed into the urn, joining himself, with physical difficulties (until achieving the coveted climax), to the beast, who responded zestfully to Don Diego's brutal thrusts.

The mermaid, in a cloud of infinite longing brought on by her confinement, enslaved to the daily coos and smooches of the rakish Vallidolidian, somehow survived his abuses and the incomparable Ocean crossing, which for her especially must have seemed interminable. In this state of privation, at death's door, she arrived in Seville, whereat the daffy ambassador began to suspect that he would not be able to deliver alive this prey that was meant to net him great prestige at Court. Whereupon Don Diego de Medina, in a head-over-heels frenzy to keep her alive, deeply regretful of the wantonnesses he had obliged her to abide, prevailed upon the Andalusian authorities and set her loose in the shallows of the sandbar of Sanlúcar de Barrameda, with the idea that if he restored her to fictitious liberty for a few short days, the mermaid would recoup her color, her inner felicity, and the natural grace that endows these creatures of another world.

It was there, in Seville, in those ports still thronged with explorers, that Don Diego de Medina discovered that Felipe, the Prince of Hope, was about to travel away from Spain for some time. He then foresaw that what he had best do was chase after His Most Serene Majesty, now in Barcelona en route to the Italian city of Genoa. A matter of life and death, the balmy Ambassador, without waiting for the mermaid to regain all her strength, stuck her back in the crystal and rosewood urn (whose water, as mentioned above, had to be changed every little while) and shipped out for Catalonia, north on the Mediterranean, not hazarding this time, despite the temptation, more than some light caresses. She landed in Barcelona in the clutches of death, the Antillean sea cow who, erstwhile a whore in the Indies, a provisional concubine on the high seas and falsely free in the waters at the mouth of the Guadalquivir, attained after her death such royal favor that her lifeless presence was more applauded and admired than that of any live princess at the resplendent Court of Felipe in Italy. Battered by the endless voyage, she must have died when the frigid autumnal Mediterranean winds blew into her faltering lungs, and her limbs, strangers to these chill climes, began to ice over forever.

Enveloped in pomp, regally accompanied by the noblest and greatest of the topmost Court in the world, the mermaid expired en route to Genoa, the Antillean sea cow who many notabilities of the Imperial Court, misled by the garbled babble of Don Diego de Medina, took to be the legendary Mademoiselle Pernod, the Invincible Darling of Don Alvaro de Rejón, who were (the two of them) directly responsible for this odd gift presented to Prince Felipe, His Most Serene Highness, who the instant he laid eyes on this mythical marvel, this inimitable gem, and wise to the wonder waked by these rare beasts in the hearts of men of every persuasion, directed that she be included in the Imperial retinue and, dead or alive, treated as a princess of the Court. Felipe never knew—never had an inkling—that the mermaid came into his hands poorly due, in fact, to the lust of this Don Diego de Medina now in Genoa unrolling all the stunts in the world before his goggly listeners, who appeared to believe the page's renditions word for word.

If the mestizo blood flowing in his veins (half Caribbean breeder squaw, half Spaniard sprung from clinker or convent) ever altered its custo⬛ rhythm of circulation, as though to alert him to some particular peril prowling around him, he never made a sign. If he ever questioned the sentiments he knew were as shifty as the tobacco leaf the Mayans had taught the conquistadors to inhale, of the gentlemen who followed with sharp interest the unfolding of his fiery tirades, in which he preached the Emancipation of the Empire, no flinch of circumspection ever showed on his face aflame with emotion and messianic faith. If distress, distrust, or discouragement ever festered in his inner heart, in that innerness never ruled by reason, rousing hollow cries of warning, Camilo Cienfuegos never let on to fear whatever or bowed to the forebodings that tore at him. No, in all his harangues, all the impossible rebellions he meant to lead, all the meetings, public or secret, he barefacedly held, risking life and soul, the rebel half-breed always seemed self-possessed, and if anyone unjustly accused him, jesting or in earnest, of being on the payroll of piratical enemies of the Crown, he would cut him down with a scoffing glare, twisting his mouth into a fleer the colonists were intimate with in no time. He was a man with a feisty temperament, flinty in his beliefs, with an answer for every argument he came up against; convinced that the future of the new lands lay in total emancipation, what he asked of his fellow townsmen was an impossible soul-searching before thrusting to the heart of his teachings. "Them back there," he ranted, chomping his syllables, with a twang in the nose like a prophet that reverberated through the

clubs where he often congregated with a handful of insurgents, "will never have a fuck of an idea of what this is,
of what goes on over here, on the islands or Terra Firma.
They're mooning about islands and spices and gold and
other precious metals as if this new country were some
promised land of God's." He shrugged off the deaf ears he
stumbled against every day, and instead—by some
peculiar defense mechanism—hiked his voice even louder
and pounded slowly away at the hardest rock, challenging
to debate any one of those bigwigs he knew hailed from
prisons, or had shot up from the shadiest breed and
reshaped themselves on the New Continent into that
dream personality that had lured them here. When one of
these renegades of more or less murky past posed as a
loyal upright servant of Imperial law—whereas in the old
life on the Peninsula he was probably a highway robber
or a bum scrounging in the markets for his daily scrap—
his lower lip would curl, a horselaugh choked back in a
mocking scowl. Then he would cough drily, expel a thick
puff of smoke from his puro (which he kept constantly
clamped between his teeth), glower at his questioner and
light into him snidely: "Señor, you know as well as
anyone that your grace is who he is today thanks to this
land and that you don't owe the Emperor a peanut,"
shaking his head softly for emphasis. "Them back there,"
he went on, always sure of his words, "and us here. They
think they were born at the hub of the civilized world
because they live in an old territory that we feed, we
slaves over here on the New Continent, not catching on
that it's just because we pay the piper for their absurd
religious wars and have a different style of life that they
go on living and ruling the world. It's a paradox they'll
never grasp, even when emancipation's a fact." Cienfuegos spiked his words with huffy swagger, scanning the
room with his deep jet eyes to gauge the reaction to his
remarks in those present. He detested, with all the forces
of a man made of unequal halves (the violence of the
conquistadors and the bitterness of the Indians who had
no right to gripe at the abuses) the ever-hazy geography
of the Peninsula, a ravening, squandering country to the
west, on the far side of the sea, at the south end of a
doddering continent trembling to its fall in battles, owing,

plain and simple, to the pride of kings and princes. This
was Europe, war with no end. This was Spain, devouress
of riches, usurper, shrew-mother flatly dealing out orders,
drawing up law after law that might come in handy, to
be strictly obeyed in a world where they were obsolete on
arrival, fishwife exporting customs to be adhered to letter
for letter (as if indeed they were laws), who dictated religious commandments branding as heresy any stirring
toward liberty, who dispatched endlessly, to all captains,
all clergy, all the nameless ruck, her maladies and
blights, her strangling doubts, her fears and bad blood.

He had grown up in Cuba, a beggar, in a poor, filthy
town the Spanish had founded some years prior to the city
of Santo Domingo and baptized—after the bizarre custom—
with the long, sonorous, pompous name of Our Lady of the
Assumption of Baracoa, a stopover in the Antillean
islands before reaching the Terra Firma of Mexico. There,
long hours and days and months gazing at the vast blue
mirror of the sea ebbing and flowing, foaming and
muttering, thrashing like an animal caged, he first heard
word of the Empire, the pomposity of the dignities shipped
by the Spanish to the promised lands of the New World
where it clearly served no purpose, the inviolate insolence
of the swashers, magistrates, scribes, and stout swinish
governors, and the fumbling of those who had not landed
prestigious posts or sinecures they supposed represented
glory. There in Baracoa he listened to the bitterness throb
harder and harder, pulsing in his vitals, souring his blood,
chiselling in the scowl that years later would be the
stamp of his fleeting image famed all over West India. In
the drinking houses where he swilled guarapo and marc,
Camilo Cienfuegos listened to the tales about Hernando
Cortés told by those who had already visited the Land of
the Lake, where stone edifices rose regally from waters
furrowed by slews of skiffs. "Like Venice, my man," said
the unregenerate travellers, "water ringing temples and
houses, water everywhere. And Hernando Cortés is bound
and determined he will drain it off and raise on the ruins
a Spanish city like none beheld by the eyes of the world,
señores." Stone, thought Cienfuegos, stone desecrated over
sacred waters in whose depths dwelled gods alien to
Christians, ancient deities who have fled to the north to

escape the trials and tribulations brought by the conquistadors. He heard there, in that village of fishermen, ramblers, whores and suckers for the world of ambition, the name Doña Marina, La Malinche, the princess who led Cortés to glory. News of land, of empire—if one heeded the babblers who came back beaten from Baracoa— superbly rich and many times greater in size than the old Peninsula. Like so, he leapt at a tender age into the wild lands of rebellion, the constant wars of words, the squabbles, the shouting in taverns, the straying along beaches and docks built by the Spaniards to launch them always farther than foreseen, mad for world, greedy for gold, with the excuse of a cross and a religion that loomed before him, number one enemy of the rankling in his breast. As his knowledge deepened, his ideas gained a will of iron, the force and radiance of the Andalusian pony, the durability of indestructible minerals, mindful—naturally—of the encroaching shadow of death that would stalk him until it snagged him in the deep of the Caribbean Sea. Hence he always contended in favor of the conquistadors, sidestepping their perversities and their prunes and prisms, possessing as he did the shrewdness of a tiger and the stubbornness of a mule. With expressions baldly betokening his rebel persuasion, with a self-taught eloquence enhanced in his discussions by that illuminated style that blazons the brows of nugatory prophets, Camilo Cienfuegos, the stark mad mestizo, whiled away hours wound up in conversations that did not trouble to distinguish between white conquerors, negro slaves, crossbreeds of Indians and Spanish (like himself), mulattos, mere house servants, peons, drifters, or gentlemen who had come by such a status in Cuba, Española, Trinidad, Mexico or the Isthmus of Panama. "We," he cried till he was hoarse, "are different. Them over there and us here. We've got nothing in common with that tyranny, that crown or that Emperor Carlos. Him over there with his wars. Us over here with ours."

At first, after the harangues he would fling at his listeners, with fiery slogans that pricked at the edges of conviction in people on whom the royal tithe had begun to weigh like a gravestone, sensibleness would seize hold of them and they would turn their backs, returning at once to their duties and letting slip quickly into oblivion the madnesses of Cienfuegos, whose eyes, shot through with black blood, made him look like a devil, loosed on the world by the island of Cuba before his time. But the mestizo, blind and mulish, would storm back in with a fresh provocation: "Are we such shitheels as to let ourselves be jerked around by the laws of a Crown we've never seen and that's never seen us?"

Next, one after the other, came the warnings and expulsions. They pardoned his life, thinking him a raving lunatic who had lost his senses when he was young from munching on some wild wicked weeds he always carried with him and swallowed raw, half-chewed, in handfuls, as a sure cure for the attacks of asthma that cramped his already troublesome, hopped-up breathing, making him gasp and wheeze, damping the brilliance of his eloquence and turning his eyes dim and bovine. So they drove him out of everywhere like a madman who bore within him the loathsome, diabolical seed of persuasion, as if his presence smacked of evil auguries, as if his company alone could instill the heresies he preached into the hearts of the natives and even the Spaniards, whom for him were all equals. They left him to himself, first off because a voice crying in the cursed desert of the islands and the Continent could do no harm anyhow. Because a crazed recluse pulling from his sleeve stories and doctrines totally inapt in the space and time of this Conquest was doomed to die in the uttermost solitude. It would not be a matter of making him, also before his time, into a martyr whose fate would garner greatness after his death, whose curses would become reality after his disappearance. They would let him roam over the continent, a necessary evil, planting the futile flag of secession everywhere and nowhere. They let him, to see if he wouldn't be devoured by his own delirium on one of these treks, roll in the dust of deserts, scale mountains, ford rivers, traverse territories studded with volcanic peaks and craters where one could drink, every day of the year, pure water from the white snows cloaking the highlands. Cienfuegos acclimated to everything, survived as though somehow the mad demon succoring the rebel life at the quick of him were helping him, alone and muttering to

himself, to overcome however many obstacles he was met
with. These were tests that shored up his faith, that illuminated his deluded visions and made him virtually
invulnerable. Was this a cursed phantom seen flickering
like a flame through the mountains, his gruff voice only
days later resounding in some tiny village in the immense
territory of Mexico? He made friends with the deafening
whoosh of the wind and the sheets of rain that fell from
the sky. He learned to hide in the shifting geography of
deserts, at dawn showing an orographical silhouette
different from that which he had seen the night before as
he lay silent and still as a dead man, perusing the ways
of penetrating with his madness the stupid long-suffering
of the Indians and the high-flown contempt of the Spanish.
Both qualities boiled in his blood, in a battle out of which
his incendiary mind always emerged triumphant.

Next to come, inevitably and expectably, were the
constant visits to jails and lockups in the villages and
towns he stopped in, always loudly jawing his secessionist
madness. But sooner or later his spiels (eyes straining in
their sockets, voice thundering through the darkness of
the cell) would bring round his jailers, half-castes like
himself who kept him under close watch. He explained
that he was a Liberator, that he was on their side, and
needed them to help him carry on his insurrectionary
labor, a task that would bear fruit, but would die with
him if he could not go on planting it freely along the
roads, in the forests, in the remotest backwaters and
biggest cities. In those cells he knew the stinking hells of
loneliness, the reek of rotten latrine, where the crooks
doomed to hang not only snubbed him, but would try to
beat him whenever he took to spouting off the deranged
doctrine of emancipation. In Tenochtitlán, Mexico, for
instance, he began by sitting in the little markets and
speaking in a hushed voice, after the age-old Mexican
custom, though his eyes—at times betraying him—pierced
the reverent silence of his listeners. For a spell he evan-
gelized around where Hernando Cortés was erecting the
loftiest Cathedral of the New World, right beside the
Great Temple of the Aztecs, where by his decree the
palaces and mansions were constructed in strict Spanish
style to flank a vast plaza replicating, in far grander

dimensions, the main square of Salamanca. He understood that that captain, who in the very near past had been a rebel like him, had become his chief enemy, powerful and puffed up by his victories, feats he had the brass to relay in writing to His Imperial Majesty, papers wherein he grovelled at his feet like a witless serf unable to grasp the grandeur of the world beneath his feet. It was on one of those days of diligence and debate that they nabbed him without a scruple and flung him like a beggar into the deep silence of the cells. He counted back in his mind over all the jails where, for one reason or other (but always on ideological grounds, cumbered with his emancipation thesis), he had breathed the fetid air of dead men, and he nearly choked to death, in one of those frequent attacks of asthma he was pestered by. Gasping for air, he spluttered parrotlike the slogan that in his prophecies of liberty always hovered on his lips: "Unto victory forever. Liberty or death. We shall overcome."

No one knew how he escaped from Mexico. How, hiding out, hunted from village to village, the guns of his trackers echoing at his heels, he managed to skirt death, his last resort. Nor was it ever known what means or strategy he employed to slip away from the fields of water and, camouflaged in an anonymity no longer his, reach the docks of Vera Cruz, crowded with gulls he at first confused with the buzzards that had trailed him during his long flight. He rested, barely breathing, so as to be forgotten, and gazed dully at the wide sky over the sea. He traipsed like a beggar through the little markets, where live and dead animals of every variety were on display; he hung by the tobacco stalls. He smelled the brine, saw the sacks full of cassava bread and salted meats and fishes ready for expeditions which in a few short days, eagerly wending the water, would reach the islands of West India, his land, the home he had left behind, which now struck him as the safest place to recover his health, where his name might slowly slip into the uttermost oblivion. There in Vera Cruz, amid stones and sun and sea and the back-and-forth of boats spilling daily through the narrow gate of Mexico (and main access), he learned something new: to veil his fierce eyes exuding resentment and rebellion and bow his head, beto-

kening silent submission, whenever a Spaniard (as they
were wont to) perched his proud lofty eyes on him, a
mestizo, when all was said and done.

The route he took, strung along by his messianism, was
a mystery until he turned up in Santo Domingo City,
where a somewhat fuzzy sense of a more freethinking
wind—as to actions and ideas—steeped the slack habits of
the new colonial nobility and of the officials upped to positions of privilege by the Conquest and the Empire. Camilo
Cienfuegos fancied he saw, in the lands of Española, a
hotbed where his emancipation teachings might easily
breed, as he noted something of a disagreeable itch in the
colonists, who by this time were beginning to feel cheated
and snubbed by the Crown which, for just this reason,
playing on its notions and necessities, they had begun to
trick with trinkets, peacocks, parrots, exotic fruits, dwarfs,
satyrs, mermaids, and every sort of strange creature that
struck wonder in the eyes of the conquistadors, in the end
the conquered.

So he went underground for the first time soon after
coming to stay in the capital of Española. There too, Santo
Domingo being no exception with respect to the other
seacoast cities founded in slews by the Spanish on the
Caribbean shores and the coasts of Terra Firma, the
whole thing had been pitched pell-mell, and its population, drifting and divers-colored, had a shifty feel, guar-
anteeing him, on the other hand, the anonymity and
impunity he so direly needed. If he was spotted in that
city, no one squealed, maybe because each had his own
cache of remissness shimmering on his brow, or because
the Dominicans themselves were people not too given to
minding the laws of Spain or the officers of the Empire in
charge of overseeing them, dignities sent over to
constantly eye, spy on, and pry into the possessions of the
Crown and its overseas subjects. An air of revelry, of
social rot and moral depravity hovered over Hispaniola,
where the ruck never settled for its lot as a market, and
penny-pinching or profligate (depending on the freak of
fate that fell to them) scattered higgledy-piggledy upward
from the docks to the haciendas climbing beyond the city,
and forgot their dreams of finding El Dorado of legend,
the lie that had lured them from the old Peninsula, for

which, or so it seemed, they now felt no nostalgia whatever. All these experiences ended sourly, sparking a rebel spirit (like Camilo Cienfuegos') and pointing up the clashing traits of a crossbred race that had been born with the Conquest, and was, all in all, its most genuine product. Santo Domingo was the last phase in a journey of defeats, of year after year thrusting his way forward, with his fists, by fits and starts, tearing away veils that concealed the unimaginable, or shooting up from the depths of the sea like a desperate diver, gulping for breath at the very instant of asphyxiation. He let his hair grow long and bushy, till it rested on his shoulders. His thick, stiff, straight black beard covered his face, leaving exposed only his stark cheekbones, the fierce flair of his nostrils as he sucked air with the anxiety of an asthmatic, his black eyes staring always out of the deepest and into the most profound places, a facial composite topping a body taller than the norm among the natives, and even the Spanish. In Hispaniola, possibly owing to the combined effect of a maturity won in the face of the greatest obstacles and an almost perfect knowledge of the distinct human and physical geographies of the New World, Camilo Cienfuegos at last took on some lineaments of prudence in his daily affairs, in his now scarcer ideological conversations (even in the more hushed-up ones, where a certain measure of complicity with the mad mestizo was mandatory for entry), and above all, in his social dealings with those who by caste were his superiors, or those who, due to lack of breeding or ambition, he himself classed as inferiors. Meanwhile he had cultivated his memory to an extraordinary degree, to such staggering extremes that in no time he retained faces, names, chitchat, slander and life stories, and could peg each of the motley, mobile mass of the Dominican people, their vices, virtues, fortunes, frustrations and dreams.

"That man's dangerous," professed Don Luciano Esparza, the unplugger-physician, to Don Alvaro Rejón, who had become his chum due to a commonality of interests and personalities. "He's got an elephant's memory and can rattle off the story of our lives, Alvaro. Seems like the devil's helping him."

In his professional capacity, Esparza the doctor was a

frivolous man, swayable by anybody who could provide
him with the privileges he required, and obliging to the
fledgling social order in this land where colonists dwelt.
He did not insist on preferential treatment, nor did he
relish occupying a prominent spot in parades or fêtes.
"When in Rome, do as the Romans do," he liked to
aphorize when Alvaro Rejón teased him about his lack of
initiative in matters where some direct action might be
in order. He shunned novelties until they were accepted
custom, and he was, on all counts, dead superstitious. He
imagined he saw evil spirits in the least expression of or
will to change, though meanwhile he felt not the vaguest
religious attachment. In this area of Christian beliefs, he
was a lukewarm sort, worthy of biblical puke, a wishy-
washy creature who paid no attention whatsoever to
rituals and religious ceremonies. Removed from that
realm of historical fiction, he had fitted his ideas around
supernaturalism, urges already budding inside him when
he fetched up at Hispaniola, casting from his soul the
leftover religion of pomps and dogmas so as to make room
for what he termed new winds, nothing other than a
primitive natural belief in animism applied—naturally—
to all aspects of his daily life. Addled by the immensity of
the lands discovered by the Admiral, he put behind him—
as though forgotten—the urbane university life of his
youth, to dedicate himself, over the course of the years, to
an admiration for the fetishistic savagery of the natives,
in the doctor's case meaning a heartfelt respect for earthly
superstitions. "Over here, Don Alvaro, as your grace
knows, reality tops fiction. Always. All that looks like a
lie, or a concoction of the people, all the legends and
farfetched tales that spring from the lips of the masses,
come to be part of the greater truth, which is deemed a
category of reality. A covert truth," he explained, "that
reality wishes we didn't see but which begs a reading, a
mere reading. The worst," said the physician in seeming
desperation, "is that the Messiah is come, a brujo whose
mind has room for everything, who slants it all his way,
and who has words and answers for everything. A wizard
who's on the brink of legend. And over here, Don Alvaro,
my friend, legend is truth, fame, and everlasting glory."

A wild, powerful wizard known by the people as

"Horse," thought Alvaro Rejón, the colonist, nodding to the doctor's words. And indeed he too had heard word of the prodigious memory of the crazed mestizo. "A wizard," he said aloud, but as if he were thinking to himself, "a madman who smells of death," a phrase containing prophecies none too promising for Camilo Cienfuegos, the cursed breath of death licking like a tongue of fire over his soot-black head. As he spoke, Alvaro was endeavoring to fetch up the exact spot where he had hitherto seen that rabble-rousing, know-it-all half-breed, who now, at his apostolic hour, was making no bones about his proud blood trampled by History, as he himself worded it, and never disguised the brilliant glow that marks a visionary when he speaks, no matter what it's about.

Could it have been in Baracoa, on the island of Cuba, on his first quick stop there or on one of his later journeys on the way to the Yucatán? Or had he maybe seen him in Venezuela, one of those deserters from everywhere who pass through Puerto Vigía with only the shirt on their backs, like phantoms leaving no trace, and then ship out again nobody the wiser for Margarita Island, only to pop up later in Santo Domingo or Trinidad? His memory ranged over the immense lands of Mexico, from the ports on the Yucatán Peninsula to the island of Cozumel, alighting in the volcano-ringed plains, trying to force a gap in his memory and peg Camilo Cienfuegos the mestizo, a face that at times seemed barbaric, a soft hypnotic shimmer in his eyes that swayed people, that woke their deepest sympathies or their most absolute antipathies. But he never in any instance—try as he did sometimes to pass unseen—inspired indifference, and this, in Don Alvaro's view, was precisely what was so detestable, so exasperating and cocky: that some goddamn nobody, some shitass mestizo who had never met his father was strutting around stirring people up with his tub-thumping as though he were a direct descendant of God. Added to Don Alvaro's mounting dislike for Cienfuegos, getting worse by the minute, were his ugly spells of melancholic jealousy, that churned nervously in his black bile, originating vile humors in his throat that smutted his breath with an unbearable stench. The Dominicans buzzed with a secret the whole city knew yet took pains to shush, the loves of Mademoiselle Pernod, the Invincible Darling, and this no-longer-young gallant, fast-talker, womanizer, with his zany ideas.

"Have you ever met him?" Don Alvaro would ask La Pernod in these sour, edgy moments, when the jealousy murked his thoughts, clawed his guts and cranked them like a screw.

"Never, Alvaro, have I heard of him before now. The things people say . . ."

"Among others, they say he was your sweetheart when you landed here. That you came with him . . ."

"They say I've been everyone's lover, Alvaro. You know that. It's dirt. You know they wouldn't stop making up stories were the sea to drink them up."

Mademoiselle Pernod appeared calm during these repetitive conversations. She conserved the phony, monogamous poise of the whore who knows she outclasses the heap of trash she bosses, and the other heap (cultured, quasi-noble, blithering cretins) who visit her as clientele. Barely budging a muscle, possibly shooing away memories so distant she might have lived them in another life. Or maybe she was simply stating the truth.

"Where there's smoke . . ." Alvaro Rejón persisted.

". . . there's fire. I know. People throw up a lot of smoke when they're trying to kindle a fire, Alvaro. People say more than they ought."

"In any case, that mestizo is rather attractive," Don Alvaro Rejón hinted.

His eyes were pinned on Mademoiselle Pernod, seizing her, stripping her, rolling her, smothering her in his desire. "Attractive," he said again, "but I swear he stinks like a dead man." He eyed La Pernod as he spoke. "He's doomed and we're letting him sing his balls off as if it were his last wish. All the time he's got left to live is a gift from us, a favor we're doing him. Free, my love, free," he said, purring and smirking, fixated on the reactions he imagined he saw in the face of his darling, so as to ferret out the shadow of some lie or a silence that could implicate her in a relationship he was prone to think of as sacrilege. He gazed at her naked, in the darkness slowing the oblique gleam of the moon. He saw her splayed at his feet, her nipples twitching with pleasure, a liquidy moan flushing her body. He glimpsed her, a fleeting evanescence, in the arms of Cienfuegos the half-caste, much younger than when he, Alvaro Rejón, had so fiercely possessed her. Through his mind passed the image of the mestizo surrendered body and soul to the feast of the white goddess, licking her smooth skin with his caiman tongue, cooling his mouth with the white water that sprang from the nipples of the young madame. Crazed, contorted with jealousy, steaming, he sped backwards in time. Now he saw only a girl, and the mestizo deflowering her, bloodying her hot sex and licking it clean with his tongue, as if performing an ancestral rite, the revenge of a race whose blood was half of his body. Shit, he thought, squirming in his chair, if she does know him, her talent for fakery boggles the mind. Mademoiselle Pernod's face remained unruffled, as if never, in the longest past or now, had any bond tied her to Camilo Cienfuegos.

At least as far as Rejón was concerned, his first direct contact with the mestizo was sheer coincidence, in one of Santo Domingo's countless clubs near the bawdy district, the Bagnio, where the colonist had a date to meet with some common buccaneers who came to Hispaniola to do business with him, as always on behalf of his invisible partner Pedro Resaca. It was no secret, in these latitudes, that Don Alvaro Rejón had been and still was a shark, a slaver trafficking the whole line of live flesh, who had built up his business in thousands of casinos like the one wherein he now sat ringed by strangers who had halted in Santo Domingo to consult with him and receive his orders. By now, also in Santo Domingo, he had gained high social repute, in spite of the rough-and-tumble life all assumed he had had and of the rakehell (and envied) relations he carried on with the top whore on the Caribbean Sea, Mademoiselle Pernod. Yet this gentlemanly posture, now an indivisible part of his personality, meticulously masked the cruel face of the man who always plays to win, the hustler who lays his bet always with a trick that will win him every game, a characteristic of those who can scent danger in the distance (a whiff of stinky dampness) long before it can catch up with them, thereby dodging it without the slightest effort. And Cienfuegos, Rejón had often thought, was a grave danger. Folks had

taken to calling him "Horse." A satiric poet who recited
in the gambling houses—for a handout of a few coins—
about whom nothing was known but that his name was
Virgil, had composed one of his finest poems in the mestizo's honor: "The Horse Prance." It was as if he were
already a hero, his physical stature a match for his
convictions, sounded with bright, blunt determination, a
leader, this niggling, slithery mestizo who—now more
than ever—one never caught sight of face on, wrapped in
the wrangles and scuffles his teachings touched off among
the bickering customers.

"I've seen your face before. I know you, señor," the man
of mixed blood broke in suddenly, addressing Don Alvaro
Rejón, his proud-bird eyes exuding impudence that muted
half the words his lips pronounced. Rejón was seated, and
beside him, Don Luciano Esparza, the unplugger. They
occupied one of the cornermost tables in the saloon, whose
doors all but opened onto the sea, whence the smell of live
shellfish and salt, of fish so fresh its gills still twitched.
The shouts of the tipplers webbed in the air. The slakeless clientele thumped for pitcher after pitcher of wine
and firewater. There stood the mestizo, leaning his hands
on the table, a challenger, his face two handspans from
Alvaro Rejón's, every look packed with the most phenom-
enal presumption, implying (Rejón thought at that
moment) a sort of veiled insult, an invisible glove flung
in the colonist's face. Don Alvaro Rejón, recovering his
memory, suddenly placed him, but he made no sign. Nor
did he at that moment expose any weakness on which
Cienfuegos might be able to score, being that he was
(Rejón was witnessing it now) a ruthless player who would
tilt his luck to the outside limit.

Rejón eyed him, deadpan, before responding, staking out
a distance and indifference he was far from feeling inside.
"I don't know," he said tersely and then, idly, he identified himself, "I am Alvaro de Rejón."

"I know you, Don Alvaro. Don't you remember me?"

Alert, looking from one to the other of the two notables
there before him, as if between two master fencers
crossing their pointy swords for the first time, and
with almost no warning, in intimate duel, Don Luciano
Esparza shifted in his chair, chance witness to this like-

wise chancy tourney. Alvaro Rejón deliberated. Cienfuegos, he thought, had been waiting ever so patiently for
the propitious moment, knowing that surprise was his
strongest hand on the battlefield, that to win he must
always strike first. "He's a titan," the unplugger-physician said to himself, overdoing it. As the mestizo waited,
a smirk played over his bearded face, but nohow did he
betray impatience. Don Alvaro had all the time in the
world to regroup. "The first blow is half the battle,"
Luciano thought proverbially. The game is his, thought
Alvaro. Having flung down his card, the mestizo was
waiting for Alvaro Rejón to play, so as to gauge the
strength and poise of the enemy.

"I beg your pardon. I can't quite place you," Rejón
feinted, replying to Cienfuegos' attack with bald hostility.
His words took longer than usual to come out of his
mouth. They had been pronounced with studied slowness,
reclaiming the social distance that Cienfuegos had tres-
passed when he barged in and took the bull by the horns.
The memory of Mademoiselle Pernod crossed through his
mind and for an instant he was besieged by jealousy, less-
ening his lucidity and focus. He clenched his jaw, but he
alone heard the screak and scrape of his teeth grinding
against each other.

"I'm Camilo Cienfuegos, Don Alvaro. You really don't
remember me?" the mestizo pressed ahead.

Now he could act angry, sniffily spurn him as if he were
an unknown cadger who was pestering him. This is one
option, thought Rejón. But in this snub, this cocky refusal
to recognize his adversary, perhaps lay Cienfuegos'
victory. Because this perhaps was the precise occasion he
had been waiting for, and which Rejón could not afford to
offer.

"No, señor. I don't know who you are." Alvaro Rejón
rebuffed him again.

Horse remained calm. He knew he was winning the
match. Thus he refused to kowtow to the colonist any
longer, and though no one had given him license to sit
with gentlemen, took a chair (a gesture intending to repay
Señor de Rejón's blatant affront) beside Don Luciano
Esparza, facing Don Alvaro Rejón.

"Cienfuegos, Don Alvaro. Cienfuegos. Atenco Bull-

breeders, in Mexico. Velador Arena, Señor de Rejón. Now
do you remember me?"

Alvaro Rejón peered for an instant into the mestizo's
unforgettable face, as though laying eyes on him for the
first time, as if he had never heard of him before. Now he
feigned surprise, as if in that one moment he had leapt
over the Caribbean Sea, toying with space and time, and
settled somewhere near the Lerma River, in Mexico City,
where he had been on several occasions. Then, but all
within fractions of a second, he hopped over to the bull-
pens and sheds of Velador Arena, the ring where Atenco
Breeders—mounted in Mexico by Juan Gutiérrez at the
express behest of Conquerer Hernando Cortés—fought its
bulls. No less than fifteen years, Rejón murmured to
himself. He was seething inside, edgy and agitated, but
none of this would he divulge to his enemy. The mestizo—
by now it was clear—was winning the round, moving his
pawns like a champion chess player and foiling Rejón's
strategic attempt to stake out the distance dividing him
from his opponent.

"Atenco," he nodded, ceding ground to Cienfuegos helplessly. "Yes, of course. Atenco. And you are, but of course,
Camilo Cienfuegos," he declared, pointing at him. "You
were there when I visited. You escorted me to some fiesta,
or am I wrong?" Rejón asked, as if alluding to one of the
numerous servants he had run across during his long and
far-flung journeys.

"Yes, señor. I was there. I escorted you, señor," he said
grinning, as if this victory were the most that he, Camilo
Cienfuegos, could have wished for.

"You must pardon me, boy," he cut in now with false
delicacy, thrusting him back again with this treatment.
"I had forgotten you. I had forgotten your name and your
face. That was long ago . . ."

"And yet, Señor Rejón, I recall your grace perfectly."
The mestizo was beaming now as he spoke. "I advised you
against purchasing those bulls from Atenco. So you
wouldn't get yourself in a tight spot," Horse plugged
ahead, his language now embarking upon out-and-out
insult. "And now you're a big man in Santo Domingo.
Here your grace has elbowroom." The half-caste grinned

again. Was he calling him a slaver, possibly? "A big
wheel. A rich, happy man."

Was this last remark, so loathly uttered, an allusion to
his relations with Mademoiselle Pernod? Did his snide
tone hide some secret clue eluding Don Alvaro at the
moment? Elbowroom. Rich, happy man, Rejón said to
himself, stumped. Then he thought back over his trips to
Mexico, his otiose efforts to break into the Cortés family
business. He looked into the mestizo's jet eyes. He must
know. Surely what was happening was that Cienfuegos
had up till now turned up only his low cards, saving the
best for higher stakes. In any case, thought Rejón,
calming himself, he can't know all. He didn't have to
know, for instance, that he had gone to Mexico on behalf
of Leonardo Lomelín, the Genoese, a slaver with whom
the new master of this vast territory, Hernando Cortés,
had struck a deal for the transfer of five hundred negroes
from the Cape Verde Islands, or that he, Don Alvaro
Rejón, had been one of the operation's promoters and
middlemen, along with his partner, Pedro Resaca. A
purchase, a shipment destined for the Tuxtla plantations
and mill. Nor would he have to know about his doings in
the Valley of Oaxaca, Toluca and other lands of Coyoacán.
Would he know anything of his personal inspections of the
mills of Tehuantepec, of the plantations of San Andrés
Tuxtla, or those he had carried out to assess the feasi-
bility of continuing to bring negro slave manpower into
Mexico, in Tlaltenango, Cuaitla and Cuernavaca, all of
the above haciendas belonging to what was then called
the State of Cortés, the sole Spanish conquistador who
had sensed, no sooner did he arrive, the importance of the
geographical factor in what was then known as New
Spain? Shit, shit is what this son-of-a-bitch mongrel
knows, Rejón thought, peeved. Then the colonist began to
smile too, possibly stalling for time, and to nod his head
to Camilo Cienfuegos' words. This was the moment it
came over him that the mestizo indeed stank like a dead
man, reeked alive, that his whole enormous length was
drenched with death, and that even so, here he stood, all
his foxy remarks packed with the most unshakable cheek.
He could see he had no other recourse but to win the trust
of this dangerous individual, induce him to spill his

doctrine of the dispossessed and his crank prophecies into his ears too. He would have to stomach him, swap thrusts and feints of the saber, play the snaky game of false friendship so that the mestizo would unmask himself once and for all, uncap all his hidden essences and dish himself over at last, to him, Don Alvaro Rejón.

They would need to see each other almost daily, in the mum presence of the unplugger, who sat in, silent as the tomb, on the conversations and covert meetings that Don Alvaro de Rejón rigged for the relaxed unbosoming of Camilo Cienfuegos. At first these took place informally, in the secret garrets of one of Mademoiselle Pernod's houses of fallen women. Later, in the mansion of some nabob they had lured into complicity. Loosened by liquors and liqueurs, the mestizo's tongue lashed away at the lax consciences of the hacendados, who listened to him unruffled, apparently accepting their share of the blame in the relations with Spain and who step by step (or so the zealotic naïveté of Camilo Cienfuegos would have it) were being brought around to the necessity for the schism. "When that moment comes, if it comes," Rejón muttered under his breath to the unplugger, perhaps to placate his nerves, "what this mestizo slime is running around trumpeting we'll do for ourselves. We're more than enough all by ourselves without getting shit on our hands with the help of these uppity bastards."

"You don't think we'll come to that, Alvaro?" asked Luciano Esparza with some alarm.

"Relax, old man. We won't live to see the day. It's just talk . . ."

Meanwhile, Don Luciano Esparza kept on practicing his profession, his medical know-how, in all the clandestine coves at the four cardinal points of Hispaniola: the odd service of unplugging. On the secretmost paths of the sea, the dextrous helmsmen of the slave galleys, rounding shoals, islets, reefs, and sandbars, steered their cargo of human flesh to the island for Don Luciano Esparza (dubbed Clean Hands all around), to inspect the slaves shipped over from Africa and the Cape Verde Islands; for the unplugger, like an imperious, almighty god, to accept or reject the load of slaves that Don Alvaro de Rejón would then deal out among the haciendas of Santo

Domingo, and all through the island territory of West India. For security reasons Rejón had handpicked Santo Domingo as a main base for his operations and for the glitter of money, here where new haciendas and mills sprang up by the day for the shipment of sugar to Spain, ever since the Admiral turned the island into a great marketplace. So Don Luciano Esparza presided like a high priest, solo, exclusive, expert and obligatory. He would begin by peering into the yellowy sclera of the sickly slaves, then open their inflamed red mouths, sniff their dry, stinking breath, and with scientific thoroughness, examine their teeth and each of the grisly sores that almost always erupted on the palates and gums of the negroes after many days of cramped quarters, filth, and scarcity of food. "This one's hot" was his favorite expression for rejecting the ravaged body of some negro, a remark auguring the slave's imminent death. "These sores are incurable," he would comment to let it be known that this other woozy, scrawny one carried the germ of sure death in his veins. Next, for those who squeaked through this first delirious test, he would palpate each muscle, saving for last the slow, meticulous examination of the asshole, whose infernal stink he would attempt to stanch by ordering the seamen patrolling the cargo to wash them, one by one, in the shallows. He was indeed not going to let the big trick sneak by him: "Don't go and stick it in bent," he would josh. When they had sighted the cove marked on their maps and were edging up to Española, while they waited for the arrival of Don Luciano and his thugs (whom Don Alvaro had placed in his service for this chore), the slavers would shove up into the anuses of the slaves sick with dysentery and colic a wooden plug piercing many layers of tissue inside the negroes' asses, and sometimes preventing the medical experts from spotting the malady, by bringing on a total paralysis of the intestines and keeping the evidence from running out of their rotting bellies, a stream of shit, an unslowable diarrhea that could, at the instant of inspection, represent the utter ruin of the smugglers' plans. So Don Luciano Esparza, while two or three of his strongarms held up the negro, would plunge his iron tongs into the anal orifice and pull the plug from his bottom.

Shrieking, wasted by pain, the slave let loose the shit held inside and the blood-splotched feces gushed down his thighs. "Forget this one, carajo. He's a goner," Clean Hands would say. Don Luciano Esparza knew that the disgusting profession to which he lent his services and skills possessed, as did everything in life, two faces: the revulsion induced in him by these reeking, half-dead bodies, and the exorbitant sum he charged to inspect them. "If you won't work, Alvaro, you shan't eat," he would pronounce in his more relaxed moments. More than once, as he extracted the stopper from some sick slave's ass, the sack of bloody shit had burst very near the unplugger's face, splattering his skin and clothes. On balance, it was an honorable profession, away from which Luciano seemed a different person altogether, kind and refined, as though he indeed managed to keep aside his long experience as an unplugger for his moments of intense work in every hole and corner where human flesh was trafficked. Hence, Luciano knew where every path on Española led. No beach, however remote, eluded him; the doctor knew every cove, bay, inlet and hideaway like the back of his hand. After all these years, he had the island's geography, its crannies, woods, dales and wilds wrapped around his little finger. Loyal to the bitter end, Don Alvaro Rejón had sized him up him no sooner did he come ashore in these lands full of promise, and had tasked him with the sole care and inspection of his chief source of income, the market in negroes, dispatched, by the loadful, almost monthly, to the shores of Española by his partner in Puerto Vigía, Pedro Resaca. Then Rejón would personally tend to parcelling them out among haciendas and plantations, refineries and mills, an empire stretching over the arc of the Caribbean Islands and the surrounding seas, reaching even as far as the Isthmus and into Mexico.

"He reeks like a corpse, my friend." Don Alvaro de Rejón would quip whenever the doctor, a bit alarmed by the friendship the colonist seemed to be lavishing on Camilo Cienfuegos, brought him up. "He stinks like a dead man. As if his ass was rotten," Don Alvaro snickered. "Leave this to me and don't you worry yourself. You'll see, he's going to learn this lesson for keeps . . ."

As of yore, as at the turn of the century when the city was first founded, the news blew into Santo Domingo again. First it was a mere murmur hovering around the muzzy heads of the lost men who bunched in the casinos by the docks and wharves, who having nothing had nothing to lose, sunk as they were in a drab, endless ordeal without will or hope. From the docks it rose, a rumor flitting from mouth to mouth, swelling and swirling, threshing over the facts, shedding light on old, stymied projects, freeing almost forgotten passions. It tickled the slumbering imaginations of the malcontents and failures who had always believed that their fate lay not here on Hispaniola, but on Terra Firma. Last, it overtook even powerful men, like Don Alvaro Rejón, who had always felt the lure of adventure, an irresistible longing that slinked through their pores, sucked onto their vitals like a barnacle, twined upward and outward and twisted around their hearts, stealing their peace of mind, pitching them into an endless sleeplessness that reeled over the nights and days. Each alone, and in line with his prospects, sounded the air. Each scented in the distance the redolent smell of gold, floating to his ears on a hypnotic tune.

So Santo Domingo began to simmer again. Again there was brazen talk of El Dorado, the terrible obsession of the Spanish conquerors, the supreme object for whose sake they had turned countless circles around a vast, outsized territory impossible to draw on their maps or describe in their chronicles, a story for which, at bottom, they had turned an unknown world upside down. From time to time rumors of the existence of El Dorado would roll in again

like a return of prophecies and fortunes; ill-supplied expeditions put to sea and were lost without a trace, since the
legend was more powerful than the yearning that on
hearing it was waked in the breasts of men who lunged
into adventure in pursuit of a golden phantom. The
Spanish conquistadors believed—or anyway this was how
they liked to picture it—that the most coveted and
searched-for city in the universe, a kingdom shimmering
and hidden like a promise of happiness that must
someday be fulfilled, burned its sacred fires in a secret
territory ringed by obstacles rendering it invisible to the
human eye, camouflaged in the center of a jungle of
caprices whose silence protected it from all possibility of
profanation.

From the Isthmus of Panama (a hellhole of uprisings,
killings, intrigue, rumor and fear) sprang news of the
internecine wars erupting between the Pizarristas and the
Almagristas, quarrels and killings in which the former (at
least for the moment) had triumphed, madnesses perpetrated by the Spanish of that century in a faraway land
to the south, Peru, whose capital had been the inspiration
of the conquistador himself, Francisco de Pizarro, a man
weathered in defeats, heartaches, treks, and rows, who
had already sampled glory in Mexico alongside Hernando
Cortés. According to those in the know, dreamers who
hoarded in their imaginations the tales afloat in the
Spanish ports of the New World, someone with great
powers of persuasion had related the legend of the city of
El Dorado to Don Gonzalo de Pizarro. What's more,
several natives he trusted swore, upon drawings depicting
the hidden lands, to the exact location of the sanctuary of
the golden treasure. These were old caciques, wise men of
royal blood, inheritors of lost ancestral traditions which
would drift away to sleep for a time the sleep of oblivion,
only to pop up again later in the cities in the guises of
truth. They claimed it lay along the Amazon, deep in
virgin jungles whose shadows crept up the flanks of the
icy cordilleras. Or perhaps still farther, beyond the
silhouette of the mountains, huddled like an ancient
mummy in a green maze of liana vines and giant roots
which twined and tightened around the feet of the
intruders, amid cries of beasts existing solely in these

jungles of legend. It was, in point of fact, a secret sanctuary full of treasures, a kingdom like none other in the
world, a territory at once cultivated and wild, impossible
to describe with words alone. A city of gold where three
thousand artisans chosen from the most skilled among the
silent tribes of the jungle devoted themselves tirelessly to
the fabrication of sumptuous furniture made of solid gold,
sculpted with an artistry and science that the Spanish, for
all their valor, had no means to imagine. A kingdom
whose Royal Palace was also of solid gold, with cupolas of
transparent gold so that sunlight filtered through them,
lending their interior a luminosity that was the benison
of superior races which had found there in El Dorado their
earthly paradise. A staircase of solid gold with countless
steps led to the entrance of the golden palace where—
leashed on long gold chains—lions strutted that were no
doubt the last guards of this redoubt of fable. El Dorado
at last, with its gold houses, gold ramparts, streets
cobbled in gold, temples and adoratories of gold, golden
markets, even its shacks made of gold, the whole city girt
by a colossal gold wall.

Back in Santo Domingo, Don Alvaro Rejón imagined the
fever that had waked like a wild gust in the flesh of Don
Gonzalo Pizarro, who had not regained calm until he
moved out with an expedition of eight hundred of the
boldest warriors, eight thousand native Indians whose
fear mounted as they thrust deeper and deeper into the
shadows of the darkest jungles, one hundred and fifty
whinnying Andalusian ponies and upwards of a thousand
dogs trained to scent, track and kill human beings;
numbers, supplies, ammunition swam through the colonist's mind in the tropical nights he passed without shut-
ting an eye, ever since the news blew into the city of
Santo Domingo. In short, it was an adventure worth its
salt, since its ultimate goal was the discovery and
conquest of El Dorado, the sacred city on Terra Firma.
Gold at last, said Don Alvaro Rejón to himself.

Gonzalo Pizarro turned round and round jungles, forded
rivers that looked like strange seas of brown water, scaled
mountains where the cold stuck in his bones, penetrated
the darkness of jungles which threatened to swallow him
up along with all his men; on whose thresholds human

feet had never tread. He listened to his men howl with death twenty-four hours after being stung by giant ants; he pushed aside phantoms from which the natives fled in terror as if they had seen the devil himself; as the horses' steps—the Spaniards gasping for breath—slogged slower and slower. Fever, insatiable reptile coiling in their bellies, lashing and lashing its tail, stoked their ambition, sucked all their strength and all their desire. For the eleventh time, he crossed the same rivers, wound around the same lands, bogged down in the same thoughts, the same marshes, the same dreams, still tormented, still unbowed, convinced as ever that he was soon to find the golden country. He found nothing. Only lush nature replying to his search for the region of dreams with its myriad labyrinths, its mysterious and monotonous rhythms.

Ever since the rumor popped up again, Don Alvaro Rejón went to the docks more often, quiet, observant, as had always been his way, though a trifle more close-lipped, so as to ward off (at least at first) the reports about him already flying through the streets of Santo Domingo: that he himself was the first to champion the existence of El Dorado. He haunted the gossip-shops, saloons and casinos where the waifs and strays of this world Spain had cranked up at the close of the last century lumped together to recount their feats and failures. In this greasy, rambunctious ambience, the rumor bubbled with a life of its own, the tales were revamped and pumped up into legend. An unwonted craving tinged his vision, tired his eyes, made him suddenly spurn the easy, cushy life he had found in Santo Domingo, his position as landowner and gentleman, his friendships in high places and all other meaningful alliances. Even (he confessed) his affair of the heart with Mademoiselle Pernod was weighing on him a bit much; with time this love knot had come to bore him, to smack of just what the island worthies knew it was: a concubinage with a chic whore who was the regal mistress of all the bordellos in the city. A whore, in short, Don Alvaro Rejón reasoned to himself. He was no longer satisfied, either, with the tall profits brought in by the African slave trade. "A damn slaver, in short," he growled, implicating himself in the abuse. Then, flat-

tering himself, he wound up his thoughts by stressing
that Santo Domingo was turning into a hell full of churls,
and that he, Alvaro Rejón, was not prepared to wither
away like all these slouches dragging around begging,
having been grand gentlemen in bygone days. El Dorado,
for all its air of myth, all those solemn descriptions—down
to the tiniest detail—made by those it was obvious had
never laid eyes on it even from afar, was slowly rising in
his imagination, puffing in his chest like a chrysalis
pushing to pop its cocoon and flutter his dozing ambition
to life, scrambling everything, snarling up his life as a
proper gentleman and the staid habits of a civilized, organized man. To go back to adventure (he was thinking) was
to come alive again, to fling off all those years, epochs of
calm that weighed on his head like a useless crown.
Anyone who supposed he had retired from those mirages
that existed, he was sure, the realest of realities, down
south, in the lands of Peru, he would have to show him
again that he had the teeth and balls of a filibuster.
Above all, there was gold, the sole mention of which drove
him into a dither, as for him its possession had become a
must.

"Wealth, Don Luciano," he explained to the unplugger
at the time of the rumors, "is scorned only by those who
don't have it and reckon they never will." The remark, in
actual fact, was a riddle betraying the progression of his
own ideas, now spluttering and purring inside him, his
obsession with launching an expedition to El Dorado
himself, stake everything on one card, at last, but for
something worth it this time, turn around and walk out
of this dead end that had become a sheer drag, forget the
smuggling of negroes, the whoring, the swigging of strong
waters, the contrived courtly manners, and fling himself
again into the swoon of adventure in quest of the zany
dream of undiscoverable El Dorado. For this, after all, he
had come to the New World, not to be a trader trafficking
black Africans like chattel. "Sugar, my friend, won't last
forever," he would expound to Don Luciano Esparza.
"Before we know it this whole world is going to tumble
down. Santo Domingo won't be so splendid anymore and
the wealth will go elsewhere. Life's like that," he declared
with self-persuasive sighs. "It wouldn't do to wait around

for that to happen, like ostriches with their heads in the
sand, at the mercy of circumstance." These random
remarks foreran a complete philosophy of the new adventure, like textual foreshortenings of a much broader, more
lengthy philosophy that the good life in Santo Domingo
had nipped in the bud. Now it sprang back to life in Don
Alvaro Rejón with a vengeance. "Just think," he would
say from time to time, making the most of the startled
look on Don Luciano's face. "What if we found it. All for
us! What madness!" He did not mention what they were
to find, he nohow named El Dorado, but he was padding
his convictions with thoughts that were slowly bringing
him nearer to the desired vision, a monomania also slowly
driving him mad, molting his inner and outer skins. The
moment came when he spoke only of his dream. He
grimaced like a madman; his voice deviated whenever he
alluded to the sacred city. He never tired of gathering, in
writing, on slips of paper he later stashed carefully away,
every wee detail, every jot of data however slight, every
tidbit of information wheresoever it came—that made no
difference. "What matters is to move on, even if it's on
the run. Where it comes from doesn't mean a damn to me,
Don Luciano," he said to the doctor, in defense of his rash
behavior. Bit by bit he was drawing up his plan of action.
He compared stories, searching for the common threads of
the legend, as if he were caged in a mirage of many
colors. He passed the time drawing maps to reproduce as
faithfully as possible the whole vast geography of the
south. Its rivers, valleys, mountains, cities, jungles, and
desert plateaus where the winds huddled in howling
conclaves, its silences and sounds, its peoples, phantoms,
and sovereign demons. Wrought up by the fever, he frib-
bled away his nights and days, forgetting all else. He only
left his mansion, which in his frantic passion he had
turned into a mare's nest of anecdotes and apocryphal
planispheres—tossed off by his own imagination—to
mingle with the rabble on the docks, asking over and over
for El Dorado, maniacally rounding up new clues, and
going home again to scratch hieroglyphs and signs onto
his maps, seeking the city of gold, pawing at the hidden
lands like a bull possessed by a demoniacal desire, poking
beneath the words of the fishermen and seafarers who

claimed to have been at one time or another in the
purlieus of the sacred city. He rifled the adventurers'
stories for the odd clue that might point the way, in his
imagination, to the castles of gold he was dreaming of
when he woke. Yesterday his passion had been Mademoiselle Pernod. And before he succeeded in conquering her,
she had wrenched him from sleep in the small hours with
a sweaty, feverish shiver. Here was the same sensation
again, but the blame lay with El Dorado, its gold huts,
gold houses, gold ramparts, gold palaces, rivers of liquid
gold flowing through the city, endless jungles of gold from
which select native craftsmen extracted, in buckets also
of gold, the magnificent metal they then fashioned into an
infinity of objects of every size: fetishes, figurines, icons,
altars, pulpits, baldachins, relics for divine worship, suits
of armor, helmets, swords, spears, sword hilts, necklaces,
artistic reliefs, earrings, belts, breastplates, backplates, all
in gold for the especial use of the privileged dwellers of
El Dorado, priests and lords of the grandest wealth in the
universe, who tended the sacred fire entrusted to them by
the gods of the continent for its veneration and safekeeping. Gold as aim, object, and religion. "The reason,"
he said to Don Luciano, "is very clear. Gold summons
only gold. Once you have it in your power, the rest keeps
coming to you. You attract it forever and it will never
forsake you, Luciano. Bear this in mind. It's a fact." The
mere mention of the word gold, though uttered with
disdain, was the object of an aggressive defense on the
part of Don Alvaro Rejón, who would pitch into endless
diatribes until he had fatigued his listeners into defeat.
Hence everyone in Santo Domingo began to take him for
a madman, a crank and a fraud. "That's what they
always say when your reasons are beyond their power to
reason. So they shit on you. They drag your name and
your reputation in the dirt, as if that were proof of their
superiority." he said, defending himself. He was in fact
cracked, a puppet yanked about by gold, whose only
reality lay, for the moment, in words, whisked this way
and that, day in and day out, by the wind.

By now Mademoiselle Pernod knew him all too well.
She knew she had lost him, that little by little his passion
had been going slack as if it were sick and about to die.

She knew that the gold fever, in certain insatiable spirits, was an incurable and enslaving evil, like a woman driven wild by passion, crying for more, more. She, the golden girl, the Invincible Darling, had been trumped by Don Alvaro Rejón; she, the White Goddess, the most beauteous and regal female on all the Caribbean Sea, who had outshined each and every one of the legends told of her before the coming of Rejón, and who then had lowered herself with every act, cheapened herself with every lewd lunacy dreamed up by Don Alvaro; she, Mademoiselle Pernod, who had found in him her sacred city, who had licked into his heart of hearts with her smooth pink tongue, who had offered up all her deep, juicy hollows, all her hot holes, for Rejón to decant into her ever-renewing mysteries all the unutterable passions he had corked up inside him until meeting her; and now she was on the brink of losing her promised land, since in Don Alvaro de Rejón nothing stacked up against the memory of the golden dust he dreamed of finding on the southern Terra Firma, in a place hazy and crazy but more golden than she herself, a berserk land that the Spanish, by dint of thinking about it and imagining it to be real, had fashioned of air. A golden land for which, carrying forth the tradition of History, they went on conquering, killing, dreaming, and losing heart. Forgotten by Rejón, Mademoiselle Pernod's body, sated with sadness, began to wither. So she gave up her golden vespertine strolls and withdrew, like a girl taking the veil in repentance for her waywardness, into her hacienda on the outskirts of Santo Domingo, in whose pool the mermaids and mermen she had trained for love still pirouetted. Her eyes lost their famous radiance and went watery, impaired by the veil of lukewarmness and apathy that had drawn across them, while a quiver of wistfulness and that fear of being left alone hovered about them at every moment; it was as if they peered into the future at the departure of her lover for the lands of the south, and were gently girding her for her solitude. She spent the nights sighing and moaning, recalling the thrust of Alvaro Rejón's body as he sent her reeling into the stars.

Don Alvaro Rejón, meanwhile, was busy with less frivolous pursuits. Scruffy, dirty, his obsession for the sacred city shimmering on his brow, boozy and wild-eyed, he kept his resolution by reading histories of all sorts on El Dorado, comparing his notes, and advancing, in his imagination, through the jungles that would lead willy-nilly to the hidden sanctuary. During the day, a crowd formed a line at his door, that even looped around his house. One by one, scandalmongers, shammers, farcers, frauds of every feather, and jabbering dreamers told him their stories and tales in exchange for a few coins. Alvaro listened to them poker-faced, never letting skepticism show on his face. Studying alone, late that night, he would know how to winnow the truth from the lies (for which he paid the same price during the day). He had no complaints. "All roads," he conned himself, "lead to El Dorado." He quivered with madness. Solemn, nerveless, he treated as gentlemen all the crooks on the Caribbean Sea who turned up at his house to sell him information. He conversed, in the language of each, with acknowledged buccaneers and destitute tycoons who came to his haciendas to dissuade him from his prodigious self-poisoning. Guilty by confession of the crime of dreaming, he beamed at all of them with that bizarre lucidity that often illumines prophets of truth, in their early phases, and yet the citadel of his reveries was none other than a golden absurdity acting on his mind with insuperable hypnotic power.

When Camilo Cienfuegos dared to look in his eyes, he grasped at once that for his purposes Alvaro Rejón was lost. If he had at some time nurtured the blind notion of winning over Don Alvaro Rejón to the cause of the schism, now it was he who was thinking of throwing in with the colonial gentleman's venture. "Camilo, I've got my own plans. Don't tell me any more about that emancipation hokum," Rejón snapped at him whenever the mestizo began to rattle off his arguments in favor of independence for the New World. "We're about to get rich for good, and you go on with your damn delusions. You smell like a corpse, Camilo," Rejón jeered. Don Luciano Esparza quaked during these clashes, which wore out the patience of Rejón, who would finally resort to putting the mestizo in the street. But as if the daily derision had slipped his mind, he would be back on the bandwagon the following day. He would return to Don Alvaro Rejón's mansion and carry on his evangelizing, his apostolic labor, as if the colonist's heartless treatment of him, fit for a servant or a slave, had been aimed at someone else. "You too will be with me in paradise, Luciano," Rejón said to the doctor, who could not fathom how the gold fever had made such a mark on the face and mind of his slaver friend. During his long spiels, the unplugger would finally screw up his courage to speak to Rejón, to attempt to induce him to face the fact of his madness, by this time no secret in the streets of Santo Domingo. "Your behavior, Alvaro, is a scandal, an outrage a man of your category must not permit himself," Don Luciano Esparza huffed.

"Go to hell, you quack. Don't nag me with that tommyrot. Your trouble is you're scared shitless. You've said so yourself. All I'm doing is heeding your advice, letter for letter, damn it. In this land reality tops fiction. Everything the people say is more or less the truth. Everything they say exists, exists. On this or that side of fantasy. There's no difference. It exists. Somewhere it has to be found."

One dawn like any other, after passing the whole night scorching old papers and raving, Don Alvaro Rejón, who of late had gotten himself into a most sorry state, fetched a whoop of joy. "The time has come, by God! The time has come!" His envoy and trusty messenger, dispatched to Puerto Vigía to consult with Pedro Resaca, his partner, had returned. And Pedro, reported the little man, agreed. The envoy was a slave clerk who conveyed his messages back and forth across Hispaniola, and who professed an odd affection for him, a mix of fear and loyalty. Resaca had weighed up what the desired encounter with the sacred city could net them. And, on another score, his affirmative reply was directly linked to the ennui induced by his do-nothing reign on Puerto Vigía. So, it was a matter of meeting up, as soon as possible, at their hacienda on the Venezuelan shores, where Resaca at once began preparations for the trek. No sooner did he catch the messenger's words than Don Pedro Resaca too had burst into yelps of joy: "Damn," he said, "this is what I've awaited for so long. To put all my eggs in one basket." Like so he raised the hopes of the hirelings, mostly sailors who had run aground on the Puerto Vigía beach and gotten hooked into slave smuggling, and of the negroes, who having not an inkling of the jungle realm they were about to enter, seemed overjoyed, at any rate, by the sudden fever that had seized hold of Don Pedro, lord and overseer of Puerto Vigía. They would traverse the inland desert plains, mount the Andes, tilting along trails to be picked out on the maps Don Alvaro would bring with him from Santo Domingo, and without a doubt they would find El Dorado. An extraordinary

273

flurry of excitement swept through Puerto Vigía: all were
to go. What they cleared was no mere camp but a fortress
made impregnable by Don Pedro Resaca and his
henchmen, a place where to enter without leave was to
leave without one's life, a spot respected by the bucca-
neering rogues who plundered and pillaged through all
the seas of West India. Even to this slave haven the gold
fever had come!

"When you land, señor, all will be ready for the great
march," dutifully reported the messenger, also a mestizo,
beardless and slight, with a bare-boned face and body, his
eyes all but hidden in his olive mien.

So all will be ready, crowed Don Alvaro Rejón, brimming with pleasure. Don Alvaro's fusta waited at its
berth, set to sail as soon as the colonist gave the word,
with an ambitious crew that the Salbagan had been
personally priming for adventure, driving them all wild
with promises of paradise. The day he gave the watch-
word to his initiates, each would be at his post, standing
by to cross the Caribbean, to round that arc of islands
that curves into the sea, and tie up at the Terra Firma of
Venezuela. The moment had indeed arrived, Don Luciano
Esparza was likewise thinking, conquered in spite of
himself by the conviction and gusto with which Don
Alvaro Rejón defended his imaginary theories. Skeptical
of all else, Luciano had wound up leaping through the
hoop of illusory gold the Salbagan had been slowly
stretching out before him as he gabbed on about the sanctuary, the bulwarks measuring over twelve feet from the
ground and roughly five or six feet in breadth, difficult to
negotiate if and when they overcame all obstacles and
attained the sacred city. "And they're gold, Doctor, pure
gold! You'll quit that profession that makes you smell like
shit around the clock, forever. You'll forget the color of a
negro's ass and live the life of a king, as befits your category, damn it. We'll purchase an island and cram it with
riches. We'll build priceless castles and haciendas not
buyable or sellable with mere money from the Crown,
mills that will thrive from age to age, a world apart, our
world, the world of the victors!" Don Alvaro Rejón cried
fervidly. Swimming in this effervescence never to desert
him now even for an instant, he slobbered as he talked,

his mouth brimming with dry white foam. "He's gone
mad," thought the unplugger, and then, altogether sold
by now, as though yielding the palm, "but he's telling the
truth. He knows where to find El Dorado." Slavering,
lungs frothing lust, Don Alvaro Rejón laid out on the
table in his study the final result of his investigations: an
adroitly drawn map, dotted with notations and secret
symbols, numbers and letters of the alphabet. "There's no
snag, Luciano. I've traced the trail in my mind, step by
step, that will lead us to the lost region in the jungle.
There's no way to miss. Here it is! Here!" he exclaimed,
excitedly pointing to where El Dorado awaited him, in the
exact spot where by his reckonings the sanctuary lay.
"Not a shadow of a doubt," he asserted. "Even the
animals are gold! Rabbits, alligators, caimans, turkeys,
llamas, snakes, dogs, parrots, macaws, ants and beetles!
You, my friend, can't picture it the way I can, because
I've worked my fingers to the bone in these indagations,
and I feel it again, here in my balls, the sweet swoon of
glory awaiting men with grit, Don Luciano." He gabbled
like a cockatoo, from memory. But instead of acknowl-
edging that Rejón had simply gone mad, Don Luciano
Esparza had let his nerves go awry: for that irresistible
fever had become absolute truth, wiggling like a worm in
his testicles, in his gut, in the air in his lungs, making
him quake incessantly and stutter as he awaited the
moment of departure. This was the honey of ambition.
Don Luciano had never tasted it before, or at least
nothing at all like this frenzy had so spooked him he
couldn't sleep. For years, not that he regretted it now, he
had misprized this sweet bile that was giving him the
shivers now too. Not that he had no beliefs. It was rather
a matter of pure pragmatism. Simply of thinking that he
was not fit for these callings, that wanted men of another
size and substance. Don Alvaro Rejón, the doctor conceded
at last, had changed him.

Camilo Cienfuegos, the cocky mestizo, had fallen under
the same curse, won over by the euphoria and fever of
Don Alvaro Rejón. So here he was now in the Salbagan's
secretmost chambers, as if he had gained his complete
trust, become his confidant in all his ventures. In any
case, it was not a matter of dropping forever the sacred

mission assigned to him by History (to rile the blood of the conquistadors, the disgruntled mestizos, the negroes, and the Indians, and rouse them against the faraway Crown of Spain). He was merely clearing a spot among his own inanities for the dream of Señor de Rejón, a short postponement of the principles by which he lived, so as— once he too discovered El Dorado—to round up an army that would rout the realists who would stand in his path, oust them from their cities and herd them into the sea. Let them swim to Spain if they can, thought the mestizo, smitten with his new dream of gold. An army (he mused) whose armor would gleam brighter than the sun, an army of thousands of waifs and gentlemen, strays and noblemen, slaves and lords, armies firing gold harque-buses, wielding golden artillery, with culverins and cannon made of solid, glistening gold, soldiers all of them heroes, deathless and triumphant, sweeping over the Continent and the islands heralding liberty beneath a single flag, also made of gold cloth, in the center of which would glitter vengefully in the wind a five-pointed star, symbol and mother of all futures. And of this army he, the unbeatable rebel mestizo, was to be the sole captain, the single hero, and the multitudes joining his flock as he made his way through the liberated lands would hail him, the continental Liberator, who would mow down all the shit and scum Spain had shipped to the New World, perhaps to free himself of them—shit, in a word, through which streamed half his blood, half the wounds he would sustain in battle. This was his fate, a madness styled in his image and likeness. But during those spells when his ever-alert conscience chewed at his heart and an inchoate fear floated to the surface of his eyes, a depression that would seize hold of him and shake him, rattling his ideas loose and knocking his bones out of joint, in those spells of trembling the mestizo loathed and feared, he would mutter over and over, to persuade himself, a phrase centuries later to pass from legend into truth, giving shape to a whole new way of life: "History will absolve me," he said to himself solemnly, making sure no one was listening. For like nearly all visionaries, all messiahs— bogus or real—which Spain would never stop spawning to the end of time (like a hateful mama rabbit sicking on the world those hotted-up heresies she herself aimed to condemn), Camilo Cienfuegos believed that the end (the liberty he dreamed of and would never live to see; the happiness of peoples, which he sought the way Don Alvaro Rejón and the Spaniards sought gold) justified the means, with the inevitable proviso that the cure (to resign himself to a yelp of protest and wither in Santo Domingo like any other barfly, waiting for an uprising against Spain not to occur until long after his death) was worse than the sickness (to hurl himself desperately into the conquest of gold, with which he would outfit his victorious army, the liberating army beribboned in gold to enter with pomp and splendor into the memory of the History of the world).

That very day, once it was known that the messenger had come back from Puerto Vigía, farewell fêtes were celebrated. During sunlight hours, untold prayers were chanted in the Cathedral, beseeching the Almighty to guide the steps of the madmen going off on the track of gold. In turn, Don Alvaro Rejón proved munificent, counting his chickens before they hatched, and promised that on his return to Santo Domingo City he would erect upon the ruins of the humpbacked sacred edifice a new cathedral made wholly of gold out of gold stones lugged over by his men from the continental jungles, with gold cupolas, gold window glass, gold benches, gold pulpits, and gold altars. He was crazy, but he had convinced them all with his gilded madness. All over the city, rockets and fireworks shot into the pellucid sky, blotting the light of the sun and choking the air with dense smoke. Glasses clinked to adventure, to the success of the Rejonista expedition, to the glorious outcome of their grit. Down their parched gullets swilled liquors, firewaters, brandies, guarapos and Spanish wines. Whole barrels of rum and guindilla and honey liquor emptied, as though instead of fêting a fortuitous farewell they were building the house from the roof down, as if they had already come home from El Dorado and were dancing with joy through the city streets telling everyone that the legend was true, that they had found the secret golden sanctuary where metal gushed from the depths of the earth, glistening jets of golden liquid spurting into the sky that centuries of civilization had searched for and never found. They, the zany,

demented Spanish had found it, had caged the myth.
Sated, elated, stroking the legend of gold with the fingers
of their imaginations, caressing the contours of the
fantasy as if it were fact, flushed, feverish, whooping and
hollering, and hornswoggled, they slaked their goatish
desires in Mademoiselle Pernod's tarthouse. They kicked
in the doors, sprang over the walls, crashed like savages
into the shadowy chambers where the strumpets rested
away from the heat, and raped every wench—public or
private—who stepped in their path. They stopped short
only of lighting the city on fire, knocking it down stone
by stone, bumping off anyone who dared refute the existence of El Dorado. A human typhoon, they swanked stark
naked through the terraces of Mademoiselle Pernod's
locales, abandoned to lust and dissipation. Never was this
carnival to be outrivalled even by the pirates who later
ravaged the island, forcing Spain to sign opprobrious
treaties annulling her power and grip over the western
part of so-named Hispaniola. Don Alvaro Rejón, now more
than ever (and never less so again) lord of lords, had
granted them piracy privileges. He, at bottom, was lord-
consort of all these bordellos and the bevy of gracious
females being gutted in his honor. After all, to a certain
extent he was Monsieur Pernod, the Invincible Darling's
lover. And he, Señor de Rejón, had proclaimed a holiday
all hollow, deeming his departure to be a portent of odysseys that would dwarf the feats of the Admiral and the
voyage of the Discovery. From this day of insanities
onward, as there are saints and names of the defunct on
the Christian holy calendar, so in Santo Domingo the date
of the expedition's departure was known as "The Day of
the Great Debauch."
　　Echoes of the ruckus reached the Queen Madame. She
tensed all her muscles, but did not speak, for she had
always held that silence is a gun loaded for the future.
She had always allowed them to come to her with their
chitchat, which once imparted, she stowed away in
unfindable cupboards. She would smile, her maximum
concession to those who recounted the scuttlebutt of Santo
Domingo, but on her side she eschewed all commentary,
so that one could never know for certain what Mademoiselle Pernod opined. But this time, when they described

to her, with or without exaggeration, the full-tilt orgy organized by Rejón on the occasion of his departure in search of El Dorado, her face crumpled, her flesh crinkled, and her brilliant blue eyes went brittle. Her grey hairs turned to spears, her passionate love turned to hate for the man who had conquered her, who had tangled her in all the nets of love, who had tumbled her from her pedestal of glory forever. She burned with the memory of the blond man from Salbago who had been driven berserk, all of a sudden, by a word that had wafted into Santo Domingo on the wind: gold. An echo that squelched, that eclipsed all other thoughts of adventure, dimmed epics and heroic feats. Mademoiselle Pernod, shut away in her luxurious chambers amid rose perfumes and scents of lime, was a rare witness to the lunacy of Don Alvaro Rejón. From the umbra of her bedroom, she could hear a dull roar, the cries of her tarts rollicking with the Rejonista hooligans and the reprehensible riffraff from the Dominican docks. Don Alvaro Rejón—Mademoiselle now saw—had been the worst of her perversions, the worst of her punishments, the secret shadow of all the disasters now storming her, from the lee, over the prow, the first round of which they were performing for her now, at carnival pitch, the furious mob tearing up her locales, smashing the furniture, shattering order in her establishments and flinging themselves indiscriminately at her strumpets, flouting all the ranks and separate categories she had imposed with such vim in her bordellos. "All gone to the dogs for a land that doesn't exist," she managed to reason as the tears streaked her cheeks and all the demons broke loose in her body that Don Alvaro Rejón's starch, applied in irrational doses of passion, had kept shut up inside her ever since he seduced her for keeps. Still, she was not resigned to losing him. She insisted on the chance that her lover would come back to his senses. She fancied that Rejón would keep a light burning—though unseen by the herd—in reminder of each of the mysteries they had discovered together. But Captain Rejón was already in another world, on journeys altogether unlike his pitching and plunging in the bed of Mademoiselle Pernod. He had gone mad for good.

Camilo Cienfuegos interpreted this breakdown of order

in Santo Domingo, not respecting even the set-apart world
of the whores, as always in his own way. This flurry of
frivolous fiestas and capricious madnesses, thought the
mestizo, was a general rehearsal, a pale, primitive
preview of what was to be the ultimate triumph, the
eternal glory of the emancipation of the New World, the
disappearance of a breed of profaners of ancient cultures
incomprehensible to their greedy minds. Like so, in this
same riotous way, his name, the name Camilo Cienfuegos, would go down in the History he so loved. Like so,
he, the mad mestizo, would return to Santo Domingo,
hailed, triumphant, mounted upon a white horse, decked
in that golden armor on which all his victories and feats
would be etched. There he sat, in a corner of the casino,
following blow by blow Don Alvaro Rejón's preposterous
rantings and ravings, and sharing, him too, in the high
spirits. The hours passed, evening drew on, the crowd
aswim in liquor, the suffocating heat sopping the air in
stinking sweat. He heard Don Alvaro Rejón's delirious
cries ("What a fiesta, by God! But this is nothing next to
the one we'll throw when we come back from El
Dorado!"); he observed the plump figure of Don Luciano
Esparza, the unplugger, his round, rum-reddened cheeks
streaked by an infinity of reddish rills that rolled down
his face and were lost in the bushiness of his beard,
chubby fingers lifting drinks to his slakeless mouth, eyes
bulging, his whole self dished over to the sensuality of the
moment, yelping ("Tomorrow's another day, damn it,
another day that will shine its light on a new life!"), then
guffawing as he palmed the ass of one of La Pernod's
cocottes, who were darting among the tables chased by the
revellers.

Just then Don Alvaro Rejón approached him, as the
afternoon hours began to wane and shadows to take hold
of Santo Domingo. Just when the proper folk began to
think that the fiesta would lapse into shenanigans and
street scuffles, just when it was supposed that Rejón and
his men would spill into the streets and go on carousing
all night long, skirmishes and ruckuses that bode nothing
good. "You and I owe each other a toast, my friend," said
Don Alvaro. The mestizo, gulled at that moment by the
rare good spirits, felt flattered by Don Alvaro Rejón's

attentions. "A toast," Rejón said again, handing him a
huge goblet brimful of rum. "Bottoms up, chum, bottoms
up!" Cienfuegos, grinning, and forgetting the differences
that had always existed between him and Don Alvaro,
drank down in one gullible, unsuspecting gulp the brew
the colonial gentleman had brought to his table. "It's got
a terrific tang," Alvaro commented, with a secret snicker.
Cienfuegos felt the flame slide over his palate, rasp the
walls of his throat, scorch his lungs (which it only grazed
from alongside) and sizzle his stomach, provoking down
below a shrieking of burning, churning intestines. But as
always he simpered like a naked woman, baring his
yellowy teeth, and gleefully pounded the table, though his
breath was short, sweat up, wheezes coming quickly on.

In a moment or so, he would begin to feel ill. He would
lurch around the bar, half choked from asthma and
alcohol. "He smells like a corpse," Don Alvaro Rejón
reminded Esparza the doctor, who was eyeing Camilo
Cienfuegos with manifest unconcern. "He reeks of death,
Don Luciano. He's drunk a half liter of wood alcohol and
he barely noticed." Then he ordered two of his faithful
thugs to lug him to the boat and lay him out in the
captain's stateroom; no sooner did they carry him out
than he called the fiesta to a close with the same voice of
command and authority with which he had struck it up.
"Tomorrow, my friend," he said to Don Luciano Esparza
as the two strode down the cobblestone streets leading to
the docks, "the sea will swallow him. By now, Camilo
Cienfuegos is dead, done for forever. From here on out,
he'll be doing his dreaming on the bottom of the sea."
Then he fell into a deep, rapt silence that Don Luciano
did not dare disturb. He muttered to himself, mixing up
the names Cienfuegos, Mademoiselle Pernod, Pedro
Resaca, Santo Domingo, Mexico, El Dorado, Cuba, Puerto
Vigía, Salbago, in a crazed kaleidoscope that froze the
doctor's blood. Don Alvaro Rejón droned on and on, his
blond beard sunken into his chest, hands clasped at his
back, his blurry, flurried eyes lost somewhere among the
past, the present, and the future.

At break of day, drunk on glory, the Rejonistas departed Santo Domingo in quest of El Dorado, bound first, of necessity, for Puerto Vigía. The wind was not altogether favorable for the navigation of the fusta. It huffed and gusted, making the boat list and lurch, as if it did not wish him to put Hispaniola behind him forever. The afterburn of a hangover on his palate and belly, standing on the quarterdeck, blond mane in the wind, eyes trained on the horizon, suddenly Don Alvaro Rejón remembered Mademoiselle Pernod. So distracted had he been by his dream of gold that he had not even bid her goodbye! In one of those sudden moments of lucidity that are torture to madmen, he thought of the moans of love, the chirring of his bones as he burst his liquid into the deep marvelousness of Mademoiselle Pernod. But, at once, as if someone had whispered into his ear something yet to be done, he shouted to his men to haul up to deck the lifeless body of Camilo Cienfuegos, the mestizo. "He stinks to high heavens. Chuck him in the sea, before he rots History!" The body of Camilo Cienfuegos smacked the surface of the water and lay to, swaying as if wanting to evade the clashing currents that fought to sweep him to the bottom, and then, at last, it sank without a sound, vanishing from the sight of Don Alvaro Rejón forever. "Slimy bastard," Don Alvaro said to himself, teeth gritted, mind riveted on the face of Mademoiselle Pernod. He was never to know that the Madame was indeed expecting a baby, a child of Don Alvaro Rejón's, just when gold had taken her place in his heart, also forever . . .

They found nothing that might point to the existence of the kingdom of gold, no clue that might justify the hopes they had pinned on this expedition. It was a slow, wearying trek, thick with surprises, contradictions, apprehensions, sicknesses, and desertions. All through the months—even years—of the mirage's glow they wound round and round in jungles, peering like ferrets into the absurdest mazes, tracking specific details their imaginations mistook for omens and signs of the proximity of the golden sanctuary. They combed hushed centuries of heaped leaves in the virgin forests of the continent. Vertigo wove through Rejón's soul more than once as they crossed passes leading into valleys without egress, or listened to the hollow silence of the desert wind wielding its power over the dunes on dark, bitter nights. The chieftains of mania—the Salbagans Pedro Resaca and Alvaro Rejón—encased in the polar chill of despair, night after night huddled like brujos whose knowledge could not, however, stack up to this discovery; it seemed that slowly they had lost their power and found themselves face to face with the null softness of nothingness, blood in their eyes, convinced that only they knew the mazy burning trails of El Dorado that appeared nowhere about. Straggling uselessly through the space of so much time, they lost their bearings among the months and years; lacking any geographical reference, linked to the moments of their leavetaking from Puerto Vigía, they showed their utter want of reason in every remark, every impression and command they handed on to the motley human chain of the march.

"Time doesn't matter, damn it!" brayed Alvaro Rejón,

his eyes more and more sunken, lost in illusion, gazing far away into the nothingness of his own tangled thoughts. "Not in the least. All that matters is that we will find it. Sooner or later."

A droning silence, which had grown on them after so long, added to his distraction and disorientation. The world, for him as for Pedro Resaca, had ceased to exist. Save for the primitive maps they used to guide them every other day, all their knowledge was pure hunch, half blind from the senseless march, the diary lost that Don Luciano Esparza had left behind when he died of fatigue, amid satanic shrieks and curses beseeching them to return to civilization at once. But conquered by the jungle, turned into a beast like any other in that closed-in universe, mesmerized by any tiny clue, which he always misread, he went on brewing over his maps, redoing trails, cordilleras, rivers, swamps, valleys, deserts, marshes, plains and little oases almost by the day, scratching in new lands over the outlines of already explored jungles, new territories overrun by the indestructible tangle of green throwing its shadow over everything, in spite of the hotheaded sureness with which Don Alvaro Rejón recklessly pegged the precise location of the golden city.

The Indians he had rounded up in Puerto Vigía during the preparations; the negro porters, whose physical force had so fired up Don Luciano Esparza that he jotted it down in his diary, a significant detail, along with personal exclamations of approval; the Spaniards who had thrown in with this trek into the unknown, wangled into this illusion by Rejón's words, cadgers banking on the profits; all had become potential enemies who any day now would begin to eye each other like strangers, leery of one another. Even the most steadfast had gotten fed up months back with the legend Alvaro Rejón harped at them over and over that they might never forget what mission it was that had lured them into this maze. The day came. Wracked by a thousand rare maladies that hogtied the medical know-how of Don Luciano Esparza, who believed that this whole geography was jinxed by spirits having a blast throwing the trekkers off track, and seized by the desire to desert, which had seeped into the marrow

of their bones, a humor only to be allayed by flight, the
porters and the guides who claimed they could read the
geological hieroglyphs of the most awesome region in the
universe, who had hacked open the trail with their ma-
chetes and slashed away the bush, who had led them over
the bald plains, abandoned them to their fates and fled
whithersoever but bound and determined to break free of
this labyrinth of words shaped by the lunacy of the blond
Spaniard obsessed forever by the sanctuary of gold.

"We've come this way before, Alvaro," Pedro Resaca
cried out in despair. "We're going around and around in
circles like fool drunkards. We're totally lost."

No less than ten times they climbed up and down the
same scarped mountains, the provisions used up, water
often scarce. Ten times they rifled the same grubby
villages, inhabited by Indians who did nothing to stop
them, never parted their lips to utter their strange
tongue, baffled and stunned as they were by the bustle
and hurry of these white gods' every gesture. Like so,
they travelled backward along the rim of time through a
tunnel leading them to a veritable age of stone, into
regions so remote they were missing from their maps, that
Alvaro Rejón never got wind of until he saw them with
his own eyes, dimmed now but still as feverish and
exacting as an entomologist's. If they were lost, so much
the better (Alvaro Rejón brooded), as none of those still
with him and Resaca would think of escaping. And as for
Pedro Resaca (Alvaro Rejón went on talking to himself),
he didn't give a damn about the complaints he cooked up
every day, attempting to make him turn back. Just as he
had blinked at the death of Don Luciano Esparza, his
body eaten out by the venom of strange ants twenty-four
hours after being stung, he would shrug off Resaca's
moaning and groaning. He would go on, alone if he had
to, alone and escorted by Yaquís, who would guide him at
last to the gates of the golden paradise, the golden fortress
of the jungles. Let Pedro Resaca (he vowed to himself)
take a cue from the native, damn it, who never cracked
his beak to gripe about anything, who led them along
trails only he—keeper of all the secrets of the miry green
jungles—knew existed. Months since, Alvaro Rejón had
holed up in that lair fraught with lies unveiled for him

by the Indian: the ceaseless chewing of coca leaves.
Resaca knew it was a bogus cure, devised to keep the
bogey of El Dorado alive, which drifted in his imagination like a vulture luring him toward death, because
(again according to Rejón) it was all a matter of not
letting oneself be overmastered by impatience. Coca freed
him from cold and heat, hunger and thirst, the trem-
blings of fear and memory, the loneliness he was seized
by, the perceptible passing of time and the regrets twining
and twisting in his soul. He was unfazed by the changes
of season, and he floated over the land, unmindful of the
swelling rivers, the winds and storms, the sheets of water
that drenched the jungle's dense verdure. And whenever
he came upon the great river or any of its tributaries, he
duped himself: "It's the sea, Pedro, the sea. We must turn
back, must go inland, toward the sanctuary," Rejón
ranted. Yaquís, meanwhile, knelt silently beside them,
watching this scene with feigned disinterest. He was a
skeletal old man, almost a ghostly vision, whose sole
sustenance was the godforsaken green leaf he chewed at
all hours with his rotted teeth. Yaquís' green magic had
hypnotized Alvaro Rejón, who now had ears only for the
native's undecipherable counsel, and brushed off Pedro
Resaca's pleas. By now the journey was a total loss. The
three of them, Rejón, Resaca, and Yaquís, were going to
wind up nowhere at all. Sole interpreter of his own
legends drifting off into the faraway ages of his fore-
fathers, Yaquís (thought Resaca) was an imposter sucking
the last lucid thoughts out of Alvaro Rejón like a magnet.
He gazed around him, sweatily trying to shake off the
constant heaviness of the fever, noting ruefully that there
was no one left, not the nameless rabble Rejón had
shipped from Santo Domingo to Puerto Vigía, nor the
negro slaves that he himself, Pedro Resaca, had
conscripted from among the strongest in his colony, now
a place of revery that returned to his memory on weary
sleepless nights, a paradise now lost forever. He tucked
away his bitterness and glided off into his memory of the
fortress of Puerto Vigía, perusing with sad pleasure each
of the places he had built with the sweat of his brow on
the Venezuelan shore, only, the instant of his return to
reality, to chase off all thought of reaching those now-so-

distant latitudes, realms he now deemed his only heaven.
He capered in confused thoughts, in foothills strewn with
clouds, his eyes drooped in a constant doze into which
unreal El Dorado thrust itself vexingly, like a nightmare
trespassing his dreams. "Not a damn thing here," he said
to himself, writhing in lonely rage. He knew all too well
that to converse with Alvaro Rejón at such moments was
as ludicrous as it was futile. Those nights he was
tormented by untold phantoms of negresses dancing naked
in his honor, their moist pink vulvas undulating in the
sea breeze, visions summoning back, each as she was, the
wenches he had sampled with sublime pleasure on his
private paradise in Puerto Vigía. And now they returned
to him in the mazy forests, poking out their luscious
tongues and licking about his penis like live serpents,
rolling in the sand with him as he penetrated them with
the facility and felicity of an irresistible god. "When I
grow up," he bawled to his negro stewards, who were
relishing the orgy along with him, "I want to be Imperial
pimp. There's no one better fit for that office than I." Lost
in hope, he spent the empty hours muffled in memories of
Puerto Vigía, magically remaking in his mind every nook
and cranny of his hacienda, which he had swapped for the
gilded lunacy of Alvaro Rejón. Now he knew that that
hideaway on the Venezuelan shores was his true sanctuary, his El Dorado, his irretrievable dream, the mission
of his life. As at other moments of his existence when he
had believed himself on the brink of death, he scanned
back in this mind to the days of glory, the voyage to
Margarita, the subsequent hop to Puerto Vigía, the slow,
painstaking launching of the hacienda, the close-knit
slave-smuggling network that he and Alvaro Rejón had
strung up all through the Caribbean Sea. Atop his Andalusian pony, he surveyed his cane fields as far as the low
plains opening out beyond the cliffs of Puerto Vigía, the
huts and crop fields of his servants, who in those days
paid him a respect due only the gods. Yet he was a true
god there in Puerto Vigía, a god who bantered and
imbibed with the slavers who came to his haven carrying
the cargo he would take charge of selling and dealing out
all over West India. He breathed pure air on the beaches
nearby, simpering with daft pleasure at his memories,

scene after scene gladdening his old head bitten by the insects of the jungle and scorched by the sun and cold. Now he returned to the most abject of miseries, confusing the patter over his skin of ravenous cockroaches and beetles for the hot hands of his negresses.

Afar, in the dim of night, from the oasis where they rested one could easily make out the blurry line where the jungle began, a vast green lushness tangled round itself. Resaca shunned that shadow, telling himself that never again would he set foot under those unending looms of giant trees hexing every risky step taken by the intruders into that territory. Meanwhile, pepless, no wish to put in a word, Resaca watched the inane conversations in which the two madmen, Alvaro Rejón and Yaquís, wound themselves up for hours on end, diagnosing into the dirt the existence close-at-hand of the golden citadel. Without a grudge he had shed the bad habit of puzzling over what method Alvaro Rejón had used to rope him in, and to launch him on this ruinous expedition. It was true that Rejón's maps were flawlessly rendered, and that his partner's arguments dictated the project's great urgency, no question about it. But by this point in time, Pedro Resaca had passed, as it were, beyond the limits of lunacy and come back like a streak to sane judgment. If he had acted oddly, no more. It was high time for this utopian project to come to an end, before Yaquís hypnotized Rejón once again and drove him back into the jungles, to cross again through the same villages, creep like aimless ants through mysterious realms, round invisible obstacles most likely whomped up by the colonist, while the hoary trunks of the trees lidding off the sky and the light of day ogled them with disdain. "Shit," Resaca grumbled, "and nothingness, which are one and the same." But there, omnipresent as ever, dead to weariness, was Yaquís, the personification of a devil who refused to die, forever champing on coca, forever scratching the route into the desert sands, and hamming up useless sacrifices to deities only he believed in. He was (thought Resaca) the incarnation of an Indian witch doctor from the altiplano, with consummate command of human frailty, back from beyond the tomb, the imperious possessor of a rhetoric of persuasion he drummed into Alvaro Rejón. One of those shamans, no doubt, who cast their wicked hooks over the Spaniards as they struck out over the continental jungles in search of a region solely existent in the fevered imaginations of those not content to be common conquistadors, who sought glory with petty, stupid zeal which sooner or later turned them into ideal victims for devilish apparitions like Yaquís, bloodsuckers, bats, who had no life outside the jungles and adjoining deserts. This was the trap laid for him by the hellish gods of the continent, imposters that could be shooed away only with orisons, aspergillums and exorcisms, now out of reach. Yaquís was peering out of the corner of his eye at Rejón, who was soaked up in his influence. Resaca watched him champing coca, shrivelled like him and still staggered by what was left of the golden dream.

"He says" (Alvaro Rejón was talking to him now) "that there's another expedition in these parts. He smells it in the distance. The captain is another blond man, Pedro, whose cruelty is renowned all over the jungle domain. Many have seen him straying like a shadow, dipping water at the banks of rivers, steering down them on a huge raft and searching, just like us. He must be Spanish, like us, Pedro!"

Resaca looked at him. His eyes teetered between embarrassment and total disbelief. "If I say what I think, you won't listen. I'd rather not speak," he retorted crisply.

"But Yaquís sees all, Pedro, he knows all . . ."

"I think he's lying to you. Lies and wickedness lie hid in every word, every look. He's hoaxing you with those tales. He's got you hexed and you can't even see we've lost everything. Absolutely everything."

Rejón became more and more riled, more and more frenzied as he listened to Resaca's despair.

"I think," he went on, "that he must be tampering with your maps. He keeps drawing new trails you can see lead us noplace, snarl us up even worse in this damn maze, Alvaro. And you don't even notice."

Alvaro Rejón shot him a fierce look, which masked his thoughts. In his dementia, he told himself that Resaca had believed very little if at all in the golden sanctuary, that it was he who was the real jinx of the expedition, the evil spell keeping them away from El Dorado. If Yaquís said another expedition was prowling through these parts, Rejón was not about to doubt him. If he said the captain of that march was a short, blond Spaniard with a limp and blue eyes that glinted like live embers plucked from the flames of hell, Alvaro Rejón would not be the one to doubt him. Yaquís knew everything about these places, he descended from a lost race of priests, a tribe of holy men snuffed by the conquistadors themselves. He could see across deserts and jungles. His gaze was much deeper and more penetrating than that of any known human being and he could scent presences from many leagues off. And Pedro Resaca did not believe in him. Pedro Resaca could screw himself (thought Rejón): the coward, here he was turning back when they were practically on the doorstep of the most important discovery on earth. Resaca followed him with glazed eyes. He saw the sterile histrionics, the gaspy breath, the stagger, saw that Yaquís had suffused him with a jungle spirit. Then, in the dead of a sleepless night, while hundreds of hoots and howls feuded in the distance, he thought of escape. For the first time he considered fleeing from this death-threatening torpor. It was the only hope of salvation, and he petted it like a madman with a new idea. All of his hopes were now squashed forever, shunted off to one side of his life. He realized that very soon the three of them would reach a threefold coincidence tokening the end of the conversation and of this trek into lost lands. On one side, Resaca was plotting his escape, but with the ineluctable proviso that he must first kill Yaquís and deflate his body of its evil air, so as to drain his influence, smelling of poison sulphur, from the body of Alvaro Rejón. On the second side, Alvaro Rejón was brewing the same scheme as Resaca. Silent, dogged, he was plotting his friend's death, egged on by Yaquís, who had telepathically convinced him that he must do away with Resaca as the sole condition for attaining the golden city lying hid in the deepest of jungles, which he knew inside out. Yaquís, an important third side of this odd, starving triangle, watched the movements of the two mad Spaniards with his chisel eyes, slowly cutting death into their faces. With his tiniest movements too, with his thoughts, he was drenching them in despair and inducing the sluggishness in which they now seemed to be lying. This, for the moment, was his great victory. He chomped slowly and soggily on the green weed that kept him awake day and night. He spit and spit a green phlegm Resaca hated more than the jungle itself. The entire little oasis where they made their camp was spattered with dried smutches left by the witch doctor's sputum. And now he came around with this hokum about another blond man, allegedly as crazy as they, a cruel Spaniard whose eyes shot fire, who lurched and stumbled over the varying vastness of the continent following the course of the great river, bearing on his head the deaths of his own companions and of all the dwellers of the native villages they flattened as they passed. Another phantom who had lunged into the madness of this territory, armed with shield and helmet, shimmering in his left hand the sword of the Spanish conqueror, as though girt to levy that last battle he was born to fight. A Spaniard who called himself the "Prince of Liberty," a sort of catchword contrived by Yaquís to keep Rejón on the bootless track of gold. And overhead, like a pendulum careening perilously and threatening to fall on his body, was that triple coincidence at which Resaca knew they would each arrive in a very short space of time. So he had to kill Yaquís, make him disappear forever.

Resaca noted that his bones were beginning to slump, that it required more and more exertion to strike up the least conversation with Alvaro Rejón. Return to civilization, to whichever of the cities founded by the Spanish right here in Peru; go back to Quito, for instance, or Trujillo. Or Lima. To hell if need be sooner than stay planted here forever on this god-awful oasis. This was now his most lucid obsession. Every day while the sun shone a wind blew that blistered their already blackened skin. But at night the roar would thin into an icy, invisible knife that bristled the skin and sliced to the root of the bone. There, nerveless as always, was Yaquís, scurrying back and forth, scratching new trails into his map of lies, and as always, observing every move they made, every step they took. At this stage, Resaca guessed the old Indian knew everything about him, including his designs to kill him. Yaquís had picked out a spot on the oasis sheltered from the fierce desert wind. There beside the palm-frond hut he laid out the map of El Dorado, erecting out of sand the gold ramparts that girded the sanctuary, working especially hard on the lopped-off pyramids that were indubitably the temples, and leaving at the center a tidy space for the market of gold. All as though it were real, but in miniature. The maquette, impeccably squared, was now complete and Alvaro Rejón passed the days enthralled, his eyes riveted to this toy El Dorado by which Yaquís had managed to paralyze him. Meanwhile they conducted inaudible conversations, whisperings of a sort that every now and then would drift over to where Resaca was nearly always sprawled in the shade, waiting in vain for a glimmer of reaction from his friend. Yaquís observed him from afar, pointing at him leerily. The Indian's jaws moved constantly, so that over the distance that divided them Resaca could not determine whether the old man was talking, or simply munching coca. Sometimes the Indian would fall into a doze out of which he would waken shrieking as if his gods or demons had slipped him secrets in his sleep, new clues to the location and characteristics of the impossible city. Enslaved to his stories, snared by this evil hex in the image of a man who kept him lashed to the land of death, Alvaro Rejón still believed, beyond the shadow of a doubt, in the fictions of this old man who had dished him the continental hell. Pedro Resaca had no clear memory of the moment of Yaquís' appearance. He must have been (he now thought) one of those lollers who had tagged on behind them on the way out of some dingy village. Goodly numbers of natives had heeled them, when the time came to head out, back in the days when this dream of naught could still be deemed an expedition. All disappeared as soon as they saw they were not heeded. Or they remained, lost, bushed, in some hidden cranny of the jungles. Or they went back to their villages casting a thousand curses upon conquistadors and gold seekers. The same scene played itself again and again and the outcome was always the same: the collapse of these stragglers who left off sticking like barnacles to the flank of the march once they saw there was nothing to gain. Yaquís was a case apart, an exception to the rule. Resaca recalled that he had remained at a distance, as though keeping a constant watch over the trail. For many days he tailed the route of the march, paring down the distance between them with laudable discretion. Before they knew it, Yaquís was in. It was as if he had always been among the marchers. Not only that. He was a deft guide in whom Rejón placed all his trust. Then the dispersal of the El Dorado expeditionaries began. First to go were the Indians. The negroes fell sick, and the Spanish themselves were unbalanced by fevers, while this unlikely little man tripped along the wild, convoluted trails as if he were born there and faithfully fulfilling an ancient tradition Alvaro Rejón and Pedro Resaca would never grasp. Yaquís taught them to eat weeds of the forest and tap water from the insides of reeds. Yaquís had become an indispensable demon in this harsh, hostile universe. He taught them not to fear the dronings of the jungle, and how to keep the night-prowling beasts out of their camp. Now Resaca had decided to kill him. He no longer had the least doubt that within that body dwelled a wicked spirit who knew all, saw all, and whose ultimate aim was the total destruction of the trespassers and their daft expedition.

That day Resaca remarked that Yaquís never took his drowsy eyes off him. From time to time he grinned at him wickedly, with a simper of false friendship, as though he already knew that on the following night Pedro Resaca would scare up his courage and endeavor at last to cut off his head. But in any case the Spaniard had his doubts. He had always heard that these witch doctors were indestructible. That even if you hacked them to ribbons, if your sword pierced their bodies and slashed them apart, in no time they would recover their image and their life, since humans had no power to dispose of them. Not even if you whacked off his head could you make the demons inside Yaquís disappear, since they possessed not only the fabulous magic ability to read future thoughts of others, but they were immortal, omniscient, and all-powerful as the gods of their forebears. Which meant that if Pedro Resaca, no sooner did the deep shadows of night fall upon the oasis that served as their shelter, dared to behead the holy man, he ran the risk that Yaquís, headless and all, would move his body in pursuit of his head and put it back in place. So that all this hacking and hewing would be useless, since to kill a phantom was roundly impossible.

So Resaca settled for wrecking the drawings, roads, ramparts, palaces and temples that the old man had been building in miniature next to the hut, prefiguring nonexistent El Dorado. Whipped on by an unknown fury, he kicked away at the sand model, demolishing the magnificent oeuvre of this uncommon artisan. In a frenzy, as though battling an army of a thousand men, Pedro Resaca bent to this labor of destruction with the same gusto with which he had built Puerto Vigía many years back. Fighting the myth of El Dorado, he felt his body regain its lost vigor. He hallooed with victory, shouting orders to the invisible bands of negro slaves who obeyed as little as a look in his eye and raced off into the farthest recesses of the legend, lighting fire to the sanctuary where the god of gold reposed. On this night of lustful lunacy, the golden fountains and markets, the streets sumptuously paved in the metal of power knew the cruel, avenging blade of the Spanish conqueror. Hither, thither, Pedro Resaca severed the heads of Indians who bore an uncanny resemblance to Yaquís. As so often he had dreamed of doing to the old man, he whacked off their heads, but they resurged before his eyes, rushing terrified into the hiddenmost recesses of the golden sanctuaries. Resaca sweated in mock battle, clad in his finest armor, clutching the reins of a white steed that whinnied with joy as yet another of the mansions of the golden city burned. The negroes of Puerto Vigía, who had been wrested from the Cape Verde Islands, gave vent to the passions heretofore pent-up within them. They stormed, looted and sacked El Dorado the beloved. They could do what they liked so long as the aim of every action was destruction. They snarled like rabid dogs, cutting the artisans to pieces, with slashes and whacks of their sharp swords dispatching whatsoever stepped in their paths. This was his revenge. The revenge of the Spanish conqueror Pedro Resaca. Upon the golden lie, Resaca would now build a new mission, a new Puerto Vigía, noble and savage. He would found a new city to be the greatest in the New World. Here before him now, trying to hide, darting around corners and among the flames, frightened

like a small boy, was the real Yaquís. He knew his walk,
his filmy faraway eyes, his trembles, his jaws chomping
away on that herbal substance. He knew his face. It was
he, Yaquís. Don't kill him, damn it, he commanded from
his horse, save him for me. This old witch doctor deserves
a special death. He must be burned alive, as dictated by
the canons of the Holy Inquisition for heretics and devils,
damn it. May he scorch and flake, may his body be fodder
for the vultures of the desert. What a grand sight it will
be, a resounding victory for the Spanish conquistador
desecrating the caves of gold in the jungle's most secret
places. Now his name alone, Pedro Resaca, will be allied
to the legendary cruelty of the Spaniard. Never will that
other lame captain be heard of again. His name, Pedro
Resaca, will reign in the jungle, shrouded in violence and
the warrior feat of subduing the demons of El Dorado.
Now he saw the burning pyre; his horse neighed with
pleasure as he basked in the sight of Yaquís writhing in
the flames, his pale blue eyes proclaiming the definitive
death of the legend concocted by the witch doctors by
reason of the stupid ambition and arrogance of the
Spanish. So El Dorado burned in the midst of the jungle
and in the dreams of Pedro Resaca, captain of an army of
black savages who had stormed and sacked the sacred
citadel, reducing it to ash. All of Yaquís' power was pure
smoke rising in pillars over their heads into a new blue
sky shining its light on a new day, a day far from troubles and obsessions, because the gold fever was over for
keeps.

He awoke swollen, as if he really had fought a battle to
the death with Yaquís and his golden empire. Sprawled
face down on the wrecked model city, Resaca tried to clear
a lucid spot in his memory. He peered with curiosity into
the old wizard's hut. He saw no one. Yaquís had vanished.
A short way off, head slumped over his chest from grief,
lay Alvaro Rejón, hiccuping impudently, weeping and
whining to himself disconsolately and yanking at his hair
in an attack of spastic rage that made him mix up his
dreams of gold with his life on Santo Domingo, his true
golden age. As he tried to stand, Pedro Resaca caught the
words Rejón was flinging into the air: "You destroyed
him, how could you, how dare you . . ." Alvaro Rejón

chanted, lost in himself. At that moment Pedro Resaca
knew that they had become strangers, that their bodies
had slowly sagged, hunched and shrunken. Their hair no
longer shone with the radiance of proud youth. Naked,
pain-wracked, broken by the years spent straggling in
senseless circles through jungles and deserts, now they
looked up and knew one another again in the midst of the
wreckage. In all these years never had he seen another
Spaniard spanning these latitudes, and save for the story
Yaquís had tried to pull on them about the blond
conqueror floating like a phantom along riverbanks,
crossing the continent in search of El Dorado, he could not
recall receiving any other tidings of their contemporaries,
the breed of Spanish conquistadors to which they
belonged. Resaca, in any event, inwardly held that Alvaro
Rejón would never wholly come back to his senses. So
fierce had the fever been that however long the reach of
oblivion, always would traces of that delirium remain
implanted in his gut, plaguing him with memories which
in his senectitude he would confuse with reality. Now he
would spend a long while dimmed by regret, sulking
aloud, fetching back a past that existed solely in his
imagination and in his feverish, never-ending soliloquies,
quarreling with himself, berating himself, his voice taking
on Yaquís' animal modulations shot through with hysterical trembles that culminated, invariably, in a frenzied
wail. Yaquís had hexed him with his golden myths, and
now it was virtually impossible for him to live without the
herb, without chewing the green leaf of coca that was the
only gold he had found during the long march. Now
(thought Resaca) it was a matter of patience, for Alvaro
Rejón to begin to recover of his own accord and to forget
his fantasies, so as to slowly begin to adapt to the reality
they had both been remote from for so many years. He
looked at Rejón again. His hair had gone raggedy, the
color of dirty straw. The skin on his face was wasted and
puckered, spotted with tiny pockholes and lumps, scars,
possibly, from tiny insect bites or sun scorches. His eyes
moved slowly and slackly in their sockets, lost on horizons where they now knew there was nothing to find but
the irretrievable past, beginning to patch itself together
cruelly in his memory.

They were skin and bones when they came to the City of Kings, run out of every grimy village they stumbled on; the living image of misery, prodded along by the winds of the desert, when they blew into this city founded by Francisco Pizarro only a handful of years before. As they hit the limits of Lima a hurricane of goodly size was rolling over the city, hurling into the air blinding fistfuls of sand from the dunes shifting around it like living beings. They had trekked and trekked guided solely by the scant directions of people they ran across on the way. No longer did they ask after the sanctuary of gold, but for the sea, the sea they had shunned all during the march. They groped through the heavy mist that swaddled the city and sifted down over it, seeping into their pores and fogging their vision; now at last they scented like dogs in rut the nearness of the sea, a dampness flooding their lungs and their mouths with some other flavor, bringing them again into the presence of water, like a promise of healing for their sapped bodies. Wasted when they left the oasis, which they now conjured up vaguely, hazily, as they walked they talked of whatever might distract them from their troubles, Alvaro Rejón chewing coca at all times, Resaca buoying him along toward the sea, the two perking each other up with plans for the future they knew before the fact they could never bring off. They were rickety old men, crabbed skin on bent starved bones, gasped breath slogging through sick corporeal tissues.

They had not yet grasped that between raising Puerto Vigía and the vast stretch over which they had travelled seeking the sacred golden fortress, between realities overblown by the imagination and dreams of utopia that never jelled, between the spinnings round and round mountains and plains, rivers and forests, a lifetime had elapsed, an entire age during which the world had gone along reshaping itself on a path different from the one they had boldly followed. This was so. They had a great deal to tell, but this late in the century, and this late in their own lives, it was highly unlikely that anyone would believe their maps or the stories they told in an ambiguous language peppered with cryptic prophecies designed to cover up their defeat. Solely delusions of beggars beaten by life, who could do nothing now but go through the world preaching their deceptive doctrines, like straw tossed to the fire. "There are things that can never be, impossible things," Rejón parroted to himself whenever he began to bog down in memories. He couldn't say for sure if the experience of El Dorado was true, or if his golden years in Santo Domingo were a lie.

Pedro Resaca had rudely awakened him from all of it. All of it. When he screeched to him that they were washed up, washed up forever, Resaca had muffled for one instant Rejón's ceaseless whining.

"Washed up. Damned. It doesn't matter if they call you mad, you fool. Get it into your skull once and for all, we've got to climb out of this hole we're in thanks to the fantasies of you and Yaquís."

Rejón looked at him intently, with eyes of his lost self, as if just at that moment he had begun to take stock of the lethargy of centuries in which he had been sunken, by free will or not, since the age of the golden fevers. His face was that of a pampered little boy whose precious toy has been snatched away. His body, a sad, poor old man losing his teeth, all his hopes dashed, no incentive to hold him to life, every syllable quavering, lost his voice's erstwhile blunt clarity. "And the maps, Pedro?" he inquired, fishing for a hopeful reply. Resaca looked at him again with sneer, to stop his mouth. "And the gold, Pedro? What did we do with the gold?" he asked, trembling.

"There's no gold, Alvaro," Resaca retorted with all the punch he had left. He dipped up a handful of coarse sand from the oasis floor and held it out to him. "Only sand, shit, and solitude," he said at last.

He gazed with a mix of embarrassment and affection at

Alvaro Rejón, who, though he saw how things stood, still refused to face the fact of the ruin into which they had fallen.

"So are we a couple of flops?" he piped up again bashfully, his voice a thin broken thread dangling from his lips.

"Yes, Alvaro. A pair of flops. A couple of scums on the edge of death," Pedro Resaca said, finally.

Then he looked into the skies, pointing to the scrawl, in the blue over the oasis, of the turkey buzzards circling nearer and nearer as though already smelling the feast of carrion the two men were about to become. "There you have them, Alvaro. Those vultures you see up there flying over us are no dream. They're the fact that awaits us if we don't scram fast, clear out of this damn hell," he said to Rejón.

But here they were in Lima. Spattered with dust, with tiny, unpleasant specks of sand that mingled with their sweat and the grimy dampness. As if an angel of mercy had delivered them back to life, thrust them into civilization again, here they were in the so-named City of Kings, a town that since its beginnings had been the scene of ceaseless rows, insurrections, intrigue and brawls between the Spanish conquerors themselves. A city where the murmur of maliciousness was a matter of course among its residents, who were divided into two parts: those on top (the conquistadors and their talk rife with machinations and rebellions) and those beneath (the Indians they had profaned, plunged into silent witness of the conquistadors' never-ending rows). A city years hence to be dubbed "La Horrible," as a high compliment, in incontestable contempt for the string of pretty lies tagged to it through the centuries by the illustrious and incessant travellers who came merely to visit. As good as on the edge on the world (not without cause was the day to come when the Spanish would coin the phrase "from here to Lima" to express, metaphorically, an insurmountable distance) they walked and talked and gazed around as though floating among clouds, but with more paradoxical clarity than ever before. By their side—glancing over with cool contempt as if they took them as servants or mere slaves—passed dandified Spanish gents, retired warriors

doing their utmost here on the far side of the world to live
out their courtly dreams, mimicking customs mentioned
by visitors who came south from the Isthmus of Panama.
Here, since the days of the settlement, lived a mood that
looked toward the past, into a sort of veil hiding behind
it the myriad secrets that glinted in the Indians' silence,
as though the city bristled with a fierce fluorescence
cached in tombs and graves, a long silence of millennial
melodies that would play on and on through the centuries, secreting the ciphers to another empire, another civilization, another religion profaned by the insatiable sons
of the Conquest. That fear so unmistakable in the eyes of
the Indians would last time without end. But the depth of
their gaze hid a sublime power of mind far superior to the
brawling conquerors fighting each other to extinction.
Pizarro's conquistadors had come here from Jauja, seeking
a friendlier place, far more genial climes. There, beside
the Rimac River, on a rectangle of one hundred and
seventeen parcels, each to be broken into four plots, and
leaving—so as not to part from tradition—an open space
for the main plaza, around which would be built the
governor's mansions, the civic edifices, and the palaces of
ecclesiastical power, brimming with suspicion, on the
watch out for heresy, strewing its vengeance of fire in
every direction. At the start there were a mere sixty-nine
townspeople. And at the time of the coming of Alvaro
Rejón and Pedro Resaca, it was a luminous, airy, open
place, a land that seemingly satisfied the nesting ambitions of the Spanish settlers, who gazed, through the hazy
air, at the shore and the blue sea where it lay like a pane
of sleepy glass.

They slunk in like hounds after a bootless hunt, looking
for the bars bunched by the docks. They did not know that
their lives were behind them, that it all lay in the past;
now the gamble of the world was too broad and strange.
They'd come back, or so their eyes told them, too late.
They were dross in the universe and no one knew their
names or doffed their cap to them as in days gone by. For
them Lima, with its tidy streets and rows of huts—one-
story mud with roofs of adobe and mud—was an exotic
city, mixing an orientalism solely conjured from travel
books and the lavishness of those little palaces and

mansions of the Spanish, presaging, even then, the unimaginable greatness to which this faraway place would someday rise.

"We're at the edge of the world," Alvaro Rejón deduced, pondering the spectacle of the city that opened before him. "We're not worth a damn here," he growled as Pedro Resaca looked on in sullen silence. Sprawled out on the damp sand at the edge of the water, the breeze buffing his face and salting his skin, Resaca basked in the sea breeze, felt how this place soothed his spirit. He scarcely heeded Alvaro Rejón's words, mouthed always between the slurp and smack of his gums as he chewed his coca. The clean sea waters cooled his feet, and for the first time in so long, Pedro Resaca felt that true luxury of liberty in his mind: he could think for himself what he would do with the few years of life he had left.

"It might be the edge of the world," Resaca said slowly. "But I won't budge. I'm staying here forever. Until I rot."

By now, Alvaro Rejón was looking better. He had altogether forgotten the gold mania and the legend spiked with lies. Far behind him, wrapped in musty cloths, fading in time, was the memory of Mademoiselle Pernod and Santo Domingo. So it was true they were washed up. That after so long, after so many comings and goings, they were the mere shadows of longings scattering away into the past, in dribs and drabs, lost snatches of a universe of dreams never had they held in their hands. All that was past. They were two helpless, histrionic old men shuffling through the streets of the port, running messages, feeding on what the young seafarers doled to them, out of charity, in return for the tales Alvaro Rejón, their storyteller, spun them in their hours of liquor and leisure.

"But all that, friends," he grinned, champing on a coca leaf, "is a lie. It never happened." With this remark he would close each of his lengthy accounts. "Yarns whomped up by the greediness of men to gull themselves and while their lives away dreaming of hitting it rich."

The mariners (like those in Cartagena of the Indies on his subsequent short stop there on the way back to Salbago) were tickled, clapping for his face-pulling, his miming, his nuances of a tale-teller, the voices he put on and off like an actor. They paid almost no attention to his little tales. They rooted him on, scrutinizing the responses of the old man who was such a show.

"You tell them as if they were so," they said to butter him up. "You act like one of those fellows who got lost with mad Agüirre searching for El Dorado."

When they noted the strain in the voice of that man old beyond his years, when his stresses and rhythms began to slur and go flat, they left him to indulge his vice, so as to win back his strength. Later, they said to perk him up, you must tell us the story of the Caribbean mermaids and the time the Ambassador took a sea cow to Felipe II and all that. Or the one about the strumpet who made love wearing gold high heels.

Tell us the story of the rebel who wanted emancipation from the Crown of the Empire, tell that one too.

Tell them a thousand and one times, for they are such funny stories and you tell them so well, like nobody else, as if they had really happened.

Alvaro Rejón smiled, displaying his spoiled teeth. He implored patience. He chomped briskly on the green gum, spat a wad on the floor, and braced, unrolled one more of his tales, tidbits of a very near past for the conquerors on the far side of the world . . .

From the slopes beyond Royal de Salbago, Alvaro Rejón squints his eyes to improve his view of the city. A crescent unconcern for everything around dulls and drowses him, as if life had gone out of him.

The wrongheaded siege the Dutch rover Vanderoles has wreaked on the island, for many days now, intending to waste it by means of hunger and boredom, doesn't matter a straw to him. Boredom, it would seem, is the Dutchman's word for prostration. The pirate wonders, however, whether hunger is a workable means. Hard-hearted hellion, unflagging in his gusto, his long craving to conquer Royal de Salbago and place it under the Dutch flag, Vanderoles has deployed his fleet so as to cut off passage to and from the sea. He suspects the blockade will bring the hoped-for success, since Salbago is flagging and on the brink of buckling before the forces of the European pirate, a man schooled, by the by, in travel books and seasoned in patience, mother of all victories. He has lusted, with a heat that melts the inner flesh, to possess the island as one might a woman of royal blood, a forbidden princess, adored in the secrecy of nautical ages, worshipped in silence as he coursed long lonely hours over the sea. In his mind was inscribed the distant silhouette of Salbago, and in all his voyages, the length and breadth of the oceans, he blazoned his fixation abroad: to conquer that no-man's-land marooned by God in the middle of the Sea of Shadows.

Cabeza de Vaca is a luckless, clumsy captain who quakes at the reality impinging on his eyes whenever he turns them toward the bay: a forbidding display of naval might rocking upon the waters that ring Salbago, a song

of foretold victory sung with passionate purpose by the
pigheaded Dutchman with the imperious eyes, chest in
the wind, whose one good eye pegs all his pleasures on the
land Cabeza de Vaca fancies he governs for the Crown of
Spain. The ships of Vanderoles' fleet—like a watercolor,
stock-still, their half-furled sails lightly riffled by the
wind—fiercely scrutinize all motion made in the city.
Vanderoles knows he is the most hated and feared of the
island's enemies, by just desserts. His resolve became an
obsession when, during his first siege of Salbago, a dead
shot of artillery fire took his right arm and all but cost
him his life. It was nothing, he said, but the memory
remained fettered to those forts he meant to smash with
the force of his will, to that forever half-built Cathedral
he vowed he would raze, and rout its ghosts.

Henceforth Vanderoles' arm, which had fallen into the
sea in battle and beached up on the yellow sands of the
shores of Royal, a trophy of war bestowed upon the
islanders for their valor by the gods of the sea, was
preserved in formaldehyde by Cabeza de Vaca, the
Commander and acting Governor of the island, and exhibited as a symbol of resistance and victory over the Prot-
estant Dutchman in parades, religious rites, civil
functions, and other like events. So the pirate's arm had
become a crucial good-luck charm for Cabeza de Vaca,
who was convinced that owning it would block the entry
of the roving Dutchman into the city, and its subsequent
sacking. In Vanderoles, meanwhile, anger flashed and
flashed like lightning, pounding his passions into a red
heat, a fire torturing his thoughts, his ideas, his plans, a
fire flaring deep down in his gut he swore he would stoke
until he had trampled the city and beheaded men, women,
and children, a whole people rankling under the hardships visited upon them by the Dutchman.

Alvaro Rejón lived apart, like a hermit, feeding on some
weeds whose seeds he had brought over from the Continent. In a cave in the hills he made his home, his last
dwelling, perhaps for a view of the vengeance of the stars
raining over the charred earth, razing it. When he heard
the first cannonballs caroming off Royal's adobe buildings, it struck him that the end of the world was nearing,
just as he had always had a hunch it would. Sunk in the

bleakest forlornness, Alvaro Rejón fetched up the shambles of his life, the journeys that now seemed lies, the
adventures crusting and hazing in his memory. Broken by
coca and despair, he doubted the truth of his existence. Up
there in the slopes, he had planted great tracts of land
with the green leaf and he conducted himself like the
apostle of a new religion which held, as a basic command-
ment, devotion to the chewing of the leaf at all hours.
"The world's colors are a dream," he ranted to the novi-
tiates who came furtively to receive his teachings. "When
you're on the leaf there's a solution to everything," he
contended.

Nor was he fazed when he saw the first puffs of smoke
from the cannonballs showering over the city. First came
the strike. Then fire swept through Royal, dealing death,
driving inland in terror the townspeople who survived the
Dutch pirate's cruel attack. Here stood Vanderoles,
announcing to the world a foretold conquest Salbago could
no longer elude. Here he was, seeking the impossible
recovery of his arm, wreaking vengeance as his part in
the history (later to be created by the chroniclers) of the
sieges and looting of the island. Gripped, thrilled by their
perfect array on the battlefield, he watched his men
racing straight for Royal's prime targets. Ravished he
observed, upon the maps sketched for him by his strate-
gists, the victories he had begun to land shortly after
launching this last assault. He imagined he could hear
the cries of the citizenry as into them plunged the swords
of this history he was the hero of. A gorgeous sight, he
thought, fire crumbling a whole city-enclave of the
Spanish Empire. It was worth it, he thought, to have lost
an arm and an eye to witness today these triumphal
scenes that were to hallow his memory for all eternity.

Was blood running through the streets of this damnable city? he asked. It was running, señor, running,
rejoined his closest councillors, whom by now he would
not deign to look at, stunned as he was by the attack, by
the bursts of smoke from the cannon and culverins firing
away into the ramparts of Royal. Could they see the
advances? How victory neared on this glittering day, a
radiant sun shining on the demise of a Spanish city? They
saw it, señor, saw it, and they were thrilled too, thunder-

struck by the rhyme and reason of the troops as they
fanned through the city on the brink of collapse.

Then Vanderoles saw that the moment had come to leap
to shore and command, in his own voice, the final assault
on the symbol, the Cathedral whose memory had muddied
his mind, the Cathedral as supreme object of his revenge.

Alvaro Rejón hummed as he watched, elixirated to the
core, with a silly simper on his lips shooing him even
farther from fact. The spectacle of fire and smoke, some
miles away, titillated him as if he were inside a dream
and drifting back to the finest days of his golden age on
Santo Domingo. "Mademoiselle Pernod," he said mysti-
cally, the magic utterance of that name conjuring all
kinds of memories, skewed memories of his lifetime,
soothing him and slipping him into a delicious and
arousing drowse. "Mademoiselle Pernod," he said again,
stubbornly, trying to bring in the image of that white
tropical goddess who had lulled him and inflamed him
like no other. Now the cannons were booming again and
the smoke rose in a great pyre swiftly eclipsing his view
of the city.

Royal was in flames, the Cathedral on the verge of
siege. Vanderoles had divined, with dead accuracy, that
there, on those holy grounds, Cabeza de Vaca would
resolve to resist to the death tumbling in around them.
Just then, in the purlieus of the Grand Plaza, Vanderoles
the pirate was issuing the command for the final capture
of the Cathedral, while his warriors chased the citizenry
into the wilds beyond the city and struck them dead.
Heads rolled and in every hole and corner lay headless
bodies, for thus indeed had been the order of the Dutch
pirate: let it be said that not a stone was left standing,
and the heads of the Salbagans were parted from their
bodies, even after death, as revenge for the stiffnecked-
ness of a people who believed they had a right to resist
when the hour of resistance was past.

Alvaro Rejón could not see the massacre: on every
corner, inside every house, beheaded bodies are flung to
the fire, the assailants rioting in revelry, dead Salbagans
scorching and crumbling to ash in the bonfires built high
and low by order of the captains of the Dutch Admiral
Vanderoles. For this proem to his most thundering

triumph, the sea rover sports his finest regalia, his royal
medals trumpeting a lifetime weathered by the waters of
the sea and the lonesome suns, the life of a corsair wafted
on the wind to the most sublime glory. His hair, grey
though he was still in the prime of life, betokened an
experience beyond the ordinary, a maturity beyond his
years, and the zeal of a dreamer who always sacked what
he set his sights on.

The first fires to catch on the walls of Salbago Cathedral filled the Dutchmen with glee and struck horror in
the few Salbagans who had slipped out of Royal, who had
fled along the slopes and hid in the nearby forests. There
it could not reach, at least for the moment, this dan-
tesque fire rising in the very heart of Royal, desecrating
the holy Cathedral into which the island's self-styled
noblemen and the bishops tailing one another to the Epis-
copal throne of the Rubicon had poured so much vigor,
vim, and money. The Cathedral took like dry straw, wood
pulpits and altars crackling and sparking, threads of fire
slinking upward into the darkest crannies, the lost
passages, the crypts, the blind staircases, the Cathedral's
ghosty secrets. Now shrieks rang out hither, thither, like
the hectic cackles of hoary bats who had nested there
since the days of the settlement, phantoms never to
retrieve their rightful human image, who would stop short
of nothing to keep living after death. This was the
memory set down in the annals of Juan Rejón, once
Governor of Royal, Salbago, and founder of the city; the
bloody tale of Hernando Rubio, Inquisitor, smeared into
the walls as if melded to their very essence; the wisdom
beyond time of Master Architect Herminio Machado; the
always proud head of the rebel Pedro de Algaba; the
strange memory of Martín Martel, Commander, who was
the first ghost to dwell in the Cathedral, the first other-
worldly being to slide its shadow through the church's
naves and spark rumors among the people of Salbago; it
was as well, though the sacred site spurned her memory,
the sashaying shadow of Zulima the Moorish girl, young
and splendid as the grass in a meadow stroked by wind;
it was Maruca Salomé and the echoing bark of a fierce dog
surging and swelling through the dense blaze, razing the
Cathedral, leaving nothingness. Salbago, the completed

cycle of a history that had commenced in the dawning of
the age of Discoveries and was closing now, at the hand
of the Dutch rover Vanderoles, a slaughter, frightful and
final.

Like black cinders the ghosts of Salbago flitted over the
great fire engulfing the Cathedral of Royal. In the air they
pirouetted, mouthing moans muffled by the exultant cries
of the victors. No cobwebbed chessmen were there now, in
no palace of no governor. And no other conquest but this
one, levied by Vanderoles the maniac, Admiral of a null
navy and falsely decorated by kings who never existed. No
memory of any other massacre but this one. No Salbago,
no Rejóns, no Cabeza de Vacas, no runs to the Continent
nor razzias nor Catholic Inquisitions imposed by the
power of the ages wherein the sun never set over the
Empire. Now the sun was witness for the prosecution, to
the smoke and flames swallowing Salbago, the new
conquerors hooraying their victory, fêting their patience,
ghosts of upwards of a century of history licked by the
flames to which they had sent so many men. Now,
Salbago and its memory were only this: cinders fleeing for
the sky like swallows shrilling or swifts mouthing their
last dying shriek.

Alvaro Rejón watched it all in a blur. But when
Vanderoles' men found him in the slopes, a scraggly old
sot, he couldn't squeeze out a tear. They hacked off the
colonist's head forthwith, severing it from a body that was
nothing but skin stuck to bone. And then they took up the
march again, victorious conquerors, lighting fire to all the
little villages they came on. Such were Vanderoles' orders,
and the pirates obeyed, scouring all the island, and all the
city, for an arm in formaldehyde they were never to find.
The sun blazed on in the Imperial sky. A blistering heat
bore down on Salbago. So hot the waters gushed up
boiling from the depths of the earth.

WINNER OF THE 1982 NOBEL PRIZE

GABRIEL GARCÍA MÁRQUEZ

*The Best in
Latin American Fiction*

ONE HUNDRED YEARS OF SOLITUDE
01503-X/$4.95 US/$6.95 Can

"You emerge from this marvelous novel as if from a dream, the mind on fire.... With a single bound, Gabriel García Márquez leaps into the stage with Günter Grass and Vladimir Nabokov. Dazzling!"
John Leonard, *The New York Times*

THE AUTUMN OF THE PATRIARCH
01774-1/$4.50 US/$5.50 Can

"A book of incredible depth, breadth, richness, vitality, intelligence, humor, wisdom, subtlety...Like all great fiction, it contains endless layers of experience and meaning, and a first reading can only give hints of its richness." *The Miami Herald*

IN EVIL HOUR
52167-9/$4.95 US/$5.95 Can

A dreamlike tale of the violent secrets and hidden longings that haunt a small Columbian village.